"I'd r...... .... be caught by Grant's men," she said, watching him boldly. *"Trust me."*

He nearly laughed, but shook his head. "I am not easily beguiled as you might think."

Her eyes narrowed, their color pale and bright, irises a clear gray, candlelight reflecting there.

"If you leave off the chains, I will stay," she said quietly. "You have my word."

Her allure was astonishing. He could not define its power. She did nothing but stand there and look at him, nothing but breathe—no wiles, no coquettish glances, no suggested words. But she exuded a wild and natural magic.

"And what is your word worth to me?" he asked, leaning forward. "Is there something to secure it?"

Her eyes fluttered, shut again. "What do you want of me?"

He knew what he wanted. He inclined his face toward hers. His heart thundered.

And then he kissed her . . .

Other **AVON ROMANCES**

Sarah Gabriel

Keeping Kate

AVON BOOKS
An Imprint of HarperCollinsPublishers

This is a work of fiction. Names, characters, places, and incidents are products of the author's imagination or are used fictitiously and are not to be construed as real. Any resemblance to actual events, locales, organizations, or persons, living or dead, is entirely coincidental.

AVON BOOKS
An Imprint of HarperCollins*Publishers*
10 East 53rd Street
New York, New York 10022-5299

Copyright © 2005 by Sarah Gabriel
ISBN-13: 978-0-06-073610-1
ISBN-10: 0-06-073610-0
www.avonromance.com

First Avon Books paperback printing: November 2005

Printed in the U.S.A.

10 9 8 7 6 5 4 3 2 1

*For Mary Jo Putney and Patricia Rice,
for sharing brilliance, patience,
charm, and glass beads.*

Prologue

London
March 1, 1728

One glance spared for the golden beauty standing in the crowd nearly cost Alexander Fraser his life, and certainly his timing. Stepping back, he lifted his sword to parry again, aware that his opponent could have taken the advantage while Alec's attention had been briefly diverted.

Fortunately, swordsmanship was not Jack MacDonald's strong point. But Alec was not about to prove that by being inadvertently skewered in front of the afternoon assembly of King George's court at St. James's Palace.

Captain Alexander Fraser, Highland regimental officer, laird of Kilburnie, and heir to a fortune he did not want, sidestepped in a wary dance. With his targe shield braced on his left forearm, he waved the dirk in his left hand like a wicked thorn and gripped a basket-hilt broadsword in his right to parry Jack MacDonald's oncoming stroke. The clash of steel rang out in the great hall, echoing against vaulted ceilings, wood-paneled walls, and a slate floor laid two centuries earlier.

Turning, Alec saw the dazzling girl again, closer to him now. Who the devil was she, he thought—and why should he care? Yet he noticed her sparkling presence even in the midst of a fight, noticed her blond beauty, her gown of cream and gold, and the silk tartan shawl tucked at her elbows.

A beautiful young Scotswoman, bold enough to wear the plaid in this nest of Whigs and Englishmen, in the presence of the king: he ought to know her, but did not. Shifting on his feet, he angled his back to her and regained his focus.

Taking catlike steps to the right, he swept his blade down. The broadswords struck together, hard enough to vibrate along his arm to his shoulder. He smacked his hilt backward into Jack's left hand, loosening the dirk clutched there. Flexing his empty fingers, Jack glared at Alec.

With a quick upward thrust of his long dirk, Alec stabbed into the wedge of space between Jack's torso and his sword arm. In return, Jack whipped his blade wildly, and Alec tilted back to avoid the sweep. He circled sideways, wary and watchful, while he and MacDonald gauged each other's next move.

2

The audience stood several deep in the hall now, a mass of colored fabrics, powdered wigs, unfamiliar faces. The press of bodies warmed air already thick with perfumes, pomatum, wine, and sweat. King George, portly in green damask and a silvery wig, occupied a gilt chair on a decorated dais. His queen sat beside him, lush and blowsy in flowered silks.

Alec saw all of it in a blur, but for the beautiful girl who glowed like a sunbeam. She leaned sideways to listen to a woman dressed in black. Whirling away, Alec lunged, pulled back.

Quarter guard, parry, stepping together, then apart in a lethal dance. Gasps fluttered through the crowd as Alec's next thrust deliberately missed his opponent. Leaping to one side, he met Jack's next advance with a hanging guard, sword tipped downward, then flicking up to catch and tear cloth, all the while keeping a steady rhythm of breath and motion.

Lifting his blade, MacDonald overshot just as Alec stepped aside, and steel bit into slate. Alec brought his blade in a swift upward arc within an inch of Jack's side, and tapped his blade against the plaid and shirt over the man's ribs—a deadly blow had he put force into it—and he held the sword in position, while Jack froze under that lethal guard.

Breathing fast, Alec waited, shirt clinging damp to his back beneath his wrapped plaid.

She was there again, just at the corner of his vision. He sensed her wherever she was in the room, foolish as it seemed, though he did not take his gaze from Jack.

Finally, MacDonald opened his hands in defeat,

3

dropped his sword with a clatter to the floor, and stepped back, bowing graciously. Alec only inclined his head.

Jack smiled, quick and boyish, then turned to bow as the crowd erupted in applause. His bright grin and handsome, chiseled face, his black hair clinging in curls to his brow, his romantic Highland plaid, coaxed ripples of sighs among the ladies. Jack MacDonald had many talents, Alec thought, among them natural charm. Women loved him no matter what sort of rascal he could be.

Jack turned, clapped Alec amiably on the shoulder. Silent and somber, Alec nodded, wiped his sweaty brow with his forearm. He held no grudge against his friend, but he was no showman, only glancing at the audience before laying his weapons on the floor, but for the basket-hilt sword. Jack collected more smiles, applause, and three perfumed silken handkerchiefs tossed his way, and as the applause ended, he turned with Alec toward the dais.

King George nodded his approval, and a solemn valet in a bag wig and a green coat beckoned the Highlanders forward, indicating that they should bow.

Alec hesitated. He was loath to bow before the German elector when the rightful king of Scotland and England, James Stuart, lived in exile in Rome. But James had nearly given up hope, they said, and would prefer Providence, or Jacobites, to make the effort to restore his throne.

As an officer in a Highland Independent Company,

Alec knew he must conceal his true loyalties here. Discretion and secrecy were the wisest choices when working covertly for the Jacobite cause. He inclined his head slightly, while Jack bowed without his usual flourish.

"Your Majesty," Alec murmured.

"Very goot demonstration," King George said. "Dat is a clay-mer?"

"Aye, *claidheamh mór* in the Gaelic, Your Grace," Alec said. "It means 'big sword.'" As he spoke, he saw the golden young woman glide closer to where he stood. The older lady in black was with her like a duenna. Alec wanted to turn, feast his gaze upon her, learn who she was—a finer reward for demonstrating Highland fighting technique than an audience with this particular king.

"I thought dey were bigger, dose swords," the king observed. Tittering laughter spread through the assembly.

"Your Majesty," Jack replied, "early Highland claymores were much larger, with two-handed hilts and blades near as tall as their owners. They were suited for brutal battle, not close combat. Broadswords now have shorter blades, and the basket hilt is a Scottish improvement. Our weapons have German blades as well." Jack bowed again. Alec stood ramrod straight and silent.

"Goot German steel, yes! But all weapons is confiscated in da Highlands now." The king snorted a laugh.

"Sire, we are aware of that," Alec said stiffly.

"A goot performance for da queen's birthday," the king went on, "better dan dat *Beggar's Opera* in de theater house now." He turned to speak to Queen Caroline, seated beside him. Plump and pretty in silks and pearls, she smiled at the Highlanders, then leaned toward her husband to murmur in confidence.

Dismissed, Alec thought.

The valet came toward them, gloved hand extended first to Alec, then Jack, as he dropped a gold guinea into each man's palm. "For your trouble," he murmured haughtily.

Staring at the insulting payment, Alec felt himself flush to the roots of his golden brown hair. Neither he nor Jack were hired performers. They had been invited at the king's request to demonstrate sword technique for the queen's birthday.

Alec spun on his heel, turning his back to the king, and strode to the center of the room to retrieve his weapons, while Jack followed. Shoving his dirk into the sheath at his belt, Alec fumed in silence.

"Between the journey and waiting here in London for the royal summons," Jack muttered, "we've spent over a fortnight on this damnable task."

Alec glanced at his cousin without reply and snatched up his sword.

Nearly three weeks ago, Alec had been reviewing lists of confiscated weapons at Fort William, in Scotland, for General Wade when the general had asked him to travel to London to display Highland fighting skills at the king's court. Wade had chosen Alec as the logical choice, since he was a trained swordsman under the tutelage of an uncle who had written a training manual on the subject. Alec had brought Jack MacDonald, his cousin and ghillie, along to act as his opponent in the mock contest.

Once in London, waiting upon a royal summons, Jack dove happily into court life while Alec—by nature keen on his solitude—strolled alone through the streets and court gardens, or tended to correspondence generated by his position as a lawyer for the Highland company in which he was also a captain. The work made it increasingly clear to him that he needed to be in Scotland, not cooling his heels in England.

Now the show was over, and he and Jack were free to go. Glancing up, he saw that the crowd had dispersed. The Highland "performers" were no longer of interest.

The beauty stood nearby, fluttering an ivory fan and murmuring with the older lady. As Alec watched her, she glanced his way again. Her gaze, charming, coy, and entrancing, struck him like a spark.

He returned his attention to attaching the scabbard to his belt. Jack picked up Alec's short red military coat and captain's sash, but he refused them. He felt obstinate. If the sight of his Highland gear made Whigs and Londoners uncomfortable, so be it.

While Jack bundled their things and tucked them under his arm, Alec glanced his way. "Jack, who is that lass there?"

"*Och*, the lovely creature? I do not know—but I heard that she and her aunt are here to petition the king on behalf of Jacobite widows who are entitled to pensions following the deaths of their husbands. The executions of their husbands," he added. "She's Highland, I would guess."

"Aye, by that plaid. Did you hear her name, or clan?"

"I did not, alas. I do fancy a mystery." Jack looked speculatively at the girl.

She glanced toward them again, directly at Alec over her fan. Her gaze was like a true arrow straight to his heart.

"Surprising to see Jacobite ladies here at court," Jack said, "but the king favors their petition, I hear, because the girl is such a beauty. Championing widows is a respectable cause, and what her Highland kinsmen might do up north may not affect her here. Plaid is so rarely seen at court that she could be taken for a spy if she were not . . . so utterly charming."

Nodding in silence, Alec saw the two women pick up their skirts and cross toward him. He stood with his broadsword clutched in his hands, steel point pressing into the floor. His heart pounded like a hammer. Beside him, Jack said something mundane—collecting their belongings at the inn, paying their stable bill—then he, too, fell silent.

Grace and magic turned to woman, she moved toward him. Though not tall, she was slender and elegant, her slim hands resting upon wide silk skirts the color of rich cream, embroidered in gold. The tartan shawl caught at her elbows was patterned in light colors. A choker of pearls wrapped thrice around her slim throat, and a twinkling crystal pendant on a silver chain rode above a lush bosom made demure by a translucent mantle of lace.

Alec stood like a statue and drank in the sight of her: heart-shaped face, flawless skin, rosy lips, a slightly up-

8

turned nose, and extraordinary eyes of light gray. The deep gold of her hair, caught high, was tucked beneath a lacy cap. Without powder, paint, or overdecoration, she was a vision.

"My God," Jack breathed. "A fairy queen."

Alec silently agreed. She sparkled. He hardly noticed her companion, a small woman swallowed in black silk. As the two women approached, he inclined his head respectfully to the other lady. Then his gaze met the girl's again, and held it.

She tilted her head in silent acknowledgment and moved past him, but an arm's length away. Her skirts brushed near his feet, and he could have touched her smooth hand.

Then she glided past like stolen sunlight.

He felt different suddenly, as if her incandescence dissolved shadows that had surrounded him for years. Motionless, he watched her depart by a side door opened by a page boy.

Exhaling, he scabbarded his sword with a swift push. Never had he felt such a headlong rush of attraction, like a physical force sweeping through him—not even for the woman he loved, gone two years now.

The delicate, mysterious Scottish beauty had sent chills clear through him. He still felt the resonance.

Beside him, Jack looked dumbstruck. "I've just seen the wee queen of all the fairies. I think I'm in love."

"Aye? The older lady seems just your sort," Alec drawled. Ignoring Jack's quick scowl, he strode toward the hall's main doors, where two liveried porters stood.

Still clutching the shining guinea in his hand, he

handed it to the porter as he left the hall. He did not want the English king's gold.

She felt taken up by a whirlwind and left trembling. Setting a hand over her thumping heart, Kate MacCarran watched the taller of the two Highlanders through the narrow gap of the doorway.

With only a few searing glances, he had captured her attention utterly. His handsome strength, agility, and the aura of quiet power that surrounded him fascinated her. Blue eyes piercing under straight brows, dark hair touched with sunlight, he seemed as rugged as the mountains of his origin, as strong as earth and rock, an honorable Highlander like her own kinsmen. His comrade was a lean, dark young man of startling beauty, but Kate noticed only the taller of the two and wondered at his identity.

Her aunt touched her arm to urge her onward, but Kate waved her ahead to where others strolled in the gallery. Left alone, she braced a hand on the doorframe and watched as the two Highlanders departed the hall and vanished in the shadows.

She felt a sudden wild longing, wishing she could go with him, back to the Highlands, into adventure. But she had business here before she could return north, and she could not allow herself to become infatuated with a stranger. The dream might be pleasant, but the risks were far too great.

On its silver chain, the crystal pendant at her throat sparkled. She touched her fingers to it, reassured by its presence, which subtly enhanced the gift of the fairy blood within her, the legacy of her family.

Love makes its own magic, said the motto of her clan. Kate had been born with the gift of the glamourie—the ability to cast a spell—in her case, she could captivate a man with a mere touch or a glance. But the tall Highland swordsman had not wavered under her glance, had not turned adoring and obedient, ready to do all her will. His silence, his stillness and pride intrigued her deeply.

Yet she must not let herself be captivated by a stranger, though he made her heart beat faster, in a way she had never experienced before. She must use her gift of charm to help her Jacobite kinsmen—that was why she was here. She must not lose sight of her purpose.

Yet somehow she felt as if the unknown Highlander had thrown a glamourie over her—she was the one caught, for a moment, while he walked away without a backward glance.

Closing the door, she turned, smoothing the skirt of her satin gown. Across the room, her aunt conversed with a blustery lieutenant general who had spent years plotting military strategies against the Jacobites. Kate felt sure she could coax a smile or two from him—and soon enough, learn some tidbits of information to benefit her northern kinsmen.

Summoning a smile, she moved forward.

11

Chapter 1

~~~ 🞰 ~~~

Scotland, the Great Glen
October 1728

"**P**reposterous," Alec muttered as he regarded the broadsheet in his hand. The creased, worn page had just been handed to him by the young officer standing before his makeshift desk in the field tent. "'Highland menace,' it says here. Do you agree, Lieutenant Heron?"

"Perhaps, Captain." The young officer turned his black cocked hat nervously in his hands. "General Wade asked me to come here to tell you about my encounter with this, ah, menace."

Alec sifted through some of the papers on the table

surface. "I've read several accounts in the few days I've been here, but you're the only one I've interviewed personally regarding the matter. This is the first I've seen of this broadsheet. She's rather fetching," Alec drawled, eyeing the page.

"Not so much in that drawing, perhaps, but she's very fetching in person." Heron cleared his throat.

"Ah." Alec tilted the page toward the lantern's glow to read the text again. In the silence, rain and wind battered the canvas shelter, and the door flaps billowed. The tent was crammed with a cot, a wooden chest piled with papers and books, the narrow folding table, and a rickety folding chair that Alec occupied. With nowhere to sit but the bed, the tall young lieutenant stood beneath the tent's peak.

"'Katie Hell,'" Alec read aloud. "'Notorious Highland wench.'" He tipped a brow as he scrutinized the illustration above the caption. "'A thief and a spy, a threat to the crown . . . possessing a most peculiar magic.' What the devil does that mean?" He looked up.

"She's notorious among General Wade's troops, and she will lure a man like a siren—before she steals documents out from under him. There is . . . a peculiar power about her. I cannot quite explain it. Have you come here intending to capture her, sir?"

"No. I'm a lawyer, not a constable. But since I was here reviewing legal documents, General Wade asked me to look into this matter as well. I'll take a written testimony of your encounter with this Katie Hell, if you don't mind, Lieutenant." He pulled a sheet of paper from a stack, picked up a pen, and dipped the point in a small inkpot.

"Of course, sir. She must be caught."

"Indeed. She's making a mockery of all of us with these antics." Alec turned his attention to the woodcut image printed on the page: a slender young woman with a pistol in one hand and a knife in the other. She was dressed in tartan knee breeches and a snug matching jacket, with a plaid sash crossing her ample bosom, and jaunty buckled shoes on her feet over stockings that clung to shapely calves. A Highland bonnet with a feather sat upon her hair, which was pulled back by a loop of ribbon, with fat curls spilling over one shoulder. A beauty mark graced her cheek, and her eyes were large and clear above a pouting mouth.

Alec began to read aloud.

Katie Hell, Notorious Highland Wench, acts as an intriguante *for the Jacobite Cause. Using feminine wiles, this Highland wanton lures governmental soldiers with her charms, then renders her victims senseless and purloins the property of crown and king. Of a wild and unpredictable temperament, this siren is thought by superstitious Highlanders to possess the magic of the Scottish fairies . . .*

He looked up at the young officer. "Was that your experience? Rendered senseless, and so on?"

"She, er, did hit me in the head with my pistol."

"Aye?" Alec glanced up, intrigued. "Go on."

"She's not like the silly strumpet in that drawing, though she has a quality to her that seems . . . almost magical, I'll admit. When I saw her, she wore a modest

gown and had fine manners. I was enchanted, in a way.
It never would have occurred to me that she practiced
espionage, though I could believe she might possess . . .
well, fairy magic. That is, until she took up my flintlock
and knocked me in the head with it."

Alec nodded, perusing the page. "She looks more
like a pirate than a fairy. Could you identify her if you
saw her again?"

"I am not sure. It was dark, and there was only candlelight in my tent. She was a lovely and gentle young
lady, innocent and educated. Not that painted harlot."
He gestured toward the broadsheet. "She left a token
behind. A white ribbon sewn like a rose. The white
cockade of the Jacobites."

"Aye, she's left them before. I've seen other
accounts—what was your experience of her?" Alec
poised the pen to write.

"Just as the sheet says, she is a siren. I could not resist
her charms. There is something delectable about her."

"Siren. Delectable." Alec made a few more notes. "So
you enjoyed a tryst with her?"

"I, uh, do not know." The black hat went round in circles in the officer's hands. "I cannot remember all of it."

Alec frowned. He had read the same in the other tes-
timonies: the officers were never quite sure what tran-
spired after they met the Highland wench, though they
mentioned kissing, then they either fell asleep or
passed out drunk. Alec suspected the girl might have
used potions of some sort to affect the men. Upon waking, each officer found a white cockade and discovered
documents missing from his quarters.

Heron shrugged. "And when I woke, the girl was gone."

Alec scratched his pen over the paper. "This girl is clever, Lieutenant. None of the officers seem to know who she is, what she looks like, or what exactly happened. They all seemed bewildered. Her ruse of having fairy magic is quite clever," he said wryly, "and even practical soldiers seem to believe it. Go on. Was anything missing from your tent?"

"Maps and chocolate."

"What?" Alec looked up in surprise.

"I do cartographic drawings for General Wade to chart the Highland roads his crews are constructing. My maps were gone, and a tin of chocolate powder was missing. Our family's preferred variety of chocolate drink, if I may say so, is always Fraser's Fancy Imported Cocoa Powder, which I understand your family manufactures. Most excellent."

"Thank you. I will convey your compliments." Alec shifted papers, unwilling to discuss, or even think, about his neglected role in the Fraser chocolate import business. "How do you know this girl took the things?"

As a knock sounded on the wooden post between the tent flaps, Alec glanced up, and the lieutenant turned.

A Highland woman peeked through the flaps, a bulky plaid wrapped over her head and form against the wind and rain, worn over a shabby green dress. Holding a basket filled with folded linens under one arm, she spoke in Gaelic and pointed toward the bed, then the basket. Her hand was swathed in a moth-eaten fingerless glove.

"The laundress," the lieutenant told Alec. "I've seen her around camp. Harmless. A bit of a lackwit."

"I see. Miss, come back later, if you please." Alec half stood out of habit in the presence of a female.

She came inside regardless, mumbling in Gaelic and waving a hand to indicate she only needed a few moments. Brushing rain from her hood, she went toward Alec's narrow cot, set down her basket, and began to strip away the blanket and bedsheets.

"Miss, we are busy here," Alec said, sitting again.

"She doesn't understand much English," the lieutenant said. "A few local women tend the chores in this camp, and none speaks a comprehensible word. They do their tasks well enough, but come and go as they please without regard for manners or protocol."

The woman hummed to herself, and seemed not only plump but clumsy, dropping clean linens on the earth floor and picking them up to shake the dirt off. Unable to see her face well, Alec noticed that under all her clothing, she had a womanly shape and was perhaps not as plump as he thought. And a glimpse of a very pleasant face under the shadow of her plaid showed a younger woman than he expected.

She took a clean sheet from her basket and snapped it out to spread it over the mattress. The crisp scent wafted through the tent, pleasantly dissipating the musty smells of grass and earth.

"Miss," Alec began. "Please—" But the girl ignored him.

"It's no use, Captain," Heron said. "So long as we set up military camps in Highland areas while General

Wade's road-building campaign continues, we must hire help from among the locals. Many of them only speak the Irish tongue, and while they are genial—and the women are bonny," he added, glancing at the laundress, "they can be a stubborn and superstitious lot."

"To be fair," Alec murmured, "Highlanders are also a generous, polite, hospitable sort. And there is no more handsome race on earth, so they say." He cocked an eyebrow. "I was raised in the Highlands."

"I, ah, beg your pardon, Captain," Heron mumbled.

"Now," Alec continued, "I presume the sentries check the identities of all women entering this camp, given the events of the last several months?"

"Of course." Heron waved his hand. "They're often kinfolk, sharing the work among themselves."

"Not reassuring, given the bonds among Jacobite families."

"Aye, but we've had only two incidents here, myself and Colonel Grant." Heron cleared his throat. "Ever since the colonel met this Katie Hell himself, he makes certain no female goes in or out of camp without identifying herself. He was furious about his experience. Still is—claims she was a harlot and threatened his life. Though he was not crowned with a pistol butt, sir."

"I've read the testimony. His pride was more wounded than anything else," Alec agreed. "To continue, Lieutenant, how do you know the girl took your things? The maps and the, er, cocoa?"

"She complimented my drawings and expressed interest in the chocolate, even made us each a cup with boiled water and sugar. Said she was devoted to chocolate and must have some."

Having tucked the sheets, the laundress lifted the blanket to shake it out. The movement rustled the papers on Alec's desk, and several of them scattered to the ground.

"*Tcha*," she muttered, turning to catch up the pages, stepping on some and crumpling others in handfuls as she bent to fetch them. Her hands were swallowed by the shabby sleeves of the overlarge dress she wore under her plaid cloak. Alec noticed that her hands were slender and pale in the fingerless gloves.

Mumbling in Gaelic, she slapped crushed pages on his desk and bent to fetch the rest. Alec leaned down to do the same, and their heads knocked with an audible sound. She gasped and glanced up at him.

Beautiful eyes, he saw, of an extraordinary silver color. He stared, and his mind flickered over a memory. Had he seen this simple Highland woman before?

"Sorry," he said, stretching out a hand to touch her plaid-swathed head. An odd ripple plunged through him, an instant need, a craving. Had it been so long since he had been near a woman?

She rose quickly, and Alec turned back to his work. "Pardon, Lieutenant. We were saying." Alec picked up the broadsheet to look at the image of Katie Hell again. "So the vixen snatched your pistol? Why was that?"

"Well . . . I attempted to demonstrate my affection by, ah, kissing her. Then she hit me with the butt of my pistol."

"Ah." Alec glanced up. "And why was she in your tent?"

"I found her wandering in the camp after dark. She said she was looking for a kinsman but seemed to be in the wrong encampment. She was weary and lost, and I offered my help."

"Did she give you her name?"

"Marie. It's . . . all I remember, at any rate."

The laundress picked up a feather pillow and smacked it hard, then laid it on the bed and smoothed the blankets again.

"Was she Scots or Highland?"

"She spoke excellent English, without a trace of brogue. And she understood French when I, er, recited some poetry to her."

"Poetry." Alec wrote it down. "Would you say she was bonny?"

"Yes. Quite young, and delicate in appearance. Her hair was blond, or perhaps ash or reddish, and her eyes were blue, or green. Could have been gray. I remember that her gown was dark, and she wore a lace cap and a dark cape and hood. She smelled like lavender. Her hair was so soft," he said dreamily.

Alec took up the pen. "Eyes of an uncertain color, hair of an indeterminate shade, speaks French and English, dark clothing, smells like a sachet . . . not very specific. Can you add anything?"

"She had a rare quality," Heron said, nodding. "A sort of allure and innocence all at once, so that I wanted to protect her as much as . . . make love to her. An irresistible combination and hard to define. I felt besotted, even bespelled. Perhaps the rumors that she is a fairy, or practices magic, are true."

Alec set down the pen. "The other officers reported similar impressions. You may have been drugged by something she put in your cup of chocolate."

"I find that hard to believe—she was so appealing, so tender and gentle. I desired her completely——"

"I hope your sore head convinced you otherwise," Alec added with chagrin. While Heron nodded and fidgeted with his hat, Alec glanced again at the laundress, who took a shirt and a pair of tartan stockings from the basket and laid them on the bed.

The garments were not his own, but he'd accept them regardless, he thought. Wiggling his feet inside his buckled shoes, he realized he had worn the same shirt, plaid, waistcoat, and stockings for far too long. Clothing often had to last indefinitely in the field, but he preferred fresh shirts and stockings whenever possible. The clean bed linens the laundress had brought were an unexpected boon. The local washerwomen were efficient at their work, he thought.

Narrowing his eyes, he studied the girl, whose back was turned. She seemed plain enough, with no trace of the irresistible female described by the men who had met the *intriguante* Katie Hell. But for those lovely eyes, which he had glimpsed when she had dropped the papers . . .

Thoughtfully, he watched the Highland girl.

Katie Hell would have to be stupid as well as bold, he decided, to enter a tent with two officers inside. He glanced at the lieutenant. "That will be all, Lieutenant.

21

I'll give the notes to General Wade. He's anxious to find the woman who has been harassing his officers."

"Sir, I would not call it that. It was more like . . . a few moments of bliss, sir. A taste of magic. She is enchanting."

"She's a clever vixen, who has turned some soldiers' hearts and turned the rest on their ear."

"Yes, sir. I suppose that's true." The officer glanced down.

"Dismissed, Lieutenant. But first, allow me to replace your supply of cocoa powder." Alec stood. "My aunt posts tins to me often. Far too often." He indicated a small table that held cups, spoons, a silver pot, and a stack of black-and-gold tins of tea, cocoa, and coffee. Choosing three tins, he handed them to Heron.

"Thank you. That's very generous."

"Not at all. I prefer stronger drink, but my aunt will not post whiskey." He grinned.

Heron laughed, nodded his thanks, and left the tent.

Alec returned to the desk. The laundress pushed the used bed linens in the basket, then picked up the load and prepared to leave. He looked up, and again something tugged at his memory—had he seen her before?

He studied the concealing drape of the plaid, the up-tilt nose, the curve of her cheek. Just a bonny Highland girl, he thought, with a bonny shape hidden under all that clothing. She did not look at him, and the notion passed from his head. She was nothing like the clever wanton in the descriptions.

He folded into his chair and took up the broadsheet illustration once again. "Katie Hell," he murmured, "you've tied a few knots in the British military fabric, lass."

The laundress walked past him, basket in her hands, heading for the doorway. Again a feeling nudged at him. "Miss," he said.

She stopped, back turned. "*Oiche mhar*," she answered.

"Oik-uh var," he repeated, his accent stiff with disuse. "Not 'good night' just yet, Miss. Come here, if you please."

Chapter 2

~~~OO~~~

Kate's heart sank as she faced the tent flaps. Dear God, did Captain Fraser remember seeing her in London?

He would need only a small leap of reason to realize that a Scotswoman who had appeared at the king's London court, then turned up in a governmental officer's tent posing as a Highland laundress, must be an *intriguante*—and might be Katie Hell, the spy wanted by the military. If he asked Lieutenant Heron or Colonel Grant to identify her, the ruse would be over, and she and her kinsmen, too, would be in grave danger.

She kept her head turned away, knowing she could not allow the captain to recognize her as the lady from St. James's Palace.

Upon entering the tent, she had seen with sudden shock that the captain was actually the Highland swordsman she had seen in London. The other man was the young lieutenant she had met weeks ago. Yet neither man paid much attention to her as she had moved cautiously around the tent. For weeks she had come and gone in the camp on the pretense of doing laundry, which she delivered to some local cousins who did the actual work for the soldiers.

Even now her heartbeat quickened foolishly in his presence. Months ago, she had learned that the Highland swordsman was a Fraser from a family of tea and cocoa importers, a younger son with an officer's commission, not uncommon for sons of wealthy merchant families. Certain she would never see him again, she had nonetheless dreamed of another meeting and acquired a passion for Fraser chocolate.

But she had never dreamed of encountering him like this. The man could have her arrested. Had he asked about her that day in London, as she had done? Had he learned her name?

"Miss," Fraser said firmly. "Come here, please."

"Oiche mhar," she repeated, hand on the tent flap. Her knees had begun to tremble, and she did not turn around.

She had taken great risk in coming to his tent to search for some vital documents for her Jacobite kinsmen. She had learned that the new captain had the lists of recently arrested Highland prisoners—and her kinsmen needed that list. Even now, one of her cousins waited outside in the darkness and the rain to get the paper, and to spirit her away to safety.

"Miss, come here, please," he repeated in a stern tone.

Running would only raise his suspicions. Turning slightly, she ducked her head under the shadow of her plaid shawl.

"Shirt," Fraser said, plucking at his sleeve. "*Leinen*?"

"*Leine*," she corrected in surprise.

"My Gaelic is not what it was when I was a lad," he explained. "My *leine* needs laundering, if you will take it." As he spoke, he undid the buttons of his waistcoat.

Kate pointed to the garments folded on the bed, careful to answer in rapid Gaelic. "Your clean shirts are there."

"*Leine*," he repeated.

"For a Highlander," she went on, "you do not know your own language very well." He blinked at her and smiled vaguely. Then he lifted his shirt high to remove it. "*Ach*, but you are a beautiful Highland man," Kate murmured.

She moved close and stretched out her arm for the shirt, which he quickly stripped over his head, then tossed toward her.

Catching the garment, she stared, stunned. He stood bare to the waist in lanternlight, taut and beautiful as a god. His wide shoulders and chest were smoothly muscled above the wrapped plaid draped around his taut abdomen. His shining brown-gilt hair slipped loose from its ribbon to brush his shoulders. He looked more like a proud Celtic warrior than a loathsome king's man.

Again, as in London, she felt the strange effect he

26

had on her, powerful and somewhat entrancing. She could barely think.

Holding the shirt, she spun away, and her basket knocked against the table. Papers fluttered to the floor.

"Blast," Fraser muttered, and bent below the level of the table to fetch the fallen pages.

Kate took that moment to quickly scan the papers on his desk: the dreadful broadsheet depicting the "Highland Wench" as a virago or worse; Fraser's interview notes; a few long lists written in a clerk's hand. Those pages must be what she needed.

She reached out, but Fraser stood again. Kate whipped her hand away so quickly that next she tipped over a china cup perched at the edge of the table. Liquid—strong hot tea, by the look of it—spilled over the papers, soaking the broadsheet. She snatched at the page just as Fraser did, and it tore.

As he grabbed at the other papers, Kate dropped her basket and snatched a linen towel to sop up the spill. Fraser took the cloth from her to swipe at the rapidly blurring ink, swearing under his breath as he did so.

More flustered now, Kate righted the cup and set it on a table that held the silver pot and tins. The pot contained steaming tea, so she refilled the cup, wondering frantically how to get a closer look at the lists that Fraser was salvaging from the mishap she had caused.

With the other officers she had encountered, all she needed most of the time was to let her charm work its magic through soft conversation, smiles, flattery, a laugh, a touch on the arm. More often than not the men fell into a dreamy daze, particularly if they had already been imbibing. Then she usually found a moment to look through papers and slip important pages into her pocket.

She could not risk taking time to use her natural magic on this man. Not only might he remember her from the London court, but she had the sense that her fairy gift would not work with him as easily as it had on others.

She must find the pages and get away quickly. Slipping a hand in her skirt pocket, she touched the glass vial tucked there, which held an herbal sleeping infusion. She had sometimes used it in officers' drinks to protect herself from their advances.

Slowly she opened the little vial with her fingers. A swift glance had already showed her that Ian Cameron's name was on one of the pages that Fraser was holding. Ian had been arrested indeed, and her brother and kinsmen needed to know where he was being kept. Finding Cameron, Kate knew, would not only save the man. It would also prevent the government from learning his secret, which could protect the lives and the welfare of hundreds, perhaps thousands, of Highland Jacobites.

Fraser stood then, and Kate set the cup on the desk without a chance to add the herbal drops. He glanced at her in silence. Kate turned away, heart pounding, having missed the chance to dose his tea.

Another choice remained to her, a method she had heard about but never tried. The very thought made her uneasy.

According to MacCarran family lore, those who inherited the gift of charm from their fairy ancestress also had the power of throwing a glamourie, a spell of enchantment that could bedazzle another, suspending awareness and even time itself.

She had never tried it, relying only on natural-born charm and good luck. Unsure how she could even throw a spell, she did not honestly believe herself capable of it, despite family legend. As a young girl she had found it hard enough to accept that she had an engaging effect that went beyond the ordinary. Putting that to good use to help her clan was well enough. Spellcasting was another matter entirely.

Several years ago, when her family still lived together happily at Duncrieff Castle, her grandmother and aunts had been experts on the family legends. They had cautioned Kate to cast a glamourie only if she understood its power. Certainly she could never understand it—others in the family knew the MacCarran lore far better than she did. An old, enormous manuscript, its pages added over centuries, contained the family's fairy and magical traditions, but the thing was a daunting piece of scholarship. Kate had scarcely opened its pages.

Besides, she felt sure that the MacCarran glamourie would never work on Fraser. The man did not seem the least bit bedazzled by her charm.

In fact, he seemed annoyed, scowling under lowered brows as he gathered the scattered papers. Kate had rarely faced that sort of reaction from men—in fact, not since her father had once caught her looking at a book in his library, a collection of Italian engravings show-ing naked couples joined in all sorts of interesting posi-tions. To others, Kate could do no wrong, a quality her mother claimed did her daughter no good at all.

While Fraser was occupied, Kate took a chance and emptied the glass vial into the fresh tea. Bitter-tasting but otherwise harmless, the herbs produced sound sleep. Finding a bowl of fine sugar, she spooned a healthy serving into the cup.

Handing him the cup, she felt uncomfortably like a spider spinning out its web to catch its unsuspecting prey.

He accepted it. "Thank you . . . *tapadh leat*," he trans-lated.

His slight Gaelic gave her a sense of quick guilt. Most of the officers she had met were puppets in red coats, Whigs all, and as a Highlander with a Jacobite father who had died in exile, she had good reason to dislike them. Every one she encountered had become infatu-ated with her to some degree, and some had been cloy-ing or lusty fools, easy to dislike and dismiss.

But Captain Fraser was none of that. Even in the coat of a red soldier, even knowing he was not quite the Highland warrior she had once imagined him to be, he still made her blood quicken.

Oh please just drink it, she thought, fighting the urge to snatch it away from him. *Drink it and forgive me.*

He raised the cup in salute. "You're a clumsy wee thing, Miss Washerwoman, but a bonny lass for all that, and I hope you're better at the laundry than the house-keeping." He drank.

Her sense of guilt increased sharply, but she leaned down to fuss with the laundry in the basket. His discarded shirt still smelled of him—traces of warm comfort, of strength and manliness. She picked up the basket and moved toward the tent entrance, then glanced back.

He sat in the chair, sipping as he sorted the papers. Lifting a hand to his head, he shoved his fingers through thick, wavy hair, gold threading through darker strands.

Just as she left the tent, Kate saw him tip his head on his hand as he studied the page, as if he felt fatigued.

Quelling the feeling of guilt, she stepped away and glanced around anxiously at the shapes of the tents in growing darkness.

As she ran forward, a figure emerged from the gloom—a tall Highlander by his shape. Kate gasped, then rushed toward her cousin. Allan MacCarran caught her by the shoulder and pulled her out of sight to a private spot.

"What happened?" he murmured in Gaelic. "I was listening in case you might need me—you were in there a while."

"All is well," Kate whispered.

"Did you find the list of arrests, then?"

"I saw it but had no chance to get it. The officer is still awake. Allan, listen," she went on urgently. "He saw me months ago, when I was in London last. I gave him the herbal infusion, but it is too risky for me to go back. He could easily realize that I am involved in espionage, being both a lady and a laundress. He's not a stupid man, this one."

Allan shook his head. "You can charm him as you've done with all the others. That tincture will put him out cold. Search out the pages and get away fast as you can."

She panicked suddenly, torn between an urge to flee the camp and an inexplicable yearning to return to Fraser's tent. The pull of the strange and wonderful magic he exuded over her was strong—and she knew better than anyone the irony of that.

"We've got to have that list," Allan said. "We must discover where the redcoats are keeping Ian Cameron since his arrest. Your brother's friend knows where that Spanish cache is hidden, and we must get Ian out before the English can force information out of him. He was taken down before he could meet your brother. We'd best get to him quickly."

"I understand," she replied. Although she did not know Ian Cameron personally, she was aware that his involvement was essential to her kinsmen's covert work. "But if this captain catches me out, and recognizes me—it's too much chance to take."

"A few moments only, and you'll be gone from there," Allan assured her. "Cameron knows where those missing weapons are, and if the red soldiers should find out the location before we do, the insurrection will suffer. This means a good deal to your clan and kin, lass."

Kate sighed. Her loyalty to her clan and to her brother was unquestioned. She would do anything for Robert, chief of the MacCarrans of Duncrieff. If he considered Ian Cameron a steadfast friend, and this mission imperative to the Cause, that was more than enough reason to do whatever she could.

"Fine," she whispered. "I'll go back."

Allan turned with her. "I'll be just here. Call out if you need me."

A chill ran through her, but she hurried back to the tent through drizzling rain. Pushing her way inside, she knotted the ties behind her to seal out the world.

Setting the basket by the door, she approached cautiously. Captain Fraser rested his head on his arms, eyes closed, and seemed asleep. The infusion had finally taken hold. Coming closer, Kate looked at him curiously.

He was tall and large-boned, with an almost leonine elegance in face and form. His profile was classically handsome, partly obscured by a sweep of thick hair, deep brown and sun-streaked. She noted taut skin and good bones, straight dark brows over closed eyes fringed with dark lashes, an aristocratic nose that sloped toward the tender curve of his mouth.

His eyes opened, and she saw a flash of dark blue. "Ugh," he muttered, and raised his head, groggy as a drunkard.

Regret rushed through her—he had not attacked her as some other officers had tried, yet she had dealt him this repercussion. He sat up, batting an arm out, clumsily sweeping papers, inkpot, and the china cup off the table. As he stood, stumbling, the chair tipped back and fell over.

Kate bent to fetch the broken cup, setting the pieces

33

aside. The potion she had given Fraser was strong, yet even the full vial had not taken him down completely. He was still alert, though weakened.

As she straightened, he grabbed her upper arms and pulled her toward him. Alarmed, Kate pushed at his chest, and her arisaid slipped from her head, dragging with it the white cap pinned over her hair, exposing her face and bright golden hair to his full view.

He frowned. "My God . . . I've seen you before." His words were low, slurred.

"No," she whispered. "Let go, please." She wriggled in his hold, speaking English without thinking.

"Blast it, I feel dizzy . . . what the devil did you put in that tea?" With an iron grip, he held her so closely that she craned her head to look up at him. "Too sweet, it was . . . with a hint of bitter. What have you done?"

"It will not harm you, though you will sleep some," she said. "Lie down over there." She pushed him toward the cot, for he was unstable on his feet and in danger of falling.

"You spoke Gaelic before . . . damn, I am befuddled." He shook his head. Then he teetered, and his knees buckled.

"Here, let me help you." Kate fitted her shoulder under his arm to support him.

Leaning his weight on her, his hand capping her shoulder, he looked down at her. "I swear I've seen you before."

With an arm around his waist, she guided him to the bed. "You're dreaming. Sit, now."

He collapsed rather than sat, falling to the mattress,

feet still on the floor. He kept hold of her, and Kate went down with him in a fast tumble. His arms felt so good—but she wiggled away and got to her feet. She struggled to lift his legs onto the bed, though he was tall and muscular, and greatly outweighed her.

He lay sprawled on the narrow cot, one knee raised, his rucked plaid revealing the knotted thigh muscles. His broad chest was bare, the red coat falling open, brass lapel buttons gleaming. She pulled the folded blanket over him and stepped back, but he snatched her wrist and tugged her toward him, so that she fell once again into his embrace.

"Oof," she said softly, pushing.

"No, stay," he murmured. With one hand, he swept his fingers over her hair, now loose of its pins. Blond strands spilled free in the lanternlight. "Fairy gold."

"No—please, I must—" she shoved at him.

He resisted easily, despite his weakened state, wrapping her hair like a skein around his hand to pull her close. "You're the one," he said in a husky voice. "The fairy queen."

She caught her breath. Surely he did not know about her ancestry. The herbs had addled his brain so that he spoke coincidental nonsense. "What—do you mean?" she whispered.

"I saw you in London," he answered, his face near her own, his breath soft upon her lips. "We called you the fairy queen."

She felt relieved. "My ancestress was a fairy, so they say. But no matter. You will not remember this in the morning."

"I've caught you." He drew her close by the winding of her hair, and with his other hand he cupped her face. "And now I'll keep you."

He kissed her then, his mouth warm and tender. Kate felt herself begin to dissolve under that luscious kiss, the sort of kiss to dream about.

She should flee. But his fingers slid along her jaw to cradle and tilt her head, and his mouth claimed hers again, deep and stirring. Heart pounding, she surrendered utterly.

Never had she been kissed like this—never. The power of it swept through her, took her breath. Sinking in his arms, she savored his kiss, the next, another, each one more delicious and tender than the last. She brought a hand up to cup his cheek, and the whiskery growth of a day or two felt like sand under her fingertips. Moving her hand upward, she found his hair, so thick and soft that she sighed. His lips moved over hers, divine and warm and vital.

She opened her mouth to his, pleading silently for more. But he paused, sighed, and his head sank to the mattress. He closed his eyes, drawing her down with him. She waited, realized that he was finally succumbing, and reluctantly drew back.

Leave, she told herself. *Let him dream, and wake without a good recollection of the night, wondering who I am.*

In spite of herself, she leaned toward him again, longing for one more kiss. She felt as if she were the one bespelled.

He stirred and pulled her more fully into his embrace, rolled to his side with her and touched his lips to hers again.

She had tasted a variety of kisses—dry, forceful, timid, mushy as pudding, many of them nice enough. But each one she had been able to dismiss from her thoughts and heart later. No man's kiss had ever touched off such a needfire within her.

Oh, his were kisses to remember, to cherish. His lips caressed hers, kneaded, sending deep shivers of pleasure through her. His breath warmed her, his hands upon her excited her so that she wanted to melt in his arms and do all his will. When his mouth took hers again like a storm, she gave in to the passion building within her, and met his lips with maddening hunger. His hands traced along her shoulders, her arms, grazed lightly over her breasts until she wanted to cry out. Each touch, each kiss felt perfect, beautiful, something she must savor.

Had she gone mad? Logic reminded her that she must go, that her cousin waited for her. She must find the papers and run.

But she felt overwhelmed by a strength of passion she had never before imagined, felt herself succumb to the fragile will of the body against such a divine onslaught.

And she knew, then, suddenly, that a kiss could be food for an inner hunger, a caress warmth for a chilled and lonely soul. She had craved this for years and had not even known how much until this moment. She only wanted more.

She felt the wild pulse of his desire all through him,

felt it echo in her, so that she trembled, moaned. His mouth found hers again, the kiss this time so deep and rich that joy poured through her, pure and astonishing and wholly unexpected.

"Oh God," she whispered against his mouth, "dear God—" And he took her again in a kiss, his hand cupping her breast, her body throbbing sweetly throughout at that single exquisite touch. Anticipation pounded within her like a drum as his hand moved over her in sweeping caresses. She kissed him in fervent response, forgetting where she was, who she was, and that anyone waited outside for her.

Chapter 3

Looping her arms around his neck, she sighed as his hand tucked into the small of her back, and she felt the hard press of his body against hers.

She could not stay—but let herself savor more, sighing as his hands moved over her in delectable rhythm, while his body tightened against hers like iron. Only a moment more, she told herself, and she would run from here. . . .

His tongue swept hers, his fingers slid up her back, over her shoulder and down, grazing over her modesty kerchief, over her stiffened bodice and the warm flesh beneath. She shivered, arched to welcome his explorations.

Another kiss, and one more, and she realized she was starved for this sort of touch, for true passion, deep and genuine. He kissed her again, lips tracing over her cheek, her ear, his breath warming her.

For a moment she felt as if she were falling, and she clutched at him, her hands upon his bare chest beneath his red coat—that hateful red jacket. His skin felt warm, smooth, his heartbeat bounding beneath muscle.

Never had she let a man touch her like this, or even go beyond a few kisses—Katie Hell was still a virgin, though it might not fit her persona. Her kinsmen would kill any man who went so far with her, yet she did not, could not, put an end to what was happening.

She knew she was the one captivated, helpless against his charm and the surprising depth of passion he tapped within her. Lost in that current, she met him with her own hunger, sensing that she could discover something magnificent if only she would let her feelings flare. A little longer, she promised herself, gasping as his mouth traced along her throat.

Soon enough he would sleep, and when he woke, Katie Hell would be gone. His memory would be dim, but she would have her own memories to treasure and a sense of what passion, even love, might be like—a secret she could take into the rest of her life.

Silent, aware that her cousin waited outside to defend her if he perceived trouble, she sighed as he touched her, as her breasts tingled under her chemise and bodice. She nearly cried aloud as his other hand traced over her skirts, as he pushed aside her layered skirt and petticoat. When his warm palm grazed her knee, then her thigh, she caught her breath and tucked her face against his shoulder.

Sublime madness, she thought, as her heart pounded harder. She kissed his jaw, felt the rasp of his beard, the tender swell of his lips, his moist tongue upon hers. She groaned on a breath, and as his hand cupped her breast, she arched against him.

He was hard and insistent against her now, and she shifted her hand and found the shape of him, began to explore him, her fingers curious, trembling. She moved her hand over his kilt, pulled at the plaid, and he slid his fingers beneath her skirt. Each touched intimate flesh in the same instant, each gasped in harmony.

And she let him do what he would, this man, only this man. The wanton of the broadsheets, the fairy seductress, did not even exist. No man had ever touched her thus.

His exploration of her was astonishing, quickly thrilling as he found the innermost pulse of her body and brought it to heat, then flame. She cried out, the soft sound taken by his kiss. Consumed and released by bliss, she lay quiet and astonished in his arms.

Then she turned her face against his cheek in silence. The exquisite tenderness of his touch had erased, in mere moments, any other kiss or caress she had endured for the sake of her loyalty to her clan and to Scotland. If nothing else came of this night, for that taste of freedom and passion alone she felt in his debt.

He held her—just held her, so that she sighed against him—then she slid her hands downward to find his

41

hard and vibrant shape, wanting to return to him what he had given her. Instinct and common sense told her what he needed. The hard length of him was warm, smooth, like heated iron within; but he put her hand away from him and turned with a low groan to sag against the bed. When he did not move, Kate pushed at his shoulder and realized that the herbs had finally taken him down.

Time was slipping past, and she knew she must leave, though some foolish part of her wanted to stay. But she could not.

She simply could not, no matter how her heart began to stir, began to awaken.

Besides, the lore of her clan held that she could only accept true love to preserve the fairy gift and the well-being of the clan. Anything less would diminish the power within the clan.

And true love, she knew, was rare enough that she need not even think about finding it—particularly not so quickly, though what burned within her, newly lit, gave her hope.

She could imagine, at least, and could treasure what he had shown her about herself, and about loving. She kissed his temple, soothed a hand over the dark silk of his hair, and eased away.

She must hurry—the list must be found. Her cousin waited to see her home again, with several miles to travel on foot to safety.

Kate stepped away, limbs trembling, and went about her work.

* * *

He rarely dreamed, and never of fairies, yet this one had slipped into his arms and his dream as lightly as a summer breeze. Exquisite, luscious, she felt divinely real against him, though he did not know if he imagined, or truly experienced, his body's throbbing response or her soft cries of pleasure at his touch. He only surrendered to the magic.

But he finally realized she was gone, had slipped away into the mist that seemed to surround him. Sinking into sleep, his mind was foggy, and he disliked the sensation. Something was not right.

Struggling against the miasma, refusing to give in, he inhaled, forced himself to surge upward. Opening his eyes, he saw slanting tent walls above him, lantern-light playing crazily on the canvas. He felt dizzy, dry-mouthed, impatient with the sensations that drained his strength.

Noticing a shadow on the canvas walls, he turned his head.

She was there, the girl he had held and loved in his strange dream. Her hair, haloed by the light, was like spun gold. She stood over his writing desk, searching through papers, unfolding pages, sifting through his notes, his correspondence, and several military documents.

No blasted fairy at all, he saw then, but the laundress. He scowled, rubbed his eyes, looked again. Dear God. Had he just played bedsport with the Highland laundress?

Silently, carefully, Alec raised himself on one elbow. Her back was turned to him, and she seemed intent on her task of pilfering his papers. He sat up, slid his feet to the floor, watching her. The room spun.

The girl turned her head a little, and Alec saw her profile more clearly. She was the girl in his dream, most definitely—a delicate beauty with flawless skin, a slightly upturned nose, eyes of silvery gray. He had most certainly seen her before.

The realization hit him like a shock of cold water. She had been in London, gowned in yellow and gold. She was neither fairy nor laundress—she had to be the spy they had all been searching out. And he had been seduced and drugged.

What a fool he had been not to realize it sooner. She had been clever, her ruse easy enough to believe . . . and she had managed to take him down before he could stop her. Like all the rest, he had fallen for her.

Rustling frantically through his papers, Katie Hell did not glance behind her. Though his head whirled, Alec sat up and reached out toward the small table. His fingers closed on his pistol.

The little hellion selected a few pages, folding and tucking them in the pocket of her skirt. She slid another sheet into her bodice, into the warm cleavage that he had touched, kissed. Her scent, lavender and clean, still clung to him, and the strange influence she had over him—quite apart from the effect of whatever she must have dumped into his tea—whirled him around, head and heart.

The girl snatched up her plaid and stepped away from the desk, neglecting to look behind her in her haste to get away.

Alec cocked the pistol, the click loud in the silence. She whirled.

"Katie, my darling," he murmured, aiming the barrel at her. "How very good to meet you at last."

Chapter 4

Voices droned behind her though she hardly listened to them. She stood in stockinged feet, hands manacled with iron. Since earlier that day, her guards had not permitted her to sit or even to move. A short length of chain, pulled taut, ran from the manacles to a bolt high in the wall, and any attempt she made to sink down or significantly shift her weight would jerk the chain until it pulled painfully on her arms. Not long ago she had fallen, and a guard had appeared to prop her up, giving her a gruff warning to be careful before he left the cell.

Weary, near collapse but determined not to move, she watched darkness gather in the tiny prison cell. Cold seeped through the straw on the stone floor, making her shiver. Somewhere behind her, lanternlight cast her shadow, slim and straight, on the wall in front of her, where the iron links bit into stone and held her in place.

Through the golden tangle of her hair, she saw other shadows—the stripes of iron bars, the shapes of guards out in the corridor. Dizzy again, she closed her eyes, but her head only seemed to whirl. She swayed on her feet, and when her knees buckled, jerked upright. Loose of its braiding, her hair spilled in a thick curtain over her face and shoulders.

She knew she was in the dungeon at Inverlochy Castle near Fort William, where governmental troops were garrisoned under General Wade. Days ago, after her arrest in Captain Fraser's tent in the Perthshire encampment, she had been taken away by dragoons, enduring a long journey north by cart through rain and cold winds until they reached this place in the Great Glen.

She could never forget how Fraser had watched her as the dragoons took her—how he had frowned in silence, then cautioned her guards not to fasten her bonds too tightly and to see that she was kept safe. Then he had turned his back and walked away.

For an instant, her foolish heart had broken, stunned by a sense of betrayal and abandonment—and by a strange feeling that she had lost hold of a precious dream. Within moments she had gathered her wits and fostered her anger, hoping she would never see Fraser again.

But even the thought of that hurt deep within, as if something pulled hard and tight, more forcefully than the damnable chains that held her now.

She sighed, tried not to think about that day. But Allan—what of her cousin? She had not seen Allan MacCarran since that night, and she had feared at first that he had been caught. But none of her guards had mentioned it, and so she clung to the hope that he had escaped and would bring word of her dilemma to her brother, Rob, and their clansmen.

After her arrival at Inverlochy, Colonel Francis Grant had come to interview her—the same colonel she had met weeks ago in Wade's Perthshire encampment. When he had questioned her, Kate had refused to answer—and so he ordered that she stand chained in her cell until she decided to talk.

Her strength was waning, but she still had her stubbornness and loyalty. She would not give her surname to her captors, for that alone would reveal her kinsmen. Grant would have sent troops out to Duncrieff to arrest them, too.

She understood the risks very well, and though her mind was muddled, she knew that Captain Alexander Fraser, who had showed her such tender passion, had arrested her and abandoned her to this fate. He had not accompanied her here. She told herself that he was not at all the man she had hoped he was. In a way, that conclusion made her feel better about despising him.

She stretched a little to ease her aching shoulders, but discomfort nagged at her everywhere—in overtaxed muscles, in chilled hands and swollen feet, in her full bladder. Ignoring all that, determined to endure, she stared ahead in silence.

After a while she heard more footsteps in the corridor, the scrape of a chair, low murmurs. On the wall, she saw shadows moving and heard the creak of the door as more footsteps padded over the straw behind her.

"Katie Hell." Francis Grant's voice, quiet and nasal, the very air around him seemed to hold loathing in it. She tensed for what might come.

Black boots and cream breeches entered her view, and she saw the thin, angular shape of his legs and the long tail of a red coat, crossed by the sash of an officer.

Glancing up, she looked into long-lidded brown eyes set in a pale and narrow face made paler by the silver wig he favored. She said nothing, though she glared at him.

She remembered Grant in the encampment weeks earlier, when he lay sprawled and snoring in shirt-sleeves and loosened trousers, a silver flask in his hand. He had been quite fond of the contents of that flask, she recalled, and she had needed neither herbal potion nor a thump on the head to subdue him—only more whiskey. Grant had sucked it up eagerly, when he was not pawing at her bodice and sucking at her mouth like a kelpie sprung from a river. Strong and wiry, his advances had left bruises on her arms that had lingered for two weeks.

Her kinsmen had nearly gone out to kill him, but she had stopped them, not wanting revenge on her conscience. After all, she had told them, no real damage had been done to her, and for the sake of the Jacobite cause, her kinsmen could not chance deliberately harming a regimental officer.

Staring at the wall, Kate wished she could tell Grant

49

that she had saved his life—and that he owed her in return for it.

"Kate," Grant said. "I'm sure you're thirsty and tired by now. Tell me what I want to know, and you'll be permitted to rest and given a hot meal."

Even the thought of rest and food made her tremble. But she stared at the wall, willing the strength of that immovable rock into her legs to keep her from collapsing.

"Tell me your name, and who sent you." She heard an edge in his voice like a knife in velvet. "Tell me why you returned again to that encampment. Your mistake, my dear, and our good fortune."

A greater mistake than anyone knew, Kate thought, thinking of Fraser. Her eyes stung. She closed them, silent.

He touched her arm, and she jerked in surprise, and when his fingers tightened, she gasped out in pain.

"Four days since they brought you here to Fort William," he murmured. "Four days without a word, and now over eighteen hours on your feet. How much can you take?"

She stared at his boots and swallowed, her mouth dry.

"Stubborn little strumpet," Grant hissed. "You will not last out this game with me. You'll talk, or die on your feet."

Panicking inwardly, Kate wondered if he was right. She struggled for breath and against the pain of his grasp.

"I do not wish to see you suffer. I remember when you came to me before . . . so tantalizing," he whispered, as he stroked her shoulder now. "You did not stay long enough, my dear. We would have enjoyed such delights together." He leaned closer. "I could have been the only man to know all Katie Hell's secrets, the only man to sample all of her intoxicating magic." His fingers stretched, grazed over her bodice, over the fullness of her breast above the stays. "I still could be that man."

She shuddered and leaned back, chains clanking, but that only extended her arms uncomfortably. Grant stood close.

"Either you tell me what I want to know, or I will tell everyone that Katie Hell was mine," he said, his breath hot and meaty on her cheek. "If you do not cooperate, you will be mine for certain, every night," he growled. "Every goddamned night."

Hearing that, her heart pounded, her knees nearly gave way. She said nothing in reply, turning her head as Grant waited.

"So be it," he hissed. "Remember, I offered you mercy." He let go of her so suddenly that she rocked with it. His boots disappeared from sight, the iron door clanged open and shut, and she heard the furious thud of his retreating footsteps.

Standing there, Kate flexed her cold, stockinged toes. Her shoes had been taken earlier, along with her plaid arisaid. All she wore was the shabby green dress, simple stays, chemise, and petticoat that she had worn as the laundress.

Her silver chain and pendant—one of the fairy crystals of Duncrieff—had been taken from her, too. Her father had plucked the crystal from the rim of the golden Fairy Cup at Duncrieff Castle for her to wear. Her sister, Sophie, had been given one, too, in a small family ceremony to mark the privilege for both of them. According to clan tradition, each child identified with the Fairy's Gift—extraordinary abilities inherited from an ancient ancestress born of the fairy folk—was given a crystal to keep with her or him. Without the protection and enhancement of the little stone, Kate knew that her inborn gift could become unreliable or even disappear altogether.

MacCarran blood held a trace of fairy, diluted over the centuries. In recent years the magic had appeared rarely in the family. Both Kate and Sophie had inherited magical talents from their fairy ancestress, abilities that could affect not only their lives but the lives, luck, and well-being of the entire clan.

Kate sighed, lowering her head. She had often questioned her own gift, even the truth of the family legends. Now, without her little crystal necklace, she felt defenseless and frightened.

Katie Hell, she thought, would not so easily charm her way free of this.

"How long has she been standing there?" Alec demanded in a low growl, gazing into the dungeon cell. "And who the devil ordered it?"

"She's been standing there since last night," the sergeant answered. "Colonel Grant's orders, sir."

Alec swore under his breath. He should have come earlier, but Wade's damned documents and tasks had delayed him.

Standing in the dark cell, the girl looked like a wisp,

a shadow of the girl he had seen before. He frowned to himself, watching her through the barred door. Her back was turned, and he could see that chains and fetters held her upright. She was shoeless and unkempt in the drab green gown, and her hair cascaded down her back in loose waves in a dingy tangle that he knew would be golden ripe in sunlight.

She wavered a little, straightened, hair rippling, feet shifting in the straw. Her weakness was obvious, but Alec also saw the steely will inside of her. The sight was heartrending.

Guilt had tormented him ever since he had called the guards into his tent after discovering the girl going through his papers. When she had been whisked away for interrogation, he had not been able to follow immediately. Once free, he had ridden northward in a grim fury. Even his ghillie had complained of the pace—and Jack MacDonald enjoyed a little madness now and then.

Alec, by nature, did not.

Dear God, he thought as he looked at her now. She appeared frail and harmless—had he made a terrible error in having her arrested? How could she be the wanton described by so many officers, the virago depicted in the broadsheet? Somehow, this fragile, determined waif was the laundress, the notorious Katie Hell, and the dazzling young woman at the king's court all at once. But how, and why?

Some said it was fairy magic, he remembered wryly, but that was nonsense. The girl had added something to his tea, pilfered documents, lain in his bed with him.

She was a schemer, a spy, a hellion, worse. Nothing fantastical about any of that.

Yet he remembered the passion he had felt for her, the comfort of holding her in his arms, the sweet taste of her kisses, her smooth skin beneath his fingertips. Had she been a harlot, or even well experienced, he would have known, but he had felt sure, that night, that an innocent had come into his bed.

He was definitely sure she was no damned fairy princess.

None of it made sense, he thought, bewildered. Whoever she was, she had a changeable nature and a host of secrets, and he meant to discover who she was and what she was about, preferably before the English military got the information out of her.

Seeing her, so tormented, he felt an angry protectiveness toward her, part compassion and part something deeper he could not define.

The girl was driving him a little mad, and he did not like that. He preferred life to be orderly, even a little predictable. At least, he tried to convince himself that he did. But her unpredictability intrigued and challenged him.

He turned. The guard sat on a wooden stool, back propped against the wall behind him, one leg extended outward. In the larger cell next to the girl's, two men reclined in shadows—one man in breeches and shabby coat, the other a large and unkempt Highlander wrapped in a plaid. Both slept.

"Has she been interrogated?" Alec asked the guard.

"She refused to reply, so Colonel Grant says she is to

stand there until she does." The sergeant struck a match and lit a pipe. The tobacco glowed, and pungent smoke filled the air.

Francis Grant. Alec frowned, remembering the man's written testimony about his meeting with Katie Hell. Alec had met Grant before, here and there, and though the colonel was his superior, Alec had scant respect for him. Grant was tense, critical, and temperamental, and carried a grudge a long way. "Sergeant, surely the girl is permitted to rest, and allowed basic courtesies."

"Not until she answers questions, says the colonel. She's hiding Jacobite secrets, Grant says, and so we'd best use strict measures. Will you be interviewing her, sir?"

Alec glanced at the girl again. She swayed, jerked upright. Then she turned her head and saw him. Recognition, and keen anger sparked in her eyes before she looked away.

"Aye, let me speak with her," Alec said. "Open the door, if you will." The soldier complied, and as the door grated open, Alec entered the cell and walked quietly toward her.

She stared at his feet through a skein of tangled hair.

"Kate," he murmured. "How are you faring?" When she glanced away and did not answer, Alec leaned close. "You'll need to talk, lass. Tell me your family name. We'll start there." He spoke quietly, watching her.

She looked away, but let out a soft, disdainful huff.

"I know you do not want to speak to me after what happened," Alec said. "But I may be your best ally here."

55

Kate rolled her eyes a little in silent disbelief.

"Captain," the sergeant said, "there's no use talking to her. She's Highland, and may not know much English."

"Or chooses not to speak it," Alec murmured, watching her.

"You're of the Highland Watch, Captain—do ye know the Irish tongue yourself? She might speak to you."

"I haven't used much Gaelic since I was in skirts on my nurse's knee," Alec replied. "And I'd wager she'd refuse to speak in any language. Isn't that so, lass?" he added softly.

Kate kept silent, but leaned toward him, her exhaustion so apparent that he felt a tug at his heart.

"We thought she'd break by now," the sergeant said. "It's an amazement she's lasted so long."

"Highland stubbornness," Alec murmured. He felt a strong urge to reach out to her and tear away those chains. But she sent him another bitter, furious glare. He knew that if he tried to help her, she might struggle against him.

"Ask her why she was spying on Wade's troops," the sergeant remarked. "Colonel Grant wants to know. She's likely working with Jacobites, though some say she's a harlot plying her trade and got caught out at it in an officer's tent. D'you think so, sir?"

Alec heard the sly question and did not comment. "How has she been treated otherwise, since her capture? Do not mistake the question, Sergeant." Alec did not take his eyes from the girl.

"Well enough, and I take your meaning."

"See that it stays that way. Kate," he said, "talk to me." He touched her shoulder.

She tried to pull away from his touch but sagged at the knees, so that her arms were pulled up sharply by the shortened chains embedded in the wall. Alec grabbed her and held her up, and she leaned against him, her cheek resting on his jacket. His heart ached for her, and he felt a furious need to take her out of the cell, and quickly.

"For love of God, girl, tell them something," he pleaded in a whisper as he held her.

"Hey, Captain sir, excuse me, but no one should be helping the wench!"

Alec looked up. "Sergeant, you can see the punishment is useless. She cannot tell us anything in this condition." While he spoke, she found enough strength to push at him. "Be still, blast it, I'm trying to help you," he muttered.

"Colonel said to beware, she'll put on an act to fool us into pitying her. She's a Jezebel, sir. Though I will say, I feel sorry for her m'self. But the colonel ordered—"

"I'm changing those orders," Alec snapped. "This treatment is ended, Sergeant, as of this moment." He had seen enough, heard enough, and suddenly could not tolerate it any longer.

"But—the colonel outranks you," the man blustered.

Without reply, Alec slid an arm around Kate's shoulders and with the other caught her under the hips to lift her easily. Crossing the cell, he knelt and set her down on the straw. She was limp as a doll. He removed his red jacket and swept it over her to cover her, and saw then that her feet, through damp cotton stockings, were swollen and purpling.

The sergeant rushed in, protesting, and Alec looked up. "The blood has pooled in her feet and legs," he said tersely. "She must lie prone and rest, or she could die of an apoplexy."

"But she's a healthy young thing, sir. Pretty as they come, and strong, too. She'd best get back on her feet, or it's my head to an onion, sir."

"I'll take the blame. Send for water, blankets, and something hot, broth or tea if it's available." Alec stood. "And find a woman to tend her. There must be some local woman, an herbwife, a cook, anyone you can find in a hurry."

"There's a housekeeper here at the castle."

"Good. See it done." Alec reached into his sporran and pulled out a few coins, handing them to the soldier, who nodded.

"But sir, what should I tell Colonel Grant?"

"Tell him she's no damn good to anyone if she dies." Alec strode out of the cell, footsteps echoing in the corridor.

Chapter 5

❦ ❦

"**G**ood Jamaican rum, by God, smuggled in along the Solway Coast." General Wade sloshed the liquid into a pewter cup, which he handed to Alec. "We apprehended this lot before it disappeared inland. Reserved some, and sent the rest south for taxation." A tall man with a regal bearing, Wade clinked his cup against Alec's. "Here's to finishing these damnable Highland roads. May we see better weather and fewer damned Highlanders."

"Sir, you are talking to a Highlander," Alec murmured, then sipped, the cloying burn sliding down his throat.

Wade swallowed, then grimaced in apology. "If your uncle were not the chief of the Lovat Frasers, I wonder

if you would be here at all, making any sort of toast."
He tipped a brow.

"At the time, when Lovat offered me an officer's
commission in this independent Highland company a
few years back, I had the choice between the dull life of
a merchant and the dull life of a lawyer," Alec said. "I
was young and thought an officer's rank would be
more interesting than sitting at a desk."

"And now you sit at desks, acting the lawyer in a red
coat," Wade said, sipping again.

"True," Alec agreed. "But I'll not complain. It is a
privilege to toast with the commander in chief of all the
British forces in Scotland." He lifted his cup.

"I'll admit there is benefit to having the nephew of
one of the most powerful Highland chiefs among our
ranks," Wade said. "No matter what your personal lean-
ings might be as a Highlander, and in my opinion many
Highlanders are wise to keep such things to themselves,
you do a fine job with whatever is asked of you."

"Sir," Alec murmured, inclining his head.

General Wade folded into a chair behind a mahogany desk littered with papers and maps, while Alec
stood on the thick Turkish carpet. The room was spa-
cious and well furnished. Inverlochy Castle, its garrisoned town renamed Fort William, was a comfortable
spot for soldiers, though not a hospitable place for Jacobites, Alec reflected.

The general peered at Alec through brass-rimmed
spectacles perched at the end of his long nose. "So
you've seen our *intriguante*, Captain? Does she still refuse to talk?"

"Aye. And I cannot blame her, having seen the cruel conditions of her incarceration."

"Damned ungentlemanly of Grant," Wade muttered. "But we need to know what she's hiding, and Grant does have a grievance with her. I thought she might talk, but she's stubborn. Are you aware that Grant was one of her victims, too? The gel left him with an aching head and took a fine set of maps with her. Francis Grant does not tolerate looking the fool."

"I read his account of that night, General. The colonel was quite foxed, so who knows what truly happened. Frankly, we do not even know if this is the girl who was in his quarters that night. We haven't learned who she is."

"She was in your quarters, too, sir," Wade said tersely.

"Aye, but . . . I was not quite myself, either," Alec said. "She is one of the camp laundresses. We established that with the Highland locals." He had ridden out to the house where the laundry was done, but realized he was not going to discover anything useful there: *She's a cousin,* he was told, *and not quite right in the head, puir lass.*

He remembered thinking, as he rode away, that she was either not right or a very clever lass indeed.

Wade waved his hand. "Difficult to trust any Highland source these days. How many Highland gels want to look at military maps and documents? None, I tell you. She took papers from you, sir, lists of Highlanders arrested, and an accounting of weapons confiscated from all Highland men by order of the king."

61

"Perhaps she was looking for news of a kinsman. Family bonds and loyalty mean all here in the Highlands, sir." He had other thoughts on why she had taken those pages, but he intended to discover the truth himself. Instincts sharpened by a cautious nature and years of covert work taught him to keep his own counsel.

"She had the documents, and she looks like this Katie Hell, as far as we know. Clearly she was up to something."

"Perhaps I was hasty, sir. My head was not clear that night." Alec swirled the rum in the cup, stared at it. "At the time, I did take her for this Katie Hell we've been after."

"And now you are not certain?"

Oh, he was very sure the girl was the notorious Katie Hell and a Jacobite spy, Alec thought to himself. And somehow he would find out what she knew about certain matters of rebellion before the English found out. He had an interest in matters of Jacobite espionage and an involvement he kept scrupulously secret.

"I think she should be interrogated, sir," Alec said. "But her treatment here is vile. That is my chief concern just now."

"I'll leave the matter to Colonel Grant, and to you. Both of you have been Kate's, uh, happy victims." Wade lifted a brow.

Alec set his cup down. "General, if word gets about that a Scotswoman was ill treated at this garrison, there will be an uproar among Jacobite and Whig gentlemen

62

alike. The blame will fall on the commander of the king's army in Scotland. You, sir."

Wade tapped his fingers on his desk. "That's troublesome. We could lose supporters of the war in both Scotland and England."

"Exactly." Alec looked around as voices rumbled out in the corridor. A rapping sounded on the door, and it was opened.

A sentry looked inside. "Sir, Colonel Grant is here."

"Tell him to wait a moment. I'm busy," Wade said curtly. The sentry shut the door, but it was pushed open by Grant.

"General, I must speak with you," Grant said, wedging himself in the gap. "Fraser! Damn it, man, I shall have your head for this!"

"Get out, Colonel," Wade snapped, and the sentry yanked the door shut despite Grant's protests. The general looked annoyed. "I presume you know what that was about, Fraser?"

"Colonel Grant may have discovered that I ordered an end to the lady's punishment. She fainted—she might even have died. I sat her down myself and told a guard to see to her welfare."

"That was out of line. But humane, I'll allow." Wade frowned, picking up a folded letter. "We should not keep the girl here, where we have no private accommodations for female prisoners. And there's a bad lot in that jail just now—that fellow Cameron, for one. A Highland rascal. But he'll be transferred soon. Sir, look at this letter, if you will."

Alec accepted the creased page handed him, then glanced up. "The Lord Advocate of Edinburgh wants to see her personally?"

Wade nodded. "I sent a courier to Lord Hume myself the day the girl came here, knowing she would need to be interrogated, possibly charged and tried at the Court of Justiciary. Lord Hume sent a messenger immediately with a reply. She is to appear before him in the first week of November. It's mid-October now. We could keep her here for two weeks, or just transfer her to his custody now and have done with it. I could send her off to Edinburgh Castle with that Cameron fellow."

"Sir, if I may say so, it is unchivalrous treatment to send her in an open cart with a male prisoner and male guards," Alec said. "General . . . the Lord Advocate is a kinsman of mine. My family lives in Edinburgh. Allow me to escort her there."

"Then do that," Wade said brusquely, looking up in irritation as the knocking resumed at the door. "Damn that pestering little man. Fraser, find out who the devil this girl is and what she knows, if anything. The Justiciary Court will need her name and so forth. Get whatever information you can from her so that we do not all look like buffoons."

"Aye, sir."

"I'll write out the order. Take her tomorrow. I'll order a closed vehicle." Wade took up a pen, dipped it, began to write. "Also—I want you to determine if she knows anything about that horde of Spanish weapons that went missing after the rebellion of the 'Nineteen, up at

Eilean Donan Castle, when the Jacobites had help from a shipload of Spaniards."

"Those weapons have never been found, sir," Alec pointed out. "Presumably the Spaniards took them back over the sea when most of them fled after the insurgents failed."

"So we thought, but rumors persist. Recently muskets of Spanish make turned up. Two Highlanders were killed in a skirmish in the Great Glen not long ago, and they were equipped with guns of Spanish style, the sort said to have been brought to Scotland to aid in that uprising."

"It is certainly possible to acquire Spanish-made pistols."

"Not marked with the initials of the ship that brought them. And this fellow Cameron was caught with the rascals who died holding those pistols. He had two such guns himself."

"Why not ask him, then?"

"We've tried," Wade said. "Stubborn Highland breeding. Like the girl, he will not say a word. He was nearly beaten to death, but I put a stop to that myself. We'll send him to Edinburgh, and the girl as well—the courts can deal with both these Jacobites. The girl and Cameron both know something, I suspect."

Alec had a strong sense of that, too. "If these weapons came into Jacobite hands, the rebels could arm themselves again."

"Just so. Over a thousand of these Spanish weapons were hidden, rumor says. Possibly more. But where in blazes are they?"

"I imagine we could find out, sir."

"Exactly. We've worked for years to confiscate weapons from the Highlanders, and the new military roads allow us to move troops and supplies more efficiently. But our troops are nowhere safe if Highland men can shoot at us from those blasted hills."

Alec nodded. "I'll take the girl to the Lord Advocate and do what I can with her."

"Good. Make her trust you. I hear she's a charming thing, but most pretty young women are, eh?" Wade glanced up with a quick gleam in his eye. "Then turn her over to the Lord Advocate. She is his problem. Here." He handed over the hastily scribbled orders. "Take an escort in the morning."

Alec saluted and turned. As he did, the door burst open, and Grant rushed inside. "General, I must report Captain Fraser as insubordinate! He's changed my orders concerning the female prisoner."

"He has that right," Wade said smoothly. "I've given him custody of the girl. He'll escort her to Edinburgh, and we will be done with her here."

"But she is in my keeping—"

"That is my decision, Colonel," Wade said firmly.

"We cannot trust him with her," Grant snarled. "He was with the wench himself. She casts a spell over any man who comes near her. I barely escaped myself. She's bewitched Fraser."

By the door, Alec looked over his shoulder. "She's just a bonny young girl. Whatever witchery you attribute to her may be in your head . . . or elsewhere."

Wade huffed a laugh, though Grant sputtered. "You

might be as much a spy as your doxy, Captain. You're both Highlander stock. There's hardly a Highlander who is not a Jacobite."

"But for the Whiggish Campbells, and their minions the Grants?" Alec asked smoothly.

"You should know, being in Lovat's pocket," Grant snarled.

"Gentlemen, that will be all," Wade interrupted. "Colonel, are the arrangements made for Cameron's transfer?"

"The brigand is to be moved tonight," Grant answered, still tense. "The man's near a beast. This will not be easy."

"Indeed. Fraser, I suggest you be on hand to assist. It may take several men to load him into that cart if he protests. Do you have command of the Irish tongue?"

"Some, sir. I'll be there." Ignoring Grant's protests, Alec saluted again and opened the door.

Kate pressed her back against the stone wall and watched the two men in the cell with her. Not long ago, guards had escorted the prisoners inside just as she woke, aching and groggy, from a dreamless sleep. Both men appeared asleep, one lying on the floor, the other seated in the corner opposite her.

Shivering in the chill, she stretched her back and legs, stiff from hours of standing. Darkness filled the cell, and she realized it was night. She had nearly slept the day away.

Raising her knees and tucking her feet under her skirts, she glanced around warily. One prisoner, a Highlander by his wrapped plaid, lay on his side, back turned toward her. His long dark hair hid his features. The other man, dressed in a brown coat and breeches, reclined in an opposite corner.

The seated man opened his eyes and looked intently toward her. Then he touched his brow in salutation, lifted a brow. Kate glanced away.

Through the barred iron door, she saw the shadows of the guards in the corridor and could hear them talking. An iron-trimmed door opened and rattled shut, and more male voices sounded in the corridor, out of sight of Kate's cell.

The man in brown snorted. "Hey, girl. Come sit by me."

She ignored him, resting her head on her arms.

"*Och*, too good to talk to me, hey? Look, Donald, they've brought us a lady to share our quarters!" With his foot, he poked at the man on the floor. The Highlander did not respond.

The man glanced at Kate. "Look at that, they near killed that lad afore they dragged him in here. Ah think he's dead."

Kate looked at the prone fellow in alarm. He was motionless, but could have been sleeping as much as dead. His plaid and long-limbed, athletic build made her think of her brother and kinsmen. Lowering to her hands and knees, she crawled toward him and touched his shoulder tentatively.

"Sir, are you well?" she asked in Gaelic. He did not move when she pushed, though she rocked the weight of his big body.

"*Och*, that lad's gone for sure," the seated man

68

drawled. "So 'tis thee and me, lassie." He grinned, showing rotten teeth. "And I find I canna resist ye."

Kate scrambled backward toward the relative protection of the wall and pulled her knees even higher under her skirts, wrapping her arms around herself. She had to find some way out, she thought desperately. The barred window was too high and narrow for anyone to wriggle through even if he could reach it, and the cell door, a framework of iron bars, was latched shut by a stout iron lock.

She studied it, recognizing the style of the lock—she had some familiarity with the things, having spent many childhood hours in the company of the Duncrieff blacksmith. Given time and a small knife or a set of scissors, she could probably loosen it, she thought. But she had nothing but the few silver hairpins left in the tangled strands of her hair, and they were too pliable for the purpose.

The scruffy man still watched her, and after a few moments came toward her in a half crouch. She had dreaded that, and glanced toward the corridor. No guards were in sight.

"Hey, lass," he said, sitting down beside her. "Cold in here. Let me keep ye warm." He slipped his arm around her, leaning heavily against her.

Kate pulled back. "Get away from me," she snapped.

"*Och*, lassie. We need to watch oot for one another in this place." His hand gripped her upper arm hard. "And Ah know they put ye in here because Ah've been cooperative, hey?"

Kate tried again to pull away, feeling dizzy and still

weak from her earlier ordeal. "Get off me," she demanded, wriggling in his hold. He pressed close, smelling unwashed and vile.

"Oh, lass, ye're a bonny thing, and it's aye so nice to share me quarters. Ah heard them sayin' ye like to share beds wi' men," he growled, and slid his hand into her hair, pulling so hard she cried out with the pain. His face moved closer, his lips grazing her cheek. Kate shuddered, braced both hands on his chest, chains clanking, and pushed against him with all her strength.

Chapter 6

A shadow fell over both of them, and Kate saw a pair of muscled, half-bare legs under a rumpled plaid. Just then, a huge hand descended to grab her assailant's coat, lifting the man away and dumping him on the slate with a thud.

"Leave her be," the Highlander said.

"*Och!*" The man half sprawled on the floor and came to a seated position. "Ah thought ye was dead!"

"I am not, and you will keep away from the lass."

Kate gaped up at her rescuer—he was an unkempt, unshaven giant, face and hands dirty and blood-crusted, an altogether frightening appearance. She had never been so glad to see anyone in her life.

"Thank you," she murmured.

"*Och*, Highland Donald," the man drawled. "She's a wee harlot, this one. We'll each get a turn." He slid toward Kate again, though she writhed.

"Get—off," the Highlander growled, leaning down to grab a handful of brown coat, hauling the man up in one great fist. He flung the Lowlander aside like a sack of beans. The man hit the wall with a dull thud, rolled over, and sat up looking dazed. Then he scuttled into a corner to glare at them in silence.

Kate stared upward. The black-haired Gael had taken a beating recently, for one eye was bruised and swollen, and his cheek and lip were cut. But his expression was calm, his jaw square and reliable, his mouth sober yet tender. In his blue eyes she saw weariness, gentleness, and no threat.

"Thank you," she said again.

He grunted in reply and turned, walking over to the small man in brown, now bunched against the wall. "Stay there, you."

"Just a bit o' fun, lad." He waved a hand. "Ah'm Jacobite, like you. Friends, aye?"

"I have all the Jacobite friends I need, and so does she," the Highlander said. "Stick to your corner if you value your crop of lice and the head they're living on."

Kate stared at him in utter gratitude as he turned and came back toward her. He sat an arm's length away, leaned his head against the wall, and closed his eyes.

Kate noted the bruises and the caked blood. "Are you badly hurt?" she asked in Gaelic.

"I'm fine enough," he replied.

"I'm grateful for your help, sir."

He nodded, eyes still closed.

"I'm Kate," she said. "And you are Donald?"

He snorted. "Donald is a name some Lowlanders use to refer to all Highland men, lass. I am Ian Cameron."

"Oh!" She gasped and scooted closer. "Ian Cameron—we've been looking for you," she whispered.

He opened one eye. "And who would be looking?"

"My kinsmen." She kept her voice low, though she did not think the Lowlander or guards would understand Gaelic. "I'm Kate. My brother is Duncrieff."

Both blue eyes opened. "Robert MacCar—"

"Hush," she whispered. "They might recognize the name, even in our tongue. We knew you were taken but did not know where you were held."

"I've been here a few weeks." He rubbed his head. "But how is it that Rob's sister is here?"

"I was arrested for . . . helping my kinsmen." She leaned closer. "We thought you might be in Edinburgh Castle."

"Not yet, but they will send me there soon, I hear. Colonel Grant and his men took me down about a month ago. He's a madman, that one. But at least I earned the right to be here." He smiled in impish contrast to his bold size.

"Earned it?" She looked at him, puzzled.

"I slept too long that morning, and they found us—killed my two cousins and took me. But I wounded two red soldiers and made fools of the rest. Knocked some heads together and went down roaring like a bull." He winced and touched his swollen eye.

73

"I am sorry about your cousins. And I'm not surprised to hear what you did. Ian, did you ever find . . . what you were searching for?"

He shook his head. "I know what you are asking. I have not found it yet, but I know where to look now. I was taken before I could get there and before I could send word to Rob."

"Where is that?" she asked breathlessly.

He studied her. "If I told you what I know, and they tortured you as they did yesterday, damn them all"— he spat in disgust—"you might speak of it."

"I would not," she said.

"Well, then, I'll say this." He leaned close, glancing past her, where a guard paced close to the cell door. "The hermit of the Highlands knows the secret."

She blinked at him. "Hermit? But where?"

"That's what my cousins said, when they found the weaponry," he whispered in Gaelic, watching over her shoulder toward the door. "A hermit near Glen Carran, they said. They would not tell me more until we were closer to the place—caution on their part, but they did not think to be killed. I was on my way to tell your brother and to go searching."

"They told you nothing else?"

"They died too soon, lass," he said somberly. "If you see your brother, you must tell him this."

"I will see him soon," she said. "Somehow, I will."

"They mean to take you to Edinburgh Castle, too, I have no doubt. Does your brother know you're here?"

She shook her head. "I have not told anyone my name, so they cannot send word to anyone. It's possible one of my cousins knows, and he will tell Rob. If the red soldiers learned my name, they would go after the MacCarran and arrest him. The officers believe my kinsmen sent me to spy."

"Did they?"

She lifted her chin. "They did."

Ian dropped a shoulder toward her. "Listen to me, lass. You're right to keep quiet. Whatever you know about Rob's business, let it remain secret. Do not tell me anything more. If they torture me, I would tell." His tone grew wry and teasing.

"You never would," she said, her tone lighter. She felt suddenly glad to have found a friend in this dismal place.

"*Ach*, I might. I do not have your strong will, to survive what they did to you in there." His expression darkened. "I heard it all. Making you stand for hours—brutal. I'd kill them for you if I had the chance."

"I'm fine. An officer decided it was enough punishment and put an end to it."

"Ah, the tall captain? I saw him. Good man."

"I owe him for it . . . though he was the one who arrested me."

Ian cocked a brow, an almost comical sight with his eye swollen shut. "But he relented? Ah, the fairy charm of the MacCarrans is at work in you, hey?"

She looked at him in surprise. "You know about that?"

"Your brother has mentioned his sisters, and he spoke of the clan legends." Ian leaned close again, waved a hand. "Can you get us out of here, lass? Spirit us away to a fairy hill?"

She shook her head. "It's a useless gift if it exists at all. Here we sit, and I cannot help either of us."

"Pity." He grunted thoughtfully. "Well, if it's real, it will serve its purpose one day, or so your legend claims. Now get some sleep, lass. Do not fret about that one there," he added, indicating the Lowlander. "I'm your guardian here."

"And I am forever in your debt."

He smiled crookedly through the scruff of his black beard. "*Ach*, you're like a bit of sunshine in this wretched place. Hush, now. The guards are coming back."

Kate closed her eyes and tried to rest, but she heard heavy footsteps and male voices, with a new voice in their midst. She opened her eyes suddenly, all her senses alert.

She knew that deep, calm voice. Looking toward the door, she saw Alexander Fraser standing beyond the iron bars. She felt the shock as his piercing gaze caught hers. For a moment, he was all she saw, despite the other men in the corridor with him.

Colonel Grant emerged from the shadows followed by four dragoons in red and white. One of the soldiers produced a set of heavy keys and unlocked the cell door to pull it open. Fraser stepped back, and the dragoons came inside, crowding the cell. One of them held stout iron chains and a set of manacles.

She gasped and pressed her back to the wall. Beside her, Ian sat up, and the man in the corner did, too.

"Ian Cameron," one soldier announced. "You'll come with us."

Kate looked at Ian in alarm. He regarded the men calmly. "Where is it I am going?"

"Edinburgh Castle," Grant answered, stepping forward. "Your trial date will be set soon. Likely you'll be executed."

"A bit hasty, Colonel." Fraser leaned against the doorframe. "Mr. Cameron, you're to be interviewed by the Lord Justice Clerk and perhaps tried before the bar in the Court of Justiciary. You will have a chance to speak on your behalf. Execution is not guaranteed," he added grimly. "You could be sent to the Tower of London and held for a length of time."

"Thank you, sir." Ian stood to his full height. Kate stood up with him, feeling small and insignificant in the crowd of tall and robust men. Her heart pounded with dread for her friend.

"Come with us, Mr. Cameron," Fraser said, then sent Kate a quick, somber glance.

Two dragoons took Ian's arms and placed manacles on his wrists, though he already had fetters on his ankles. He resisted the additional bonds, twisting hard, flinging one soldier aside, while another stumbled backward. The third dragoon stepped toward him, tripping over the other.

Fraser came inside the cell to help, shouldering past Kate to take hold of Ian's arm. She went to Ian's side, too, her own wrist manacles and chains jangling as she took hold of Ian's broad arm and pulled.

77

"Let go, Kate," Fraser growled. "This is not your matter."

She ignored him. *"Iain mo caran,"* she said: *Ian, my dear friend.* "What can I do?"

The Highland brigand looked down at her, while the dragoons, with Fraser's assistance, clapped the irons around his thick wrists and added another length of chain to join the ankle and wrist bracelets together.

"Get away from here however you can," Ian answered in Gaelic. "Get word to your brother. Tell him about the hermit. Hurry, get word to him before I am dead."

"Ian!" Kate sobbed out, and grabbed for him.

"Get back," Grant snapped, shoving her against the wall, so that she struck her shoulder.

Fraser growled something and pushed Grant out of the way just as Ian lunged for the colonel. The dragoons grabbed hold of Ian and yanked him forward. Stepping through the commotion, Fraser calmly took Kate's arm and pulled her aside.

"Are you hurt?" he asked, looking down, his hand on her arm.

She shook him off. "Leave me be. *Ian!*" She ran forward.

Cameron turned. "One kiss before I go, my dear, a little touch of magic," he said in Gaelic. Quickly, he leaned down, and touched his mouth to hers in a fast, poignant farewell kiss.

"Ah, the magic is there." Ian gave her a little smile as the soldiers hauled him toward the doorway.

"*Ach Dhia*, Ian," Kate moaned.

Cameron glanced back at Fraser. "You watch after her," he called. "She can trust no one else here. I give you charge."

Fraser nodded, standing just at Kate's shoulder. He walked past her as the others led Ian away—and as he went past he touched her elbow, a gentle, subtle reassurance. The contact sent shivers through her, and she stared after him, but he did not turn back. One of the guards clanged the door shut and locked it.

Kate stood in the middle of the cell, listening to the footsteps as the men walked away. The shivers continued, subtle and pleasant, as if his touch lingered, a sense of safety with it. Closing her eyes, she took a long breath.

When Ian had kissed her, she had felt no magic—it had been like kissing her own brother. And in all the kisses she had shared, heartfelt or not, the only true magic she had ever known had been in the arms of the officer who had just left to escort Ian to his probable death.

"Hey, lassie," the Lowlander in the corner crooned. "Ye're a right witch, to buss that Highland Donald when ye refused me. But now it's thee and me again." He grinned.

"Stay where you are," she snapped, sending him a dark glare, "or I'll cast a spell you'll never forget."

He gaped at her and did not move.

Kate sat against the opposite wall, pulled her knees close, and covered her face in her hands, chains clinking.

* * *

"The fairy queen?" Jack stared at Alec.

"The very one." Alec opened a canvas satchel and crammed in a clean shirt, tartan stockings, and a thick sheaf of papers tied with string, documents he still needed to review.

"And just where are you taking her?" Jack was still gaping. "She's a spy? Why did you not tell me before?"

"I wanted to be sure," Alec muttered. "She hasn't confirmed it herself, but I would not be surprised if she is."

"She has to be," Jack said. "So she's a clever wee fairy."

"It seems so, at least the clever part. I'm to escort her to Edinburgh to see the Lord Advocate."

Jack snorted. "Your uncle, Lord Hume? He'll chew her to bits and wash it down with your uncle Walter's hot chocolate."

"Aye well. That may be, unless I can intervene."

"Oh, I just now remembered—the post rider brought this for you from Edinburgh." Jack handed him a packet. "I suppose if we ride along with the dragoons, 'tis better than the lass going alone with 'em."

"We're not riding with 'em," Alec said, slipping the package into a coat pocket. "I want you to go into Fort William tonight and hire a carriage and horses. Do not charge it to the army's account. Pay coin for it—use this," he said, taking money from his sporran.

Jack accepted it. "Why not use one of the vehicles in the stables here?"

"I cannot get one of those until morning."

"So we're off tonight, then? On our own, I presume?"

Alec nodded, closing the satchel. Jack leaned a shoulder against the wall, studying him. "I wondered why you were packing in haste. This isn't like you, man, being the staid sort of Fraser and all. I'm shocked." He said it teasingly, but his gaze was serious.

Alec shrugged. "I'm a bit shocked myself. Nonetheless, it will be done, before anyone has the chance to interrogate her any further. Francis Grant cannot be trusted."

"I could have told you that. But there's something else at stake here. You are not the sort to go snatching women in the dark of night."

"Tonight I'll call up a little madness from the other side of my family, how's that," Alec answered wryly.

"She must be quite valuable, this wee spy of yours."

"She is. More valuable than the government even realizes, and I want her out of here before it occurs to them."

Jack frowned. "What is it? Jacobite business, but what? Those missing weapons? I know you've had a letter about the rumors of those things from your uncle, MacDonald of—"

"I'll explain later." Alec lifted the satchel and tossed it to Jack. "Right. Off with you, then. And be quick about it."

"If we're set to rescue the fairy queen," Jack said, "I'll do whatever is necessary."

"We're not going to rescue her. We're going to take her to justice in Edinburgh," Alec growled.

"Hey, that's not the gentlemanly thing."

"Does that matter to you, with a lass in every county?"

"Ah, but only one of those has my heart," Jack said. "I'm under the wee fairy's spell, too, and I'm not ashamed to say it." With a grin, he shouldered the pack and walked out the door.

Scowling, Alec followed in silence, not about to admit that he, too, had fallen a little under whatever magic Katie Hell exuded.

Chapter 7

Removing his cocked hat, Alec shook the moisture off, then brushed raindrops from his sleeves. Standing outside the dungeon cell again, he peered through the iron bars.

The girl sat with her back against the wall, knees propped up, head tucked on her folded arms. Shuddering with the chill in the air, she looked forlorn.

When Alec and the others had escorted Cameron outside, a raw autumn storm had burst while they waited for a cart and horses to be brought round for the escort. Rain and wind delayed their efforts, but Grant ordered the dragoons to travel without stopping, regardless of the weather.

Overhearing Grant as he ordered one of the dragoons to move the female prisoner later that night to be transferred under cover of darkness, Alec had slipped away at that point to pack his bag and make his own arrangements with Jack MacDonald, knowing that he had to get Kate away from here, and Grant, as soon as he could.

He stood by the cell door, yet Katie Hell did not glance toward him. Sheets of rain pounded the high, narrow window, and chilly air blew through the dankness. The girl shivered again.

"Kate," Alec said, reaching into his pocket.

She lifted her head then. Disheveled and weary, she still retained an indefinable, enchanting quality. Her remarkable silvery eyes snapped anger as she looked at him.

He dangled the silver necklace from his fingers, letting it catch the light. Minutes ago, he had claimed it from the sergeant for a bribe of a few shillings. As it swung in his hand, he saw Kate's eyes spark.

Oh aye, he thought, he could have no more doubt that this was the woman he had seen in London. He remembered that she had worn the silver and crystal bauble around her throat, beneath strands of pearls. The sparkling little necklace had suited her fairylike appearance: the pretty crystals, which could be plucked along many Highland slopes, were sometimes called fairy crystals.

"What do you want?" she asked, her voice hoarse.

"I came to see how you're faring," Alec replied.

"You've seen. Now go away."

"Come here." He let the silver necklace swing.

She narrowed her eyes. "Leave it there and go away."

"I must speak with you first."

"We have nothing to say. You had me arrested, or have you forgotten?"

"What choice did I have, Kate?" he asked quietly.

She paused. "Though you wear a Highland plaid, you're a red soldier all the same. A true Highlander would never have arrested me, nor would he take away one of his own."

"You mean Ian Cameron? What is your interest in him?"

"Go away, unless you mean to open those doors and let me out of here." She glanced uneasily at the other man in the cell.

Alec had already noticed that the fellow watched her in a way that made his skin crawl. He wanted to get Kate out of there as much as he suspected she wanted to go. "Come here," he said.

By nature and habit, he was cautious rather than reckless. Yet tonight he found it rather easy to call up a little of the madness he hid inside himself, the wildness he had smothered for most of his life. It was there, waiting to be tapped.

The girl was indeed the beauty he had seen in London, and therefore was more valuable a prisoner than Grant or Wade even suspected. The woman hobnobbed with King George, yet had such interest in government documents that she disguised herself and went into officers' tents at great risk to get them. She had some sort of intrigue in mind, no doubt of it. As things were, that meant Jacobite scheming.

And she was certainly no other than Katie Hell, yet she would admit to nothing more than her first name.

He meant to question her until he was satisfied—then he might just let her go. But he was not about to tell her that.

Dangling the silver chain as it caught the light, he tucked it in his sporran and turned away.

"Wait." She came toward the cell door, the chains on her wrists chinking. Alec turned, leaned close to the bars, aware that the sentry was now approaching along the corridor. "What is it you want of me?"

"You must come with me," he murmured.

She scowled. "Where?"

"Elsewhere," he said, and glanced over his shoulder. "Sergeant," he called, "I'll need the key, if you please."

"Begging pardon, Captain, but Colonel Grant gave new orders concerning the wench."

"I know. I've spoken with the colonel. He's tending to other business now and asked me to supervise this."

The sergeant nodded. "Aye, then."

"It's all arranged. As it happens, I have a vehicle waiting, since I plan to travel to Edinburgh myself. I'll see to her transfer. Discreetly, just as the colonel wanted." Alec removed Wade's preliminary orders from his pocket and waved the page without giving the sergeant time to look closely. "It's an awkward matter, and we're pressed for time, as you know. Unlock the cell, please. And I'll need the key to her fetters. Keep this to yourself, sir, as long as you can."

Reaching into his sporran, Alec produced a shiny guinea, which the soldier snatched before relinquishing a small iron key. The sergeant opened the cell door with a larger key.

"I'll see to this, Sergeant." Alec stepped inside and took hold of Kate's arm while she gaped up at him.

"Where are you taking me?" She pulled back. "I do not want to go to Edinburgh with you."

"Go there with me," he murmured, "or Grant."

"I'll go with neither," she snapped.

"Very well. Good luck to you, then. May you be safe and well," he said—but he said it in awkward but sincere Gaelic as he turned away.

"I'll go with you," she returned in rapid Gaelic.

Alec released a breath and turned to take her arm and lead her through the door. He was glad the exchange had been brief. His scant Gaelic would not have stood up to the challenge.

As they moved into the corridor, the other prisoner rose from his corner to grab the bars as the sergeant shut and locked the door. "Hey! Ye took the Highlander away, now the wench. Let me out, too!"

"You don't want to go where she's going," the sergeant growled.

"To her death, is it? She's a witch, that one. Ye'd best burn her if you take her to that place." He laughed.

Kate gasped as Alec pulled her along. "Could they do that? Try me for witchcraft?"

"Have you turned anyone into a pig lately?" Alec muttered.

"I'm thinking about it," she snapped. "Do not pull so hard. I'm not a sack of wool to be dragged about!"

"You'll not be burned as a witch—they no longer do

that in Scotland, fortunately for you. But we must hurry." Alec drew her past the sergeant's post.

"I could hurry if these chains were off, and if I had my shoes." She stopped short and lifted her bedraggled hem.

Alec looked down at her stockinged feet and the heavy chains around her ankles. He sighed. "Be damned. I forgot about the shoes."

"I will have my shoes and buckles, too. And my good plaid, and my silver necklace, which you have stolen from me."

Frowning, one hand on her elbow, he led her back to the guard. "Sergeant, fetch the rest of her things, please."

While they waited, Alec crouched to lift the hem of her dress. Seeing the manacles around her slim ankles, he felt a jolt of anger. Her slim ankles and the torn fabric of her stockings were crusted with blood.

He brushed his fingers over her ankle. Then he took the small key from his sporran, unlocked the cuffs, and skittered them and the joining chain away over the stone floor.

He glanced up. Her eyes looked beautiful, sad. "I'm sorry," he said. "I did not realize."

She shrugged. "Hurts mend."

"Do they?" he murmured, thinking of hers, and his own, layers deep and invisible. He stood.

She held out her hands, where another set of iron fetters and a swag of chain linked her wrists. "And these?"

"Not yet." He dropped the key back into his leather purse, buckling it shut.

She huffed in annoyance, then turned as the soldier

returned clutching Kate's plaid and shoes, leather bro-
gans with silver buckles and stout soles.

Sturdy shoes to run off in, Alec thought as he took
them, and the plaid, and slipped another coin to the
sergeant. He handed the shoes to Kate and draped the
plaid over her shoulders.

"And I'll have the necklace, too," she said.

"It's safe. We've no time. Put your shoes on."

She stooped and tried, her hands clumsy with the
manacles on her wrists. Alec bent and took her foot in
his hand to slip one shoe on, then the other. She balanced a hand on his shoulder as he buckled the shoes.

"That's too tight," she said.

He adjusted them impatiently, then stood and
tugged her toward the stairway. As they rounded the
corner, he headed for another staircase not used regularly. He had no desire to meet anyone else just now.

"Where are you taking me? Did you bribe that soldier?" Kate yanked futilely under Alec's sure grip.

"Outside, and aye," he said curtly, and guided her to
a dim stairwell, where stone steps circled a central post.

"Sending me to Edinburgh is unfair. I've heard no
charges yet, no judge has interviewed me, and I have
not seen a lawyer."

"You're seeing one now." Alec pulled her up another step.

"You'll take me to a lawyer, then?"

"I *am* a lawyer. Blast it, will you pull us both down
the stair?" He stepped down behind her to lift her by
the waist, setting her on the next stair tread to hurry her
along.

"You? My case is lost for certain, then. You're prejudiced against me," she muttered irritably.

"I'm not *your* lawyer. I am *a* lawyer. A Writer to the Signet, trained at the University of Edinburgh and Leiden, and currently employed by the army to review documents. You reviewed some of those documents yourself, as a matter of fact."

She looked back at him, began to speak. He hefted her up yet another step. She was lightweight and no trouble to lift.

"A pusher of papers and a wretched turncoat. Why would I want you for my lawyer?"

"Be damned," he grunted, urging her upward again, "I am not your lawyer, as I said, and will you keep silent?"

"I will not. Look what you did to dear Mr. Cameron."

"Dear Mr. Cameron has knocked more redcoat heads together than you or I could count. Though you seemed quite eager to kiss him," Alec added, not sure why he mentioned it.

"A kiss of friendship. You'd wait an eternity for the same, I promise you," she snapped, stopping on the step above him, so that her face was near on a level with his.

"Would I?" He stared at her in the darkness. The memory of the kisses they had already shared flooded his mind, seeming to fill the small space between them with palpable tension. His body pulsed, and he was sure she was affected, too, for she glanced away in silence.

He gave her a gentle shove up another step or two

with a hand at her lower back. She drew a breath, clearly in pain.

"What is it?" Alec asked.

"Nothing," she said. "Just that every muscle aches, I'm tired, I'm hungry, and I do not care to hurry to my trial and execution though you are in a rush to get me there."

"You can rest and eat later. Up you go."

Kate took the next steps, reached a landing, and turned. "What sort of law do you practice, and what do you charge for your services?"

"Hire me later," he answered, a hand at her waist.

"Are you worth hiring? I probably cannot afford you. Most long-robes charge absurd fees. Stop that," she said, when he urged her upward again. "I will be climbing by myself."

"Then please do so," he said between his teeth. She had a way of speaking, he realized, that was as wholly charming as the way she moved, the way she looked, her scent, her kiss—

Stop that indeed, he told himself.

"If I could afford to pay you, would you swear to the military that I've done no crime?"

"I was the arresting officer. I cannot defend you."

"Tell them you made a mistake. After all, you did."

"Shall I lie for you, and benefit by funds from your bank account, if you have one? That's *criminis particeps,* my dear, which is Latin for—"

"I know what it means. I can read and understand Latin, French, and Italian."

"Excellent. An accomplished lady. Then what the devil were you doing sneaking about a military encampment, dosing my tea, and stealing my papers?"

"I gave you a soothing tonic. You looked tired."

"How kind of you. At least you admit to that much. This way," he said, when they reached the top of the stair.

"I did not intend to steal anything that night."

"Did you just intend to memorize it?"

"You surprised me with that pistol." She turned, mere inches away, and rested her hands on his chest, heavy iron links banging against him. "Captain Fraser, please let me go. Leave me here, and I'll slip away," she pleaded quietly.

Somehow his hands found the sweet curve of her waist, and his fingers settled at the small of her back. Her eyes held some kind of magic, beautiful eyes of pale gray, extraordinary in shadows. He stared down at her, frowning slightly.

He could indeed release her. For a moment, he felt as if he had captured a fairy creature whose innocent allure had cast a net about him, drawn him into her spell. She was fascinating, unpredictable. He wanted, blast it all, to help her, though he would risk a great deal if he assisted her to escape.

For a moment he was deeply tempted to do just that. He had not cared about helping or pleasing anyone in a long time, he realized. Still he did not answer.

"Please, Captain. I must be free," she whispered.

She glowed, this girl, vibrant and exciting, shining like a candle flame on that dark landing. His body throbbed as memories of delights he had shared with her rushed through him.

He had never known anyone like her. Even Amy, who had once possessed his foolish, pining heart, had not been so enticing as this girl. With Kate, a mere smile, a sweep of those dark lashes over silvery eyes, made his body pulse, his thoughts blur.

The rain pounded outside the doorway ahead, and the rainy light illuminated her upturned face. Inappropriate to the time, the place, the situation, he felt increasing desire. Reaching out, he brushed a hand over her cheek, could not stop himself.

He pulled away. "We must go," he said brusquely, grabbing her elbow.

"I do not think I want you for my lawyer," she muttered.

Chapter 8

⁓◦◦◦◦⁓

Emerging into the dark courtyard beside Fraser, Kate felt the cool bliss of raindrops and wind on her face. She lifted her head, glad to be outside for the first time in days, regardless of the circumstances.

Hastening beside him, she stumbled. He put a hand at her waist and guided her with him. Ahead, she saw a post chaise in the shadows by the main gate, harnessed to a pair of horses.

A man opened the door and lowered the hinged step. He was young, lean as a whip, wearing dark clothing, his features hidden by a cocked hat. He was not military, she noted, puzzled, as Fraser urged her toward the open door.

Quickly, he lifted her around the waist and dumped

her inside the coach. Kate scrambled onto the bench seat as he came inside to sit beside her. The seat of squabbed leather was comfortable, though the vehicle was small, intended to hold two or three.

Windows pierced the sides and the door, and the sloped front wall of the coach had one small window. Through that opening, she could see the horses' heads and saw the coachman leap onto one horse to ride postillion.

"Sit back and hold on," Fraser said. "Our rider will be in something of a hurry, I think."

She settled back against the seat, thought at first the coach moved slowly, stopping at the gate as the postillion rider spoke to the sentry. Fraser lifted a hand in a brief salute, and the coach rumbled out over one of the stone roads that Wade's construction crews had been cutting throughout the Highlands.

Suddenly the rider urged the horses on, and the vehicle lurched and began to race. Kate slid across the bench seat into Fraser, who righted her. Quickly she moved back to her own corner by the window.

She watched outside as the chaise rolled along. The rain lessened, and the sky, still in gloaming, was a hazy lavender above the dark shoulders of the distant mountains. She leaned her cheek against cool glass and watched the stars sparkle through a veil of scudding clouds.

After a while, she glanced at Fraser, who sat an arm's reach away. A damp chill pierced the coach, and she shivered, trying awkwardly to pull her plaid closer around her.

He reached out and helped her drape the arisaid over her shoulders, since she was hindered by her shackles. His hands were deft as he fixed the silver pin, caught in the fabric, more securely for her.

"Silk-lined woolen tartan," he remarked, fingering the fabric. "You make quite the living as a laundress."

"Laundresses can have nice things, too," she said, and he was silent, fastening the brooch. For a moment, she savored his closeness, the warm scents of soap, man, and a surprising hint of something sweet. "You smell good," she said impulsively. "I noticed it before."

"Thank you," he murmured.

She held out her hands. "You may take these chains off me now, if you please."

He regarded her wryly. "We might bargain for it."

"I will not bargain." She opened her palm. "I'll have the chains off, and I'll have my necklace from you, too."

She thought he pinched back a smile. "The larger chains will stay for now. And the finer chain is in my safekeeping."

"But it's mine," she protested, feeling frantic suddenly. The necklace was more precious to her than anyone outside her family knew. From the age of seven, she had never been without it. "I must have it."

He lifted a brow. "And you said your name was . . . ?"

She caught her breath and looked away. Fraser propped an elbow on the window frame and rested his chin on his knuckles. For a few miles they rode in silence, Kate continually glancing over at him.

Still, though she would not admit it, she was grateful to be in a fine coach, warmed by her own plaid and on her way somewhere, anywhere, rather than sitting in that dungeon. She was grateful to Fraser for taking her out of there. Although she did not want to admit it even to herself, she felt a subtle but definite thrill running through her as she sat near him.

The coach rumbled along, and Kate bounced a little on the seat. The shackles, resting in her lap, clanked. "Where are we going?" she asked.

"Away from the Highlands," Fraser said simply. His piercing gaze made her flutter inside, then he looked out the window again. In the dim light, his chiseled profile blended elegance and strength, so easy to admire that it made her feel pleasant inside. But his dark, straight brows were pulled tight.

"We're following Wade's road down the Great Glen into Perthshire," she observed. "Will we head to Edinburgh from there, or take the lesser road straight east?"

"We'll travel through Perthshire, then southeast for Edinburgh. If weather allows, we'll make only one stop, since MacDonald recommends that for the sake of the horses."

"MacDonald?"

"My ghillie and my cousin, John MacDonald. Jack."

She nodded. "Your kin are MacDonalds?"

"Aye. My mother was born a MacDonald of Keppoch."

She blinked. "The Keppoch clan are strongly Jacobite. But you're a regimental officer, and a Fraser. What sort of Fraser are you—the Whiggish sort, or the Highland sort?"

He smiled. "*Comme çi, comme ça.*" He waved his hand.

She narrowed her glance. "A captain in a Highland Independent Company, wearing Highland gear and speaking only a smattering of Gaelic . . . you must be one of Fraser of Lovat's own kin, since you are an officer."

"That's quite astute," he said, sounding surprised.

"I would not be proud of the association, either, if I were you. Simon Fraser of Lovat has long toed the line in this dispute, when he is not turning in Scotsmen whom he has befriended. And now they say he refuses to acknowledge James as Scotland's true king."

"Well informed, lass." He folded his arms.

"Your chief is well-known among Highlanders and Lowlanders alike. He began the first independent companies himself to form several companies of the Highland Watch. A good thing, until he gave control over to the British. Surely Lovat would place his own trusted kin as officers so that he could maintain a hand."

"He likes money and the convenience of no longer having to supervise the companies," he answered.

"And now you supervise one for him?"

He shook his head. "My father bought me a commission when I was younger, and Lovat made me a captain in one of his watches, the company called *Am Freiceadan Dubh*—"

"The Black Watch. I've heard of it," she said. "So you are in Lovat's pocket! Do you flip and flop as he does to protect yourself?"

"I am firm as a rock," he drawled, "in my convictions."

"I cannot argue that," she murmured. Then she scowled, for his answering chuckle thrilled her too much. "But I cannot trust a turncoat, even one with Highland blood."

"I am not a turncoat. And are you so willing to forget that we enjoyed . . . a friendly encounter previously?" he asked softly.

"It did not end on friendly terms. And," she said emphatically, "it will not happen again."

He was quiet. "Agreed."

She felt disappointed by his reply rather than validated. Looking away, she watched the passing landscape in silence, then glanced at him again. "When we arrive in the city, will you deliver me to the Tolbooth, or to Edinburgh Castle?"

He settled back, glanced at her. "So eager to be confined?"

She lifted the chains, shook them. "I would rather be free. You could easily do that for me."

"If I let you loose, you might decide to fling yourself from the carriage and run off."

"What an interesting idea," she drawled. "But my back and my limbs are still sore from the courteous treatment I had at Inverlochy Castle, thank you."

"You can thank Colonel Grant for that. Tell you what," he said, reaching into his sporran. "Promise me something, and we will bargain."

"For my necklace?" she asked.

In answer, he waggled a small iron key with two fingers.

"I promise my good behavior," she blurted.

"I was thinking of a more reliable token than that. Your name would be good for a start."

"Kate."

"Now, now. Full name." He flipped the key, caught it.

"Katherine."

"Pretty, but it won't win the bargain, Miss Katherine. Or shall I call you Katie Hell?"

"You may call me Miss Hell," she said primly.

He laughed. Kate had not expected that, or her reaction to its quiet warmth. She wanted to hear the sound again.

"Miss Hell," he mused. "What clan is that? MacHellion? Are there many like you, Amazonian Jacobites snatching documents, hefting pistols and poison, and using female wiles on unsuspecting governmental officers?"

She lifted her chin, unsure how to reply. There was little point in denying that she was Katie Hell. Fraser and Grant, too, had sorted out that the laundress, the widow, the old wisewoman, the young woman in search of her brother—all the roles she had played over the past year—were the work of Katie Hell. Part of her secret was revealed—but Fraser alone knew more about her than any other man.

Not only had he claimed her body and captured a little of her heart in ways no man ever had—but he also had seen her in St. James's Palace last spring. His testimony, if he chose to give it, would be enough to hang her as an *intriguante*. He could place her not only in the military encampment but near the king.

And if he learned her name, he would have enough evidence to arrest her kinsmen as well.

"Kate," he prodded, as she remained silent.

She did not answer as she watched scenery flash by the window. The rain clouds were clearing, and she saw the glitter of water beyond the lacy shapes of the trees. The chaise rushed over the road, and Kate shifted in her seat, chains jangling.

"Those irons look beastly uncomfortable," Fraser said.

She shrugged. The chains were painfully heavy.

"Why did you come to my tent that night?" he asked. "What did you expect to find among my papers?" His gaze was intense.

Any information she gave him could condemn her and her kin. This man had showed her some small kindnesses, but she could not trust him—did not know if she ever could.

"What did you think to gain by seducing me? Not that I minded that part," he added.

"What?" She blinked, looked at him quickly. "Seduce you? I never did that."

"Have you forgotten?" He leaned over a little, his shoulder touching hers, the pressure sending a delicate shiver through her. "We made love that night, if memory serves. Or nearly so. I do recall enough," he said, leaning closer and lowering his voice to a murmur, "to know that we shared more than just some kisses."

"I recall nothing of the sort," she said, lifting her chin.

"Do you not? I will not be ungentlemanly, Miss Katie—Katherine—what-you-will, but truthfulness is best here. You and I both know what happened. You perhaps more than I."

"If you want truth, then you should recall that *you* seduced *me*," she snapped. "I had every intention of leaving that tent as fast as I could." She turned her head away again, heart pounding.

He had turned the tables on her that night, something she could not say aloud. Katie Hell had fallen, hard and fast and foolishly, for his kisses and his touch. And that dreadful mistake had resulted in her arrest.

"Seduced you? My dear, I was barely conscious after you put whatever it was in my tea, but I do remember what we did, or most of it. No, do not look away again. You're no prim lass, if rumor serves. And I am not prone to bedding laundresses . . . or ladies of the royal court either." He lifted a brow.

"Rumor does not serve." She raised her chin. "And you are an insufferable cad."

"That was you, wasn't it, in London, last March?"

Her heart raced. "I don't know what you mean."

"Perhaps you'll remember soon." He extended his open hand, the key upon his palm. "Sooner or later, Kate," he murmured, "you must talk for even a chance at freedom. I do not mean now, from those chains. I mean . . . altogether."

She shook her head, glanced down. "I cannot."

"Then I presume you know something. Tell me," he went on quietly. "I'll listen. I promise not to use whatever it is against you." His voice was soft, compelling.

"I cannot trust you." Crazily, she wanted to do so. She wanted to forget all this and go to him, feel his arms around her again. But that desire made no real sense to her—the world had gone topsy-turvy. He had arrested her. She did not know what he wanted of her. And yet, he made her feel good. Safe.

Fraser slid the key back into his inside pocket and inclined his head to watch her in silence.

Kate sighed. "I suppose you think I am a true wanton. But I am not. Nor am I a criminal in need of restraint." She shook the cuffs and chains. "You could free me here, in this chaise, if nothing else out of plain courtesy."

"I would, if I believed that *I* could trust *you*." He settled back. "I suggest you sleep. It will be a long ride."

"Please," she said. "The cuffs are hurting me."

He tilted his head, relaxed and in control, an ease of manner rather than arrogance. She hated it all the same. "Just give me a little of the truth, Kate."

"The truth is you are a damnable beast."

"Ah. The lass needs a tongue-scrubbing." He closed his eyes as if to sleep.

She sighed. "What can I bargain other than my name?"

"Do you really want an answer to that?" He opened an eye, closed it.

She knew what he meant, knew her own reputation. Remembering deep, luscious kisses, Kate glanced at him, at his lips, his hands. Blushing furiously, she was glad of the darkness. "Very well. My name is Marie Katherine. I cannot tell you more than that. Please understand. It would endanger too many."

"Well, that's more than we had." He took the key out.

She lifted her hands. "At least loosen the manacles."

"Iron cuffs cannot be loosened, darling. They are either on, or they are off."

"Off, then. Please," she added. Darling—somehow it melted her, weakened her utterly. For an instant, she felt tears sting, but drew a breath against them.

He played with the key. "Why were you in my quarters?"

"Laundry," she said.

"What do you know about Spanish weapons?"

She nearly gasped aloud. If she gave him any clue that she and her kinsmen and Ian Cameron were searching for those weapons, and if he then learned her name, everything that her brother and the others had struggled toward would be destroyed. They would all be arrested ... perhaps executed. Unless she could trust Fraser to keep it to himself—and that thought was preposterous.

"Spanish weapons?" She shrugged. "They are quite expensive, being imported from Spain. That's all I know."

"Spanish weapons," he said, "hundreds, perhaps a thousand or more guns and such hidden away by Jacobites nearly ten years ago and recently found. I think you know where they are located."

"If they were recently found, then why ask me?"

He sighed, then reached out and placed his hand over hers. The warm contact felt stunning in the darkness. Twisting the key, he took the heavy bracelets off, one by one, and pooled the chains and manacles on the floor at his feet.

"Thank you." Kate rubbed her chafed wrists. "Why did you—"

"I was bewitched into it," he said sourly. "But you'll have those back on later. There's a good deal more you can share with me, Marie-Katie-Katherine, and I'll not let you go." He spoke intimately, his voice a velvety caress.

"Not ever?" Her heart beat very fast now.

"Well, of course, when the Lord Advocate decides what's to be done with you," he said, waving his fingers in dismissal.

Kate sighed and settled into the corner by the window, leaning her brow against the window glass. Watching the landscape fly past, lulled by the motion of the vehicle, she glanced again at Captain Fraser. He appeared relaxed and lost in thought, legs extended, arms folded.

She studied his form, the square, broad shoulders, wide chest, and strong, taut limbs. If he fell asleep, she thought, then she would have a chance to get away.

But how? Was she brave enough, or mad enough, to throw herself out the door as Fraser had suggested? She did not think so, but she would not rule it out. Any risk was preferable to trial and incarceration.

Later she would consider the possibilities, she told herself. For the moment, she felt achy and exhausted. She closed her eyes, not wanting to think about Spanish weapons, or kinsmen and friends in danger. Nor did she want to think about the man who sat so close to her now, though her mind constantly returned to him.

She wanted only to sleep, and soon enough surrendered.

Chapter 9

Alec reached over to adjust Kate's head to a more comfortable angle as she slept. He paused, tracing his fingertips over her cheek—her skin was incredibly soft, the shape of her face graceful in the moonlight. He was aware of his strong attraction to her and knew the trouble that could cause for both of them. Even without this complicated situation, he kept himself clear of deeper ties and feelings.

He had lost his heart once, and it had led to betrayal, then tragedy. The chances of that happening again were very remote—he had no other brother, and no former betrothed to jointly betray him—but he never wanted to feel that hurt again.

No matter the temptation, he must not develop tender feelings for this girl—not because she was his prisoner and likely a spy, but because he could care deeply about her, given the chance. He could love her, were she fairy queen or laundress. And that frightened him when little else did.

His thoughts in turmoil, he closed his eyes again but could not rest. Reaching into his jacket pocket, he retrieved the small, thick envelope that Jack had given him earlier. Another letter from his aunt. He had not yet found time to read it, but he already suspected part of its contents.

The envelope had a sweet odor, which Kate had detected when she had leaned against him. It could not be a good thing, he thought, for a man to walk about smelling of chocolate.

He undid the string and opened layers of brown paper. Inside lay a letter folded around a little packet wrapped in waxed paper. He opened it, peeled the wax covering away. A sweet, rich scent wafted outward that made his mouth water, but the dark, amorphous glob that fell into his hand would kill any appetite.

He rolled it between his fingers, grimaced, tucked it back into the waxy paper, and set it aside. The letter also reeked of cocoa as he scanned his aunt Euphemia's flourished and formal handwriting.

My dear Alexander,

Enclosed is Walter's latest Eating Chocolate, which he insists you sample. Taste the wretched thing if you dare. Your uncle says it is his best effort yet.

Your compliments over the last batch only encouraged him. Had you told him it was vile and tasted of rotten eggs, as I did, he might have ceased his silly experiments, and we would be safe.

Rosie thinks this latest effort is not so bad, but Lily was confined to bed for a day with the headache after only a taste. She and I share a sensitive constitution. Daisy was not allowed to try it, though Walter would have permitted it had I not rescued the wee lass. Chocolate should not be given to bairns, I told him.

Alec smiled. He did not doubt Lily's delicate nature, but his aunt was robust, despite her claims to the contrary. She competently managed the household belonging to Alec's late brother, Edward, and fostered Edward's three orphaned daughters with bustling efficiency. Effie was married to Alec's uncle Walter Fraser, and they now lived in the Edinburgh town house, Hopefield House, which Edward and Amy had preferred to Kilburnie, the family estate, because of its proximity to the business. Following Edward's death, Alec had inherited both properties and the business as well.

As the younger son, all that had come to him upon the deaths of his parents had been a house on Kilburnie's property and a share in the business. He had been content with that, but Edward's death had left him greater shares of Kilburnie and Fraser's Fancy, with considerable portions set aside for each of Edward's daughters once they reached adulthood. Alec would not have quibbled had all of it been left to the girls—he did not begrudge them a penny of the family fortune and had little use for luxury himself.

He did not visit either Kilburnie or Hopefield House often anymore, although military matters and holidays required that occasionally he visit the family town house. He possessed a fortune, a thriving business, a Highland estate, and a handsome town house, and he had family who cared a great deal about him.

Yet at times he felt alone, without a real home or close family. That was his own perception, he knew, for he had closed off his heart that much. Frowning, he looked at Effie's letter.

Walter is sure that his Chocolate Confections will invigorate Fraser's Fancies, but he is not a practical man, I fear. Your brother had such a gift for business. Tea is a reliable commodity, Edward used to say, and chocolate is a luxury, yet Walter expects his Confections to become household fare in Britain and on the Continent, too.

Please come home as soon as you can and talk Walter out of his mad scheme. Other matters require your attention as well. May this note find you in good health, which I pray Walter's Nasty Concoction will not interrupt overmuch, should you be so brave as to consume it. The lasses send their love.

Yours affectionately, Euphemia

Postscript: Rosie will send a letter when she masters penmanship.

At the bottom of the page, in a childish and ink-spotted scrawl, was another signature:

Rose Alexandra Fraser

Frowning, unwilling to admit how much the little signature affected him, Alec folded the letter quickly and tucked it, with the untasted chocolate sample, back into his pocket. He sighed and shifted on the bench seat. That single line of blobbed ink had wrenched his heart.

He was guardian to his three orphaned nieces, though he knew they were in better hands with Effie and Walter than with him. The business was in better hands, too, for his uncle had been devoted to the success of Fraser's Fancies since its inception in his youth. Alec served only as a silent partner, issuing bank drafts as needed and acting as legal advisor. That suited him, but Walter and Effie were in their seventies now, and could not continue to watch the girls and tend the business indefinitely.

He should go back to Edinburgh, resign his commission, and take a larger hand in running the Fancies. He knew that day would come. But each time he saw Amy's daughters, he felt such longing and loneliness that he resorted to keeping away altogether.

As for "eating chocolate," Alec felt that, despite Effie's fears, Walter's dream had merit, given a good recipe. But so far that recipe had eluded his uncle.

Watching the landscape in the darkness, Alec realized he had not visited the Edinburgh town house since midsummer. Edward had died months ago following a wound taken in a sword fight—though a skilled swordsman, his brother had lacked Alec's level head. Edward's quick temper, combined with a love of whiskey and late nights in oyster bars following Amy's death in childbirth, had put him in one last predicament, a duel that he had not survived. Alec had been grateful when his aunt and uncle had offered to continue to manage household, children, and business, leaving him free to resume his military duties.

Though he was named heir to his brother's estates and guardian to the girls, he could not nursemaid a pack of tiny females on his own. Nor did he want to be a chocolatier, but his father had trained both sons in the family business. That training and experience would suffice when he needed it.

Alec did not consider himself competent to raise children, especially small girls who had lost both parents within a span of three years. They needed more than he could possibly provide.

Despite her outward bristly quality, Euphemia loved the girls with a generous heart. Amy would have been glad to see her daughters raised with warmth and security. Alec, unmarried and a commissioned officer, could not provide that for them.

This time, when he returned to Hopefield House, he would arrive with a guest who refused to divulge even so much as her full name. He wondered how to explain her away to his family.

Kate gave a soft snore and slid sideways, her shoulder pressing his arm, her head tipping against his chest. He let her rest there. Moonlight bathed her face so that she looked more like a fairy queen than a hellion or a spy.

He sighed. What the devil was he to do with Katie Hell?

She shifted in her sleep, and Alec settled his arm rather comfortably around her shoulders. The rocking of the coach brought them close together, and she snuggled against him.

Sitting with her in so cozy a fashion, he relaxed a little further. Feeling tired, he rested his chin upon her head and closed his eyes, enjoying the sway of the coach and the warm, sleepy weight of the woman against him.

She made a sound like a mewling kitten, her cheek resting on his jacket lapel, her breath tickling his chest, blowing warmth through the fabric above his waistcoat.

"Oh," she murmured, her eyes still closed. Her hand lifted, her fingers splayed on his waistcoat. "You smell so nice."

Alec glanced down. Her face rested inches from the pocket where he had tucked the wrapped chocolate.

He smiled and brushed a hand over her hair, quickly, almost furtively, so that she would not know, and he would not have to acknowledge it even to himself.

A sudden lurch of the post chaise startled Kate out of a soothing dream that was lost the moment her eyes opened. She sat up, mortified when she realized that she was leaning against Captain Fraser's chest. His fingers cupped her head, but he was awake, tense and braced.

"What the devil—" he growled as the chaise careened sideways, undercarriage creaking. Kate bounced on the seat as Fraser held her tightly by the shoulder, keeping her in place. He peered through the window, twisting to view the road behind them as the vehicle skittered around a curve.

He swore under his breath. "We're being pursued."

"Who is it?" She craned her head to peer over his shoulder, the angle of the carriage on the road allowing a glimpse of the road behind them. For a moment, she saw the moving shapes of horses and men. "Red soldiers! Is that an escort?"

"No," Fraser said. He rose from the seat, half-bent in the cramped space, swaying with every jounce of the chaise. Grabbing the door handle, he opened the door just enough to stick his head outside. "Jack!" he called. "Jack MacDonald!"

The next wild bounce of the post chaise threw Kate off the seat, and she fell in a heap on the floor. Fraser braced himself with a hand clamped over the doorframe. "Jack! Get off the main road!" he bellowed.

Trying to stand, Kate lost her balance and knocked into Fraser, who supported her with one arm while he pulled the door shut. With another bounce of the carriage, both of them tumbled onto the seat. Another sharp turn in the road tossed them into a corner, so that her cheek met Fraser's. The raspy feel of his whiskered jaw, the hard brace of his arms felt secure—felt safe. She clung to him.

"Hold on," he said—unnecessarily, as she had no intention of letting go just yet. "Jack knows the tracks

113

and paths in this area. He'll lose those fellows in the darkness."

The post chaise rumbled down a steep hill at a reckless pace, swaying dangerously. Sliding from the seat again, Kate felt Fraser's hands around her arms, pulling her back into a hard, practical embrace. He leaned back to balance the wild rumbling of the chaise, which tilted down a steep incline.

"Your ghillie is a lunatic!" Kate looped her arms around his neck as the world tumbled and leaped around them.

"Fortunately," he answered.

The chaise careened to one side, righted, and stopped. Kate heard the snorting and stamping of the horses, and heard the ghillie call out. "All's well in there?"

"Aye," Fraser called back, sitting up, one arm around Kate. "Are you hurt, lass?"

"I'm fine." She sat up, limbs shaking, and pushed her hair out of her eyes, shoved her skirts down over her legs.

"Stay here." He stood and opened the door, stepping out into the cool night air.

Not about to take orders, Kate followed, nearly tumbling to the ground when she discovered that the drop step was still up.

Fraser spun, caught her deftly, and set her on her feet, then turned her toward the ghillie. MacDonald clamped an arm around her shoulders, while Fraser walked away.

"He's gone to look for them. You'll stay here with me, Miss," Jack MacDonald said.

Hearing the soft accent of a true Gael, Kate glanced at him in surprise. He smiled down at her. He was only a few inches taller than she and dressed in Lowland gear, yet in the moonlight, she saw a lean and muscular man, younger than she expected, with a startlingly beautiful face, clean-chiseled and perfect. And he looked familiar, which she had not noticed earlier upon hastily boarding the vehicle.

"We'll wait here, you and I," Jack said.

Nodding, still trembling, Kate glanced around. Fraser was nowhere in sight, and the post chaise had come to rest at the bottom of a long hill, which faced another steep hillside, forming a pass far below the level of the road. They had taken a drover's track down the hillside. A thick fringe of trees and underbrush screened the gully from the road above.

Catching her breath, Kate realized that not only was Fraser gone—her confining chains were off, and she was outside. This might be her only chance to run. If MacDonald released her even for a moment, she could slip into the trees and disappear. She glanced at him again—and nearly gasped.

Now she knew him: MacDonald had been in the London court, too, as Fraser's opponent in the swordsmanship demonstration.

Her thoughts whirled. This was trouble indeed.

Both Fraser and his ghillie could place her in the royal court, with access to the king—a true threat of treason if Fraser also identified her as the girl who had come in disguise to his tent intent on stealing documents. All of it would spell Jacobite intrigue and danger for her and her kinsmen.

She looked around, increasingly desperate. In the darkness, she saw that a tangle of trees and underbrush edged the track that led through the hills. Black mountains thrust into the night sky, feathered with mist. Kate recognized the profile of those hills: they bordered Perthshire from the north.

Duncrieff Castle, her home, lay just west of those peaks, and not so far from here. A day's walk between a gap in the range of hills would bring her to Glen Carran. Her brother, Robert MacCarran—chief of their clan—and several of their kinfolk would be at Duncrieff even now. Her sister, Sophie, had recently married Connor MacPherson of Kinnoull, whose Highland estate was not far from the family seat. Anywhere in that long, narrow glen, she would find kin and clansmen willing to hide and protect her.

If she could only get there, she would be safe.

She hoped that Allan MacCarran had already brought them word of her capture. If so, her kinsmen would be looking for her. Somehow she had to reach them, and she needed to let them know that she had seen Ian Cameron, that he was on his way to trial and probable execution, and that he had a message for them concerning the hidden cache of weaponry.

Overwhelmed by a sudden need to be home, to be with her family, to be free and safe, Kate gasped aloud and put her hand over her mouth.

"What is it?" MacDonald asked in Gaelic.

"Nothing," she replied. "I am only weary."

He squeezed her shoulder, but did not let her get away from him. Moments later, Fraser emerged from the trees.

Kate's heart leaped inexplicably—so tall and handsome in moonlight and shadows, clothed in dark tartan and regimental red, he exuded both wildness and authority. She watched him almost hungrily, in spite of herself.

But any hint of the romantic warrior dissolved when he went straight to the chaise, opened the door, and retrieved the manacles and chains. He dumped them into a canvas satchel that he dug out of the luggage hold at the back of the chaise. Shouldering the pack, he came toward them.

"How many were after us?" he asked MacDonald. Kate glared at Fraser, thinking about the chains, but he only glanced at her before listening to his cousin.

"Six or eight," Jack answered. "We lost them coming down here. They did not see us in the darkness and rode past."

"They'll be back. But that was well-done, Jack."

"Well done?" Kate burst out. "He nearly killed us all!"

"Jack did what he had to do," Fraser pointed out calmly. "It was necessary to lose the soldiers somehow."

"Why lose them?" Kate snapped. "They were accompanying us."

"Not exactly." Fraser took her arm as MacDonald stepped back. "Jack, go on ahead with the chaise. We'll walk from here."

"I am not walking to Edinburgh! Tell me what is really going on here," Kate demanded.

"Later," Fraser said curtly.

Kate punched him in the arm—a petulant, futile, impulsive response, she knew. Fraser sent her an irritated glance and put a hand on his canvas satchel. She backed away, and Jack caught her.

"Huh!" Jack grunted. "A walk with that lass would be like strolling with a wildcat. You take the chaise, Alec, and I'll take charge of her."

"Oh, no. You'd enjoy that too much. I'd wager the two of you would hie off somewhere, and I'd never find either of you again. We're due in Edinburgh soon, and that's where we'll go."

"*Ach*, the lad does love his rules," MacDonald whispered loudly to Kate. "His da bought him a commission in the army because of it. But he has a wildness, too, that he will not show to anyone—not even himself."

Kate blinked at Jack, then Fraser.

"If you two can stop chatting," the captain drawled, "we'll leave now and meet you at MacLennan's, a few miles from here."

Kate looked up. "Is MacLennan another wicked regimental officer? Does he run a local jail?"

"MacLennan's Changehouse. An inn," Fraser said. "Fortunately it's not far, it has good stables, and it's owned by friends."

"Yours or mine?" she shot back. Jack laughed.

"Take that damned chaise and get out of here," Fraser barked to the ghillie. "Lead the soldiers as far away as you can."

"I'll lose them in the hills where the military road ends, and I'll meet you tonight, or by dawn at least."

"Fine. Be careful, lad."

"Aye, Alec. Tell Jeanie MacLennan I'll see her soon."

"If I do that, you'd best keep your promise to her this time," Fraser rumbled ominously.

As Kate glanced from one man to the other, she saw Jack grin and shrug before turning to run toward the chaise and horses.

Guiding Kate with him, Fraser walked away. He seemed calm, but his fingers flexed on her arm, and she felt his urgency, taut as a fiddle string. Behind them, Jack chuckled softly to the horses as he turned them, and the vehicle began to roll toward the earthen track that led up to the road.

Chapter 10

"**A**lec—such a normal name for a madman," Kate grumbled as they walked along. "And you must be mad to drag me about like this. What is it you want from me?"

"I'm not a mad sort, according to my family," he answered, so blithely that she felt tempted to stomp on his foot out of sheer frustration. He had simply ignored her question. The man was so consistently unruffled that it irritated her. Kate was the opposite much of the time: high-tempered, direct, and expressive. Serenity of character, such as her sister Sophie possessed, eluded Kate, though she craved peace often enough.

"Our branch of the Frasers," he went on, "is traditionally said to be made up of 'mad' Frasers and 'staid' Frasers. I am not one of the wilder ones."

"Really," she said sourly.

"When I was a lad, my Highland nurse dubbed me *Alasdair Callda* in the Gaelic."

"'Dull Alexander'? I could see it . . . though Jack Mac-Donald says you have a touch of the wildness in you."

"I make up for staidness in other ways," he murmured, and his fingers flexed on her arm.

An unbidden thrill poured through her like a spiral of flame. Kate remembered his compelling touch upon her body on another night, when matters had been very different between them.

"Besides, more to the point here would be to learn your name, Miss Hell, not mine," he said.

"*Alasdair Callda* . . . You may call me *Catriona Allta*," she replied quickly.

He chuckled. "Very good. Wild Katherine. Alas, not quite what we're after."

"Alas," she echoed.

Within minutes, he had led her along a diagonal path over the slope, far from the drover's track, keeping below the level of the military road. As they mounted another hillside, Kate yanked out of his grip. Fraser let go long enough that she stepped away, but he snatched her arm again.

She twisted. "Please, just let me go."

"If I did, you'd soon be lost out here."

"I know the area too well for that—" Instantly she regretted the words.

"Do you? Interesting. So your home is near here, is it?"

"No," she said hastily. "I've . . . just been through here before. On my way to Edinburgh for shopping," she added.

"Shopping? So the laundress shops in Edinburgh?"

"No, the fairy queen does," she snapped.

"The mysterious Miss Kate," he drawled. "Even if you know the area, if you were to wander alone, Grant's men would find you, I promise you. They'll search the roads and the hills."

"And the inns," she pointed out.

"We'll take that risk together."

Together. A feeling stirred in her, something she did not want to awaken, a deep and real need for companionship, for a partner in life, for love. Captain Alexander Fraser was not the remedy for that, she told herself sternly.

"'We'?" She spoke defiantly. "I would not go anywhere willingly with you, nor would I go with Grant's soldiers."

"That's an odd remark for Katie Hell," he growled.

Without thinking, she slapped his face.

Angling his head to one side, Fraser stared down at her. In the moonlit gloom, she saw the flushed mark of her hand on his cheek. Heart pounding, she stared upward in silence, breathing hard. Tension rose between them, palpable and pulsing.

"I am not a whore," she said between her teeth.

"And I'm usually more of a gentleman," he murmured. "I beg your pardon." He took her arm and walked onward.

Over the shoulder of that hill and along a weathered track that led beside a burbling stream, Kate allowed him to guide her. Then she tried again to pull away from him, another futile attempt. Although she was determined, he was simply stronger.

"Please, you must let me go."

"You're a stubborn wee thing," he muttered. "You're not off to a certain beheading. It's just a judge's inquiry."

"Which could lead to a hanging. I've done nothing wrong. And I want . . . I just want my freedom."

"So do we all, lass, in our ways."

"What sort of freedom could you want? You have what you need, seems to me—a man of privilege and rank and good family, with only the thought that he must do his duty or be damned. You crave nothing more than that, I'm sure."

"You've a mouth on you," he ground out. "I crave the sort of freedom that brings peace of mind and peaceful lives. The sort that helps make a man's life what it truly could be."

"Then get rid of your red coat, Lovat Fraser," she replied.

He exhaled audibly. "Careful of the rocks here," he said, and she realized in that moment how patient and tolerant he could be. "Listen to me, Kate. You'll go to Edinburgh with me, or with Grant. I'd far rather you were in my company."

"Why should you care who takes me to prison?"

"It is the manner of the taking that concerns me."

His implication was clear, and Kate felt grateful for his protectiveness. But she could not stay with him for that, or any other reason. "Releasing me would solve this for everyone."

"It would solve it for *you*."

"Just tell them that I escaped from you."

"But Colonel Grant would be so disappointed. He and I do not see eye to eye about some matters as it is." His tone had a wry, teasing note in it.

"You agreed with him about packing me off to prison!"

"I'm following orders, as you point out. General Wade assigned you to my custody. I'll keep close watch over you until the courts decide what's to be done with you."

"They should just release me."

"I hope for your sake they do, my dear. Or Miss Hell," he amended carefully.

My dear sounded so much better. "Where are you taking me, if not directly to prison?"

"To my home in Edinburgh for a few days," he said.

"That is the first good news I've had from you. If I must go in your custody, I at least want a proper bath after the hospitality of your prison."

"It's not *my* prison, lass. You can have all the baths you like at Hopefield House, and clean clothing, too, until it is time for your interview with the Lord Advocate. It would greatly help matters if I could give his office your name."

"It would be so much more helpful if you just let me go."

He sighed. "I suppose I will have to register you with the courts as Marie Katherine Hell. Or do you prefer MacHellion?"

"Register me as the Queen of Nonny-nonny, for all I care. Why did Colonel Grant send soldiers after us if you already have custody of me?"

"Because he is a blethering idiot."

Kate laughed, surprised. "We do agree on that."

Alec glanced at her. "Apparently he has some personal grudge with you and would like nothing more than to see that you pay for that. I suppose you know what he's upset about, Katie Hell?"

Her face burned, despite the cool wind. "I did not seduce Colonel Grant, if that is what you are thinking."

"Just as you did not seduce me? No fists, now," he said, feinting with a hand. "You have better manners than that. I would appreciate an honest answer, not a display of your temper."

She looked away in silence, more frightened than fuming. "I remember clearly the night I encountered Grant," she said in a low voice. "He treated me roughly, quite overcome with . . . lust. I feared that I would not get away unharmed."

His fingers flexed on her arm. "Go on."

"I defended myself. I struggled, then I planted my knee in his . . . trousers before fleeing the tent. He was so drunk that he fell, hit his head, and collapsed to the floor. I suppose he blamed all of that on the wicked Katie Hell."

"As a matter of fact, he did."

"I did nothing to that man, I tell you."

He was silent for a long moment as they traversed another hillock, the breeze blowing hard against them on the ridge. "Had I been there and seen that—"

"Then you might believe what I'm saying now?"

"No. I'm saying I might have killed the man."

She glanced at him, astonished, even pleased. "Then you do believe me. I do not seduce men, though they may say it of me."

"Kate, whatever you have done or have not done is not proven—and if it remains so, that is in your favor, for it is a legitimate verdict under Scots law," he added. "But if Grant and other officers identify you as the girl who came to their quarters and took papers and maps, your denials will do no good. As for seduction, I only know for certain that something happened between us." He pulled her along with him.

She could not deny that something had occurred between them, and she cherished the memory of it. "I cannot help it if—" She touched her throat, where her silver necklace was still missing. No one beyond her family knew of her inherited fairy power. "I sometimes have an effect on men," she ventured.

He huffed. "I know all about that. Come ahead." He urged her onward, righting her when she nearly stumbled.

"I see trying to explain myself to you would be futile."

"You do not have to explain that part of it. I know what happened with us, and I would guess you've been in that . . . predicament before, Miss Hell."

"What happened with you—was different."

He stopped, turned her toward him. "What do you mean?"

"I have never . . . done that before," she admitted.

126

He frowned down at her. "Do you tell all of them that?"

She sucked in a breath, feeling as if she had been slapped this time. "I am not a harlot."

"Then who are you, and what is your business with officers?"

She looked away, heart slamming. "I cannot tell you."

"Whoever you are," he growled, "what happened between us in my bed should be forgotten."

She glanced up then. "Forgotten?"

"It has no bearing here and now. It's best for both of us if it is forgotten." He resumed walking, shouldering his satchel and tugging her beside him. "As for Grant— I warn you, he is not the sort to forgive and forget."

"Unlike you," she drawled.

"Unlike me." He said it so calmly that Kate felt a little swirl of stubborn defiance. Planting her feet, she refused to move. Alec turned.

"Katie my lass," he said, as he groped inside the satchel and drew out the chains and manacles. "Come with me now, or you'll come along in chains."

"Just leave me. I will be fine and off your hands."

"I will not leave you anywhere that Grant's men can find you," he said firmly.

"Why not? Either way I'll end up going to prison!"

"You do not want to go that way, if you take my meaning."

She scowled at him. "I take it."

"Good. Now what do you choose?"

"If I have no choice but to go with you, I'll want my

127

necklace, please." She opened her hand. "I'll bargain my cooperation for that."

"Something tells me I could get the poor end of a bargain with Katie Hell," he murmured.

"Take that chance." Kate knew that she was taking the greater risk. She often felt bespelled in this man's presence, yet Alec seemed capable of resisting any charm she might have—but for one night she could not forget as easily as he could.

Dipping a hand into his sporran, he opened his palm to show her a moonlit pool of silver and crystal. Kate reached out, but he closed his fingers over the necklace and over her hand.

"I wish this wee bauble was all the chain you'd ever need, Kate." His voice was quiet.

She felt her knees go weak. "Give me my necklace, sir."

"I have no desire to put irons on you, but I don't want to have to bargain continually either. I have to trust you to come with me. But my guess is that you'd leave first chance." He stated it quietly, as fact.

Kate sighed. "I would."

"An honest answer. I'll keep the bauble as an assurance of your good behavior. I've nothing else to bargain with."

She gazed up at him, heart pounding, breaths fast. He had so much to bargain with, she thought. Had he bargained a kiss such as he had given her before, her resistance might dissolve.

He leaned so close, nearly nose to nose with her, that for a moment she thought he might kiss her as he had done before, and she impulsively craved it, like a hunger rising fast in her. Tilting her head back, she waited, and her wildest thought was to allow it, to revel in it, to let that erase the threats and stress she felt otherwise. She half closed her eyes.

"Later, darling." He dropped the necklace into his sporran. "I think we will not gamble like this just yet."

She blew out a breath, trying to shake off the effect he had on her, the subtle, powerful influence that made the blood rush in her veins. "The inn is this way?" She strode past him, limbs trembling.

Fraser caught up with her and took her hand to guide her through a cluster of trees. "I warn you to behave yourself, lass. No escaping, no arguing, no slapping or punching your custodial officer."

"You're crediting me with evil thoughts." She lifted her chin in defiance, shook her hand loose, though the contact felt dangerously pleasant.

"Have all the evil thoughts you like. Just keep them to yourself."

"I'll consider it."

"Good. Give me your word on it, one Highlander to another."

"Highlander? You're but a Lowland officer in a plaidie."

"I'm a captain in Lovat's independent company, and I'm considered a Highlander by all but you, apparently."

"You live in Edinburgh, you're a red soldier, and likely a Whig. You insist on keeping my personal property when you've no right to it, which is not the natural courtesy of most Highland men. A Highland oath would mean little to you."

"I was born and raised in Inverness-shire, spoke Gaelic until I was given knee breeches, have worn the plaid all my life," he said, "and oaths mean all to me."

She returned his gaze, breath quickening as she wished she could believe him. When she had first seen him at St. James's Palace, he had looked like a magnificent Highland warrior. That day, she had fallen a little in love with him—but since then, he had proven himself other than what she thought.

"If you were a true Highlander, you'd be Jacobite."

"Not necessarily so. The *Am Freiceadan Dubh*, the Black Watch as we are sometimes called, police our own—which is what I'm attempting to do now," he said wryly. "We are not a Jacobite faction, but a goodwill extension of cooperation between Scots and the crown."

"Many will say we should not be cooperating with them at all. And I'll make no oaths with a man I cannot trust."

"You can trust me, you just do not know it. I'll have your promise, or it's chains with locks for you." He shifted the satchel, chains chinking inside.

"That's not amusing."

"It's not meant to be. I'll have your word, now." His voice deepened from teasing to somber.

"Only until we reach the inn. And only because I'm starving and tired."

"I'm sure you are." He walked beside her, his hand on her elbow, leaves crushing underfoot, the air moist and cool. "So we'll call it a truce."

"For now," she warned.

Chapter 11

Moonlight bathed the inn as Alec led Kate toward the stone two-story building. Windows glowed with warm light through red curtains, and a tin lantern burned on a hook beside the door. To the left Alec heard sounds from the stables behind the inn: horses snorting, a groom calling out. He doubted Jack Mac-Donald would be here yet, and he only hoped the fellow was safe.

Glancing at Kate, he reached down to pull up the plaid arisaid she wore to cover her blond hair. She was too noticeable, Alec thought, with hair like a lantern flame. Luckily, her lightweight, silk-lined plaid was long enough to cover her from crown to knee.

"Best if you're not easily recognized," he explained as he opened the door. Guiding her inside, he ignored the glare she sent him, knowing very well she did not want to be with him, and he certainly understood her need to be free.

Her gaze caught his, and for a moment he saw uncertainty beneath her rebellious frown. Setting a hand on her shoulder, he leaned close to murmur at her ear. "I promise no one will know you're my prisoner so long as you behave. Agreed?"

She nodded, and her next glance tugged at his heart again.

The main room was dim, smoky from candles and tobacco, and filled with voices, music, and the savory smells of good food. Near the fireside, an old man played a fiddle, the plaintive tones wafting outward. Scarred tables and benches were arranged throughout the room, occupied by men and a few women.

Alec quickly saw that some of the men wore coats and breeches and spoke English, while the rest were Highlanders in bulky plaids. He saw with relief that there were no soldiers present.

"Keep quiet, and please keep your head down," he told Kate.

Hearing his name called, Alec turned. Behind a high counter, the gray-haired owner, James MacLennan, raised a hand in greeting. Beside him stood his daughter, a pretty, dark-haired young woman holding a swaddled infant against her shoulder. Seeing Alec, she smiled and hurried toward him.

"Miss MacLennan, greetings." Alec removed his

cocked hat, still keeping a firm hand on Kate's slender shoulder. His prisoner was silent, tucking her head in the shadow of her plaid. Jean glanced toward her curiously.

"Welcome back, Captain Fraser. And welcome to you, Miss—"

"Jean MacLennan—meet Kate," Alec said, while Kate mumbled a greeting in return.

Jeanie smiled, her pink cheeks, glossy black hair, and dark eyes all sparkle and warmth. All the while, she patted the infant, a squirming bundle on her shoulder. "Is Mr. MacDonald with you, sir?"

"He'll join us later this evening. We had a slight mishap with our carriage and walked here ahead of him. 'Twill take him some time to repair the, ah, damage." He smiled. "Your little one is doing well, I hope." He could not recall what gender the creature was, or its name, though he had been introduced to it during a visit two months earlier. It had been newborn then, he remembered.

He hoped Jack remembered, the thorough rascal.

"Oh, aye. He smiles now, and sleeps through most nights," she said proudly, while the child whimpered. "He won't keep you up the night this time, Captain Fraser."

Kate looked squarely at Alec and lifted a brow.

"I generally hire the room above Jean's," he explained.

"We have that room ready for you tonight, Captain. I'll tell Father." Jean hastened across the room to speak with the innkeeper, who tapped ale from a keg into a pewter pitcher. The man turned to grin as Alec approached.

"Welcome, Captain. Will you be hiring another room for the lady?" he asked.

Kate began to speak, and Alec squeezed her shoulder. "One will do . . . for my wife and me," he said impulsively, knowing he could not chance putting Kate in a separate room. Kate jerked her shoulder under his hand in protest.

"Wife?" The innkeeper looked astonished, while Jean gaped at Alec, who only smiled.

"Bride," he corrected. "We've just been wed."

"Only just," Kate muttered.

"So it's Mrs. Fraser, then! Congratulations," Jean said brightly, patting her infant son. Her father handed her a key. "Come this way. Will you take the lantern for us, Captain?"

Alec took the glowing lantern MacLennan handed him, and he and Kate followed Jean up a flight of wooden steps to the second floor, and onward to the corner room that Alec usually hired on his trips back and forth between Edinburgh and Fort William. Opening the narrow, creaking door, Jean stepped back, soothing the baby again, who squawked and quieted.

"I changed the bed linens a week ago," Jean said. "No one has slept here but either you or Jack MacDonald. And most of the time he keeps company elsewhere. It's three shillings more to change the linens, as you know, sir."

"These will do," he said, though Kate made a choking sound. "Can you provide some supper for us? I know it's past nine, but my wife is famished." Kate would need a decent meal after several days in prison, he knew, and he could do with something himself.

"My father would tell you to take bread and cheese tonight, and wait for bacon to be thrown on the griddle after dawn. But there's mutton stew left, and half a loaf of brown bread. I'll fix that up for you both and have it ready for you downstairs."

"Thank you." Alec fished a few coins from his jacket pocket.

"Will Jack MacDonald want a meal and bed when he returns?"

"I'm sure of it," Alec answered, "though he may not arrive until morning."

"I'll watch for him. Oh, we also have new casks of ale and a good Spanish rum. Captain, and Mrs. Fraser," she added as she turned to go. Alec held the door open for her.

"We'll be down directly." He steered Kate into the room, then slipped Jean the coins, which she fisted against her child's swaddling.

When he turned, shutting the door, Kate was staring at the bed. "I am not sleeping there."

Two steps took him to the bed, where Alec sat on the mattress, which sagged and groaned beneath him. He patted the lumpy surface. "It's comfortable. I've slept here often."

"So I gather." She folded her arms.

"If you're thinking I'll take advantage of you while we're alone, don't worry. You're perfectly safe." While he craved another night of delight with her in his arms, he could not allow that to happen. "I give you my word."

She frowned, brows tight, her gray-blue eyes like captured moonlight. Then she lifted her chin. "You can hire another room."

"I'm frugal. We'll share this one. I'll sleep on the floor."

"I'll sleep there. The bed linens are old, and used."

"As you heard, I'm the only one who's slept here," he pointed out. "Perhaps Jack once or twice."

"And who knows who else!" She wrinkled her nose.

"I hire the room out for a month or more at a time, since I travel back and forth to Fort William rather frequently."

"You gave the lass a coin, but did not ask for fresh linens, nor even another blanket."

"I gave her the coin to keep for herself, not to pay for services, since she turns every penny over to her father. And I will not ask her to do extra work for one short night's rest here. You've just spent days in a prison cell. I would think this would seem a Pasha's paradise after that."

"I was raised to certain standards."

"Oh? A gentle upbringing, I assume. And where was it that you were raised?" He cocked a brow.

"At home, with clean linens on my own bed." She glowered at him. "As long as we are here, I'd like a bath. A private one."

He stood and looked down at her. "You can be a fine, spoiled, wee thing when you get a notion in your head. So the mysterious Miss Hell apparently had a privileged upbringing."

136

"I just need a bath, not an interrogation. I'm tired."

"I understand that. At this hour, you'll have to make do. I won't ask Jean to heat water and climb the stairs to fill a hip tub for you. She has enough to do, and a small babe to care for, and no husband. Her father runs her ragged as it is. He's been no less demanding of her since the babe's birth."

"Is she not wed? Whose babe is it . . . yours? Perhaps you should sleep with her instead and leave me here," she suggested.

"The babe is not mine, I promise you. It's Jack's." He set his hat on the bed, ruffled a hand through his hair, rubbed his eyes. God, he thought, he was more weary than he realized. He wanted to take off his jacket and just go to sleep. But the enticing thought of resting in that bed with Kate gave him more than a moment's pause.

Potentially a very dangerous night, he thought.

Kate watched him. "So Jack MacDonald is the father?"

"The girl refuses to say, though I'm sure of it. And Jack would marry her, I think. He's fond of the lass, but he's not inclined to settle down. Jean has not pressed for it, either."

"Perhaps she loves him that much," Kate said quietly. "Enough to give him his freedom."

He paused to glance at her. "I suppose that's it. She's a decent lass. No one holds it against her that she got with child before marriage. We Scots are very good about tolerating missteps within families. How does your family tolerate your, ah, wild ways?"

"Fine, since it was their idea." She clapped a hand to her mouth. "I mean—"

"Aha," he said simultaneously. "So you admit to a wee bit of mischief."

"Any mischief I have committed was mostly with you." Kate folded her arms. "I can easily understand how Jean got into her dilemma. Jack MacDonald is a true charmer."

"Is he? I suppose so. What of me?"

"Chaining women is not very engaging." She turned to look around the room. "Tell me, will Jack accept responsibility for his child?"

"Jack acknowledges it, but taking responsibility is another matter." Alec shrugged.

"Then do you trust him to return with the carriage?"

"Don't look so hopeful. He'll be here. Jack keeps his word, once given. But in the matter of ladies, he can be a fickle soul and avoids giving his word like the plague. As for your bath," he went on, "there's a basin and pitcher in that corner, where you can wash up." He indicated a table that held a large ceramic pitcher and a wide bowl. "We can ask for hot water later. If I know Jean, what's there now is clean, and the towels will be fresh, too. I pay an extra fee to have clean towels and plenty of soap and water on hand—though I'm not so particular about bed linens, since I'm hardly here to use them, and the room is not hired out otherwise."

Kate wrinkled her nose, then walked toward the washstand to peer into the white pitcher. A thick chunk of soap sat in a small dish, and a linen towel was folded beside it. On the wall above the stand hung a small, round, cracked mirror. She glanced there, lifted a hand, and dropped back her shawl, so that her golden hair tumbled over her shoulders. Pouring a little water into the bowl, she washed her hands and rinsed her face.

At the simple sight, Alec felt a strong urge rush through his body—straightforward lust, he thought, nothing more. She held no real magic over him, he tried to tell himself.

But when she removed her cloak and tossed it aside, when she lifted her modesty kerchief away to pass the linen towel over the exposed tops of her breasts, he felt that magic begin to work.

And realized he was staring. He glanced away, fiddled with the lantern, slid open the horn plate, lowered it again. The flickering shadows and golden light only made her seem more beautiful, more lush and perfect, when he glanced her way again.

She sent him a little glance. Interesting how her eyes could look like precious silver one moment and storm clouds the next, he thought. She turned her back, and he turned away.

He heard more water sloshing in the bowl. Then the splashes stopped. "Captain Fraser, I do need some privacy."

He stood, his back discreetly turned. "I'll be just outside the door. There's no other way out of this room," he added pointedly, as he left.

Standing in the dark, narrow corridor, he heard further splashing in the bowl. When it stopped for a decent interval, he knocked and entered again.

Kate stood by the dresser with her skirts hiked, one bare foot propped on the bed while she slid a dampened towel along her calf. Alec glimpsed her slim,

SARAH GABRIEL

shapely limbs—taut and smooth, skin like cream—
before she dropped her skirts in a flurry.

He spun away, heart pounding so that he felt as if he
were under a spell. She was fey and beautiful, her
scrubbed face glowing, her hair in damp tendrils. Alec
felt stunned, though he tried to convince himself that
he could resist whatever power she seemed to have
over men.

He waited in silence while she splashed further, then
he heard her pouring the water from the basin into the
slops bowl, and pouring fresh from the pitcher. Then he
felt the towel slap over his shoulder.

"Your turn, sir." She breezed past him to sit on the
bed, rope-sprung mattress creaking even with her
slight weight.

At the bowl, Alec rinsed his hands and face and
splashed his neck, grateful the water was cool. He felt
hot enough already, hot to the core of his being. He removed his red coat and matching waistcoat to stand in
his rumpled shirtsleeves and the wrapped and belted
plaid that he so often wore, its dark blues and greens
hiding the grime of his constant travels.

He did not turn but felt her gaze upon him. In the
small, clouded mirror hung above the washstand, he
glimpsed her, a lovely creature, fairylike in the dim glass.

Washing his hands thoroughly, then raking his fingers through his hair to comb it, he tugged at the queue
with its black ribbon—he rarely wore even a bag wig,
for he hated the itch of the things—then paused to
cover his eyes with his palms for a moment.

"Tired, Captain?" she asked.

140

"No," he answered curtly, though he was. He generally kept matters to himself. He straightened the banded collar of his shirt and turned.

"Shall we eat now?" she asked, sitting up eagerly. She stretched her arms high, as if savoring the feel of hands free of irons. Her breasts shifted deliciously under the stiffened bodice that elegantly defined her slim torso. Standing, she rested her hands at her waist, fingers tapping.

Alec stared, feeling again the sudden burgeoning in his body. He would have to suppress that if they were to spend a night together in this room, in that bed.

"I am starved. Let's go." She walked to the door and took the handle, then tapped her foot impatiently.

"A moment." Alec fetched the satchel he had left on the floor earlier, reached in to remove the chains and manacles.

"Not those," she said warily, backing away.

"You could too easily escape from the public room." He moved toward her.

She stepped backward again. "You cannot expect me to go down there chained like a prisoner."

"Lass," he murmured, approaching her while she pressed against the door. "Remember, you are a prisoner of the crown."

"I am Mrs. Fraser here in this place, so you told them. You would not bring your bride to a public room in chains."

"Likely not," he said amiably. "But then, you are not really my bride, are you." He took her right wrist and clapped the manacle around it.

She watched him in fuming silence as he closed the latch on the cuff, then grabbed the other manacle and chained it to his left wrist. Snapping the bracelet shut, he pocketed the key.

Then he picked up the canvas bag, thinking he would use it to disguise the chain between them once they were in public. He was not interested in humiliating the girl, just keeping her in one place. He took her hand, chain swinging between them.

"We'll share the burden," he said.

"I do not need to share anything with you. Undo this!"

He wove his fingers tightly with hers. "Tell me why you came to my tent, who sent you, and your full given name."

"I brought clean linens, the washerwoman sent me," she listed, leaning close, her eyes snapping indignantly, "and you know my name—or all of it you need to know."

"I'm going to enjoy our meal together, Marie Katherine," he said, "and our bed should be cozy tonight." He rattled the chain, aware that he rattled her spirit a little, too.

"So soon as you close your eyes, I will have that key."

"Kate, my darling," he said patiently, reaching for the door handle. "I consider myself warned. I am hungry, and I am going downstairs. Which means you'll come, too."

She huffed in protest but followed him into the hallway.

Chapter 12

◦◦◦◦◦

Kate leaned her cheek on her free hand, her other manacled to Fraser's beneath the table, and watched Alec polish off the last of her stew, having finished his own. The man had not lost his appetite, she thought. Nothing seemed to disturb his cool, constant equilibrium.

She had eaten only a little, though her own appetite was normally good. Watching Alec from beneath her gathered brows, Kate refused quietly when he offered her the last heel of buttered brown bread. She waited in silence while he polished it off then took a long draw of ale from a pewter tankard, apparently not bothered by the fact that his left hand was chained to her right hand beneath the level of the table.

Kate touched her throat out of habit, missing the cool delicacy and reassurance of the little crystal. She could well imagine that her kinsmen would advise her to charm her captor and get away—but they had always had better faith in her abilities than she had. And without the fairy talisman, charming anyone might not be so simple a thing, for she had always been told, had always felt, that the polished bit of crystal had some power.

Besides, she felt more resentful than alluring tonight. Had she turned up her charm like a lantern wick, had she waved the pendant under his very nose, had she transformed into a fairy queen before the man's eyes, Captain Fraser would scarcely notice. Staid Alexander was immovable, impenetrable, infuriating.

He did not seem to melt whenever she looked at him a certain way, as most other men did. Nor did he sigh, gaze at her like a calf, murmur poetic descriptions of her form. And he certainly did not agree to whatever she asked of him. Suddenly she realized that she had come to assume men would be fascinated by her—and at the same time, she realized she should not expect it at all.

To her disbelief, she was the one staring, the one sighing and conjuring descriptions: his eyes, blue as a twilight sky; his hair, the color of oak gilded with sunlight; his physique, as perfect as a statue of some ancient god. She was the one melting whenever he looked at her.

She was baffled. The man who had shown her deep,

wonderful passion the night she had lain in his arms seemed indifferent, even impatient with her.

Yet that was oddly refreshing. Here was a man she could not predict, control, or influence. His aloofness challenged her, and she savored it. He did not bore her. Instead, she was glad to discover that her power did not always prevail. He offered her a release, of a sort, from the constant presence of the Fairy's Gift.

Only she knew that Katie Hell, the wild and alluring one with the fairy power, was nothing like Kate Mac-Carran, who had a strong spirit and temperament but preferred to live a quiet life, with an ideal of peace and serenity that did not suit Katie Hell or a MacCarran blessed with the glamourie.

Kate had never liked the inborn gift in her fairy blood. She could not always admire the men who succumbed to her allure, and feared she might never find a man to respect and truly love.

Fraser was different from the rest. She was attracted not only to the powerful magic of a virile, handsome, intelligent man, but to the indefinable allure of his strong will and steadfast character. How ironic that she was not really free to pursue her interest in him, but rather had to escape him.

Seated beside him on the wooden bench, her right hand and his left joined by the manacles hidden beneath the generous folds of her arisaid, she studied him.

Although he had intrigued her the first time she had seen him in court, she had not fallen in love with him. Fairy magic might enhance love, but it could not create it. Despite his charisma and her fascination, despite the astonishing passion she had felt in his arms, he was an officer, she was his prisoner, and nothing but trouble could come of that.

He glanced up as she watched him. "What is it?" he asked, around a mouthful of bread.

"Are you a Whig or a Jacobite?" she asked.

Looking startled, he swallowed. "I find it wise to keep such opinions to myself. I presume you are Jacobite?"

She rolled her eyes. "That hardly needs answering."

"Just take care to keep it to yourself. There are too many in and out of here who might not share your fervor for the Chevalier de St. George," he murmured, referring to the discreet name sometimes used by James Stuart. "You do not have much of an appetite," he added, looking at her trencher.

She lifted her hand, and his, beneath the folds of her plaid and quietly shook the shared iron chain.

"Ah. So that bothers you. It's not for much longer."

"What if Jack does not come back? What if he's in danger?"

"He can take care of himself. I know him well, and I trust him. My parents took him in when he was a waif who had lost his family and had come to Edinburgh to wander the streets and beg for whatever jobs he could find. He sought us out, and my father's carriage nearly ran him down in the street as he approached. Even if he had not been my mother's kin, my father would have felt an obligation to the lad."

She tilted her head. "You were raised in Edinburgh?"

"Partly. We spent our summers near Inverness, in the

Great Glen. My parents, my brother and sisters," he added.

"Are they there now—in the Great Glen?"

"Kilburnie House? No, they're gone, most of them. My parents died of fever seven years back, and my brother passed away less than a year ago. My sister lives at Kilburnie with her husband."

"Are you Laird of Kilburnie now?"

"I am, though I rarely get the chance to go up there. My sister and brother-in-law run the household in my stead. They have small children, and Kilburnie is a good place to raise little ones. And where are you from?" he added casually.

Kate slid him a sour look, then sipped cool brew from the pewter cup in front of her. "The Highlands," she answered.

"And what do you know about those Spanish weapons gone missing in the Highlands?" He said it low and deliberately, his fingertips tracing a wet ring on the table surface.

"I've told you I know nothing about that."

He leaned so close that she felt his breath stirring her hair, the warmth of it, and the feeling of his closeness, plunging through her. "Tell me your secrets, lass, or we will both run out of time, and the Jacobite cause along with us."

She stared at him, stunned. "What do you mean?"

He glanced up as Jean approached, and Kate watched him, wondering what he really wanted, what he really thought about Jacobites and hidden Spanish weapons . . . and captive female spies.

"All done here?" Jean had the baby with her again, swathed in a plaid blanket. When she had served supper earlier, the child had not been with her.

"Aye, thank you," Alec said.

"The food was excellent," Kate added. "So the wee one is awake again?"

"Aye, and fussy tonight, he is, but there's no one to watch him but myself. My brother Davey usually helps in the tavern room at night, but he's out courting." Glancing about, Kate realized how little help Jean had at the inn—there was no sign of the innkeeper or any other servant.

Alec glanced meaningfully at Kate. "We'd best go upstairs, love. We're both weary, and we'll have an early start tomorrow."

Love. The softly spoken word sent a wonderful shiver down her back. "We'll leave, providing Jack MacDonald arrives," she pointed out pragmatically.

"I'll save him some stew," Jean offered, as she reached for their pewter plates. Kate stacked them with her free hand to help out, keeping the manacled hand with Alec's below the table level.

"Look," Fraser murmured, tightening his fingers on hers.

Glancing up, Kate saw three redcoat soldiers entering the inn just at that moment. "No," she breathed. "Is there another door we can take to leave the room?"

"Too late," he whispered. "They'll see us if we go."

"*Och*, look, more patrons." Jean turned. "Soldiers, too, and my da's gone to bed and my brother's not here. I'll have to see to them." She shifted the child, who fussed again, and patted its back. "You'll want to speak with them, Captain?"

"Not really," he said quickly. "Go on, Jean. My wife can watch the babe while you tend to your work." Alec prodded Kate with an elbow.

"Aye, let me take him." Kate suddenly realized what Alec intended—the child could provide her a needed disguise. The soldiers were not searching for a young mother.

"Oh, thank you. I'll be back. If you want to take him upstairs with you, I'll fetch him later." Jean set her bundled child carefully in the crook of Kate's arm and turned away.

Kate awkwardly supported the infant with one hand manacled to Alec's own. "I cannot hold this child if you keep the chain on both of us," she whispered, while she tried to balance the lightweight, warm, surprisingly active bundle. "And I'm not going to run off with Jeanie's bairn in my charge. But I think you knew that," she added suddenly.

"Aye." Beneath the table, he set the key in the lock and turned, then discreetly dumped the irons into the canvas pack that sat on the bench between them. He draped the generous folds of her plaid to shadow her face. "Sit there and stay quiet."

Fraser stood and turned his back to shield her from view, bracing a hip on the table as he lifted his ale tankard and drank casually. Kate huddled in the corner of the bench, jiggling the baby, who began to cry while squirming fiercely.

"I have no experience with babes," she said, lifting the child to her shoulder and desperately tapping its back.

Alec glanced at her. "Don't beat on the poor lad like that, he's not a drum. Just use that famous charm of yours, and he'll do all your will."

She shot him a scowl. He smiled and turned away.

Across the room, the soldiers saw Fraser and strode toward him, while Kate sank deep into the shadows, leaning over the baby. Alec stood as they came near.

"Evening, gentlemen," he said.

"Captain Fraser," one of them greeted him somberly. Kate peeked over the baby's shoulder, while keeping her head ducked as if she was concerned only with her child.

Jean's son was crying piteously now, long, tremulous cries that wrenched Kate's heart and added to her panic. She was not sure how to soothe him, but was glad of one thing—the soldiers would be less inclined to bother a woman with a shrieking baby in her arms.

"Greetings, Corporal," Fraser replied. "What's your business here, if I may ask?"

"Sir, I think you know. We've been following you since you left Fort William earlier tonight with the female prisoner."

"Oh, was it you we saw earlier?" Fraser asked easily.

Kate missed the next part of the exchange, which was drowned by the baby's staccato wailing. She rubbed his back and cupped her hand over the small head, whispering nonsense, kissing his brow. His soft infant scent was unexpectedly wonderful.

"Colonel Grant demands that you turn her over to

us, sir," the corporal then said. "If you won't, we are ordered to take her."

Kate ducked her face beside the baby's head, her heart pounding hard.

"I would gladly give her up if she were here," Fraser answered. "She proved to be more trouble than I thought."

The officer looked around. "Where is she, sir?" His glance took in Kate and the baby, and passed over them.

Jean's son stopped crying, the silence only a suspended breath prefacing the terrible wail to follow, long and quavering. All three soldiers glanced at Kate, and Fraser took a sideways step to block their view of her.

"The girl is not here," Fraser said.

"You should be aware that Colonel Grant intends to bring charges against you unless you give the girl into our custody. He did not give permission for you to take her away from Fort William, sir."

"But General Wade did. Remind the colonel of that. And besides, Katie Hell is not here."

"We saw you with her, sir, in the carriage."

"The damned wench escaped." Fraser sipped from the tankard, wiped his mouth on his sleeve, then shook his head. "The horses took off—you lot frightened them. When we finally stopped, the girl leaped from the carriage and ran off. I chased her while my man went looking in another direction. I was lucky to find my way here to wait for my ghillie. He'll know to come here. That Highland lass is damned clever, though," Alec went on. "I lost track of her quickly."

"We didn't realize, sir. Colonel Grant said you were . . . not to be trusted."

"Did he? He did not like General Wade's orders, I will say that," Alec remarked.

Kate watched them all, heart pounding, while part of her wondered why Fraser was so willing to help her at the risk of his own reputation if the truth was discovered.

"You will want to return and inform Grant that the girl is gone," Alec suggested. "I'll be going on to Edinburgh in the morning. I was heading that way with or without the prisoner."

Kate strove to listen, but the baby rolled out another loud wail, writhing under its swaddling.

"Sir," the corporal said loudly, over the child's cries, "we should continue to look for the Jacobite wench!"

"She's Highland. She'll disappear, fast as a fairy perched on a hillside."

How I wish I could do just that, Kate thought frantically. As Jean's infant continued its rant, Kate knew that she had to remove him, and herself, or attract more attention than she wanted.

She stood, clutching the child to her shoulder. Heart slamming, she walked boldly past the men.

One of the soldiers stepped in her path. Kate glanced up, hiding all but her eyes behind the baby's blanketed form. "Sir," she murmured. "Let me pass. My bairn is fussy tonight."

He touched his fingers to his cocked hat. "Mistress, excuse me. My wife and I have a small one around that age. I haven't seen my daughter since she was born."

Kate pushed back the swaddling to allow the soldier

to peek at the babe. He touched the baby's cheek and smiled.

Fraser looked around at her then, but Kate turned her shoulder away from him. Then the young officer stood back, nodding to Kate. "Thank you, Mistress. You must see to your child. Good evening."

"Sir," she murmured. "Come, hinny," she soothed. Carrying the fretful infant, she crossed the room to climb the wooden stairs. She turned the corner out of sight of the tavern below, ducked into the room Fraser had rented. Shutting the door, she leaned against it, breath heaving.

She carried the baby to the bed and sat, pushing pillows behind her so that she could lean against the wall and hold the baby in her lap. Then she did her best to appease him as he wailed. She cooed, smiled, spoke softly, and was rewarded with further fretting, while the baby wiggled in its swaddling.

Fraser had pointed out that a male child might succumb to her charm. She was feeling desperate enough now to wish it were so. But her fairy charm did not seem to affect this unhappy fellow any more than Fraser. She could not charm either of them.

"Perhaps the captain is your father," she muttered. The baby cranked out another quavering wail. "No? Good. I did not really want him to be your da."

She got to her feet with the child in her arms and paced the room, swaying as she walked, murmuring and patting him. Eventually he grew quiet, his limbs relaxing as he settled his head against her shoulder.

"Soft you, soft you," she sang in a gentle voice, re-

membering a lullaby her nurse had sung years ago,
when Kate, Sophie, and Robert had been very small,
and the world had held no threats for them. "Smooth
you, soft you, how well I love you. . . ."

The baby's head drooped on her shoulder, and he
found his fingers and sucked noisily. Continuing to
sing, Kate sat down again and held him, watching his
eyes drift closed as he listened to her singsong lullaby.
When his breaths lengthened out, she smiled to herself.

With a sense of surprise, she realized she had
charmed this small male creature all on her own, without any fairy gift, without the fairy crystal. She had offered comfort, compassion, and a little love, and he had
responded sweetly.

However small, the accomplishment pleased her,
and she smiled to herself, holding the child close.

Chapter 13

Her voice was like whiskey and honey, smooth and sweet, with an earthiness that sent a sensual shudder through him. Alec leaned his brow against the door and listened, eyes closed, while she sang, soft and low.

More than lust coursed through him—a deep longing, too, so that his heart pounded.

Below, he heard the soldiers talking to each other as they finished their ale and another game of cards. Fortunately, the corporal had been satisfied with the tale of Katie Hell's escape from the carriage, and no one had thought to question the identity or presence of the young woman with the baby.

After Kate had left the room, Alec had shared a

round of drinks with the soldiers, served by Jean, who sent Alec nervous glances to communicate her concern about her child. The soldiers kept her busy with requests for ale and food, though she served them only bread and cheese at the late hour. When the child's shrieks had quieted, Jean had relaxed, going on with her work.

Alec had taken his leave of the soldiers' company as soon as possible, claiming fatigue after a long evening supposedly spent chasing Kate over the hills.

But as he headed upstairs, he heard the corporal ask Jean about hiring out a room for the men to share that night, remarking that there was no more searching to be done in the black of night, with more rain threatening.

Now he stood by the door, eyes closed, until the song ended. He knocked softly, eased the door open, stepped inside.

Kate swayed gently by the window, the infant cuddled in her arms. No harlot, no wildcat hellion, just a lovely young woman soothing a child. He thought of a Madonna by some Flemish painter of long ago: a delicate woman with gray eyes and golden hair, and tender, graceful hands.

Then she turned, sending a shiver through him with a quick, unguarded smile. Alec nodded silently, loath to disturb the infant, and he closed the door silently. He could not help but remember Amy, with her sweet face and dark hair, her serene smile. She had married his brother Edward while Alec had been attending school in Leiden. He had returned to find her nearly a mother. The last time he had seen Amy, she had been holding a

156

small child in her arms, another clutching her hand, the third rounding her belly.

Her welcome had been warm, but uncertain, her abiding affection implicit in her brown eyes. Could they not be friends as before, her eyes had asked silently, could they not forget the hurt and resentment that had come between them.

But he had never answered her unspoken question. She had gone to childbed a month later, slipping away after birthing a scrap of a girl who had fought to be born. By days and degrees, Alec's heart had seemed to form a shell. The hurt was a little easier to carry that way.

Now another beautiful Madonna stirred his emotions, golden and fiery rather than dark and quiet. He looked at her silently, his torn heart in need of mending, and no one aware of it but he.

When Kate smiled at him, he sensed compassion and caring in her lovely eyes. He came toward her, entranced, drawn.

"Where is Jean? I hoped she would come fetch him soon."

"Still serving tables." He removed his coat, flung it on the bed, and sat, mattress groaning beneath him. When he leaned backward, the headboard whacked against the wall.

"Hush!" Kate patted the child as it whimpered. "Please don't wake him. It took me so long to get him to sleep. I'm not very good at mothering."

"You're doing well enough."

"He'll be hungry soon, and he needs new cloths." She wrinkled her nose.

"A natural hazard with babes. Have you no wee kinfolk?"

"Not close. Many of my kinfolk went to France years ago."

"Jacobites? Did they leave after the 'Nineteen, or earlier?"

"After the 'Nineteen. Most of us left then, with my father. My sister returned earlier this year, and she's already wed and expecting a child by year's end. Now I will have a little experience to lend her. An hour's worth, at least." She smiled, tucked her head against the baby's head.

His heart melted, but he only lifted his eyebrows. "A sister? And what would her name be?"

"Would I tell you?" She laughed, rubbing the infant's back, pacing. "And you? Do you have wee kinfolk?"

"Two nephews—my older sister's sons—and three small nieces . . . the daughters of my late brother."

"Then you have ample experience with children," she said, coming closer as she held the baby in her arms.

"Not a whit. I avoid them like a plague, haven't visited for months—*oof!*" Alec opened his hands as Kate deposited the infant in his arms. "What the devil—"

"Do not swear. He listens carefully, so watch what you say."

"He's two months old," Alec pointed out. "He doesn't understand the language yet. Blast," he said, feeling the bundled behind resting in his hand. "It's wet."

"I've no extra clothes. What do you have in that satchel, besides chains?" She went over to his canvas bag. "Clean shirts?"

"One washed by your own hand, or so you claimed at the time. But that's good Flemish lawn," he protested, as she rummaged in the bag and pulled out the shirt.

"It can be cleaned," she told him, shaking it out.

"The hell it can, a baby could turn that stuff to saffron, and it would never come clean."

"So you do have experience!" She crowed with glee. "Only an expert would know that."

"I have better experience with almost anything than bairns, my dear. Jeanie won't be long. This wee beastie can wait. Put that shirt back—look, he's fine." He jiggled the child, who regarded him with such a bewildered expression that Alec chuckled. "He resembles the wee monkeys I saw in the Tower zoo . . . which means you are Jack's bairn for sure," he told the baby playfully. The tiny creature grimaced, and Alec laughed again softly. Kate tipped her head, watching them.

"I think Jack is quite handsome," she said.

"Most women seem to think so," Alec remarked.

"I think you are, too." Her eyes sparkled.

He glanced up and smiled in return, could not help it. He felt bespelled again. She dazzled him, without benefit of silks or jewels or deliberate allure. A natural, indefinable quality about her fascinated him. He wanted to savor the sight of her, and savor more of her—much more.

He turned his attention to the baby, who burped. "Oh, aye. There's definitely Jack in this lad."

"I hope Jack turns up soon, and safe. I feel responsible, since he led the soldiers away from us. But they're here this evening," she added. "Does that mean he's come to harm?"

159

Alec frowned. "Honestly, I've wondered about that myself. But none of the soldiers mentioned an accident involving the carriage, and that's encouraging. Jack has friends throughout the region, so he could have gone somewhere for the night, planning to meet us at dawn. There's naught to do but wait." The baby began to squirm, tiny fists waving, face reddening. "Here, Kate, take him," Alec said. "Matters are about to get worse, I fear."

"He's yours for now." She stretched, yawned. "Are you sure he's Jack's and not yours?"

"Of course not. I don't go about bedding innkeepers' daughters. Laundresses, on the other hand. . . ." He lifted a brow.

Had he been made of steel, the searing glance she sent him would have melted him to the core. He pursed his lips, finding that he was enjoying this all too much.

Kate sat beside him, mattress sagging so that she leaned against him. "He's so calm now that you're holding him."

"It's because he's just done his business," he grumbled.

"Not that—I meant that your hands are large and strong, and your voice is deep and quiet, and you're so . . . steady and calm. He feels secure in your keeping."

Alec glanced at her, a little surprised.

"You'll make a good father someday. Won't he?" she asked the baby, taking the tiny hand.

The world seemed to go still around him. Alec sensed the warmth of the child and of the woman beside him, and he inhaled against the pull on his heart. This was what he had wanted for so long—a woman by his side, an infant between them, himself protecting them, at peace. That possible future had been taken from him, all at once, years ago, and he had not recovered the capacity to dream of it again.

Somehow Kate had cast another spell over him that led him back to those dreams. He exhaled, shook his head. "*Och*, this laddie does not care who has him. He only wants his needs met."

"We're all like that," she said, stroking the baby's head.

"Aye," he murmured, keenly aware of her shoulder against his, her hip beside him. God, he thought, this ease and comfort between them felt so good, so natural. He frowned slightly.

"If Jack is the father, will he and Jean marry?" she asked.

"Ask them," Alec said, shrugging. "It's their business." He spoke too sharply, and Kate must have felt it, for she rose abruptly and walked away. Going to the window, she looked outside, profiled chin lifted with pride and a spark of temper.

"I do not know why I am still here with you," she said. "I should have escaped when I had the chance."

"Don't be silly. You would not have left the child alone."

"No, but I could have found a way. You're disagreeable as an old bear of a sudden. It was so nice for a moment . . ." She paused, fingers tapping the windowsill. "And if I stay with you, I'll just end up in prison. I should just walk out right now while you're holding that bairn. No one would stop your *wife*," she bit out defiantly, turning, glancing at the door.

"You could ask a ride from Grant's men," he suggested, his own temper stirring. "Or you might try that window, though it's a long way down in the dark."

She pursed her mouth in silent irritation and seemed about to reply. Then a knock sounded at the door, and Alec looked up on instant alert. Kate whirled and put a hand to her bodice.

The door creaked opened and Jean peered inside. Alec felt a sense of relief—not only would she take her infant off his hands, but Kate would have to stay for now.

"Captain Fraser—you're here, too. Oh, my laddie," Jean crooned as she entered and saw her child in Alec's arms. Holding a bundle of clothing under her arm, she deposited that on the single rickety chair in the room and took the baby from Alec. He stood, arms folded, and smiled.

"Thank you for watching him," she said, cuddling her son.

"He was no bother," Kate replied. "We enjoyed watching him."

Alec nodded. "Jean, I'll remind you that we plan to leave early tomorrow, once Jack comes. We want to keep our departure a secret should the soldiers ask where we went."

"Do you want me to pretend I know nothing?" Jean's brown eyes gleamed. "Was your wedding a secret one? Has Mrs. Fraser's father sent out the military to search for her, is that why you want to avoid them?"

"Something like that," Alec said, glancing at Kate.

Jean smiled. "*Och*, I understand. Dinna worry, the red soldiers are below stairs, so you will likely not see them again if you stay up here tonight, then leave very early."

"Good," Kate said quietly.

"I nearly forgot—I brought something for you," Jean said, reaching for the bundle. "You're so kind to watch my bairn, and I wanted to help you. I know you're stranded with the carriage being broken and all, and while you wait for Jack. But here—this gown and these things do not fit me so well since the child was born. I thought perhaps they would fit you."

Kate accepted the things and undid the linen toweling that was knotted around the garments. She pulled out a chemise and a few other garments of embroidered cotton, then drew out a long-sleeved gown and attached bodice in a deep, rather glorious shade of red. She gasped and held the dress against her.

"Oh, it's lovely!" Kate smiled. "But I cannot accept it."

"I tell you, 'tis too tight for me now and will only gather dust. Jack gave it to me two years ago, and I've only worn it a few times, to dances on market days, and to a holiday concert in Perth . . . but now . . ." Jean shrugged. "The color is very fine on you, with that hint of copper in your hair. And the red puts some roses in your pale cheeks. Captain Fraser, what do you think?"

Alec tilted his head as he studied Kate, who glanced at him almost shyly over the draped bodice of the gown. Dark as rubies, the red fabric lent a warm glow to her ivory skin and made her golden hair seem all the richer. "I like it very well," he said.

His mind elaborated how beautiful she would look in

163

the gown, then he thought about taking it off her again. He cleared his throat, sat up. "She'll look like the queen of all the fairies in that thing, gowned in scarlet and gold."

"Aye, it's true," Jean agreed.

Alec leaned his shoulders against the wall, feeling relaxed, enjoying the moment, "That's a generous gift, Jean. We'll replace the dress with something new. Do you prefer red?"

"Oh! I love red, but it's not necessary—"

"Nonsense. I'll have something sent from Edinburgh."

"I would be happy to help choose it," Kate ventured. "Provided I'm . . . free." Her glance met Alec's.

Jean turned, set her hand on the door handle. "When Jack MacDonald arrives, I will let you know."

Kate came toward her, and Alec stepped toward the door to open it for Jean and stand guardian so Kate did not try to escape. "Thank you, Jean," Kate said. "And good night, little one. I don't think I've heard his name," she added.

"John Alasdair MacLennan. I call him Wee Jack." Jean smiled.

"Ah," Kate said, "it suits him."

Jean bid them good night, and Alec then shut the door after her, turning. Kate busied herself folding the gown neatly, along with the underpinnings Jean had given her. She glanced at him.

"What now, Captain Fraser?" she asked.

"You could put that dress on if you like," he murmured.

"I would if you let me go," she retorted. "You could

164

get a quick glimpse as I left the room and the inn and your life altogether. How would that be?"

"Always bargaining. Perhaps you do have some fairy magic, as they say of you in the propaganda sheets." Alec bent down to pick up the canvas satchel and lifted the irons from it in a heavy, clanking mass.

Kate took a backward step. "No—not that." She edged toward the door, then slipped a hand behind her to grasp the handle.

With one step, Alec was there, too, wedging his foot against the door to keep it shut. He pressed his right hand against the wood above her head, the chains dangling from his left.

"I cannot bear to be shackled again," she said.

He leaned toward her. "I have no other assurance that you will stay here tonight."

"I'd rather stay with you than be caught by Grant's men." She watched him boldly, and Alec saw a spark there, felt his body answer, like a top spinning, surging. "Trust me."

He nearly laughed, but shook his head. "I am not so easily beguiled as you might hope." He was leaning close enough to kiss her, he knew. The awareness plunged through him.

Her eyes narrowed, their color pale and bright, irises clear gray, lanternlight reflected there. "If you leave off the chains, I will stay," she said. Her glance did not waver, but her fingers closed on the door handle, white-knuckled. "I give my word."

His breath stirred her hair. She tilted her head, closed her eyes. Breathed, he saw, and waited. So did he.

Her natural allure was potent just then, so that he felt
pulled toward her power, like a gentle but compelling
stream, or a spinning vortex. She just stood there
watching him, without wiles, coquettish glances, or
suggestive words—yet she exuded a wild and natural
magic. He felt wholly susceptible, although he had
tried his damnedest, all along, to withstand it.

"I'll need a way to . . . secure your promise," he murmured. His heart slammed, his body clenched rhyth-
mically, anticipating. Bending toward her, he let his
nose brush against hers. God, he wanted to kiss her.

Her head tipped back, her eyes fluttered shut and
open again. "How . . . can I prove my word?"

He knew what he craved of her. But she had insisted
that she was no wanton, and he believed her. He inclined his face near hers. His heart thundered. Kate
tilted her face a little, just enough, and he kissed her.

Her lips were so tender beneath his, sweet, almost
poignant. At first her lips were soft and still under his,
tentative but permissive. He sensed a longing, a vulnerability in her that matched what he felt within himself.

She needed this as much as he did. Wanted this.

The realization tore through him, and he sucked in a
breath, cupped her shoulder, felt her sag against the
door and surrender to him. The kiss renewed itself between them naturally, hungrily. A melting touch of lips,
a slow drawing away. With a new rush of breath and
urgent need, he kissed her yet again, and lost himself
utterly, completely, in that moment, as her hands lifted
to take him round the back, and she curved her body
against his.

Chapter 14

She moaned under his mouth, her fingers clutched at his shirt, his waistcoat. She returned the kiss with a wildness that drove him on, that matched the fire stoking within him.

Stop, he told himself, and yet he pressed her against the door, his palm flat on the wood, his other hand sliding from her shoulder down her arm. His thumb grazed the side of her bodice, and she sighed. Her hands slid up and sifted through his hair. She moaned again, low and needful, and the sound plunged through him. Her hips pushed against his, and he grew hard and urgent against her where their bodies arched, pressed.

Madness, this was madness, he told himself, his

heart slamming, his breath quickening. She pulled at his shirt, her fingers gliding over him as if to savor the feel of his shoulders, his neck, his jaw. Alec had never felt like this, ever, as if a vein of lightning crashed through him without warning, white-hot and wild.

He pulsed all through for her, burned for her, lost his reason further with every hungry kiss. She pulled at his shirt now, straining the buttons of his waistcoat, as her mouth opened beneath his. Her tongue was cool and moist and divine, sending a keen flare of passion through him so that his body filled and hardened further, until he thought he might burst.

His long fingers cupped over her bodice, shaping the upper curve of her breasts. Her heartbeat was strong, her breath as fast as his own, and he traced kisses downward over her cheek, the arch of her throat and graceful curve of her collarbone, until he kissed the tops of her breasts. She did not protest, only mewled a little and leaned her head back. His fingers worked the lacings of her green gown quickly, and the front bodice pieces loosened, exposing her plain chemise, then the sweet fullness of her breasts. Somehow he managed this, driven mad by her fingers, gentle and deft where they ran through his hair, traced along his jaw, tugged at the buttons of his shirt.

She seemed as intent in her passion as he was, and he lifted his head to kiss her again, pressing her back against the door, while his fingertips found her nipples, one and the other, turning them to warm pearls, flicking them gently as she moaned and sagged against the door. She began to slide downward and Alec went with

168

her, sinking to his knees, holding her, kissing her as he knelt with her, dimly aware that he hovered on the brink of control.

Wrapping his arms around her, feeling her arms tighten around him, he held her tightly for a moment. That in itself felt so damned good, the bliss of comfort enhancing desire. Stop, he told himself, stop now; but he was caught in a strange, hot fog of passion that would diminish only if she put a stop to it—that alone would clear it.

She nudged at him, sought his lips for another kiss, the most luscious he had yet experienced with her. When she arched against him, her heart thudding against his own, her breath mingling with his, he could not think.

So he savored every kiss like a drunkard, freed by her returned hunger and desire. He sensed joy as he tasted her, touched her, felt the wildness of her touch, the exquisite sensation of her skin under his hands. She was lush, warm, giving. Her gown—shabby green thing that it was—came away easily, nearly tearing, and two thin petticoats and a simple set of stays came with it. She pulled at his waistcoat, his shirt, his wrapped plaid, all lost somewhere between the floor and the bed. All the while, every motion, every step forward woven in a net of kisses, caresses.

Laying her on the mattress, Alec shoved aside the coverlet to reveal the bed linens she had not preferred, and he stretched out beside her. Her chemise was fine cotton or lawn, he saw, and translucent, so that the lanternlight glowed through it when she lifted an arm,

169

raised a knee. The curves of her body were taut and beautiful. Lowering his head, Alec rained gentle kisses over her lips and then her throat, and he slid the chemise down to touch her breasts then with his fingers, his lips.

A wild and passionate memory, half a dream, came to him then—he had loved her like this before. He remembered the wild sweetness of it, the pleasure and the sense of disbelief. Now he could savor every inch of her with his head clear, his intent clear. But it was truly madness—he should not be pursuing her like this though she allowed the chase with such willingness.

Breath heaving, he paused, then forced himself to draw away, stilling his hands, eyes closed, fighting desire and the deep attraction he felt toward her. Surrendering to that was all he wanted, and yet he could not give in to that urge.

She was in his military custody, in his protection. He could not treat her as if she meant nothing to him. Already she was coming to mean too much.

He rocked away and sat back against the wall. "I am sorry, Kate," he said in a husky voice.

Silent, she reclined on the bed and watched him, eyes wide and wary, lips lush and tinted with passion. Then she sat up, tugging at her chemise, and curled her knees high beneath it. She ducked her head on her folded arms and said nothing.

Alec remembered that she had sat like that in the prison cell, too, looking so forlorn. He touched her arm, and she jerked away, batted at him with her hands. "Leave me be," she said.

"Kate, this is just not right," he murmured.

"I know. You think I am just a harlot, and you want nothing at all to do with me," she said, head tucked, voice muffled.

"That's not so." Shoving his fingers through his hair, he sighed. "It's not right, this. You are my responsibility."

"Oh," she said, an arm waving upward, head down, voice catching on a sob, "oh, and you must follow your duty and your orders, and resist at all costs the wicked little wanton in your keeping." She looked at him then, her eyes pink-rimmed.

"It's just not right to do this," he said helplessly. He needed to explain, but he was never one to articulate, much less filet, his emotions to reveal what lay hidden. He reached out again, and she slapped him away again. "I did not mean to hurt you, or insult you—" he began.

"Just leave me be. I'm tired. I want another room, please." She threw her feet over the edge of the bed and stood, snatching her clothing, her gown and stays, her petticoats and the plaid.

Despite her distress, he noticed the lightning decision she made, choosing Jean's red gown over her own shabby dress. He nearly smiled, finding the feminine gesture disarming. Had he been snatching up garments in a hurry, he would not have noticed, or cared, what he grabbed.

She pulled the fresh chemise on over her own, yanked the newer stays on over that, while he watched with a sort of bemused fascination, seeing how easily she managed the laces at the front—he would have thought they belonged at the back—and how quickly

171

she figured out the red gown, whose design puzzled him, split wide at skirt and bodice, yet meeting snug in the middle, like an hourglass. She pulled it on like a coat, overlapped it somehow at the waist and fastened it, so that the chemise and petticoats showed. He watched, his body surging of its own accord at the sight.

When she stomped to the door, he stood and stepped forward rapidly, though she grabbed the door handle to turn it. "I'll need to borrow a few coins to pay for another room."

He took her wrist. "You will stay here, Kate."

She yanked. "And we'll forget about what just happened?"

"I did not intend that. I apologize." He leaned a shoulder against the door, fingers around her wrist.

This was where it began, he recalled, not long ago, and his body still throbbed with need. Be careful, he told himself.

"I do not think of you as a wanton, and I apologize, again, if I implied it. But you must remain in my keeping."

She jerked her hand away, but he held on. "For how long?"

Forever, a voice murmured inside of him. "Until I turn you over to the Court of Justiciary."

She tried to wrench away. "I'm leaving," she said.

"Then again, I'm sorry." He dragged her away from the door, sat her firmly on the bed, and held her there with one hand. With the other, he snatched up the iron bracelet, forgotten in the madness of moments earlier, and clapped it around her slim wrist. Holding that, he then turned the key. "Truly sorry, Kate."

"No," she whispered, almost a cry.

He snapped the other metal cuff around his own wrist, as before, and locked that shut, too, dropping the key into his sporran. "It's better this way. Safer."

"For whom?" Her voice had a smoky warmth, sweet and earthy.

"For me. You're far too much of a challenge for me, Miss Marie Katherine What-you-will." The words were wry, but he gazed at her somberly.

She stared at him, wild and disheveled, eyes pink and nose sniffly, hair in a tangle. So vulnerable and lovely, and deliciously desirable, he thought. She was not a goddess, a siren, a fairy queen—she was a simple girl who fitted to him, heart and mind and body. And he needed her, felt the urge rise up and grab him fast by the heartstrings.

Her breath caught, a remnant of a sob that wrenched his heart, and she gazed up at him.

"Do not look at me like that," he said. "Please. Lie down, if you will. We both need some rest." He gave her an encouraging push. "Stretch out by the wall. I'll lie on the outside."

"So you'll know if I try to get away."

"Exactly." He gestured for her to move. She scuttled backward and settled on her side, her back to the wall. Alec sat and took a moment to turn down the lantern wick. Smoke twirled upward in the darkness.

He stretched his legs out on the bed, mattress sagging beneath him as he shifted. Kate curled on her side, forcing Alec to extend his left arm because of the short length of chain.

He rested against the single flat pillow, feeling awkward. Thin moonlight through the window illuminated the girl's form beside him. "If you would come closer and sleep on your back, we'd both be more comfortable."

"I like sleeping on my side. I rest that way at home."

"And where is that?" he murmured.

"Besides," she continued over his words, "I do not want to lie near you. It's just not right, remember."

"Kate." He sighed. "Just get comfortable."

"I think I should leave. Who knows what will happen here in the dark, with you."

"Will you accept my apology and let this go?" he asked irritably. He folded his hands, chain pulling. "We have to lie close, since the chain is short. And you're a prisoner of the crown, unless you've forgotten."

"You forgot it," she snapped, though the bite was not sharp.

"I'm remembering it now. You're a very valuable prisoner."

"Valuable to whom?"

"To me," he said quietly. "And I cannot risk losing you." His words echoed in the space between them, took on more meaning than he wanted. Or was that just his blasted, inexplicable, undeniable yearning for this girl?

"I need to be free," she whispered. "And I do not want to be . . . hurt. That is all, Alec."

Her use of his name cut through to his heart. "That's

all I would want, too, if I were you. And I could give you that, if you would give me a little information."

She half sat. "You might free me?"

He shrugged.

"If I have no guarantee, why would I tell you anything?"

"Because," he said, "I am your best chance."

She narrowed her eyes. "But you're following orders."

"If I were the sort to obey all the orders I get, you would still be in Grant's keeping."

"Oh? Were you not supposed to take me out of Fort William?"

"I have custody over you, but my method of removing you from incarceration was . . . not exactly as ordered." He sent her a wry glance. "I stole you away."

"*Tcha.*" She shifted to a seated position. The mattress bounced. "You did that because of Colonel Grant?"

"In part."

"Then I will thank you for that, at least. I suppose you will be in a kettle of trouble for this."

"That could be. It's not so important."

"Could they imprison you for it?" she asked quietly.

He regarded her through half-closed eyes. He could not tell her all that he knew, and besides, she distracted him mightily, the sight of her alluring, his yearning to touch her unsatisfied. "It's possible they could imprison me, aye."

"Anything I could tell you," she said carefully, "might be used against my kinsmen. The government would go after my family, and other Jacobites through them."

175

"You'll have to trust me," he murmured.

"Would you tell your superiors what I say?" Her hesitant tone told him that she considered revealing her secrets.

If she did so, he might be able to let her go. But he felt a deep twinge at the thought of losing her. "I keep things to myself when I choose. I'm not a wee tin soldier, my friend." He leaned back his head, watched her, kept his hand still beside her, the chain between them. He waited.

She narrowed her eyes suspiciously. "I thought you were a staid Fraser who always follows orders."

"We staid ones do think before we act. Usually."

"You do too much thinking sometimes, Alasdair."

His body pulsed secretly. "Perhaps. I must ask something."

"No more questions about my name and that." She rested her head on her arm and waited.

"Who is the hermit?" he asked slowly.

She watched him. "Why do you ask?" Her voice was husky.

"It took me a little while, since my Gaelic is not so good anymore, but I finally realized that Ian Cameron mentioned a hermit . . . and something hidden away."

"I do not know who the hermit is," she admitted. "Some nonsense Ian was saying. Perhaps he would rather be a hermit than be jailed and waiting for his execution. Do you think I know some grand secret and would help you undermine the Jacobites when I will not even tell you my full name?"

"Talk to me, and perhaps the Jacobites will not be undermined," he said urgently, his heart pounding. He could give up his own grand secret—he would, if he thought she would believe it and accept it of him. "You have to trust me, Kate."

"I would like to, sometimes . . . but I cannot."

"So you do know something."

"I am very tired," she said suddenly, and put her head down, reclining. A fall of golden hair covered her face.

Well, they had made some progress, he told himself. Those few, fiery moments of passion had altered their relationship and changed him somehow. Perhaps it had affected her, too. He had nearly told her that he was engaged in secret Jacobite activities himself, despite being a government officer.

He was beginning to trust her that much, and it scared him.

"Good night, then," he said, thumping the feather pillow and lying on his back. The chain jangled. "I promise not to touch you." He thought it might kill him to keep that promise.

"What if I said I did not mind if you did?" she asked in the darkness.

He caught his breath. "That was not the way for your custodial officer to behave, and I apologized for it," he finally said, eyes still closed. "If it came out in court, it would not help your case, lass, believe me."

"I thought," she murmured, "that you . . . did not even notice that I am a woman, after that night when we—"

"I noticed," he said gruffly. "I have always noticed you, from the first day in London." She was silent, an affirmation of sorts, for she had not yet admitted to

177

that. "So I suppose I am like all the rest, pandering after Katie Hell like a blethering fool." He folded his free arm behind his head.

"No, you are the only man who ever—" She stopped. "The only man who ever apologized, and the only man who could have . . . done his will with me."

He opened his eyes to stare at her, dumbstruck.

"Good night, sir." She stretched out, moved around, sighed. Every time she shifted, Alec felt more than the poor mattress sagging. He felt his own fierce response, a longing that would soon turn to flame if she did not quiet down and go to sleep.

"I need a pillow, too," she said.

He opened an eye. "Were you demanding as a child, too, or is it a recent habit?"

"Only since I met you," she answered, and caught the pillow Alec tossed at her.

Chapter 15

As moonlight filtered through the window, Kate knew she must try to leave, though an inner voice urged her to stay. Soon it would be dawn and too late to slip away without being seen.

She glanced at Alec, who reclined asleep beside her, his profile clean and handsome. The sight of him, the warmth of his body beside her, sent a subtle quiver through her. But she could not be here when he woke. Her body contracted with dread at the thought of further confinement in Edinburgh, or anywhere.

Outside, she knew that the military road that ran past the changehouse also cut through lands near Glen Carran. She could not openly follow Wade's route that way, but she could make her way over the hills to home and kin from here.

All she had to do was get the key and slip out quickly.

Alec's hand lay warm and heavy upon her own, their wrists shackled together. His occasional soft snore told her that he was truly asleep. Remembering that he had dropped the key into his sporran, she edged closer, covering the chains with the bedclothes to smother their sound.

Shifting even closer, so that she could feel his warmth, feel his breath dancing upon her cheek and stirring her hair, she stretched out her fingers toward the sporran.

His bearded chin brushed over her forehead, and she closed her eyes, involuntarily sighing. She could not think about how it would feel if he wrapped his arm around her now. She could only allow herself to think about that key and the temptation of freedom.

He stirred, moved a little, and as the mattress shifted, Kate rolled a bit closer to him, her face just a breath from his own. She grew still and waited until he settled. Then she traced her fingers over his waistcoat and kilt toward the sporran at his waist. Finding the buckle and leather strap, she slowly worked the clasp to open the pouch.

Of stiff leather and hide, the Highland purse rested just below his belt, shielding an essential part of his body beneath his plaid. As her fingers dipped inside, she felt him stir, boldly and certainly, on the underside of the sporran.

She caught her breath. The key lay near her fingertips, stretched inside the pouch. She could feel him
rouse again just under her hand, only leather and
wool between them. Suddenly a wild need overwhelmed her, and she nearly moaned aloud, wanting
to be in his arms, to feel his kiss again, to explore him
and love him as he had begun to do for her not so long
ago. Her body aroused easily at the very thought, the
slightest touch, still throbbing inwardly after that earlier encounter.

This was no time to indulge fantasies and feeling,
though suddenly she ached for him. When he moved,
sighed out, Kate grew still, her hand inside the pouch.

His free hand came up and found her shoulder,
rested there for a moment. Then he traced his fingers
upward to sift through her hair, raising such shivers in
her that she closed her eyes. His thumb grazed along
her cheek, and he breathed out again.

And then he stretched forward and touched his
mouth to her cheek, his lips tracing until they found
hers and settled there.

She melted, turned liquid under his touch, moaned
softly. Uncertain if he was awake or asleep, she hardly
cared—

"What the devil," he whispered, his mouth against
hers, "are you doing with your hand in my sporran?"

She caught her breath, and he caught her wrist, and
she felt the pressure of her hand, and the pouch,
against him, where the bulge rounded, hard, insistent,
glorious, and mysterious all at once. He groaned, a lit-

tle grind of sound, his hand still cupping her cheek, and he nibbled his lips over her own, then drew back.

"Take your hand out, darling," he whispered. "And leave the damned key."

"Damn it," she swore under her breath, and thought he laughed he kissed her, taking her breath away. At the same moment, he tugged at her wrist.

Slipping her fingers out of his sporran, she yet managed to trap the key in her fingers, and dropped it somewhere in the nest of bedclothes before he snatched her fingers, curling them in his own. His thumb slid over her palm to make sure her hand was empty. She splayed her fingers for him, and he entwined her hand tightly in his own.

"Now," he murmured, and his lips slid along her jaw, his breath heated her throat, making her shudder with reluctant delight, "what are we to do with you, Miss Hell?"

She gasped out, a little burst of protest and surrender all at once, and his mouth took hers again with powerful insistence this time. This was what she wanted—needed—far more than that key, though why it should be so, she could not have said. She could not think.

He let go of her hand to take her by the waist, snugging her close to him, and she rested her fingers over his plaid again, beside the sporran, where the shifting bulge stirred again. She was excited, curious about the mystery of his body, the beauty of that hidden power. Her heart raced as his kisses continued. Sighing against him, she promised herself a few moments to savor

182

this—then she would stop it, as he had stopped it. He only deserved it, she thought.

But a moment later, she would not stop him, not now, for his hand found her breast just where the bodice and chemise gapped away from her skin. The contact made her gasp, then writhe, for her body responded like a leap of flame. His lips covered hers again, and she tipped her head back and opened her mouth to his, and his tongue flicked gently over hers. She sighed, edged closer still, and dismissed the key, just for now.

He took her hand, manacled beside his, and squeezed her fingers, interlocked them with his own. With his other hand, he swept down over her skirt and pulled it up slowly, surely.

He paused. She could break away at any time, she knew, for he made that clear. He would respect her wish and pull away. The decision lay in her hands. And as before, she wanted this fiercely, though she could not name all the reasons—even if she fell for whatever unspoken magic he held over her, she wanted this with such hunger that she had no other choice but this one.

Sighing, she shifted, opened her legs a little for him, and felt his fingers graze upward, felt his touch as it found her, as he gently slid a fingertip within at the same moment that he slipped his tongue between her lips. The sensual echo nearly pushed her to madness. She gasped, swayed against him.

Under her free hand, he took on a turgid, insistent shape, and she pressed closer to him, as much as she could with the heavy bite of the metal between them, locking them together. His lips felt like a taste of ecstasy over hers, his fingers teased just inside of her, coaxing and tender, and she arched as a frisson of sensation seared through her. Breathing fast, she slid her hand under his plaid and along his thigh until she found the firm, heated length of him. Sighing out at the beauty and power of it, she closed her fingers about him. He groaned low under his breath, thrust a little against her, the sporran edged out of the way between them. Kissing her, he slid his tongue over her lips, and his fingers touched her exquisitely now, stoking that extraordinary fire within her to a sort of wildness.

She felt almost drunk somehow with sensation, swept onward, allowing herself to plunge headlong into what was happening as he explored the most intimate region of her body, as she did so for him, thrilled by the intimacy of that secrecy, that closeness between them. All else—all but touch, breath, desire, and the moment—ceased to exist.

Her body quickened as a burgeoning power caught her, held her, rocked her along with him, while her fingers eased over him just as he stroked within her. Lost in kisses, in caresses, she was just where she wanted to be, in this wildness with him—only with him, her most secret dream come true.

He thrust against her at last, sporran and bedclothes and wool between them, frustration woven into passion and urgency, and she held him, felt him holding her, poignant, inexpressible moment of joy, and then she released a sigh just as he did, her head tipped to meet his, and she breathed quickly with him in silence.

"My God," he whispered after a moment. "Kate—"

"Hush," she said. "Hush. All is well," and she kissed him as she spoke. He wrapped his arm around her, pulled her close, the iron manacles pushing against her ribs, and as soon as her heart calmed its beat, she felt herself falling asleep beside him.

A little while later, she awoke, and knew he was sound asleep again, his breath deep and slow. She remembered, then, that the little key was caught somewhere in the bedclothes between them. Groping about, she found it.

Slowly, hardly daring to breathe, she picked up the key and inserted it into the lock on her wrist, quietly turning it.

She had no choice. Truly she did not, for she was like a bird, and the cage had just opened.

Kate winced at the creaks in the old wooden floor as she tiptoed through the empty, darkened public room. If the dragoons discovered her leaving, things would go worse than if she had stayed with Fraser. But she moved toward the front door, which was tucked in the entrance alcove.

The door was locked. She was not surprised, but it would not be simple to open. No key was tucked anywhere nearby, either beside or above the door. Standing on tiptoe, she stretched her fingers high to check. She leaned her head against the door in frustration and recalled that the innkeeper carried a large ring of keys at his belt. It must be there, and so she had no chance of obtaining it.

Dim light and cool air leaked through a tiny window beside the door. Breath frosting, Kate peered at the lock, bending close to examine it.

She was familiar with this sort of lock, just as she had recognized the lock in the prison. All she needed to free it was a narrow, straight tool and a little time. Glancing about, she walked into the main room with its tables and benches, and saw a nest of spoons and two-tined forks sitting in a box on a cabinet. Snatching a fork in triumph, she raced back to the door.

Jiggling the hasp of the lock, listening to the mechanism inside, she finessed the tines of the fork into the keyhole. Angling carefully, she glanced into the empty room. Listening not only for the barrel of the lock to fall, she was also on alert for any footsteps from above, where her Highland officer slept with one hand shackled to an empty manacle.

As a girl she had often watched Duncrieff's blacksmith at work making locks, bolts, farming tools, and kitchen implements. Fascinated by the puzzles the iron pieces presented as the smith fitted them intricately together, Kate had watched and learned. While the fire blazed at the forge, and the smith and his apprentice had worked, she had helped with some tasks, while she and her brother had played endlessly with the bits and pieces, her mind sparking with curiosity at the patterns and details.

But her stern, if good-intentioned, father had ordered Kate out of the smithy, and her sister Sophie out of the ornamental gardens where she happily mucked. Chief of his clan, he regarded both activities as unsuitable to his fairy-blessed daughters, who must marry not only well, but for love, the time was right.

But the proper time never came, for her father had been arrested for rebellious activities with MacPherson of Kinnoull and a Cameron chieftain. He had been fortunate, being only exiled to France while his friend MacPherson had been executed, and the Cameron laird imprisoned. After years in France and Flanders, where Kate spent time being educated in a convent, which sat very ill with her, she had finally returned to Scotland with her brother Robert, after their father's death in exile. Her sister Sophie, adapting well to convent life, had remained in Bruges, and their mother had remarried in France.

Sophie had returned several months ago, but even as the three siblings reunited, and Sophie found true love and married the son of the executed Lord Kinnoull, Kate knew that life at Duncrieff would never be the same.

She felt again a powerful yearning to be home. She twisted the fork fervently in the lock, desperate to be on her way back to Duncrieff. She could not bear confinement, and she could not bear being away from her family at Duncrieff.

Then she heard the satisfying click as the inner ratchets turned and released. Catching the hasp, she set the bent fork on a table, opened the door, and slipped outside.

The night air was fresh and cold as she lifted her face to the stars. She had snatched her plaid up when she left the room, and she wrapped that around her, grateful for its warmth as well as the dark cover it provided her as she crossed the inn yard quickly and quietly, skirt whipping out in the breeze. She found the pale strip of stone road that ribboned past the inn yard and over the hills, and crossed that, too, heading for the moorland and west to the wilder hills to which she belonged.

After more than a week in prison, the sweet draft of pure Highland air revived and cleansed her. Its essence was power, clarity, magic. She ran over the moorland until she left the stone road far behind, until she was breathless and felt part of the earth again, part of the air.

She thought of Alec Fraser, imagined him waking to find her gone. Though she should have felt only happy about her escape, she could not shake a sense of longing and even loss. For years, she had believed that she would never find a man to love her, whom she could love—perhaps she was losing her only chance by running away.

Yet he liked his orders and rules too well, she reminded herself, and the whole thing was best forgotten entirely.

She ran westward toward Glen Carran, miles away over the hills, but within reach. By evening, perhaps tomorrow morning, she knew she would be home.

Chapter 16

Standing in the inn yard in the darkness, Alec swore under his breath. Without a horse, he had little chance of catching a Highland girl running over terrain that was no doubt familiar to her. Even with a horse, he would find it slow going in the rugged and rocky hills if Kate had indeed gone that way.

And he did not know which blasted direction she had taken. Swearing again, he turned to glance from one direction to another as the cool night wind ruffled his hair and lifted his jacket. He saw no one out in the moors and hills beyond the road anywhere he looked. She was gone—but where?

The little wildcat had bespelled him in his sleep after all, but he was determined to catch her and determined

189

that he would not be fooled again. The fever pitch of passion and release while she lay in his arms had been astonishing in its intimate power, but apparently that had not changed her mind about acquiescing to her custodial officer's wishes.

Damnation. He spun on his heel and walked toward the stables to rouse the sleeping groom, offering him three times the usual fee if a horse could be saddled quickly. Within minutes, Alec was mounted on a good bay mare. Turning her head, he cantered out of the stable yard.

Pausing in the middle of the cobbled road, he listened to the wind, to the burble of water, to the sound of night birds. Scanning the hills in the darkness, he did not know which way to go. He closed his eyes and imagined her walking the hills. She was a wild and fey creature who would not keep to the road. She was a Highland girl from a staunch Jacobite clan though he did not yet know which one.

Ah, he thought. She would go west—even northwest, toward the true Highlands. It was a guess, but likely the best one.

He turned the horse and headed away from the road. In the matter of Katie Hell, his heart seemed to know readily what his head could not always sort out.

Before long, a pale and silvery dawn lifted over the shoulders of the hills, and Alec saw the landscape around him more clearly: turf and rock, water racing through burns, and the vast bulk of the mountains in the distance. He had not ridden very far, perhaps a few miles over the moorland, before he saw her climbing the shoulder of a hill.

In the dawnlight, he saw the bright blur of golden hair and the bell shape of her red skirt. Blasting out a sigh, he cantered the horse toward her.

Soon he halted at the foot of the hill and tied the reins to a tree, then ran up the slope with long-legged, sure steps.

Ahead of him, she walked steadily, perhaps tiring on the incline. Riding had conserved his energy, and being a Fraser of the Great Glen, he had spent much of his youth in the Highlands and knew how to pace himself on a hill, just as she did.

Coming closer, he picked his way over the incline, which was rough with stones and tangles of heather and gorse. Kate glanced back then and saw him. She ran, hair fanning out like sunrise, that red dress like a beacon as she crested the hill. Closing the distance behind her, Alec hurried upward, his legs longer and stronger than hers, and soon enough he was very close.

He reached out and took her by the arm. She jerked around in impatience and temper, and as she stumbled, he went to his knees into the heather with her. Catching her, he rolled with her and made sure she did not take a bruising as she fell. But he made sure she went down and had no chance to get away again.

She spun in his grip and began to crawl away on hands and knees, but Alec snatched her by the skirt, the ankle, the waist, wherever he could find a hold, and pulled her toward him.

She writhed and twisted like a water beast, and he fell partly over her to stop her. A pointed elbow to his stomach made him grunt, but he managed to pin her to the ground, on her back in the heather, his knees beside her hips.

Her eyes were wild, and she bucked under him. That could be delightful, he thought, in other circumstances—but he was not enjoying this at all.

"Settle down, lass," he said breathlessly, pinning her arms.

She twisted. "Are you mad? Get off me—"

"Ease up. I would not hurt you." He dropped his weight on his hands, pressed them to the earth beside her shoulders, keeping her trapped under him. "Do you think I would chase you out there for a tumble I could have from any number of willing lassies? You're a plum, my dear, but I'm not so overcome by your legendary charm that I'd go to the trouble just now," he bit out. He sat back on his heels, keeping her under him.

She glared up at him, breath and bosom heaving. She snarled something in Gaelic—he knew it was no compliment—and managed to free an arm, striking upward. Alec snatched at her wrist.

"Wherever did you learn such manners," he said calmly, and rose to his feet, hauling her up with him. "Come with me."

"I won't go anywhere with you." She brushed at her skirt.

"Would you rather sleep in the heather? Last night you were very particular about your bed." He pulled her with him, and when she stumbled, he put his hand on her elbow. "I've no great whim to be chasing spoiled young lassies over the hills in the middle of the night."

"It's dawn," she said, as if determined to contradict him any way she could. "I have to go home. That's all."

"Tell me where it is, and we'll both go. I've questions for your kinsmen as well."

"We will not be troubling them with Whig business."

He huffed. "My horse is at the foot of the hill. Home, hey?" he asked, as she tramped along beside him, her arm rigid in his grasp. "It must be a grand place, with you in such a fever to get there."

"It is. But I'll not tell you where to find it."

"Katie my dear, your intractable nature does you no good. Think how poorly it will go with the Lord Advocate if you refuse to identify yourself."

"I can avoid trouble for both of us by just going home."

"Oh, for my sake? Or just to ignore this whole business?"

"If you would leave me here, I know these hills—"

"Ah, so you do live near here somewhere." He led her toward the waiting horse. "If you want to protect others, take my advice and do not be the saintly, sacrificing sort. It does not pay in the end."

"I am not sacrificing anything. My sister is more that sort. She considers others first, always, sometimes to her detriment. But I am not like that."

"So I see," he drawled. "If your sister does not have your wildcat ways, then bless the lass for a saint."

He thought Kate laughed. "My brother used to call her Saint Sophia. She's a patient soul, though she has a temper when she needs it. One day she was stolen away by rebels and had to find the courage and spirit to defend herself. And now she's married to the very man who took her away."

"Brave man indeed," Alec grunted. "Watch your step."

"She's sacrificing and loyal, but I'm loyal, too. That's why I must get back home. If you have any true Gael in you, you'll understand that."

"Loyalty can be overdone. I lost someone once by being too loyal." He wondered why he mentioned that.

"What do you mean?" she asked as they walked.

He sighed. "A few years ago, I lost my betrothed when I was in Leiden studying. I wanted her to be happy, urged her to do what she most needed, while I was gone. She decided she most needed my brother and could not wait for me."

Kate halted, stared up at him. "Oh! I am so sorry."

"Aye, well," he muttered. "She had her reasons, I suppose."

"It must be hard for you to visit them."

"At the time, aye, but they're both . . . gone now. He died months ago of a sword wound, and she . . . passed away over two years ago in childbirth. I am guardian to my three nieces now."

"Do they live in your house in Edinburgh?"

"Aye."

"I would like to see them," she said.

That surprised him. He glanced at her. "Why, after this great urge of yours to be shut of me?"

"If I cannot get shut of you, and if I do have to go to

Edinburgh, I'd rather visit your wee nieces than meet the Lord Advocate," she said reasonably.

"Understandable. But you'd see the Lord Advocate at any rate. He's my uncle."

She stared at him, slowing her step. "Is he a Fraser, too?"

"No, but an uncle just the same."

"Then I need not worry. Why did you not tell me before?"

"Do you think I can buy your way free with him for that reason? Hardly. Though you might try your wistful, bonny charm with him . . . so long as you do not expect the old gentleman to chase you through the streets."

"That's just for you," she snapped.

"I doubt anyone could charm the old man," he mused. "He is wretched and disagreeable. I wish you luck of it."

She muttered something low in Gaelic and stomped away. Alec strode with her, his hand firmly on her arm. "Lass," he said between his teeth, "I think you are not so much an irresistible siren, as they say of Katie Hell, as a spoiled and overindulged young lady who suits herself."

"How do you know that I am not thinking of others every moment," she said hotly, "including now? Would I be in this fine pickling if not for them? I would not!"

He chuckled, for her slight trace of accent and her Gaelic speech patterns showed now and then. "Pickle," he said. "Fine pickle. And we're both in it. Asking who the devil you are is not intended to harm your kinsmen, but to help you," he pointed out.

She tilted her head. "How could that be?"

"Obviously you are fiercely devoted to your Jacobite kin, though they seem to have sent you into the mouth of the lion to fetch information for them. But what have they done for you?"

"They are not cowards," she burst out. "They are utterly loyal to their clan and their rightful king!"

"All a fine bunch of rebels within one clan, is it? I see. Are you MacDonald, then? My mother was of that ilk. Or MacDougall? They're loyal to a fault when it comes to the crown of Scotland and the king over the water."

"I'm no MacDougall, though I respect their stand in this rebellion. And if you're a Keppoch MacDonald through your mother, then why are *you* wearing a red government coat?"

"We're discussing your kin, not mine. You could be a MacGregor," he went on, "since you refuse to give your name. The Gregorach are a proscribed clan, and Miss Kate prefers to remain nameless. Hmm," he said, tapping his chin, sliding her a glance.

"Wrong, though I'll admit to having some Mac-Gregor kin."

"This is a fine game, but I'm losing patience. Perhaps I'll just call you Rumpelstiltskin when we go to Edinburgh."

She laughed then, an enchanting chime. "I've read that tale in the German, sir, but I'm no Hanoverian. In Scotland you'd have to call me Miss Whuppity-Stourie. It's also a tale of guessing and magical names."

"My nurse told me the story often enough. Magical, I agree, though you're definitely not a gnomish sort. Let me see," he murmured. "You were heading northwest. If you kept walking in that direction, you'd come across MacPhersons . . . and those devils the MacCarrans of Duncrieff, a small but troublesome nest of Jacobites. Fiercely loyal, and clever, too."

"I am thinking that Miss Whuppity-Stourie is a nice name."

"Aha! MacCarran! They have a legend about fairy blood, I think. It makes so much sense, I should have realized it earlier." He crowed with victory. "Kate MacCarran!"

"Now what?" she asked bitterly. "Shall I turn around three times and disappear?"

He grinned. "How about spinning me a barnful of gold?"

"I'd rather turn you into a frog," she sulked.

"Marie Katherine MacCarran." He hooted softly, saw her grim expression, and grew sober. "Are you the daughter of a rebel, or sister to one? The MacCarrans are a fine lot, but gone to rascals of late. Your chief was imprisoned a while back, though it was established as a false charge later. He's young . . . and I would guess you're his sister. What is his name? Robert MacCarran."

"Oh, hush up," she muttered.

"Sister to a chief," he said, pleased with himself.

"And you thought I was just a fairy queen," she snarled.

They reached the bottom of the hill, and he led her toward the waiting horse. "A pity I did not learn your name that day in London. It would have been easy to put all this together."

197

"I learned yours," she said. "I learned about the chocolate, too, but not the Whiggishness."

"What have your kinsmen talked you into doing for them?"

She tried to jerk her arm away, but he gripped her securely. "I do what I please, and no one orders me."

"I do not doubt that," he said. "But you're helping your kinsmen for some reason."

"MacCarrans have always been loyal to the Stuarts, which you, as a red-breasted puppet of Lovat, may not comprehend."

"Aye, the lass has a mouth," he muttered. "Why did the rogue MacCarrans send a lass to do their work for them?"

"Because they would look odd carting laundry about."

Alec chuckled. "Miss MacCarran, you keep your secrets close. Come on." He walked her forward, lifted her into the saddle, and swung up behind her, shifting her onto his lap.

She turned. "You learned my name," she said, holding out her hand. "We had a bargain. I'd like my necklace now, please."

He lifted a brow. "I had to guess the name."

"You enjoyed it," she pointed out, and Alec smiled. "Now I'll have my crystal and chain from you."

"Very well." He sighed, and stretched two fingers into an inside pocket of his jacket. "You did not look there earlier, did you," he said wryly, pulling out the silver chain and quartz crystal. "You were too busy looking elsewhere, weren't you." He pooled the silver into her palm.

She cupped her hand, and such joy lit her face that he felt foolishly glad to see it. "Thank you. And as for looking elsewhere . . . you liked it well enough."

"I did. So did you." He watched her.

She shrugged, and in the pale dawn he saw her blush.

"What is so important about that bonny wee bauble?" He helped her to fasten the clasp behind her neck, his fingers straying a little to trace over her neck. She bowed her head, and angled away from him, the gesture a silent reminder that he was, after all, her captor and not really her lover, even if he felt so tempted to change that.

"This is a fairy crystal, handed through my family for generations," she answered. "I've got a touch of fairy blood in me, and . . . a hand for the magic now and then." Her eyes sparkled, their moonlight gray enchanting.

"I could almost believe that, Miss MacCarran, if I believed in fairies and such." He took up the reins. "Hold tight. And try to resist your unrelenting urge to be shut of me."

He turned the horse toward the Perth road, and was glad to see that Kate wrapped her arms around his waist without protest.

She rode dozing in his arms, giving him the sort of trust he wished he could earn from her when she was awake. Supporting her with one arm, he slowed the horse beside the road and sat watching the dawn turn from cool pink to brilliant fire over the ridge of the mountains.

He often felt grateful for such things—the rising sun, the breath in his body. He knew how quickly it could vanish, and he had built a shell around himself to protect against such loss.

Lately, most particularly when he was with Kate, he sensed that shell beginning to shift and crack. He felt a warm burst of gratitude, of emotion, in his chest. He had felt that only since he had met Kate MacCarran.

For too long he had allowed himself only safe feelings, emotions he could control. Since this fey and lovely girl had walked into his life, that had changed. He knew that now. And if it continued, the gates that shielded him would crack.

Either he would then face his old hurt—or he would find that it had healed and he could be reborn, in a way. He did not know what might happen, nor could he guess if Kate was a permanent part of that. But he knew she had a kind of magic indeed.

All his careful resistance had fallen by the wayside now, for he realized that he was succumbing more than any other man ever could. He had gone the fool for Katie Hell. And he did not mind so much as he thought he might.

He pressed his cheek against her hair, kissed her head, allowed himself that—no one to see, no one to know. He held her quietly and watched the new day birth out of the old.

Kate stirred, half sat, looked about sleepily. "Oh, it's lovely," she said, looking at the sky.

"Aye," Alec murmured, and urged the horse forward.

Chapter 17

The bed beneath her sagged, but no more so than her spirit. Seated in the upstairs room at the inn, Kate gazed out the window at a sunny sky, heathered hills, and trees blazing with autumn. She wanted to be out there, on her way to Duncrieff. Instead, she was locked in his room, with a couple of guards posted outside.

Alec Fraser was taking no chances that she might try to escape again—or so he had told her when he had left her there earlier that day. Before departing, he had found two old women to sit outside her room and make sure she stayed put inside.

"I am not so foolish as to post a male guard outside your door," he had told her when he had returned to

201

SARAH GABRIEL

the room to fetch his canvas bag. "I'm concerned about Jack, and I'm going to ride out looking for him. It's best I leave you here, where you can be confined. Old Mrs. MacLennan and her sister will act as your chaperones. They're not very talkative," he had said, opening the door while Kate gaped at him in disbelief. "They fear you'll try to cast a spell on them."

"Why?" she had demanded, jumping up from the bed to rush toward the door.

"I have no idea," he said lightly, and closed the door, but not before her shoe, yanked off and thrown at him, narrowly missed his head. Then she heard the turn of the key in the lock and his footsteps on the stairs.

Kate was not sure what explanation Alec had given either of the old ladies, but when they had delivered luncheon to her shortly afterward, they both gaped at her in silence, deposited the tray, and scuttled out with scarcely a word. Again the key turned, and she was alone.

At least she was free of shackles, and she had her crystal pendant back in her own keeping. After closely examining the lock, and seeing through the keyhole the two old ladies perched on chairs in the corridor—one of them sending such dark scowls toward the door that Kate was certain she was the only one in danger of a nasty spell—that she had finally decided just to spend some time resting. The past week had been exhausting.

Later, awake and refreshed after a long nap, she heard a male voice outside her door, but it did not belong to Alec, nor was it the gravelly tones of the old lady with the dark scowl.

202

She went to the door and tapped on the wood. "Hello!"

"Aye?" the man answered. It was a young voice, a bit quavery and quite pleasant. "What can I do for ye, Mrs. Fraser?"

"Who's there?" She pressed her hands to the door. "Where are the old—where is old Mrs. MacLennan?"

"*Och*, the ladies were weary, 'twas a long time for them to sit here, so I offered to watch the door for a bit. I understand you're not to leave. Are you sick? By the way, I'm Davey, Jean's brother."

"Oh! No, I'm not sick at all. I feel quite well. And I'm pleased to meet you, Davey MacLennan." Kate smiled to herself. Oh, she thought, Alec Fraser would regret leaving her this day.

"And you, Mrs. Fraser." His voice had not yet settled into its masculine resonance. "What d'ye need, Mistress? Would ye like some food or drink?"

"That would be lovely, Davey, thank you."

"Yer husband says ye're no' to be let out of there, no matter what."

"We had a silly spat, my husband and I . . . I'm sure it's fine if I come out now."

"He said ye're no' to go even downstairs. Says ye're a bit of a wildcat, and we're to keep an eye over ye 'til he returns."

"Oh, Davey. That's not really necessary."

"He was quite firm aboot it, Mistress."

"Oh," she said tentatively. "Do you know where he is?"

"He left a while ago, riding out, and hasna come back. He said ye shouldna come down to the public room for any reason, wi' the dragoons down there.

Worried aboot his wee bride near soldiers, I suppose."

"I see," she said, oddly touched to think that Alec might have had her safety in mind after all.

"He has a temper indeed," Davey said, "for he was arguing wi' two soldiers. These dragoons came stormin' in and accusin' him o' hiding something—"

"Davey," she said urgently, "what are you talking about?"

"Them dragoons said they'd arrested two braw Highlanders today wi' some guns they shouldna be carrying," Davey said.

"Weapons that should have been confiscated?" She held her breath, palm flattened to her chest.

"I dinna think they meant the auld, rusty bits that Highlandmen turn over to the army, swearin' they have no more weapons when they do," Davey went on, referring to common Highland practice, "but fine, shiny flintlocks o' Spanish make. Fine enough to make the Englishers mad, hey."

"Spanish! Did they say who these Highlanders were?"

"Nah, just that they were men from the western hills, which describes much o' the Highlands, to my mind. Then the dragoon said they would send troops into the hills to look for others with the same arms, which they shouldna have. He said that Captain Fraser might know more about these than he'd let on and that he shouldna protect those that had the Spanish pistols."

"Oh, no," she said, distress mounting. "What did Captain Fraser . . . my husband . . . say then?"

"He was angry. I saw it 'round him like steam, but he

were calm enough. Said 'twas so much kerfuffle and he knew nothing about it. Then he went off to find his ghillie, who may have come to harm along the road. Rode off like a hellhound, did Fraser."

Kate nodded to herself, breath coming anxiously. Someone else knew of the missing Spanish cache and was using the weaponry, and the government troops were after him in force. And Alec Fraser, she suspected, wanted her to tell him what she knew because he meant to stop this or even protect the Highlanders who had found the weapons.

But why? Frowning, she leaned her head against the door.

Davey tapped on the wood. "Mistress? Ye're quiet."

"I'm just . . . Davey, could you fetch me some food? I am hungry, and thirsty, too."

This might be her only chance to get free of this place and run to Duncrieff to warn her brother. If her kinsmen had found out what Cameron tried to tell her, two of them might be the men who had just been arrested.

"Sure, I'll bring you summat. We've hot chocolate drink, too, Jeanie made a pot not long ago. Would ye like some?"

"I would love some," she said, distracted by her thoughts.

"It's Fraser's Fancy Cocoa," he said, sounding pleased.

"I'm sure it is," she answered. "Thank you, Davey. You're a gentleman."

"Thank ye. I'll be back. Ye'll be safe alone for a few minutes, Mistress?"

205

"How could I get past a locked door?" she asked sweetly.

Davey laughed in agreement, and she heard his footsteps pounding down the steps. Then she dropped to her knees to examine the lock once more, peering through the keyhole.

She could see the shadowed upper hallway, and at a certain angle, a gleam of light from below, where she also could hear the sounds of men laughing in the tavern. Someone called for another ale, and she heard Jeanie call out an answer.

The mechanism of key and handle was simple enough, but she had nothing at all with which to try the lock. She wished she had saved the fork from the night before. Hearing footsteps, she stepped back. A key was inserted from the other side, and the door swung open.

A lanky youth with a wild shock of rust red hair stepped into the room and closed the door behind him. He carried a covered dish in one hand and a cup in the other. He smiled, his fair skin blushing, his brown eyes sparkling.

"*Och*, Mistress Fraser," he said. "You're younger than I thought. And . . . bonny."

"You're bonny yourself," she answered, accepting the cup of cocoa. "Thank you so much."

"*Och*," he sputtered. He held out the covered dish nervously, almost dropping it. He was clumsy as a colt, stepping on his own big boot, lurching forward to catch the dish as it toppled.

She scooped it out of his hands before it hit the floor.

"Thank you," she said, and set it carefully on a small table.

"I'm sorry you must be in here, Mistress," Davey said. "Perhaps Captain Fraser doesna appreciate his Highland bride."

"I'm sure he does. We'll clear this spat up soon enough," she said brightly.

"I'm Highland, too," Davey said. "I'm for Jamie o'er the water m'self, Mistress, though I darena say it around here."

"I understand. And it's so nice to have a brave Scottish lad to look after me in this place."

"*Och*, aye." He watched her earnestly, with an innocence and guile that reminded her of a puppy. His big brown eyes lowered, then lifted as he looked at her and blushed even deeper.

She took up the cup of chocolate and sipped. It was hot and thick, though quite bitter, with very little sweetening added to it. She could barely swallow it, but did her best.

"Thank you, Davey." She knew she had him—she could tell by the wide, limpid gaze, the slight droop of his lower lip, the hot flush in his skin. He was really very young, and she felt a small qualm, not wanting to mislead him.

This had happened before, with young men especially. She need only smile, say something friendly, and they swam in like fish to the bait. She rather liked the lonely puppyish sorts and was kind to them; she avoided other types—men with an edge to them and no need for affection and men who wanted only to satisfy their sexual hunger. She could charm them, too, with a look or a tilt of the head, but she kept away because of the risk. Francis Grant had been one of those, but she had gotten free of him.

Alec was neither yearning nor needy, and she found his solitariness and restraint compelling. But she would not think of him now, she told herself.

She smiled at Davey MacLennan and saw him blink. He was the adoring sort, an easy snare, so very young. She glanced away, almost asked him to leave, wanting to let him loose gracefully. She knew how easily lads his age fell, how easily they felt foolish. But with Davey to watch her, she had a real chance to slip away from the inn.

Touching the stone at her throat, she smiled at him.

"Go ahead and eat, Mistress," he said. "You look pale. The food is verra good, I had some of the stew earlier."

She smiled again and sat on the bed, the only seat in the room besides one simple wooden chair. Davey went red to the roots of his carroty hair when she chose the bed. Uncovering the dish, she broke off a bit of the steaming pie with her fingers and ate it quickly, dipped her fingers for a little more, then licked her fingertips and looked at him. He watched her with a strange expression, as if he had turned to a half-wit.

"It's very good," she said, "but there's too much for me. Will you finish the rest?"

"I canna. I should go." He stepped back toward the door and put his hand on the doorknob.

"Oh, Davey." She sighed. "I could use some fresh air. Will you walk outside with me?"

"Captain Fraser would have me head if ye left this room."

"He won't be angry at me when he returns, I'm sure. And I do so want to apologize as soon as I see him. I'd like to wait for him outside."

"He'd like that," Davey said, watching as Kate dabbed her lips with the linen napkin he had handed her with the dish.

She stood. "You go downstairs, then, Davey. I do not want to get you into trouble. I'll remember you for a kind friend."

He hesitated. "I could finish the pie."

"If you like." She handed him the dish, and he began to scoop his way eagerly through the remaining food.

A glance through the window showed her that it was late, nearly sunset. She did not have much time. Alec would be back.

"Thank heaven!" she said, turning away from the window. "I just saw my husband returning!" She felt awful about that, for she had not seen him. And she liked Davey.

"He did say he'd return by end o' day. I'd better go." Davey paused. "But if ye'd like to greet him, I suppose I could walk ye outside, if he's just there on the road."

"That would be so kind." She picked up her plaid shawl and wrapped it around her, then went to the door, rising on tiptoe to kiss the tall lad's cheek. "You are a true friend."

"I am?" he asked, and opened the door for her as Kate hurried past him and down the stairs.

Halting his horse along the road, Alec sat and stared in disbelief as Kate crossed the road away from the inn, boldly and openly. She had not even waited for cover of darkness. Stunned, he simply watched as she headed in the same direction as last night. The little vixen had not bothered to vary her route, he noticed.

Shaking his head, he lifted the reins, urging the mare to a fast canter. He would have to go after her. The temptation to just let her go flashed through his mind—but he could not. She knew something about those Spanish weapons, he was sure, and he had to find out what.

He watched her for another moment. Well, at least if he lost track of her this time, he would know where to find her—with the MacCarrans. Some inquiry, here and there, would lead him straight to the glen and castle where her kinsmen no doubt waited for her.

Frowning, he thought about what sort of kinsmen would let the lass face the sort of risks Kate had taken. But until she trusted him with more information in that regard, he should not make judgments.

But he had to go after her. He urged his horse forward.

He had ridden as far as the next large town to find some trace of Jack and inquire about recent arrests. Aye, he was told at an inn there, two Highlanders had been taken near Edinburgh and whisked off to the castle. One of them was said to be a MacCarran.

Somehow he had expected that. Riding on, he had

searched for sight or news of Jack MacDonald without success. Finally, on his way back to MacLennan's Changehouse, he had found the man himself at a private estate no more than two hours east of MacLennan's.

First Alec assured himself that Jack was fine: the chaise had collapsed in a ditch and Jack had taken a bad knock to the head, finding help and hospitality nearby but neglecting to send word, which was only typical of him. After securing Jack's earnest promise to follow quickly, Alec had started back to the changehouse, anxious to return. He knew he had left Kate too long under makeshift guard.

Now he knew just how busy she had been that day. Next time, he vowed, he would set a dozen old women to watch her.

As he rode closer, he saw Davey MacLennan walk out into the yard, looking baffled as he turned in circles. Alec urged the horse forward into the yard as the lad spun again.

"Hello, Davey," he said calmly. "Did she get away?"

"*Och*, sir! I'm so sorry—I know ye wanted Mrs. Fraser to stay here and wait nicely for ye."

"Aye, your grandmother and great-aunt were to watch after her. What happened?" Alec waited, hands folded on the saddle.

"They grew weary and asked me to watch out for her. She's a fine lass, your wife. She said she wanted to meet ye out here and give you her sweetest apology. And now I dinna ken where she's gone. She's disappeared!"

Alec nodded. "You did a fine job to keep her as long as you did. I'll fetch her. Go on inside, lad." He tossed

Davey a gold guinea, then chucked to the horse and cantered across the road toward the moor.

Sweet apology indeed, he thought.

Moments later, Alec saw Kate as she topped a low hill. He followed at an easy pace, for she was but half a mile ahead. The sun spilled glorious color through the sky as it sank behind the hills; in that glow, Kate's hair, slipping loose of its knots as usual, shone like pale bronze.

And Jean's red gown was as bright as a flag. Bless Jean and Providence, he thought, for making his life that much easier.

He saw Kate walking in the open, where the grass stretched over gentle swells to the rim of a hill. She glanced back then and, seeing him, broke into a run.

Riding steadily, Alec soon pulled near her, and she raced faster, hair and skirts whipping like banners in the wind. He leaned hard from the stirrups, precariously low, and reached out to scoop her around the middle with one outstretched arm. Though she flailed like an albatross, nearly pulling him from his horse, he managed to drag her upward and dump her over his lap. Then he clamped an arm around her middle, and turned the horse.

"Oh, no you don't," he grunted, as she almost wriggled away. He snugged his arm tight around her, trapping her arms under his, while he handled the reins in his left hand. He had planted her firmly in his lap—a little too much so, for he felt the blunt discomfort the moment he brought her into his lap. Ignoring the pain as best he could, he held her tightly, though she wiggled and writhed in her effort to break free.

"That," he growled, "is enough!"

Quieting suddenly, she stared at him, mouth open. Then she began twisting in his arms again.

"By God, I've endured enough of this," he said. "Next time you try to get away, I shall just let you do that!"

"That would be fine," she snapped back.

"And then I'll just follow you to that nest of Jacobites you're protecting and get all my blasted questions answered," he said between his teeth.

He rode onward, while she sat silent and frowning.

She had made him furious, yet he felt the vigor of it, the challenge of it—for her sheer contrary stubbornness was the equal of his own. He had to admire her spirit. Having lost some of his own spark somewhere along the way, he had long felt some self-imposed restraints. He understood her need for freedom far better than she could know.

The other feelings that tumbled inside him had no name as yet, but he suspected that they were all part of the birthing of a new part of himself . . . and by the way she had him spinning about like a whirligig, he wondered if he was beginning to feel a wild sort of love. He had changed some, and just enough, in the last few days, to feel that might be the case.

She did not ride peacefully in his arms, pushing against him now and then, resentful and frustrated. He slowed the horse, holding Kate with one arm, the reins with the other. Reaching the road, he let the horse walk to cool, then halted it altogether. He looked at Kate, held her while she twisted, and waited.

"Stop, now," he said quietly. "Just stop. I cannot let you escape, and you know it."

She sighed, quieted, looked away. He felt strangely caught in a mythic conflict, like a man from an ancient tale restraining one of the wild fairy folk in a battle greater than both of them.

And he realized that both he and Kate were resisting something greater than any individual grievance. If a bond was forming—if he truly was beginning to feel love for her—that had the power to remake and re-shape him, and her, into something finer than when they began.

Someday, perhaps, he could accept that he could indeed love this girl, if he dared think about it. And if it proved true, sooner or later he would have to tell her the truth: that he, too, fought for the Jacobites in a covert way.

But that time was not yet, and there were things he had to do, duties to fulfill, secrets to plumb. He held her, feeling her continued tension and resistance.

"Kate," he murmured. "I am no threat to you."

She looked up at him. "Then tell the court you lost me out here. You told the soldiers so already. Let me go on my way, and you need never bother with me again."

"I will always bother with you," he said, and the word lingered: *always*.

She looked at him in sudden wonder. Alec leaned down then, could not help himself, as if drawn forward, and touched his lips to hers. That gentle meeting of lips

214

plummeted through his body, hardening him then and there for more. The kiss dissolved into another when she sighed and returned it before pulling back.

"Stop that. You muddle my head. Why will you not listen to what I am saying and just let me go?" she asked.

"Perhaps I like kissing you," he said wryly. "Perhaps you should say more so that I'll understand—tell me what your kinsmen put you up to with those trips into the military camps. Tell me what you and yours know about those damned weapons."

Kate scowled. "You know I am far too much trouble to keep, and I intend to be even more trouble. I will not let you take me so easily off to prison."

"I realize that. But you'll stay with me, Kate MacCarran, no matter what your wilder blood wants. Make of that what you will."

She looked at him in startled silence, her frown pensive as he guided the horse down the hill through the gathering darkness.

Chapter 18

Glancing toward the inn, a mile or so away through twilight shadows, he saw its windows glowing with lanternlight. As his careful gaze swept the length of the road in the opposite direction, Alec saw a vehicle moving not far in the distance.

"Ah," he said. "It's Jack, at last."

Kate sat straighter. "Jack? Thank God! He's not harmed after all! I was so worried."

Hearing the concern in her voice, Alec felt a pang of envy. He guided the mare down the slope, reaching the stone road at a point between the inn and the oncoming post chaise. Soon Jack slowed the horses and drew the vehicle to a halt.

"There you are," Alec said, as Jack dismounted and came toward them.

"Jack, all this time and no word!" Kate said. "Are you well? What happened?"

"Met with a mishap, but it's fine now. *Catriona Bhan*, so good to see you again," Jack added in Gaelic, and tipped his hat.

Fair Katherine, Jack had called her. Alec frowned as Kate smiled brightly. He had never thought to gentle her with the compliments that came more easily to Jack MacDonald.

"Alec found me earlier today," Jack said, "recuperating from my adventure. I was just about to return here."

"He did not tell me." She glanced at Alec.

"I had no chance to tell you while you were shrieking like a banshee," he muttered, only for her to hear. No, he thought, he did not have a knack for facile pleasantries.

"I'm sorry to be late," Jack went on. "What's going on? What are you two doing out here?" He seemed to notice Alec's taut grip over Kate, who sat across his lap.

"A wee dispute," Alec said.

"He will not let me go home where I belong," Kate said.

"It is my opinion that the lady should stay at the inn," Alec said, "but she prefers to traipse about the hills unescorted, especially by her assigned custodial officer."

"Aha," Jack said, and Alec was grateful his cousin had the wisdom to say no more.

Kate inquired in Gaelic, then, if Jack was well, and he

replied, and asked after her. Alec listened while she answered that she herself was fine, but that Fraser could sometimes be a military . . .

He frowned. "*Baobach*—what is that?"

"Blockhead," Kate answered, and resumed her conversation with Jack in Gaelic.

"Alasdair Callda is trustworthy, never doubt that," Jack said, "though he likes his secrets and his sulks." He added something in Gaelic, and Kate laughed.

"If you're quite done now," Alec snapped. "I trust you will want to spend some time with Jeanie, now that you're back?" He added that sternly.

"Of course. Though I know you need to go on to Edinburgh, and I thank you for waiting. You could have gone on ahead."

"I wish I'd thought of that," Alec grumbled, with a touch of sarcasm. He felt unaccountably irritated with Jack and realized it had to do with Kate—only with Kate. He turned the horse, while Jack ran toward the chaise, leaping up to ride postillion and follow Alec's lead to the inn.

"Are you not glad Jack has safely returned?" Kate asked.

"Aye. But I saw him earlier today and told him so already. I'd like to move on now, but he'll want to spend a day at least here with Jean and the bairn."

"You can both stay at the inn as long as you want," Kate replied. "And I'll just go on my way."

"You're as stubborn a lass as ever existed," Alec said, shaking his head slightly. "I should be shut of you myself." Aye, he thought, he was deeply irritated. Jealous. It did not suit him, but there it was.

"You do not find me charming, do you?" she re-marked, tilting her head.

"Charming enough, but I'm not one of your fools, lass."

"I know that," she murmured.

"How did you get out again, by the way? Did you bedevil poor Davey? Did he adore you enough to do all your will?"

"He was glad to help me."

"I'm sure, the poor lad. Shall I do that?"

"What, help me? Of course."

"I mean adore you," he said. His voice was a low growl—his heart pounded. Earlier he had thought his closed-up heart was softening some, but now he wanted to indulge in some of the old, familiar edge and annoyance that he used to keep others away.

She lifted her chin in that way she had, not haughty but proud, confident, knowing her worth—the way of a fairy queen. "You could do so if you like," she said. "Adore me, I mean."

"What if I already do?" His heart thumped hard, and a feeling turned within, that same whirligig set to motion.

She laughed softly. "If you did, I would know."

"Would you?" he asked, watching her, knowing how easily he could adore her—perhaps already did.

He heard her breath catch. "If you did, you would not drag me about in chains, would you," she replied.

He touched the crystal dangling at her throat. "You're wearing this chain, and no other, just now."

She touched it, her fingers covering his. Then she looked away. He loved the clean grace of her profile. Aye, adored it.

"Kate," he said suddenly. He was not sure what he wanted to say, or do. He only knew he had to touch her, felt the pull of it like a storm within.

But they had reached the inn yard, the chaise rumbled past them, and Davey himself came running out to take care of the horses. Seeing Kate and Alec, he stopped uncertainly.

Alec saluted, Kate waved, and the lad smiled. Then he ran to help Jack bring the horses into the stables. Alec dismounted and reached up to lift Kate to the ground.

But he hesitated, holding her against him for a moment, her hands on his shoulders, her body curving so sweetly against his, even here, in a public yard, though it seemed as if only the two of them existed for a moment.

"If I set you on your feet and let go, what would you do?"

"Run," she said.

"That's honest." Setting her down, he held her firmly about the waist and turned as Jack approached. "Jack, if you want to go inside and see your lady, go ahead," he said. "I'm going upstairs with mine. We'll wait for you there."

"Aye then," Jack said, and smiled at Kate.

She was looking only at Alec, neither smiling nor frowning, her gaze thoughtful.

* * *

"So you have the urge to run, hey," Jack murmured. Much later that evening, he sat with her in the small rented room. Alec slept on the bed, his back turned to them, snoring deeply. He had been so tired that he had asked Jack to stay in the room and keep watch over Kate while he slept.

"I do," she admitted. She sat on the bed, her back propped with pillows while Jack occupied the single chair.

"I can understand that." He leaned back, stretching out his legs and crossing his feet and buckled shoes. He wore a brown frock coat, breeches, and waistcoat with white stockings, with no Highland gear at all. If he did not wear the full Highland kilt, then wearing a tartan jacket or waistcoat was grounds for arrest as a Jacobite. But for all his finery—snowy white linen ruffles showed at his jacket cuffs and neck, and his buttons were good silver—he was a thorough Highlander, Kate sensed, inside.

And he was that rare thing, a truly beautiful man, with expressive hazel green eyes beneath straight brows, glossy dark hair, a ready grin with a hint of a dimple. He looked more like a gentleman than a servant. He spoke to her mostly in Gaelic, his manner respectful but casual, so Highland in his manners that he set her at immediate ease. She felt as if she had a trustworthy friend already in Jack MacDonald.

"If you understand that I need to be free, then please let me out of here," she murmured, glancing at the door.

221

Jack waved a hand in dismissal. "I would if I could. But we'll do as Alec Fraser wants."

"Why?" She crossed her arms. "I have kinsmen I must see, a home to return to. I must go west, not east."

"I know. MacCarran. *Tcha*," he said. "You could have told me. I'm a Keppoch MacDonald. Our kin are allies."

"If you are Jacobite, then why are you with Alec Fraser?"

"I'm loyal to the great cause," he said amiably. "And loyal to that cause, too." He pointed a thumb toward sleeping Alec.

"I do not need to stay here," she insisted.

"That may be," Jack said easily, leaning his chair back until it thumped the wall so that he could rest his head there. He closed his eyes. "You will have to think on that for yourself. Who will benefit if you go? Yourself? Your kin? Alexander Callda? Who will benefit if you stay? It could be you and Alec both. That is what I think. But you must decide."

She frowned, taking in his meaning. Jack was silent then, seemingly intent on sleeping. Slowly Kate stood, watching him warily. But his hand lashed out to grip her forearm and coax her back down to her seat.

"I would not be doing that just now," he murmured, opening one eye.

"You closed your eyes. I thought it was a signal that you would look the other way if I left."

"I wanted to keep from looking at you, lass. You've a blinding sort of beauty. Makes a man lose his wit. I thought I'd best not look upon you, with all your fairy magic."

222

She touched the crystal at her throat. "My what?"

"MacCarran—I know the stories. I do not know if Alec does, but I do. And you and I both know that I would fall at your feet like all the rest, subject to your fairy gifts. So I'd best not look at you too often." He closed his eyes again.

She laughed. "You have your own charm, Mr. Mac-Donald."

"So I do. But I'm not such a fool as to flirt and fiddle with the lass who's taken Alec Fraser's heart."

Her own heart beat very fast, suddenly. "I doubt he would truly give his heart to any woman."

"He has given it to you," Jack murmured. "I can tell you that. He might realize it himself one day." He opened his eyes to fix her with a piercing glance. "And when he does, you'd best take care with his heart. That's no man to trifle with."

"I know," she said quietly.

"Good. And I'm no man to trifle with, either, should my kinsman be heartbroken by a fairy-blooded lass who does not even know her own power."

"No need. He does not love me," she said.

"Mm," he grunted. "He does, or he will, or he can. Do you?"

She was silent, glanced at Alec. "I . . . could."

"This is hopeful. But we'd best change the subject. This one is dangerous. I might be tempted to look at you, and you might look at me, and we'd both be lost forever in our own wicked charm, my darling. And then where would our Alasdair be?" He smiled with wry satisfaction.

She laughed again. Jack made her want to do that. Yet despite his beauty and smooth charm, she did not feel the sense of irresistible attraction with him that she felt so clearly with Alec Fraser. That both puzzled and thrilled her.

And she began to wonder if Alec could be the one man with whom she could find true love, the only sort of love she could ever accept in her life because of the fairy legend. She touched the fairy crystal again, thoughtfully.

"I'm sure you and I could manage to behave," she said.

"We could. I'm that loyal to Captain Fraser that I'd not allow anything else. Would you?" Jack opened his eyes again.

She shook her head and glanced at Alec, at his broad back and strong shoulders, his tousled brown-gilt hair, all she could see of him, but for his hand tucked over the coverlet as he slept. He had strong, graceful hands, she thought.

"I'm glad you came to no harm these last two days, Jack. You took a risk for Captain Fraser and me, and I thank you for it, even if the captain is not so appreciative."

"In his way, he is, though he keeps things to himself."

"He keeps to himself why he is so determined to rush me to Edinburgh," she said. "I am in no hurry. And I suppose you want to stay here for a while."

He looked at her. "Me?"

"To stay with your lady and your son," she said bluntly.

A frown puckered his brow, and he was silent for a moment. "I do want to stay with them," he said.

"He's very bonny, the bairn. You must be very proud."

"He looked like a dry apple when I saw him last, but he looked bonny tonight," he admitted.

"He is beautiful," she said. "I love his laugh."

"He did not laugh for me."

"Just wait. You will fall in love, Mr. MacDonald. And Jeanie is a very good mother."

"I know. And I am . . . not so good a father. I offered to marry her, you know, but she refused me," he added. "Said she would wait until I knew for sure what I wanted. And all I have wanted to do, for the last year, is marry Jeanie MacLennan, if I could only convince her. I fear my wicked past follows me about."

"I know what that is like. And I think you are a very good man, Jack MacDonald."

He huffed a laugh. "My secret is out. What about Alec Fraser? What do you think of him?"

She glanced away. "He . . . puzzles me. Befuddles my brain."

Jack laughed. "You befuddle his brain. And more."

"I know he's one of the good ones," she said quietly.

"He would prefer we not know that," Jack whispered.

"If you want to spend more time with Jean and your son before we go to Edinburgh in the morning," she ventured, "you had best go down to her now. It's late."

"I promised Alec I'd sit with you while he slept."

"I'm sleepy myself. I think we should all rest." She yawned a little and stretched.

Jack looked at her, eyes narrowed, and chuckled. "I'm not a silly young lad, Miss Katie Hell," he drawled.

"Cut more of the cloth of your employer than I thought."

"My cousin," he corrected. "Through MacDonald of Keppoch, where I was fostered as a stray and an orphan."

"He mentioned that."

"Did he? I'm surprised. He keeps his past and his thoughts to himself, does Alec."

"All those rules and such. A good Whig."

"Hardly that," Jack said.

She leaned toward him. "What do you mean?"

"Ask him yourself. He might tell you."

"Is he . . . a Jacobite sympathizer?" Once dawned, the idea thrilled and would not go away. "Is he?"

"I cannot speak of another man's politics. It is very personal. You will have to ask him. But even so, either way," he said sternly, "his politics would not erase your arrest and your upcoming hearing."

She frowned, feeling somber suddenly, dreading what awaited her in Edinburgh. "Jack, what do you know about Spanish weapons and some recent arrests of Highlanders?"

He no longer looked in a teasing mood. "What I know is that you must tell our friend Alexander whatever you know before men lose their lives."

She drew breath to speak, sitting up quickly. Alec stirred beside her, rolled over, a hand over his brow.

"Still talking?" he asked groggily.

"Aye, listing all your fine points," Jack said. "But the

226

lady still thinks you are descended of a water beast, and she will have none of it."

"Go to the devil," Alec grunted, and rolled over.

Jack stood and bowed his head to Kate. "I'd best take my leave of you now, Katie MacCarran, for it is late. And I will give you a little time to decide what you most want."

He smiled ruefully at her, took up his hat and went to the door, opening it, then closing it with a quiet click.

He did not lock it behind him.

Chapter 19

~~~◦◯◦~~~

She walked steadily, stubbornly through rain, now
and then wiping away the tears that kept coming.
Slipping on a muddy hill, gasping, she lifted the red
dress, its hem sopping and filthy in the time since she
had left the inn. Jean's lovely gift, ruined—perhaps
that was what made her cry, she told herself.

Surely she would not cry over leaving Alec Fraser
asleep on that bed, would not cry over the dreadful
feeling that she was betraying him, that she was losing
him, that she would never see him again. None of that
should matter a whit to her.

She was free, and that was most important. No one
could have expected her to stay when the door was
open and Alec lay snoring softly, his back to her as she

slipped out of the room. Her brother and kinsmen would be worried for her sake, and they needed word of Ian Cameron and his message about the missing weapons. Had she been able to explain that to Alec, she might not have left him as she did.

But she had slipped away without a word, pausing to gaze at him before leaving. All had gone well this time. She had traversed the long moor and was nearing the foothills already, and still she had seen no one behind her.

She sniffled and told herself to ease up, as Alec would have said himself, had he been there to support her choice instead of adding to the clash between his purpose and hers.

Turning, she felt an odd flicker of disappointment that she did not see him behind her. Yet when he found her gone, he could easily follow. He knew her name and could find her clan—and she felt sure he would follow her. But she would reach Duncrieff first with her message, and she could send her kinsmen away.

And then she did not know what might happen. For the moment, reaching home would have to be enough.

She hurried on through cold, drizzling rain and pockets of thick fog, the morning so beastly that she kept her plaid drawn snug about her head and shoulders and slowed her progress over the challenging terrain. Ahead, she saw the mist-covered mountains that shielded her family's small glen. Every step took her closer to her goal—so long as she did not think about the man she had left behind at the inn.

She plodded on, the pattering rain soaking her. Jack had urged her to trust Alec Fraser, and her own feelings did as well—much more so than before—but she could not remain in military custody. No matter how trustworthy Alec might be, he could not protect her from what might come.

And she realized, suddenly, that she did not want to put him in any situation that might endanger him. If she escaped, simply got away from him, he would be in less jeopardy than if he tried to help her.

In that moment, her feelings crystallized, in a way, like the little pendant she wore at her throat—she realized that she was running to protect Alec as much as herself and her kinsmen.

If he did follow her, she would have to send him away for his own well-being. She had walked away with memories and secrets that would warm her always, and for her own and Alec's sake, it was best if they stayed apart. She dashed at another tear.

Feeling a stitch in her side, she stopped, breathing hard, and worked her fingers under the trappings of her dress to loosen the laces of her stays a little for comfort. Looking back, she saw only the empty moorland stretching behind her toward the military road, though much of the view was lost in gathering fog.

Topping the next low hill, she discovered a worn earthen track that dipped and wound its way between slopes and peaks. This was the drover's track she had hoped to find, knowing that it would lead her westward through the hills.

Mist turned the rain-shrouded hills dismal and dark,

and she realized that Alec could not easily follow her through the maze of hills. Sooner or later, though, he would find out which glen belonged to the MacCarrans.

Duncrieff Castle in Glen Carran was no more than a full day's walk, she guessed, heading northwest through the Perthshire hills. Kate had only a little bread in her pocket, saved from supper the night before, and only her plaid shawl for protection from the elements. But once she reached the hills that edged Glen Carran, she would be able to find Highland homes where she could stop and rest, or ask for shelter for the night if necessary.

Stopping beside a narrow burn, she dipped her hand into the fast-flowing, cold water to sip her fill, drying her chilled fingers on her plaid before moving on. The overgrown drover's track was marked well enough, and she easily found her way.

After a while, she heard cracking and rustling somewhere behind her. She whirled. The sound came again, echoing in the foggy hillsides so that she could not locate it. Again the rustling sounded—footsteps touching rock, crushing wet grass.

Alarmed, not knowing who else might be roaming these hills—cattle thieves or kinsmen, brigands or government soldiers—she gathered her skirts in her hands and hurried up another incline.

The higher she went, the thicker the fog became. Near the crest of the hill, it was white and dense as a bank of clouds. Kate climbed upward steadily, but more cautiously. Her red gown was damp and muddy, and she ached with weariness, but she moved on.

A nagging awareness lingered, for she grew more sure that someone was nearby, perhaps deliberately following her. She did not think it was Alec, for she had that much start on him. Glancing around, she could see little, for she stood in a trough between two slopes that formed a deep bowl of fog.

"*Kate!*"

She gasped, her heart jumped. She was sure the voice belonged to Alec—she knew the tone and timbre of it. He called again, and she thought the distorted echo came from far below where she stood.

He had indeed followed her.

"*Kate!*" His voice was faint, and nowhere close, and she had no idea which direction it came from. And suddenly she wanted to answer though she knew she should not.

She turned, hurried onward, stopped again. What if he was lost, what if he worried that she was lost? Rather than angry or impatient, he sounded concerned—and determined.

She would be foolish to run back to her captor, she told herself. She had gotten clear away and needed that advantage, for eventually he would find Duncrieff, and her.

At the crest of the next slope, the swirling mist thinned enough to reveal the drover's track and the raw shapes of gray rock and mossy turf. And she heard another sound, beyond the patter of rain and the eerie whoosh of the wind—footsteps crushing grass, and the low murmur of male voices. And they were much closer than Alec Fraser.

* * *

"Where in blazes is she," Alec muttered as he walked up yet another steep incline. "Damn it, Kate, where the devil have you gone this time?"

He had spread a much more colorful string of curses all the way up this latest set of slopes as he stuck doggedly to the trail. Once or twice he had glimpsed that red gown far ahead through the mist, so he knew she had found and followed the drover's track that he was now taking.

He called out again, his voice echoing, strange and lonely, in the misty hills.

His red woolen coat was heavy with dampness, its snug tailoring a hindrance as he climbed, but he was at least glad of his Highland kilt, which allowed him to make more rapid progress as he strode and leaped.

Though it might prove futile to follow Kate directly in this indecent soup, and though he knew he could find her family's castle through dogged inquiry, he went onward nonetheless. He stopped, peering around, seeing only bleak rock and muddy turf cloaked in fog. No flash of red satin, no bright golden head visibile anywhere. Had she turned off the drover's track already?

He swore again, under his breath, and climbed ahead.

After waking to a cold and empty bed and rushing furiously through the tavern room, snatching a biscuit out of Jack's hand as he went past—he had left the fellow gaping and without his breakfast biscuit, holding his swaddled babe and unable to follow, which only served Jack right, to Alec's mind—he had then made decent time in crossing the moor on horseback.

At that point, he had seen Kate's red gown far ahead through the rain, and though encouraged, he knew she was at least an hour ahead of him. Once he reached the foothills, he had left the horse at a small hut, where he discovered a withered old shepherd staying home out of the rain. The old man was glad to show the horse some hospitality in exchange for a coin. Alec had continued on foot, asking directions to the home of the MacCarrans.

Duncrieff is through those hills, the man had said, and on the other side, in a long glen. Take the old drover's track, he had advised.

Since then, Alec had seen enough glimpses of Kate's bright skirts that he had blessed his luck for red satin again. He followed the earthen path but lost sight of her somewhere amid a long stretch of rumpled foothills. The little wildcat was fleet and nimble in this territory. Though he was long-legged and fast, and not hindered by the drag of a damp gown, he did not know these hills as she did.

Glancing about as he hurried, Alec followed instinct more than logic through the fog. Time was running short for Kate's Highland Jacobites, he thought, and for any involved in a plot to conceal those Spanish weapons from the authority of the British government—including himself.

More than once, he had wanted to trust her enough, before she had taken off like this, to tell her about his covert interest in helping the Jacobites find and use that cache of weapons. Ever since he had met the girl, he had begun to feel differences within, slight cracks and chinks in the armor that he needed to lose—its constraints, he now realized, had protected him at first, and did him no good whatsoever now.

But if he lost Kate, if he never saw her again, he might just slide back into the shell in which he had existed for so long. He pursued her more for himself, he knew, than for his obligation to the government. Any questions he had for her were for the sake of his heart, not for the sake of military orders.

Like her, he was a spy, and like her, part of him felt rebellious indeed—but in his case, he realized now that he no longer wanted to be the man he was so accustomed to being—lonely, bitter, resistant to love. True, he had been getting along in life capably that way, until Kate had begun to work her magic on him.

Kate was not the only one who wanted to be free.

But his changing feelings had nothing to do with the fact that Kate MacCarran was his prisoner, and he was her military guardian. And both of them had best show up in Edinburgh soon, or their heads would share a price.

And he had best find those Spanish weapons before Ian Cameron or one of the recently arrested men—one of Kate's kinsmen, judging by the report Alec had heard—was coerced into revealing that information to the crown.

He trudged onward, distracted. He saw the need to make changes within himself, and a little struggle might be part of any rebirth, but the girl roiled and ruffled and bestirred him in every way. He would never be out here, lost in fog, but for her.

"Kate!" he called again.

He paused for breath. No wonder Highlanders were often braw and powerful men, he thought, looking at the hilltops in front of him. Regular sword practice kept him strong and limber, but this steep upward trek was still a challenge. Military duties that included riding between city and encampments, and otherwise sitting to study legal documents for General Wade and others, had made him a little lazy.

Nonetheless, he strode onward. "Kate! Katie!" he shouted, though he heard only echoes in answer.

After a while, he stopped near the feathery edge of the mist, staring into what looked like a magical realm: deep fog crowned a slope of turf and rugged rock, like a portal to another world where legends thrived and where those who entered might vanish within.

Kate had disappeared somewhere in those blanketed heights. For a moment, he could well believe she had fair magic in her.

"Where are you?" he called, voice echoing. "Kate!"

Kate . . . Kate, the sound returned to him.

If Kate had climbed this way, she could be lost, or hurt, or both. He felt as if he could not give up the search until he knew for certain that she was safe.

Searching for the best route into the fog, he heard sounds then—faint and distorted but real. And then he heard the unmistakable sound of steel sliding out of leather.

The sound sent chills down his spine.

He set his left hand on his dagger, his right on his sword. He had brought his weaponry with him, not sure what he might encounter if he, as a solitary soldier, ventured deep into Highland territory, where rebels and brigands roamed.

Waving his dirk in his left hand, his sword in his right, he turned warily. If he called out for Kate, the men would know where he stood. Bending, he grabbed up a few loose stones and scattered them down the hill.

He heard hissing whispers, and footsteps off to his left. He waited, still and scarcely breathing, then moved up the incline.

They leaped at him then, bursting out of the mist and over the rocks, three wild men waving wicked steel and looking for blood. Alec whipped his sword upward, ready for the assault. The first opponent came at him, and the sudden slam of steel jarred him to the shoulder, for the man, the older of the three, wielded a heavy broadsword.

They came at him all at once then, the older man and two younger. At first Alec thought he was seeing double in the mist, for the lads were identical. One was here, one was there, then they switched places, while the old man weaved between them, his blade smacking into Alec's, then the lads to right and left brought their swords to meet his. Alec spun, blocking and parrying as he defended himself to the best of his ability.

The younger Highlanders, who appeared to be twins, were quick, though not as skilled as the older man. Alec soon found that two at a leaping game, with the third man coming through the middle, was more than enough challenge in fog, on a slippery, rocky slope.

The oldest Highlander was grizzled, stocky, fierce as a bear. Lacking grace or finesse, he was a strong swordsman, using an older-style sword, a plain and brutal instrument. But what counted most at every turn was whether a blade struck, missed, or swept past only to return again.

Alec was schooled in Italian, German, and French technique as well as traditional Highland swordplay. His three challengers had obviously not studied any Italian manuals, but they were instinctive and ferocious fighters. Alec was hard-pressed to keep pace with all three at once. He had practiced often enough with multiple opponents, for his father and uncle, who trained him with his brother long ago, had insisted on it for sharpening awareness, agility, and for learning to think quickly.

What he had not learned, and what his opponents had mastered, was fighting on uneven natural terrain. The Highlanders were agile and swift on the slope, moving easily over rocks and tufts of heather and gorse. Alec had to glance downward now and then to avoid the natural hazards underfoot, a necessity he knew could be a fatal flaw in this fight.

The clash of steel echoed on. One of the younger men leaped on a boulder, and the other circled toward Alec's other side. Facing the old man between them, Alec beat back a volley of powerful strikes and lunged forward. His sword tip caught the thickness of the man's plaid, sliding into flesh, and the gray-haired Highlander stepped back, turning ashen.

The lads descended on him now, two at once. Alec danced back, his glance wary and his sword slashing at air, stabbing and missing. They were nimble devils, weaving back and forth, while their companion clutched his side, blood darkening his hand.

Then Alec saw her. She stepped out of the hillside and through the mist as if she stepped out of a fairy mountain, looking like a queen indeed in her scarlet gown, her hair like melting gold. If she had any touch of fairy blood in her, he saw it now, dazzling around her. For an instant, he stared—then turned back to the fight.

The Highlanders came at him from behind and beside, and Alec whirled, turned. When Kate ran toward him, Alec shouted for her to stay back. One lad swept his blade downward while Alec angled his to block it, while reaching his other hand out to push Kate away. In that moment, his opponent's heavy blade caught his arm.

He felt the strike more than the pain, and looked down in surprise to see that a cut to his left forearm had sliced through wool deep into flesh. Blood pooled in the gap. He felt oddly stunned, while the world around him began to tilt crazily.

The Highlanders dropped their swords, and Alec released his own. He stepped back, hand clapped over his arm, pressing against the warm gush that continued.

Kate ran to him, reaching out. Then Alec saw that the Highlanders were not her enemies, but her men. Like a fairy host, the warriors of the queen, they came behind her.

He sank to his knees suddenly. Kate dropped down with him to kneel in the muddy turf. Her men came closer.

Strong hands grabbed him just as the ground slanted upward.

Chapter 20

Click, clack, click-click.

He lay with his eyes closed, half-dreaming, images in his mind forming, the bed warm and comfortable, the pain in his arm receding. *Click, clack, click-click.*

Days, nights unmeasured in a big, deep bed, curtained in sumptuous green damask, the coverlets fine and warm, the linens soft. Quiet whispers, gentle and capable hands, hot soup and cool cloths, the pungent aromas of ointment and hot compresses.

Click-click-click.

All the while he struggled against draining weakness and fever. The wound on his arm had turned fierce, he knew. Someone had cleaned it, sewn it, cleaned it again. He remembered whiskey burning a path down his throat, the searing fire of the cauterizing iron, and the oblivion that followed.

And Kate was there through it all, amid the blur of unfamiliar faces and voices. He was aware of a plump, dark-haired woman with kind hands, and others, including the Highland men who had tried to kill him. A lovely woman had been there, too. She looked like Kate, but was with child. Or was she Kate in his fevered imagination, while he dreamed of life as he wished it could be?

Click, clack, click-click.

Kate's presence was security to him, was safety and love incarnate, and he clung to that, watched her when he could do little more than open his eyes and had no breath to thank her. She could have left him so easily. He did not know why she stayed.

Yet he knew he would have stayed for her. His feelings were very clear to him, as if emotions and hopes had been burned clean by the fever. Why had he not seen it before? It was so simple, so right. He loved her.

He turned his head. She sat by the fire, haloed in the golden light, head lowered, attention centered on a task. Her hands moved quickly, busily, over a small pillow in her lap. He heard the light tapping again. *Click-click-click.*

Thread bobbins, he suddenly saw, made the sound. A finespun web covered the little pillow she held, while she formed a web of thread; tiny pins fixed the design, and the pale threads were wound tight on a dozen or more slender bobbins that dangled over the slopes of the pillow. Kate moved the bobbins back and forth, plaiting and twisting, her hands graceful, adept. He had heard the noise throughout his illness.

"So you weave your fairy spells on a fine silken pillow," he said, his voice hoarse.

She looked up, smiled, so that his heart ached to see it. "It's lace," she said. "I love you."

At least he thought she said that before he slipped back into slumber. Fairy magic or none, he was in her thrall.

"We'll let your brother decide what's to be done with him," Neill Murray said. He was her brother's friend and ghillie to her sister's husband, Connor MacPherson, and he often spoke freely to the MacCarrans.

Beside him, Kate's cousin Allan MacCarran nodded grimly. "Rob will want to send him away."

"He cannot do that," Kate replied. "Captain Fraser could die if we move him now. Two days he fought fever and blood loss from that cut on his arm, and he is still weak. Your own wife helped me nurse him back to the land of the living, Neill Murray. He'll not go back." She dipped a cloth in a bowl of rose water that Mary Murray had brought, and dabbed at Alec's brow. The fever was gone and he slept, but she knew it could return without warning. "He's had a serious wound, and must recover."

"What about my wound?" Neill said, touching his side.

"Mary said it was only a deep scratch," Kate said. "How are you faring with it?"

"He's fine," Allan said. "Tough as rock, but whines when he takes a small hurt."

"Small! That lad's got a fierce sword hand, for all he's a king's man," Neill said, indicating sleeping Alec. "And he should not be here. He's a red soldier."

"What of Highland hospitality?" Kate asked sternly. "I, for one, am glad we have the care of him here."

"Aha," Neill remarked, glancing at Allan.

"What's this?" her cousin asked. "You never cared about an officer before. You could not wait to shake free of them, and with good reason."

She set down the cloth, and looked at the men who had entered the room not long ago. Standing, smoothing the covers over Alec as he slept, she turned and led the others out of the room and into the corridor, then turned.

"It seems we need a little privacy for this discussion," she said. "And you know I do not relish harm to any man, regardless of the color of his coat or the slant of his politics. There's nothing particular about that man in there."

"I am thinking he's very particular to you," Neill said. They all looked around as Roderick, one of Neill's twin sons, came down the corridor toward them. Black-haired and beautiful, he gave Kate a dimpled smile.

She nodded in return. She liked Roderick and his twin very much, and knew they were good friends of her sister Sophie and had been helpful to her when she had been stolen away by Connor MacPherson.

"Padraig has gone to find Duncrieff to tell him that Katherine has come home," Roderick said, "and he will let him know there's a red soldier with her. Other red soldiers will be out looking for them, so we must beware if he stays here."

"He'll soon be strong enough to leave here," Allan said.

"Not for a while. I am surprised Rob is not back yet," Kate said. "Do you think he is close to home by now?"

"Who can say? No doubt he's coming back over the hills with Connor MacPherson," Neill answered. "We had some trouble recently. Andrew MacPherson and your cousin, Donald MacCarran, were captured when they went to spy on the newest section of Wade's road. They were taken to Edinburgh Castle, we heard. Rob and Conn went out to learn what they could from the constable. Rob's been distracted by your arrest lately, and he's been out, along with his men, nearly every day to learn news of you. That's why the lads and I came across you, then the red soldier."

She nodded. "I'm so glad to be back, but I'm sorry about Andrew and Donald. At least my brother will be relieved that I'm back so he can concentrate on helping them now."

"And Ian Cameron, too. We all want that lad back as well. Padraig will find Rob and Connor and bring them back quickly," Roderick said. "And Padraig has Thomas MacPherson with him. If they meet up with red soldiers, both are armed with fine pistols, those Spanish-made flintlocks. We found a few, but the rest—"

Kate shook her head. "Do not speak of that matter. That's why Andrew and Donald were taken to Edinburgh Castle—did you not realize?" She spoke in a whisper.

"What do you mean?" Allan demanded.

"I heard they were arrested with Spanish weapons. Wade wants to find the hidden cache. Captain Fraser is looking for them as well. Take care not to speak too openly of that matter."

Neill frowned. "It is not safe to have this red soldier of yours here."

She returned his gaze. "We cannot send him away."

"For all he's braw and bonny," Neill said, "and for all he seems to have won your heart, he's got to leave."

Kate glanced away. "I have not given anyone my heart."

"No?" Allan asked. "Well, I agree with Neill. Your captain goes, or we'll have even more trouble."

"And you, lass, will want to keep your loyalty where it belongs, home with kin and clan," Neill added sternly.

Kate said nothing. How could she expect them to understand that she had fallen in love, when she should not have risked it, and now loved an officer of the crown? As a fairy-blessed MacCarran, she must be careful whom she chose to love. Neill and Allan knew it, and she supposed it was part of their concern. Already there was trouble brewing over Alec's presence at Duncrieff, which did not augur well for the future.

She touched her crystal pendant. "He'll stay," she said firmly, looking at the others.

"Stubborn lass." Neill shook his head.

"Katherine, you know your brother will not be

happy to find a red soldier here," Allan said. "Let alone the one who arrested you and pursued you out here. They will know where we are, whether he stays or goes, now. He cannot be trusted. I say we send him away now, tonight or tomorrow, before he recovers enough to learn more about us and our glen."

Roderick nodded agreement. "We can carry him by cart to a spot outside of Glen Carran, when he is well. He can make his way east from there."

"What sort of hospitality is that?" Kate asked bitterly. "We pride ourselves in the Highlands on helping friend and enemy alike in time of need. You cannot do this."

"In this case, it's wise. Rob will agree," Neill said.

"What of the lists, Katherine, and the weapons?" Allan asked. "With all the nursing you've done, we've had little chance to discuss these things. You said you saw Cameron. What more?"

"When Rob arrives, I'll tell you. Not now, not here." She glanced at Alec, who slept.

"You have other things to explain, too," Allan said. "You've changed somehow, lass, though I cannot quite say how."

"I have. And this man will not leave here."

"He should be out of this glen," Neill said.

"I suspect the lass has other reasons for what she says," Allan murmured. "If so, she could endanger this clan with the wrong choice if I remember the fairy legend properly."

"I will make the right choice," Kate said. "I will."

* * *

247

Later, when moonlight filtered through the windows and the castle seemed to slumber, Kate sat on the edge of Alec's bed. The fire in the hearth crackled, its smoke fragrant, making the room warm and cozy. Enclosed by curtains drawn nearly shut, the bed seemed a peaceful space. Kate dipped a cloth in the basin on the table beside the bed and stroked the dampness gently over Alec's cheek, beard-roughened and firm, over his jaw with its stubborn, handsome contour, over his strong throat, where his pulse thumped steadily though his eyes were closed.

His fever had broken early on the previous morning, though Neill's wife Mary had given him a potion that kept him slumbering through the day to speed his healing. Kate felt vastly relieved that the crisis of the illness and injury had passed, though she now felt a new anxiousness—he must leave soon, for her kinsmen had determined that for the sake of all of them.

She slid the damp cloth over his shoulders. He was without a shirt, and she skimmed the moisture over the rounded muscles of his shoulders and arms, and across his chest, where power lay banked beneath smooth skin. The cloth passed over his breastbone, his heart, over his ribs. His small, flat nipples tightened, he shifted, his breathing changed. The beating of her heart quickened, and she licked her lips a little, rocked with the motion as she pushed the cloth slowly over his chest, down his abdomen. His lips moved, his eyelids fluttered, and he seemed on the verge of waking, sighing so that his abdomen rose and sank under her hand with the damp cloth.

She did not doubt that Rob would agree with their kinsmen when he arrived. As soon as Alec's strength returned, he would be escorted elsewhere.

This night was perhaps her last chance to be alone with him.

She moved the cloth up and down, avoiding his bandaged left arm, which rested on a small pillow. Touching the cloth to his chest again, she watched drops of water trickle over his bare skin to enter the soft mat of dark hair that feathered over his chest and arrowed beneath the coverlet to his lower abdomen. With one hand, she pushed the cover down a little and brought the cloth down with it, sweeping, tracing, easing the warm, damp, soft cloth over his skin.

He roused under the covers, bold and already rigid, and as she stroked the cloth downward, she saw his unmistakable response. Her own body answered with a quickening. The yearning grew, heating her from within.

She trailed her hand after the cloth, taking up the moisture with her palm. He was a bonny and beautiful man, she thought, his skin cool and smooth, softened by a mat of hair that was delightful to touch. Chiseled in places, rounded and comforting in others, he carried strength in every fiber of his form. Flawless skin slid over taut muscle as he moved a little, the sheen lovely in the amber glow of the firelight. He stirred her within like no one ever had, ever would.

Even if her kinsmen did not send him away, she would have done so herself, knowing he could not remain here for long without raising suspicion in the government, and she could not travel east with him to fulfill the obligation in Edinburgh. Yet despite all the tugs and tussles between them, she had come to realize that she loved him.

Shifting on the bed to reach his side, leaning over him, she pressed against him and felt him arouse further, just beneath her, so that she moaned a little on a breath, to herself, and moved closer still, sliding her palm up along the muscled terrain of his abdomen.

"Kate, lass," he murmured, "either stop that now, or there will be consequences."

"Oh!" Gasping, she sat upright. "I thought you were asleep!"

"How could I be, with so lovely a creature here with me?"

"You!" She slapped him a little with the damp cloth. Laughing softly, he caught her wrist with his right hand. "And I was bathing you all this time—why did you let me go on with it?"

"That hardly needs an answer," he said, drawing her close to him. He brought his right, uninjured arm fully around her, and she fell gently against his chest where he reclined against a bank of pillows. "I was up and about after supper, but you were not here then," he said.

"I was with my kinsmen, and my sister. We thought you were still sleeping."

"Aye. Well, a servant left a fine meal, a pot of tea and one of lemonade, too—though it was not what I would prefer—"

"Lemonade and tea are all you'll get," she said, sliding her hand in circles over his bare chest, feeling the heartbeat beneath, "unless you want cocoa."

"Lord, no. I ate a little, had the tea, then had a bit of a wash myself, and I read among the books in the case over there. Poetry and such. I was dozing when you came in a little while ago. Since you wanted to give me another bath, I wasn't going to refuse."

She gasped a little and laughed as he nudged her downward to nestle beside him in the warm, deep bed. "Alec," Kate said, slipping her arm around his neck. "So you're feeling well?"

"Oh, very well," he said, nuzzling her cheek with his lips.

"If so—Alec, my kinsmen will want you to leave Duncrieff. So this night . . . may be our last . . . to be together."

He stopped, breath caressing her cheek, and she heard him sigh. He drew back. "And I suppose you will not be coming with me to Edinburgh?"

"They do not want me to do that." She gazed at him soberly.

"I see. And what is it you want?"

She closed her eyes. "You," she whispered.

He sighed low, nearly a growl, and held her for a moment, his cheek, whiskered and rough, pressed against her own. The warm, masculine scent of him filled her senses. "Katie . . ."

Before she could draw breath to ask or reply, she felt his lips graze over her cheek, her jaw, then her mouth, and she returned the kiss with sudden fervor, feeling thunderstruck suddenly by desire, by hunger.

Circling her arms around him, she pressed herself against him. He was fully awake, for he murmured her name, began to question—and she hushed him with a finger to his lips and withdrew it to kiss him again. As his hands traced over her, his kisses only deepened the fierce yearning that grew within her.

She sighed against his lips, ran her hands over his smooth back, his sculpted shoulders and torso. Her mouth craved his, and her body's hunger was greater, overwhelming, demanding, and when he rolled her to her back, she breathlessly helped him to unlace her bodice, to strip away the gown and the stays that were only a hindrance, for she knew what she wanted. Thinking about what it would be like to be without him, she could not bear it any longer. She wanted him to make her his own.

Fairy legends or none, obligations to her clan or none, she wanted to love this man here and now, secretly and deliciously, if just for one night. Soon he would leave her life forever.

He lay back and raised his outer knee, pulling her more fully on top of him, his body hard and warm and sensual against her, and when he pulled at her chemise, she sat up and stripped it away quickly, flinging it away, sliding back into the circle of his arm with a deep sigh, capturing his lips with her own.

His fingers found her breasts, caged their fullness, eased over the nipples, one and then the other. She cried out softly and slid upward as he came closer, and when his mouth closed upon her nipple she shuddered. The joy that spilled through her made her desperate for him.

The curtained bed, dark and warm, created a haven of protection. She felt free to do as she wanted and needed—and she needed to trust him, to love him, to give herself entirely within this private space. The world would never know what they did. Nothing mattered but touching, kissing, pleasures given and returned. Longing filled her with a kind of fire, a wildness that brimmed over in her, which she needed to share with him.

If she never saw him again, she would know, finally, what it was truly to love him.

Sliding her hands over his firm and beautiful body, she pushed back the bedcovers and shifted over him, sighing out again as his hand slipped down and touched her, brought her to exquisite shudders, so that she arched and gasped. When a sweet release rushed through her, she moved and placed her thighs on either side of his hips, pressing herself against him, wrapping her hand around the hard, heated length of him.

He sighed, eyes closed, arched toward her, shaped her hips with his hands. He grew still beneath her, breath heaving slightly, and she felt the deep, needful pulse of him against her. Leaning forward, she rubbed her body against him so that he groaned deep, and she felt the vibration of that all through her. She stretched to kiss his mouth, lingering there, tracing her tongue with his, over his, and she felt her own need throbbing heavily within her.

Lifting slightly, she slid her body along his and found that his body and hers formed a natural and perfect match, so that she rose and settled herself over him, taking part of him into her, pulsing over him, breathing hard—willing away the sweet pain of the first time— then she eased herself downward again. The motion was hers to make, the decision hers.

He caught his breath, grasped the tuck of her waist with his hand, then drew in a breath as he moved upward. At that moment, she slid down, fitting over him like hand to glove, and she cried out, so softly, as he filled her to the brim.

She pulled back a little, opened her eyes, saw him do the same. In the darkness and firelit glow, his gaze met hers, keen and piercing. "You . . . oh, God," he whispered. "Wait—"

"Hush," she breathed, knowing he had just discovered that he was the first—the very first. "Hush—I want this. I want to know what this is, with you. And I want you to know, too, what we would have together, if—we—could. . . ."

But she could whisper no more, for she was leaning on her arms, easing downward, and she felt the glorious rhythm shudder through him as he began to move within her. His thrusts formed a cadence that flashed into a potent, exquisite flame inside of her own body. She rocked with him, cried out as he groaned, and the strength and the wonder of it overwhelmed her then. For an instant she soared upward, his hand at her waist and his heart thumping against her own the only line

254

that kept her earthbound, and where she wanted to be—with him.

She fell forward then, her hair loosened and slipping down like a golden curtain, and felt herself emerge slowly from the heart-slamming magic that had poured through her. He sucked in a breath, another, pressing his head to her own.

Somehow she felt different, as if she had found a new clarity of heart, of soul. She would have told him so, but could not find the words, tucking her head against his shoulder.

He took her into the circle of his arm, his body lightly covered with sweat, as was her own. She snuggled against him, closing her eyes as he kissed her brow.

"Kate, I'm sorry. I did not realize that you had never—"

"Hush. We will not speak of it," she whispered. "It does not matter. You were the first, and you are the only one, and that is all that matters."

"But Kate—"

She pressed a finger to his lips. "You had better rest now." She rose to hands and knees, climbed nimbly over him, and slid her feet to the floor, gathering up her clothes. When he reached out for her, she stepped away.

"Come back here," he growled low.

She shook her head, stepped away, pausing to pull on her chemise, then her dress over that. Stopping to glance at him, blowing him a small kiss in the darkness, she whirled and fled the room.

Chapter 21

❝**O**ch, you're awake and alert today. Greetings, sir." The woman smiled as she approached with a brass tray, which she set on an inlaid table beside his bed. The table already held a tall, shining silver candelabra with three fat, fragrant candles flickering bright on a gloomy afternoon. "I think you must be feeling better!"

Alec sat up and nodded a greeting. "Much stronger. Thank you for helping me, madam. I know you've been in and out of the room all the while that I've been sick. And I know that you did not need to do that—I am aware that I might not be welcome here."

"Highland hospitality is owed to whoever comes knocking at the door," she said, "even red soldiers."

"I'm not an English redcoat, but of a Highland company," he said. "I am Captain Alexander Fraser."

"I know. I'm Mary Murray, wife to the man you cut."

He blinked. "Madam, I'm sorry—"

"No need. He's fine enough, my Neill. But oh, what a wicked wound you had!" She spoke Scots rather than Gaelic, he noticed. "Now sit up, Alexander Fraser, and have some soup." She smiled and plumped the pillows behind him and added another blanket to the bed, though the room was warm already. He smiled in return.

She was a handsome woman, Alec noticed, lush and rounded, with light blue eyes and black curls framing her face beneath a lace-edged cap. She picked up a small china bowl filled with steaming dark liquid, its scent rich and familiar.

"Chocolate." He nearly groaned.

"Aye, Kate said your own family makes the very cocoa powder we use, and the tea and coffee, too! Fraser's Fancy tins! Imagine!" She smiled, folding her hands. "It's fine stuff, that. Neill buys some for me whenever he goes to Perth or Callander for the cattle markets and suchlike. I do love a wee sip o' chocolate drink now and then. Muckle fine, your cocoa wafers."

"Ah," he said, accepting the little bowl. "I'm glad you like it. I will send you some once I return to Edinburgh."

"*Och*, I dinna want you to go to trouble for me."

"No trouble at all." He sipped. The hot chocolate was good, hot and sweet, with a thick layer of foam on the top. "Excellent, Mrs. Murray. A deep froth, and quite hot. I like the extra sweetness." He had never enjoyed

257

chocolate drink much, but he found that he genuinely enjoyed this.

" 'Tis a bitter brew without extra sugar cracked off the sugar loaf, and it needs the best cream from the first milking, too," she said. "And I whip it very well. They've a fine silver chocolate pot here at Duncrieff, with a stirring stick—whatever that's called—"

"Molinillo," he answered, "or moussoir."

"The very thing. At home I do not have a chocolate pot, so I pour it from one cup into another, which gives it a fine thick foam on top, given enough pouring."

"That's a traditional old method, and very reliable." He sipped again. "So you use the wafers in the tins, and add more sugar? Our powder is already mixed with sugar, and dried into wafers and packed in the tins. It only needs breaking off, and mixing with a cupful of boiling water."

"Aye. 'Tisna sweet enough. City folk must drink it verra bitter, I think."

"This is truly excellent." He vowed to send Mary Murray not only a crate of cocoa tins, but a good silver chocolate pot and molinillo. "I shall tell my aunt and uncle, when I see them, that the best chocolate drink I ever had was in the Highlands."

"*Och*, Captain Fraser," she said, as she took the empty bowl from him. Then she handed him a larger bowl, wide and shallow, filled with hot soup. "Sit higher, so you'll no' spill this. It's a fine beef broth with vegetables from my own garden, and they came dear this year, so you'll eat it all."

Alec shifted obediently and accepted the bowl and

spoon. "Thank you. I appreciate this, Mrs. Murray."

"*Tcha!* You were weak as a bairn when I first saw you. Your strength will return quickly, for you're a healthy man"—she said it with an appreciative smile, and he chuckled at the implied compliment—"but you must rest, and eat that broth, and more, to gain back your strength."

He nodded, sipped at the soup. Looking past the blue damask hangings on the bed, he saw a well-appointed room with mahogany furnishings, windows draped in ivory brocade, Turkey carpets in rich colors on the wooden floor.

"Duncrieff is a fine castle," he said. "A fine home."

"Aye, 'tis. Himself, the chief o' Clan Carran, is no' here at present, gone into the hills wi' Lord Kinnoull, who married Miss Katherine's sister, Sophie. You were on Kinnoull's lands when Neill and them caught you."

He nodded, touching his bandaged arm in its cloth sling. "How did they come upon us that day, do you know?"

"Neill and our sons were out in the hills, and heard you calling for Katherine. When they saw your red coat, they took it for a threat. They've been searching for her ever since . . . well, we heard she had been taken by the red soldiers. And then a miracle returned her to us."

Mrs. Murray apparently knew about Kate's involvement, Alec thought, frowning a little. No doubt they all did, here at Duncrieff. "Are you kin to Katherine Mac-Carran, Mrs. Murray?"

"Not blood kin, but friends of her family."

Alec nodded, glancing around the well-appointed bedroom, all he had seen of the castle so far. The view of the mountains through the tall windows was spectacular. "This is a fine place."

"You'll see more of it soon, when you're on your feet. Be sure to see the Fairy Cup of Duncrieff, too. 'Tis the prize of the clan and kept in the drawing room here. They say there's fairy power passed through generations of the MacCarrans of Duncrieff. Kate and Sophie both have a touch of it, and a fine lot o' mischief that has caused." She smiled impishly.

"I can imagine. Have you known Miss MacCarran a long time?"

"We've known Katherine and her sister and brother since they were bairns." Mary narrowed her eyes. "Just how well do you know her, sir?"

He cleared his throat and dipped his spoon into the soup again. "Not well enough," he finally said.

"*Och*, all the lads want to know her well. And so her kinsmen have to protect her from them." She watched him thoughtfully.

"Seems to me," he murmured, "that they could have protected her a little better than they did."

"Aye well, it may seem so. But with that fairy blood in her, they could either lock her in a tower or make the most of that charm she was born with. I suppose you might know that she has the fairy way about her, Captain."

He laughed ruefully. "I've heard something about it. Sounds like a delightful family legend."

"*Och*, there are many stories about the fairy gift of

260

the MacCarrans. Some have the glamourie about them so that they can charm and conjure, and some have a way wi' growing things, and some have the Sight, and some have a healing touch . . . oh, there are so many stories in this clan. They have their fair share of magic, these MacCarrans." She smiled, eyes sparkling.

"I'd have to agree," Alec said, chuckling.

"Eat your soup, Captain Fraser. Katherine made that for you. She's been devoted to you these days—even slept over there on that wee sofa at night." She pointed across the room.

"I know," he said, remembering vague, comforting memories of her constant presence during his brief, fierce illness. "Where is she now?" He lowered his gaze, remembering their passionate, dreamlike encounter the night before, and he realized how very much he wanted to see her again.

"I sent her to her room to get some rest. She's been doing all this for you as if she were your own devoted wife. So what I'd like to know," Mary Murray went on, "is how like a husband you've been to her."

He frowned. "Husband?"

"You know what I mean. The girl has a magic about her that makes men fall in love with her. They canna resist her if she turns that glamourie on them."

"Glamourie?" he asked curiously.

"A fairy enchantment. She bedazzles men when she wants."

He nodded and dipped his spoon in the soup.

"But I've never known her to return the interest."

"No?" Alec met the woman's serious glance.

"There's something different about you, sir, and I think she knows it. I think you've become verra important to her, Captain."

"Madam, I assure you I have no ill intentions toward her."

"I believe it," she said after a moment. "But you'd better hope that her brother and kinsmen believe it, too."

"I have nothing to hide from them, Mrs. Murray."

"Good. You know, you could make this situation better for all concerned, sir."

"Aye?" He waited, expecting her to tell him to clear out of Duncrieff as fast as he could.

She leaned toward him. "Marry the lass," she whispered. She took the empty bowl from his hands. "Marry her, and make it right for both of you. For everyone. That's my advice. And dinna tell a soul I said so. It's just for you to think about."

Dumbstruck, Alec stared at her.

"If you've bedded the lass, then you should wed her. You're gentleman enough to know that yourself."

He did not know if he was being reprimanded or encouraged. "And gentleman enough to make no comment about it to anyone other than the lady herself," he murmured.

"You dinna need to, I can see it for m'self. There would be a kerfuffle over her marrying you, but you can get 'round it."

"I'm sure her kinsmen would object," he said, folding one hand over the other.

"They would at first, but once they see she's happy, there would be a change of heart in the matter. This clan believes strongly in their fairy legends, and tradition says those who have the fairy ways, as Katherine and Sophie do, must marry only for true love—or the whole clan will suffer if a wrong choice is made. So they say."

"True love?" He blinked, startled. Was it possible? Suddenly, surely, he knew that it was.

"I think it is a bunch of blether, m'self, this MacCarran need for true love. Though Sophie did well by her Connor," she added thoughtfully. "Well, I say, just marry the one what makes yer heart flippit, the one who makes you laugh and knows you like no other. Marry the one you want to see on your pillow for all your life. That's good enough for me. But they will have their legends here at Duncrieff."

"Mrs. Murray," Alec said, "you are a woman of wisdom."

"I know." She grinned. "And if you do wed that lass, you can protect her when she goes to Edinburgh to face the courts."

"She does not intend to face the courts, from what she tells me," he remarked.

"*Och*, but if you're with her, you'd keep her safe, and the threat of it all would be lifted." Mary nodded as if she were certain that would happen. Taking the bowl, she bid him farewell and quietly left the room.

Alec frowned to himself, thoughts racing. Dear God, he realized, Mrs. Murray was right. He had not seen it quite that way before. He sat up, shoved a hand through his hair.

He had let the MacLennans believe that he and Kate

were married at the inn. At the time he had done it to keep the girl with him. But he had loved her, held her, as if she were his bride—she deserved his respect. He ought to marry her—he wanted to do that, though it stunned him to realize it fully.

Now he knew—now he felt sure that whatever charm Kate possessed could only enhance what he felt for her. Love could not be created by intent—it came from a far greater magic to blossom of its own accord.

Love or not, it was unthinkable for a custodial officer to marry his female prisoner. And marriage had been the last goal on his mind for years, ever since he had lost it so tragically.

Yet suddenly, wildly, marrying Kate made perfect sense.

Chapter 22

Tapping lightly on the door before entering the room, Kate was surprised to see Alec awake. He looked strong and healthy, if ill at ease, for he perched on the edge of the bed with the thick ivory coverlet, embroidered by her mother years ago, wrapped around him. His torso was bare, his left arm held by a cloth sling against him. One leg and foot stuck out beneath the coverlet, toes pressed to the floor.

"I've nothing to wear but this, apparently," he said, indicating the coverlet.

She crossed the room toward him. In the firelight, his bare skin was sheened smooth, and his hair, freed of its queue and black ribbon, swept softly over his shoulders, glinting like dark whiskey in the light. His gaze, blue-gray as a stormy sea, compelled her toward him.

Thinking of the way he had loved her, touched her, the other night, she caught her breath. "I've come to save you, then," she said, "for I've brought a clean shirt." She set the bundle down on the bed. "Your plaid and jacket are being cleaned and mended."

"I'll need more than a shirt if I'm to walk out of this room, my lass," he murmured with a wry smile.

She nodded, swallowed, did not want to think about his leaving Duncrieff. He would expect her to go with him to Edinburgh; she was, after all, still under arrest.

Remembering what she carried in her pocket, she drew out a thick envelope. "This was in your jacket."

He accepted it and set it aside. "It's a letter from my aunt in Edinburgh."

"It smells heavenly," she said. "Like chocolate."

"Now and then she sends me a wee sample of something my uncle is working on—an eating chocolate, something like a wafer, but it is meant to be eaten like a small pastry, all of chocolate."

She smiled. "That would taste wonderful!"

He grimaced. "It might, but my uncle is fond of chocolate in the traditional Spanish style. With pepper," he emphasized. "Believe me, it is not too pleasant when you bite into it in solid form. His experiments continue, and the sample in that letter could have hot peppers in it. It's the way the cacao powder was mixed in the Americas, where the Spaniards first learned about chocolate from the savage tribes there," he explained. "*Xocalatl* is what they called it there, and they

266

drank it cold and unsweetened, sometimes with very hot peppers added."

Kate wrinkled her nose. "I cannot imagine that—it's such a lovely, rich drink. We've always made it with lots of thick cream and sugar—it's the only way I've ever had it prepared."

"You're fortunate," he said, and she laughed a little.

"So you were taking me to their house in Edinburgh?"

"I am planning on that, aye," he said, in a careful tone.

She glanced away to pick up the shirt and hand it to him, but he looked askance at it. "I'll need my plaid with that."

"A shirt is all you need for recuperating in bed."

"All I need for bed," he murmured, touching her arm, "is you, Kate . . . my God, I do." He seemed surprised by his own words.

Her breath caught in her throat, and shivers plunged through her as he drew her toward him, opening his knees, coverlet draped generously over him, to bring her close, circling his uninjured arm around her waist, and he slid his hand along her back so that she leaned inward.

She could not help herself, wanted to pull away and could not. His nearness took her breath away, and as his lips met hers, she simply melted. This was what she wanted—tender touching, shared passion, and love. She wanted only to be with him.

And what must be said, what must be done, seemed only to interfere with what felt most real to her, what she most desired. She did not want to think, to argue, to bargain anymore.

His lips brushed over hers, yet she could not allow him to dissolve her will further. She pulled back, stepped away, picked up the shirt, and dumped it in his lap.

"You should be resting," she said, while his hand slid away from her waist.

"I've had more than enough rest," he growled, his voice hoarse with what she knew was desire. "I'm mending quickly now. And we've got to be away from here, you and I, and off to Edinburgh." With one arm in the sling, he began to pull the shirt awkwardly over his head.

"I'm not going with you," she said quietly.

Thrusting his head through the neck of the shirt, he paused, then slowly drew the cloth down over his torso, empty sleeve hanging. He stared at her. "I cannot leave without you."

"I will stay here, with my kinsmen about me. You must go," she said, drawing back farther, away from his spell. "My kinsman Allan thinks so, and our friend Neill Murray."

"I do not doubt they want me out of here, but you must come with me. I have yet to meet your brother and speak with him."

"He will say the same."

"You're expected in Edinburgh. If you intend to hide from that, you would have to put yourself into exile and leave Scotland altogether."

"My father was exiled nine years ago," she said. "We lived away from Scotland and Duncrieff for years because of it. He never saw Scotland again, for he died at

James Stuart's court in Rome. I'll stay here." She folded her arms.

Alec tipped his head. "Once you make up your mind, you never give in, do you?"

"Rarely. And I'm safe here. Duncrieff is remote enough. After a while, Katie Hell would be forgotten. Only you," she said, "would know the truth of my name outside of my own kin. You and Jack."

"So you expect me to just walk away from you?"

She glanced down, her heart aching so that she pressed her crossed arms against herself. "I would have to ask your promise . . . to keep my identity a secret."

"Another bargain? What would you give me in return?"

She raised her gaze to his. "My trust."

"That's a fine reward, lass." He reached out, took her arm and pulled her toward him again, so that her hip met his thigh, coverlet draped between them. "But I cannot leave you."

"Can you not?" She could hear the soft sound of her breathing as she waited.

He pulled her so close, then, that she leaned against his chest, so close she could feel his heartbeat under her hand lifted between them. So close that his cheek brushed hers. "There are other matters to consider," he said, as his lips grazed over her cheek to touch her mouth.

"Oh," she breathed, feeling her legs wilt. "What?"

He nudged her nose with his, slipped his tongue along her lower lip, so that she sucked in a breath and melted further, leaned against him, felt his arm encircle her.

269

"You are still under arrest," he murmured, his deep voice resonating through her. She began to pull away, and his hand tightened at her back, his lips and breath warmed her, thrilled her, even as his words threw her into turmoil. "And you remain under the legal custody of an appointed agent of the government."

"You," she said.

"Me," he breathed, and his lips took hers again. She moaned in surrender, then in protest, and pushed away.

"Do not do that," she said. "I cannot think when you—"

"When I what?" he asked. His eyes were so very blue, she thought. Had she fully noticed their extraordinary beauty before?

"When you ply that magic over me," she said breathlessly. "When you touch me, kiss me, I cannot help myself. Do you know that you are the only man who has ever made me feel like this? And yet you are the one who would take me away from here." She felt a sob rising in her throat.

"Kate," he whispered, reaching out to take her hand.

She shook him off angrily. "You had better leave."

He shook his head, sighed. "Listen to me. You are to appear before the Court of Justiciary within a few days, and I am to bring you there. If we do not—"

"You said you do not always follow rules." She glanced at him. "What would happen if you went back without me?"

"I might be arrested, I suppose, on a charge of treason, or aiding a spy. Grant would see to that. He wants you brought to justice, not for spying, but for humiliating him."

"Oh, God," she whispered, shaking her head. "I did not really think—what then, if you were arrested because of me?"

"I suppose I would have to find some way to escape—Jack would help me—and would come looking for you here."

"And then?" Her breath faltered.

"We would flee into exile, you and I."

She admired the ability he had to add a wry touch, now and then, to make even serious situations seem manageable. She was often too serious. "But you have family to consider."

"So do you." He reached for her hand again. "Kate," he said, rubbing his thumb over the back of her hand, "marry me."

She put a hand to her bodice, feeling a sort of panic. She thought of the Fairy Cup, of the legends, of her own determination never to marry. What if this love was not true, what if this red soldier was not trustworthy after all, what if her clan suffered for her choice? "I cannot. I must not."

"Do you need a finer proposal?" He indicated the coverlet. "I would look silly kneeling in this, or in my shirt alone. You'll have to take me as I am. Marry me, lass." His thumb moved over her hand, making little warm circles.

Her breath was coming in gulps. She wanted to throw her arms around him, tell him that she loved him, that she did not care about legends or arrests or what her family would say about a redcoat, or his about a spy. For so long she had not been able to do exactly as she wanted. There were more constraints on fairy-blessed Katie Hell than anyone realized.

"We hardly know each other," she finally said.

"I could better protect you in Edinburgh if we were wed."

Shaking her head, she looked away, her arm outstretched, hand in his. "My kinsmen would never allow it, so it does not matter if it would help or not."

He tipped his head. "Since when do you go by what others say?" He lifted her hand to his lips, kissed her knuckles. She closed her eyes for a moment. "There are more than enough reasons. We've shared the same bed, and what we've done there . . . and elsewhere . . . certainly obligates me to marry you, if nothing else."

Again she shook her head. "Not enough basis for a marriage. Look at Jack and Jeanie. And she still refuses to marry him."

"Jean is very stubborn. And she's not sure she trusts Jack."

"Then she and I have a good deal in common. I release you from any obligation you might feel. There," she said, lifting her chin high. Pride was the only defense she had against her stubborn heart, which desperately wanted this. But she was afraid that if she made the wrong choice, her clan would suffer.

She loved Alec, she was sure—but she was not sure if he loved her, or whether he had decided to marry her out of a sense of responsibility because they had shared a bed.

She did not know if what she felt was true love, and she did not know how to tell. How did one know such a thing?

Alec drew her closer. "Listen, Kate. Our marriage would give me a better means of protecting you. But I will not beg at your feet like a pup."

She frowned, and did not answer, glancing away.

His fingers gripped hers. "I . . . care about you, Kate."

Startled, thrilled, she stared up at him. Cared about her . . . was that enough to fulfill the demanding legends of her clan? She thought not, and shook her head. "I cannot marry you."

"When you were sitting by my bedside," he said, "weaving your bit of lace—and in my fevered state, I thought you wove a spell—what did you tell me, then?"

She remembered exactly what she had said spontaneously, when he had been so ill. "I said . . . that I love you," she whispered.

"Do you?" He held her hand.

"Why ask me this now?" she asked. "Was it . . . what happened between us? You do not need to marry me because of that."

"Hush." He touched a finger to her lips. "Sometimes . . . fever burns away what we do not need, so that we can see what is most essential to us."

She leaned forward, kissed his lips. "Alasdair Callda, with all your rules and orders. With all your *thinking*."

273

"I am not an impulsive man, true. I am a staid sort. But you have whirled me 'round and 'round, Katie Hell. Life looks different to me now than before. I am trying to find my bearings again." He half smiled. "With you."

She felt a whirling inside herself, too. Smiling sadly, she slipped her hand out of his. "I cannot marry you," she whispered. "There are too many differences between you and me. Marriage between us would not be the right thing if you are only trying to help me. I am bound by clan tradition to marry only . . . under certain conditions. Please understand."

She waited, hoping wildly that he would suddenly tell her what she most needed to hear from him—that what he felt for her was extraordinary. He only frowned.

"I understand that I am being refused," he said quietly.

She pulled in a breath, began to speak—but she could not explain this to him. To be sure of that sort of love, she must hear it from his lips—but he had said nothing of the sort.

"I'll go find out if the rest of your things have been mended," she blurted, and turned away, tears stinging her eyes.

Chapter 23

Bending over the silken pillow in her lap, frowning slightly, Kate switched the long, slender thread bobbins back and forth, back and forth, plaiting and twisting the threads to form a fine mesh for the strip of lace she was creating. When she finished a small section, she stopped to move the brass pins that held the fine net of threads in place. Her fingers moved so fast over the pillow, so deftly and without much thought on her part, that her mind was free to think.

And all she could think about was Alec. His marriage proposal last night had set her spinning, and her thoughts and feelings had not yet come to ground since then. What should she do? She had to know what was right—for her, for him, for the clan that depended so on her making the right choice.

Click, click. The bobbins tapped lightly against one another as she switched the threads around, twisted the little spindles, wove the threads in and out, in and out. *Click, click.*

The work was soothing, calming to her, the repetitive movements reliable, entrancing. She need only step aside, sometimes, and let her fingers take care of the work. She had learned lace making in the English convent in Bruges, where her sister Sophie had been educated. *Click, click, clack.* She could lose herself in the rhythms of her fingers and the long, slim bobbins as she wove them, switched them, plaiting and twisting the delicate white threads.

As she worked, she glanced at her sister Sophie, who sat at a large table perusing a rather large illustrated book. Sophie's advancing pregnancy made her favorite occupation, gardening, a little impractical, and so she had settled for another morning in the library studying about the plants she loved.

"I'd so much rather be mucking about in the garden just now than reading about it," Sophie said, flipping another page. "It's more enjoyable to learn about plants and flowers from Nature. But Connor has suggested that I study and read as much as I can about these things. He has a library full of them at Kinnoull House—he studied horticulture and farming, did you know?"

"Not the fine art of brigandry?" Kate murmured, and Sophie laughed.

"He's a master of that," she agreed. "At any rate, I

will not be doing much kneeling in the garden, with this babe coming after the new year." She smoothed a hand over her rounded belly. Her sack dress, of pale blue brocade that reflected her remarkable light blue eyes, gave her growing figure plenty of room to expand. Kate watched her flaxen-haired sister and smiled. Sophie looked lush and blooming, as bright as one of her beloved flowers, which seemed to blossom almost magically wherever their mistress planted them.

Kate would never have imagined her sweet-tempered older sister holding her own with a rogue like Connor MacPherson, but she had done so, outwitting the man at his own game. Now Kate understood how her sister had fallen so totally in love with her handsome Highlander. Sophie had found genuine love, and her happiness had contributed to a peaceful atmosphere at Duncrieff, so welcome after the tragedies and unhappy events of the years that had gone before.

So there was something to the fairy legend, Kate thought. A loving marriage had brought more magic to the clan. *Love makes its own magic*, she thought, remembering the motto on the rim of Duncrieff's Fairy Cup. Sophie's experience gave her more hope for her own future.

"I love these Dutch tulips, the variegated sort, like red and yellow flames," Sophie mused, turning another page. "I wonder if Connor would let me send for more bulbs from the Netherlands."

"The man would let you do anything," Kate said as she plaited a group of delicate threads. Gradually she was creating a pattern of linked acanthus leaves. "It will take me years to finish this strip of lace," she muttered. "I've had hardly any time to work on it at all."

And if she went to prison, she thought grimly, she would never have a chance to complete it. She thought again of Alec—did he really expect her to ride off to Edinburgh with him and marry him on the chance that she might not have to go to prison? She could not trust the outcome of that—she was, after all, a spy. And he was a redcoat, she reminded herself.

"Oh, I like this one very much," Sophie said, leaning forward at the table to peruse a page she was studying. She flipped the page of a large book filled with illustrations and glanced up at Kate. "Look at this handsome red tulip. Quite wonderful. I do love the red ones."

"I do, too," Kate said, twisting threads. "And I do not know what to do."

"Katie?" Sophie asked. "What is it?"

"Oh! Nothing," Kate said, furiously flipping lace bobbins, *tap-tap-tap*.

"Is it the red soldier?" Sophie asked gently.

"Of course not." *Tap-tap-tap-tap*.

Sophie got up from her chair and came over to sit beside Kate on the brocaded sofa. "Are you sure? You know, I went to see him this morning. I thought I had best introduce myself."

"You did?" Kate looked up, feeling a curious hunger to know more. "What did he say? What do you think of him?"

"He was resting, so I did not stay," Sophie said. "We spoke only briefly. He seemed very tired, and I pulled the drapes shut and urged him to get more sleep—that sort of injury takes a good deal from a man, though he is healing very fast. And I came close to say my greeting, just to get a better look at him," she confided, laughing a little. "He's very bonny, your Captain Fraser—a braw and beautiful man."

"I suppose," Kate said, ducking her head again to focus on the next patch of mesh.

"We said very little, but I liked him very much, instantly, and that sense never fails me with people. He seemed calm and strong. He is a good man." Sophie set her long, graceful fingers to the crystal hanging at her throat on a fine chain. "He's a very good man, Katie, despite being a red soldier. He said that you—"

"What?" Kate looked at her sister, feeling suddenly desperate, needy.

"He said you make him look at everything differently, as he's never seen it before," Sophie said. "He said he would never forget you, and he hopes you will forgive him someday." She tilted her head, watching Kate, who shrugged.

"Nothing to forgive. He was only doing his duty."

"I imagine so. He mentioned how much he appreciates our hospitality, but says he must leave soon and plans to do so today. He was not certain you would want to say farewell to him before he went."

Kate dropped the bobbins, put a hand to her mouth, and began to weep, while Sophie slipped an arm around her shoulder.

Alec walked through the hallways of Duncrieff alone, passing one well-appointed room after another, but he had no time to pause or explore. When Mary had arrived very early with a breakfast tray of coffee as well as hot chocolate drink, he was already dressed in plaid, waistcoat, and mended red coat, along with his officer's sash. He had assured Mary that he was fine, truly recovered, though she fussed over him before mentioning that Duncrieff had arrived home late the night before and now waited to speak with him in the drawing room, along with Kate and the others.

He was invited, she said, to join them at breakfast—but he thought he might decline that in favor of leaving altogether.

Expecting to meet her brother sometime today, he had dressed for the interview and now felt as if he walked toward his fate, even his doom. Although he did not want to leave Kate, he knew the time had come—he could neither force her to come with him nor force her to marry him if she refused. In Edinburgh, sooner or later, he would have to deliver her to court. As much as he wanted to protect her, he could not guarantee her safety after that.

With his arm in a sling and his jacket draped loosely, he walked along a corridor and down another flight of steps. The castle had been restored a century earlier, he had learned, to Jacobean grandeur. He passed one fine room after another: gleaming parquet floors, walls paneled in oak or painted in soothing colors. Scattered throughout were Turkey carpets, tapestried chairs, furnishings in older styles mixed with a few graceful French pieces; he saw crystal chandeliers and porcelain, mirrors and inlaid tables, paintings and bronzes—

and in every room, glass or China vases filled with flowers.

Though it was well into October, every room seemed to have fresh flowers in it—vases of marigolds, daisies, lavender fronds, pots of forced tulips, other flowers he did not recognize, all in bloom. Their fragrances freshened the air, and as Alec progressed through the halls, he began to relax a bit, to feel at home here, despite the early-morning appointment that awaited him.

Duncrieff had worked its own magic over him—he felt it everywhere, as if it were an enchanted palace, an elusive part of the Otherworld. Magic simply pervaded the air like light or music.

And he wondered if the magic was no more mysterious than just the peaceful atmosphere of a home filled with love. No wonder Kate had been desperate to return to Duncrieff. He would have done anything, were it his home, to come back.

He found the drawing room, following Mary's directions, and hesitated, hand on the doorknob. Then he drew a long breath, and opened it.

The room was empty, he saw that immediately, to his surprise, for he had expected to face an angry young chief and a phalanx of stern Highland warriors.

Filled with early-morning sunshine, the room was large and lovely, the walls painted in creamy tones, the polished wood floor covered in a long Aubusson carpet, the furnishings a mix of dark Jacobean and lighter French, with tapestried chairs and a narrow sofa, and a painted harpsichord in a corner. The back wall of the room was pierced with tall windows hung with velvet draperies, framing a view of a stone veranda and gardens that swept out to the foothills and mountains far beyond.

He strolled across the room, drawn by the spectacular view. Beyond the veranda, he saw flower beds and rose arbors, a fountain apparently kept dormant in autumn, a corner hedge maze, and orchards of fruit trees. From that window, he could see miles of the heathered hills and snow-topped mountains that surrounded the long length of the glen. The honey sandstone walls of Duncrieff Castle sat above all of it like a benevolent queen watching over her own.

He glanced around the room, and his attention was drawn by a curious object on a heavy carved sideboard. Other than flowers in vases and silver candlesticks, the centerpiece on the cabinet was a glass bell jar over a silver plate swathed in red velvet. A golden goblet sat protected inside.

A beautiful thing of hammered gold banded in silver, its surface was etched with swirling knot designs, its rim set with small crystals. A few of those were missing, he noticed immediately, as he leaned forward to peer more closely.

"The Fairy Cup of Duncrieff," Kate said behind him.

"Ah," he said, turning, nonchalant though his heart pounded hard. "Of course. I've heard a little about the fairy legends of Duncrieff." He glanced at her.

She stood silhouetted in the door that led to the veranda and gardens, a fey creature with sunshine behind her all in a glow. Her fairy ancestry suddenly seemed very real.

She walked toward him, ethereal in a gown of silver-blue damask, the snug bodice and elbow sleeves trimmed in falls of lace, the bodice and wide skirts split to reveal an embroidered floral underdress. Her hair was neatly tamed beneath a lace cap, her earlobes held tiny pearl drops. Elegant, lovely, she was every bit the beautiful creature of the king's court.

She joined him without glancing at him. In fact, she seemed to be avoiding his eyes. "The wife of the first laird of Duncrieff left this to her family. She was a Green Lady."

He tilted his head. "A ghost?"

"Not that sort of Green Lady," she said. "She was a princess of the tall and beautiful race of fairies who lived in the forests of Scotland a very long time ago . . . in the time of the mists, or so they call it."

He nodded. "Did she use this cup?"

She shook her head. "She commissioned it from fairy goldsmiths, they say, of fairy gold from the hills of Glen Carran. Long before this castle was here, the princess came to Duncrieff with the MacCarran ancestor who rescued her when she fell in a river. He nursed her to health and fell in love with her, and she became his wife and the mother of his three sons." Still she did not look at him. "One day she went back into the forest, returning to her kind, and to the green places where she was born. Her need for freedom, in the way of the fairies, was so strong in the end that it overcame her love for her human family. She was compelled to leave."

"I see," he murmured. "Wild blood."

She nodded. "Leaving them broke her heart, they say, but her nature was fey and wild, and if she had remained, she would have withered away. But she left gifts with them."

"This cup?"

"More than that, she left fairy magic through her blood, which became part of each generation of the MacCarrans of Duncrieff. Her three sons each inherited a different ability, and those have been passed along. Now and then, not even in every generation, someone is born with one of the gifts of fairy, such as healing, or the Sight, or . . . the glamourie. That's the gift of bedazzling, or charming, others."

"Aye," he murmured. "And what of this cup?"

"It holds magic for the family, or so tradition says. When one is born with a fairy talent, one of the crystals is removed from the rim and worn by that person. The stone will enhance the power, or so it is believed."

He glanced down at her. "Your sister wears a crystal necklace similar to yours. So she has this gift, too?"

She nodded. "Sophie's fairy talent is the one that encourages growth—it's related to the healing gift, I suppose. Much of the gardens here are Sophie's work—she has been restoring the garden here at Duncrieff, and at her husband's home, for months. And she's increasing, came by it very quickly, she said . . . and that is a gift of growth and healing, too." She smiled.

"Very much so. She's very like you, lovely, and charming. I see the magic . . . in both of you." Strange, he thought, how readily he was beginning to accept the

284

fairy element in the MacCarrans, though previously he would not have believed such things.

"She's much nicer than I am," Kate said wryly, "very patient and sweet-natured. We both have the Fairy's Gift, and the fairy's temper at times . . . but she got more of the gift, and I got more of the temper." She twisted her mouth awry.

He smiled a little. God, how he loved her, and it turned inside him, aching, because he had not set it free.

"Give yourself your due, Marie Katherine. Your sister seems a gentle soul, and you may have a bit more fire, but you both have a dazzling charm. I have not met Connor MacPherson. When you see him, please give him my regards, and tell him I think he is a fortunate man." He inclined his head.

"You are truly leaving?" She glanced at him, frowning, and her quicksilver eyes took on the gray-blue of her gown.

He wished he could be as lucky as Connor, but Kate had refused his proposal. He would not ask again, would not beg. He glanced away, tensing a muscle in his cheek.

He had not wanted to be hurt again in love, had shielded himself from that for so long, and yet here he was, taking the blow and using his pride for a shield again.

"I came to say farewell," he said. "It is best if I go. You said so yourself." He held her gaze and she glanced away first. "I was hoping to speak with your brother, as I must, and hoping to borrow a horse for the journey back."

"Of course," she said politely, Alec felt his heart sink even further—she did not protest his decision. "My brother and the others are outside on the veranda."

"Excellent." He stepped away.

"Alec, wait—" She paused, lifting a hand to her bodice.

"Aye?" He watched her over his shoulder, standing a safe distance from her, but he felt a strange pull in his belly, as if a cord tugged between them.

"So you truly are willing . . . to go back without me?"

"Do you want me to drag you out of here shrieking, with a host of wild Highlanders on my tail?" He felt impatient suddenly, hurting and harsh when he should not be so with her. "I'll report my prisoner lost and take my chances. It's better for you that way, my love," he finished, his voice almost flat.

He turned and walked toward the outside door. Her footsteps sounded behind him, but he did not turn until he opened the door and waited in silence for her to pass through ahead of him.

Chapter 24

On the sunlit veranda, Kate picked up her skirts and hurried to keep up with Alec's long-legged, determined stride. Several yards away, Rob, Connor, and the others turned when they saw them approaching.

Rob came forward, somber and wary, a tall ash blond man with a scholarly look, not at all the hotheaded chief of his reputation; adoring her brother, Kate had always thought him to be a handsome, strongly masculine version of his sisters in appearance and coloring. Connor MacPherson of Kinnoull came behind Rob, looking much more the Highland brigand—her brother-in-law was a large and robust man, his dark-haired good looks striking, his green eyes intense; in his wrapped plaid he looked like a savage warrior, despite his fine education. In the last few months, she had come to love him as a brother, appreciating his wry humor, his slow smile, his quiet wit.

But she did not know how either of them, or Allan and Neill who followed behind them, would greet Alexander Fraser. She had found no chance to speak with Rob yet, though she knew that Neill and Allan would have told him, and Connor, what they knew.

The hour was early, the breeze chill, and she shivered. "Robert MacCarran of Duncrieff," she said, "Connor MacPherson, Lord Kinnoull—this is Captain Alexander Fraser."

Rob eyed Alec for a moment. "Fraser, sir," he said.

"Duncrieff." Alec held out his hand. Rob, having no other choice, shook it. Alec turned to Connor. "Lord Kinnoull."

"It's Connor," her brother-in-law replied, and shook his hand. Despite their polite greetings, Kate felt the tension in the air mount as Alec greeted Neill and Allan, too.

"We were just coming inside. It's cool out here, but Connor wanted to see a change Sophie had made to the gardens here, though she has not yet joined us this morning." Rob gestured to Kate, who led the way as they walked back into the drawing room. Rob turned to Alec. "You're recovered from your illness, sir?"

"Aye, well enough to travel," Alec said. "I thank you for your hospitality, but I must be going as soon as I can, if I may trouble you for a horse. I'll see it returned to you. Your sister will stay here, by the way," he added. "I'll not demand that she go with me." His voice was deepened and serious, and Kate felt her breath catch in her throat a little.

Rob nodded, glanced at her. "Kate?"

She lifted her head. "I asked him to leave me here. He has agreed, though he must tell the courts that I ran away. He is taking a chance in doing so."

"All they will know is I . . . lost her," Alec said.

Lost her. The tone of his voice, and his implication, perceptible only to her, tugged hard at Kate. She glanced at him sadly, but he did not look her way just then.

Her brother nodded. "We are in your debt, sir, when I thought we might be in confrontation. We heard from Allan that you had Kate arrested."

"I did. Under the circumstances, the lass looked to be an *intriguante*, or at the least a thief. It was not until later that I understood . . . well, to be frank, Duncrieff, there is something I want to know before I leave."

"What is that?" Rob sounded cautious. Kate looked on with alarm, thinking Alec would ask them now, directly, about the missing Spanish weapons.

Alec glowered. "What the devil were the lot of you thinking, to send a lass out to do that sort of work?"

Kate caught her breath, and her heart seemed to flip. Rob looked startled, and all of them stared at Alec.

"But she agreed—" Neill began.

"Let Fraser speak," Rob said. "What do you mean, sir?"

"The mischief she was about was dangerous, particularly for a young woman. She was bound to be arrested, sooner or later. Arrested, or worse," he growled.

"It was her choice," Allan countered, stepping closer.

"She knew the dangers involved. We kept watch over her every time."

Neill nodded. "There were always one or a few of us there. We never let the lass do anything entirely on her own."

"But you did," Alec said. "Every time she stepped into an officer's quarters, she was on her own. She could have been—"

"I was fine," she said. "Someone was always with me."

"Always nearby. You were never entirely safe, except once, with me," Alec said, gazing at her intently.

Staring up at him, Kate was, for a moment, speechless. His concern for her, touched with outrage, and his willingness to challenge her kinsmen on the matter gave her a sudden, strong feeling that he did love her— he truly did.

Her heart began to pound.

"Your kinsmen and friends likely knew some of the risks better than you did," Alec went on. "A beautiful young woman with an irresistible charm about her should never have gone out alone to do that sort of work."

"It was my choice," Kate said. "It was not their doing."

"I would never have let you do that on your own," he said.

"Nor would I have asked you," she retorted. "I told my kinsmen that I would manage it without their assistance. They were not happy about it—they always sent someone with me."

"She's a stubborn lass," Rob said. "You know that by now."

"I am wondering," Connor said, "why the captain seems more interested in her safety than her supposed crimes."

"Aye," Rob agreed, eyes narrowed.

"She is a fiery bit of a lass, I understand that," Alec said, "and if she wants to do something it is nigh impossible to stop her. She's brave and resourceful, and . . . bonny," he continued, "and she willingly took on great risk of life, limb, and reputation for the lot of you, and for the Jacobite cause."

"You seem to care a good deal about it," Connor observed.

"I do. I care that she could have been ruined or hurt. I care that she was poorly treated in that damnable prison, and where were you lads all that time?"

"Searching for her," Rob said sharply. "We were going from place to place trying to find word of her—the whole irresponsible lot of us were at it."

"And it seems she was with you all the while," Allan said. "So the question might be, Captain, what the devil were *you* doing with her while we were searching?"

"Doing my best to watch after her welfare," he said.

"And chasing me whenever I managed to escape," she said to her kinsmen. "But he went after me each time, and that's why he followed me all the way here."

"The lad's as stubborn as she is," Connor said, arms crossed as he regarded them.

"I would guess the man treated you well," Rob said, touching Kate's arm.

"He did." She looked at Alec. "He took me out of the prison before real harm could come to me. He treated me with respect. He was always . . . careful of my comfort."

Alec inclined his head toward her, his gaze sober. She glanced away. She had never seen the full brunt of his temper, and she felt a secret thrill that the question of her welfare had stoked him to a fiery outburst.

"Then we owe you thanks for that, sir," Rob said. "And in answer to your original question, I'll admit that we did ask Kate to help with some clandestine activities. Our Jacobite loyalties will be no surprise to you, so I will not skirt it."

Alec nodded. "Why did you want to involve her in intrigue?"

"She has a certain . . . ability that makes it possible for her to go places we cannot go and obtain information that we cannot. We gave her protection, she always had a guard with her, but her own ability protects her, also."

"You are talking about this fairy business," Alec said. "You do realize that Katie Hell now has a reputation for magic and spellcasting, along with . . . certain unsavory traits."

"Those rumors were a risk we all knew, but so long as her true identity was not known, we did not think it would cause trouble for her. As for the fairy legends, though that may seem foolish to some, we know how real and powerful the fairy gifts can be in this family."

Alec shook his head slightly. "The lass has a wicked charm, and is highly clever and as stubborn as they come . . . but all of you believe in this supposed fairy power?"

Kate saw Rob and the others shrug, nod.

"I sympathize with you, Fraser," Connor said. "I have been in this situation myself."

"Situation?" Alec asked.

Connor inclined his head. "Being spun about by one of the MacCarran lasses."

Alec half smiled. "Indeed, Kinnoull."

"The fairy business, as he calls it, does not work on this man," Kate said, folding her arms. "I could spin him until we were all dizzy with it, and he could still walk away from me without looking back."

"Huh," Neill said. "Is that true? You do not see the girl's fey charms?"

"Oh, I see them," Alec drawled. "And I'm as vulnerable as the next man, where she is concerned."

"You do not seem so," she said. "I did not think you truly cared, until . . . now. And now you'll leave, and I—" She stopped.

He looked down at her. "I'm off for Edinburgh. Do you want to go to prison after all?"

"I do not," she answered.

"Well, then," he answered, as if it were final.

"But I would not mind being with you," she said, heart pounding, for she felt bold and defiant on impulse.

Suddenly she did not care if her decision suited the fairy legends or not. He was leaving, and she would not see him again, and the reality of it suddenly impacted her. She could not let him go. She wanted to plunge headlong into risk with him.

Alec stared at her. They all stared at her. "Would not mind what?" he asked slowly.

"I would love to be with you, as you asked me before," she whispered. "If you'll have me."

His cool blue gaze softened, and he huffed a laugh, shook his head as if bewildered. "Changed your mind, have you?"

"Aye," she said, lifting her chin. She took a step toward him, and another step. Tears stung her eyes. "If you still want to marry me, Alexander Fraser, I will accept the offer."

"Marry?" Rob asked. Connor silenced him with a gesture.

Alec tipped his head. "It is a great deal of trouble for a lad to work up the courage to ask a lass to marry him . . . only to be refused," he said in a soft, wry tone. His eyes sparkled. "Tell me why you have changed your mind."

"Will you not make this easy for me?" she asked.

"Should I?" In part, she knew he teased her a little to alleviate the tension, but she also realized how serious and vulnerable he was feeling. He needed to be sure of her feelings, just as she had wanted to be certain last night of his.

Neill, chuckling, grinned at Allan. Meanwhile, Rob and Connor watched her as if spellbound. She took another step forward, her gaze focused on Alec.

"I do want to marry you, Alasdair Callda." She stood close enough to touch him, yet did not breach the space between them. "I do want that, though you will be stubborn about it."

He laughed low and soft. She loved the sound, which she knew now was characteristic of him, a low, breathy, pensive laugh, so quietly masculine that it made her heart beat faster. Reaching out, he slid his hand along her cheek, sending shivers through her. "I'm never so stubborn as you, my lass."

"Well?" she asked.

"Aye, well?" Neill echoed, and Rob, Allan, and Connor looked keenly interested.

In answer, he leaned down then, his fingers lifting her chin a little, and he kissed her lips. "I will," he whispered. "Very well, I will."

She laughed, threw her arms around his neck.

"But I do not know if your kinsmen will approve of this. They may not want to welcome a red soldier into the family," Alec added, resting his arm around her.

"It would be a bit of trouble, having a redcoat in the family," Allan said with a mock frown, while Neill nodded.

"If this is what Kate wants," Rob said, "and if her choice comes from the heart, and Alec's does as well, that is more important than the color of his coat."

"It does indeed come from my heart," Kate said.

"And mine," Alec echoed. "Truly."

That was what she most needed to know. Kate glanced at him and smiled, feeling her spirit soar in that small, perfect instant.

"So that is the way of it," Rob said thoughtfully. Kate was not sure he was convinced. "You do know our family legend, sir?"

"I've heard something of it," Alec answered.

"The Fairy Cup over there, is inscribed with our clan's motto. 'Love makes its own magic,'" Rob quoted, " 'and its own miracles.' It is engraved along the rim of the cup in ancient script. The legend holds that whenever one of the fairy-blessed in our clan falls in love and wants to marry—well, you tell it, Kate."

"It must be love of the finest kind," she began, glancing at Alec. "It must be true love . . . for if it is a wrongful match, the clan will suffer for it somehow. Love is somehow part of the magic that exists in our clan. I am more and more convinced of that."

"And this is why you refused me?" he asked.

She nodded. "I had to consider my clan, because I am one of the fairy-blessed MacCarrans. Though I knew my own heart . . . I was not sure of yours."

He smiled ruefully. "You had nothing to worry about." He looked up. "Let me assure you lot, also, that you have no worries so far as I am concerned."

"What do you mean?" she asked. "That you will not tell anyone in the military that Katie Hell is here and that you've married her?"

"I mean that I am one of you. I am a staunch Jacobite."

Kate gaped up at him. The others stared.

"I've kept this to myself for good reason. For a few years," Alec went on, "I have been involved in some intrigue, working with the Jacobite council, Lochiel and the rest."

Kate stared, breathless. "You're a spy?"

"I suppose I am," he said with a shrug.

"And you're working under Cameron of Lochiel, chief of that clan?" Rob asked.

"Among others, aye, including my uncle, MacDonald of Keppoch. I've been searching for Ian Cameron, too," he said quietly, while the others regarded him with expressions of relief and astonishment. "And I've been trying to find those blasted Spanish weapons, too, before the government finds them."

"But you never said," Kate breathed out. At first stunned, she soon realized that she had felt this all along, in varying ways, and Jack had certainly hinted at it.

"Kate, you would not even tell me your whole name," Alec told her. "I was not certain who you were working with or against. I am a cautious man by nature."

"I know that," Kate replied.

"My instincts say we can trust you, Fraser," Rob said, looking somber. "I will take the chance. I think these lads will, too. If Kate loves you, that is all the recommendation we need."

"Thank you," Alec murmured.

"You say you've worked with Keppoch?" Connor asked, his slight frown revealing his sense of caution in the matter.

"Aye, most often, since he's my mother's brother. I'm a Writer to the Signet, and as an officer I review documents for the military, and sometimes for Jacobite allies, including Blair of Atholl and Cameron of Locheil." He paused. "I have learned elaborate secret codes and alphabets, I've used the trick of writing in lemon juice and oil to be held before a candle flame, and I've carried packets and notes between Sleat and MacDonald of Keppoch, between Lovat and Lochiel. I keep clear of the Earl of Mar, who reports regularly to Westminster now. And I've carried messages for Fraser of Lovat, though of late he cannot make up his mind where he stands."

"You're of Lovat's ilk?" Connor still seemed wary.

"He's my father's half brother. I trust his loyalty to family, but I know how far trust goes with him, and so I am careful," Alec replied. "I am Laird of Kilburnie, near Inverness, though for many years my family has also been based in Edinburgh to maintain the business that my grandfather and great-uncle started."

"Fraser's Fancies," Kate supplied.

Connor gave a curt laugh. "The chocolate powder? Interesting," he added.

"A good business, which my uncle manages very well in my stead," Alec said. "They are loyal Jacobites themselves, though they are very careful who knows it. The place is located very near the courts on the High Street. Have you heard of the Chocolate House in Edinburgh?"

"Near Castlehill? I've been in the shop myself," Connor said. "I've heard that the owners might be sympathetic to the cause. The word is carefully guarded among Jacobites."

"You could have told me all this," Kate murmured.

"Interesting indeed," Rob said. "What do you propose, Captain Fraser?"

"It's Alec, please. I propose we find those Spanish weapons and do what we can for Ian Cameron and for your kinsmen, who may be with him in Edinburgh dungeons."

Connor nodded grimly. "Do you know where this cache of weaponry might be hidden?"

"I do not," Alec said, "but I suspect Kate knows something that may help us."

"I spoke to Ian Cameron," Kate offered. "He did not know exactly where the weapons are hidden, but he has some idea."

"A few of them have been found, apparently," Rob said, directing his remark to Alec. "Some of the Camerons got hold of a few from the original cache—Ian said his father had them. He gave some to our lot, and said he would find the rest and get back to me when he discovered where they were stashed."

"Andrew and Donald were given a couple of arms from one of the Camerons," Allan said. "But no one seems to know exactly who found them or where the weapons are now. Ian had that news."

"He told me that a hermit has them," Kate said. "A hermit somewhere near Glen Carran."

"There are no hermits in this area, and there hasn't been for hundreds of years." Rob frowned.

"Hermit . . . could he mean hermitage?" Connor asked.

"Aye, that might be," Rob said.

"What hermitage?" Kate asked. "I haven't heard of it."

"The old name for what's now called Ossian's Hall," Connor explained. "It's a small, hidden spot not far from the old ruined tower where I lived for a long while. There's a waterfall near there, and a wee building, a sort of folly that Blair of Atholl partly built on his property, and left unfinished. It's quite remote, and there are caves behind the waterfall. I wonder—"

"The caves! Of course!" Kate brightened. "I should have thought of it earlier. When we were children, we heard stories about a saint who lived in that area. A hermit."

Rob nodded. "Right. The lads and I will go see if there's anything hidden away." He glanced at Connor. "When we return, we'd best be off to Edinburgh to see to the lads there."

"Fraser, will you be with us in that?" Connor asked. "We will not spring them free of that dungeon through legal means."

"I'm with you. You'll do better with an officer along," Alec said grimly. He pulled Kate close, and she felt the tension in him. "Kate should stay here."

"After all that, I'm going with you," she protested.

"We intend to get those lads out of the dungeon, not see you put in there," Alec said. "If you were to appear in Edinburgh with me, you would be expected to report to the Court of Justiciary. I am not unknown in Edinburgh, Kate. Your presence would be noted, so there's no avoiding your appointment."

"Did you not say the Lord Advocate was one of your uncles?"

"Aye," he growled. "The meanest of the lot."

She smiled, despite the anxious feeling in her stomach. She had a strong urge to be with Alec, no matter the danger to her. What he and her kinsmen had decided to do was genuinely dangerous, and she would not stay home worrying about all of them. "Perhaps he can be charmed," she said brightly.

"I doubt it," Alec said, sending her a sober glance.

Chapter 25

〰◗◖〰

"Watch your step," Connor said, leading the way into the shadowy cave. "It's slippery through here."

Following behind him, Alec took Kate's hand and ducked his head to enter the narrow cleft in the rock face, just above and to one side of the rushing waterfall. After one of Neill's sons had run back to Duncrieff with news of a find, Alec was anxious to see it for himself, and Kate went with him. Despite its precarious location, he would never have suggested that she wait at home. She was as good as or better than on this terrain as he was, and she had every right to see what her kinsmen had found.

"Look there," Connor said, his quiet voice echoing.

Attaining the top of the inclined cavern floor, Alec stepped into a clearing in a narrow cathedral-like space, dark but for the lanternlight that reflected the slick dark stone of the interior walls. Just ahead, he saw Rob and Neill standing beside two large wooden chests.

Rob flipped the lid of one as Alec and Kate came forward. Nearby, Neill raised the lantern high.

"My God," Alec said, gripping Kate's hand more tightly.

"Guns, aye—but I did not expect to see gold," Kate whispered in the echoing silence.

Golden coins gleamed, sending a sunny glow upward to illuminate Kate's face as she knelt to peer into the chest. Thousands of coins were scattered among hundreds of weapons, the coins spilling around the pistols, muskets, bayonets, and swords as if they were wood shavings.

Alec dropped down to one knee beside Kate, reaching out to run his fingers lightly over the upper layer of the contents of the chest. With a sweep of his hand, he touched the cold steel and wooden-and-brass fittings of a hundred flintlock pistols, and his fingers rippled over the faces and edges of silver and gold coins that filled the spaces between.

"How many weapons are there?" Kate asked. She glanced up at her brother. "And how much do you think is here in coin?"

"We do not yet know. It will take some time to count all of this out, and it cannot be managed here." He gestured

302

toward the other chest. "That one holds broadswords and blades in particular, and more coins, too."

Allan lifted the lid of the other chest, while Alec scrutinized the deadly gleam of the blades within. "Good Toledo steel. And those pistols in the other one are of the best Spanish make. I've seen those insigne before," he said, indicating the engraved maker's marks on the butts of some of the weapons.

"We'll have to move these out of here before we can safely assess what we've got here and decide what the devil to do with all of this," Connor said.

"But can Spanish coin be used here in Scotland?" Kate picked up a silver piece, then a gold coin to look more closely at them.

"Easily," Alec said. He sifted through the coins. "Silver reales and escudos . . . pieces of eight—that means it's worth eight reales," he told her, choosing a silver piece and dropping it again with a gentle *chink*. "Gold doubloons . . . aye, it can all be used as currency. Spanish coins are highly desirable and useful everywhere because they are made of pure silver, and pure gold. These coins can be traded for their value, or melted down to be used for their pure precious metals."

"How do you know?" she asked.

"I'm a lawyer and a merchant, both," he answered, then glanced at Rob and the others. "The Spaniards had their own reasons for wanting to see the English out of power in Scotland, and so the weapons and money were obviously intended to support the uprising of 1719. But someone hid it well after that rebellion failed."

"Aye, a pity, too, for that uprising was the most likely to succeed of any we've seen so far," Connor said.

"How did these chests come to be here?" Kate asked.

"I suspect they were secretly brought by our father, along with Connor's father," Rob said.

"Your fathers were in the 'Nineteen?" Alec asked.

"Aye. They escaped the northern Highlands after the attempt floundered up there and came back this way with Cameron of Lochiel," Connor said. "I remember my father spoke of it at the time, but he said nothing of this cache. Too terrible a secret to let out to anyone, I suppose, until he and the others knew what they would do. But they never had the chance."

"Cameron must have hidden away a stash of his own," Alec said. "Some of his men have been found with weapons like these, and Ian gave a few over to you lads. Lochiel has been eager to know where the rest of it was hidden. He must have suspected that MacCarran and MacPherson had possession of some of it, but he had to wait until the time was right. The last few years have not seen many rumors or attempts at another uprising, but the rumbles are beginning again. Weapons and coin are sorely needed."

"This looks like the bulk of the Spanish hoard," Neill said.

"But my father and yours were never able to do anything about getting this to Lochiel when the time was right," Connor said. "MacCarran of Duncrieff was exiled to France, and my own father was executed." He shook his head. "How did Ian find out?"

"We'll have to ask the lad," Rob said. "First we'll find

a better spot to hide this, then it's off to Edinburgh as fast as we can, before the military has a chance to break Ian for the information."

"Oh, he'd never tell," Kate said. "He teased me that he would, and that I should say nothing of your business to him. But he'd never say what he knew except to us."

"He would indeed say," Rob countered. "You don't know Ian as we do. He'd talk, if they pressed him hard enough. He's a fine man, but he has a wife and child to think about, and if he perceived a real threat to them, I think the man would speak."

"With the amount of coin here, and the weaponry, there's more at stake than I thought," Alec said. "If the crown learns that this is here, they will do anything to take it and claim it, and they'll quickly punish anyone who knew of it."

"Aye," Connor agreed. "We'd best move these chests somewhere else before we go east to the city."

Kate stood. "Why not leave them here, where they've been safely hidden for years?"

Rising to his feet beside her, Alec shook his head. "If Wade's soldiers discover anything from Ian, they'll come here as fast as they can. The chests should be moved quickly."

Allan closed the heavy lid, shutting out the gleam of the gold like shutting a second lantern. "What should we do with the hoard itself? We cannot let it sit untouched when it could be of use to the Jacobite cause."

"It should be distributed somehow among loyal Highlanders," Alec said. "Though to whom, and how, is a difficult problem."

"Should we give it to the Jacobite council?" Kate's eyes looked luminous and unsettled as she turned to look at him.

"Some of it, certainly," Alec said. "But I'm thinking about the scores of Highlanders who consigned their weapons to the government. Most of them have little thought of rebellion. They are simple men who need weapons to protect their homes and to use in hunting to provide for their families. Those men deserve these arms more than war-minded Jacobite leaders."

"I knew you were a good man," Kate said, smiling up at him.

"That makes sense—the arms to those who need them and the coin to the Jacobite council," Rob said.

"Cameron of Lochiel can convey the money to the council," Connor said. "We'll let him know. Alec can do that, since Lochiel is waiting to hear from him on this matter. As for the weapons, we'll have to spread the word somehow, but slowly and carefully."

"Some of the weapons could be transported in cartloads and on the backs of garron ponies," Neill suggested, "and some can be handed out secretly from here. Word will spread among the rebels. One by one, the Highlanders will be armed again, and they will have a measure of safety they've not known for years."

Allan nodded. "For now, where should we store the chests?"

"Up at Glendoon," Connor suggested. "My ruined tower up in the hills is a perfect spot to hide these away again and a good place from which to distribute weapons to those who are given the discreet word. No one will come up there to search. It's said to be haunted."

"*Tcha!*" Neill waved a hand. "I will not carry these heavy chests up that devil of a hill, Kinnoull."

"Then we'll get your strapping young sons to help. Either way," Connor said, "by afternoon, we'll have this tucked away and be on our way to Edinburgh."

Kate looked at Alec, and he saw uncertainty in her eyes.

"Stay here, Kate my love," he murmured. "You will be safe at Duncrieff."

"I'll feel safer with you—and I have to know that you are safe as well." She leaned against him. "Where you go, I will go."

"Too much risk," he said, putting an arm around her. "You did all you could to keep from going there with me, and now the tables have turned. I want you to stay here."

"We've each changed our stance on the matter." Her glance grew stormy, stubborn.

"And changed in other ways. I did not know then what I know now, Kate," he whispered, bending to kiss her hair.

"Neither of us did. And that is why I must go with you now." She gazed up at him. "No need to say that I am your prisoner . . . just say I am your wife."

Chapter 26

As a soft pink dawn bloomed over Edinburgh Castle on its towering rock, they entered the city by the West Bow, a steep and winding hill that led from the western hills into the city past the high volcanic crag that supported the castle. The post chaise came down the twisting incline through the Grassmarket and toward the Canongate, passing through the portal kept by the City Guards. After a question parried by Jack, who rode postillion on the lead left horse, the vehicle was waved through. The horses' hooves clopped on the cobblestones, and the air was brisk and cool, and fresh with promise of a new day.

They had traveled the whole of the previous day on garrons as far as the Perth road and MacLennan's

Changehouse, where they met Jack. After a meal and a few hours' rest, they departed in the post chaise before dawn. Kate and Alec rode in the vehicle led by Jack on the lead horse, while Rob and Connor rode behind the chaise. They had planned to enter the city separately and stay at an inn in the Canongate frequented by Jacobites, rather than stir suspicion by arriving as a group at Hopefield House.

Kate stifled a yawn and watched the sky glow over the castle. Seated beside Alec, who watched pensively through his side window, Kate wondered what awaited her here. She had been to Edinburgh often for shopping, theater, and concerts in the days before her father's exile, when she had been young and life had been so different for her family. Since then, she had made necessary trips for the household, and in the company of her kinsmen for matters of espionage and Jacobite loyalty.

At last she realized with a sinking feeling that Alec had been right. Perhaps she should not have insisted on coming and instead stayed behind at Duncrieff, where she would remain safe. She could not predict whether she would have to face a hearing and a subsequent imprisonment, or whether she would simply stay with Alec's family, as he planned, and escape the city with him after Ian, Andrew, and Donald were freed.

They were all taking risks, she knew. Alec, her brother, and Connor MacPherson were about to place their lives in great jeopardy in order to save their comrades. She could not, in good conscience, sit at home waiting for word of their mission.

Alec reached over then to lay his hand over hers, which rested on the seat beside him. "Not so long ago, you thought I meant to bring you here in chains," he said, as if he knew her thoughts. "But I never intended for you to face the Court of Justiciary. I want you to know that."

She looked at him, frowning in wonder. "What, then?"

"I was going to let you go, Katie," he murmured. "Once you answered my questions, once I knew where the weapons might be hidden and what must be done to find them, I had thought to release you. I planned to take you to the town house where my aunt and uncle live, aye. But I did not always intend to take you to the court."

"But those were your orders," she said.

"Aye." He shrugged. "But if you had only told me what I needed to know—your name, who you were working with, what Ian Cameron had told you—I could have puzzled out much of the rest. If I could have spoken to your kinsmen to learn where the weapons were hidden . . . I would have let you go."

She listened in disbelief. "You mean, all that time you let me believe I was going to be interviewed and put in prison?"

"You are scheduled for the interview, and would likely have been imprisoned afterward. But I knew there was a way out of it, if the other questions could be resolved. I had to let you believe otherwise because you refused to cooperate with me."

She smiled a little. "I am glad you came after me. But

310

if it had not happened as it did, Alec, we might never have discovered . . . our feelings for each other."

Alec tightened his fingers over hers. "You're a wise lass, Katie-Katherine. Things do happen for a reason."

"Even when we think something must be so wrong, it turns out later to be the best way, after all."

He leaned close, as she did, hands clasped, shoulders touching. He kissed her, lifting his injured arm so that he could cradle her cheek in his hand. His lips brushed hers, caressed. A simple kiss, and so tender it brought tears to her eyes.

He drew back, relaxed against the seat back. "Don't fret over it, Kate. We need never say who you are."

"What will you tell your family?"

Lifting her hand to his lips, he kissed it. "That you are my bride. It's true, or soon will be."

"It *is* true. In Highland tradition, once a marriage promise is agreed upon, even if it is privately and without witnesses, if the two people then give themselves to one another in physical love, it becomes a binding marriage. And we have done that, I believe."

"*Matrimonio consummata*," he said, nodding. He lifted a brow. "The marriage promise should be made first, and the consummation fixes it in a binding agreement. We had witnesses to our promise, which is quite binding, but we reversed the order of the events, you and I." He smiled mischievously.

"We will have to correct that, then."

His thumb made tiny circles on her hand, sending delicate shivers all through her. "We will amend it as soon as we can."

311

She leaned back, close to him as he slid his arm around her, and she smiled up at him. Sunlight slanted through the window, illuminating the side of his face, glinting gold over his hair. Lifting her face to his, she kissed him again in silence and returned her glance to the window.

Though it was early morning, the streets were already busy. Shopkeepers were opening awnings and doorways, tradesmen and women were sweeping steps, and some were setting up small carts or tables to display wares just outside their entrances.

The caddies were out, too, strolling up and down the hill on paved and earthen paths, sitting on doorsteps or street corners. A few waved to the chaise as it went by. Kate noticed that they were almost all Highlanders in plaids and shabby clothes, boys and youths willing, for a fee, to run here or there to carry messages, fetch things, carry packages, or lead anyone through the maze of streets and closes to reach a destination. Considering the hills and slopes in the city, and the towering tenement floors with sometimes a dozen staircases to climb, the caddies earned their pay.

She saw the sedan chair carriers out, too, waiting beside their chairs, ready to hire. The single seats were enclosed in boxes, sometimes elaborately painted and secured on carrying poles.

Alec leaned toward Kate. "When you go up to the castle, you'll take a sedan chair," he murmured. "It's perfectly proper here. Ladies frequently move about the city on their own in Edinburgh, with the chairmen and the caddies to carry them and guide them. You will not find a safer city than Edinburgh for that. And it best suits our plan that you go alone to see Ian and the others, without an escort."

She nodded, aware of the basic plan, which she had discussed with Alec, Rob, and Connor at Duncrieff, and again at MacLennan's before approaching the city. "You would be too recognizable," she said, "and my kinsmen too conspicuous."

"Exactly." He took her hand again. "Are you nervous?"

"More because I am about to meet your family than because of any prison escape we have planned—that part is at least an expected danger. Your family is an unknown element."

"They're nothing to fear. Just don't accept experimental chocolate from my uncle Walter."

Laughing softly, she watched through the window as the post chaise followed along the Canongate and past the palace of Holyrood. She craned to look at the massive towers beyond the gates and the hulk of the volcanic hill called Arthur's Seat in the background.

Moments later, she saw Rob and Connor ride past the chaise, the Highlanders resplendent in plaids fixed with silver brooches, wearing snowy shirts under leather waistcoats and dark jackets. Waving briefly, they headed straight along the Canongate.

"They'll stay at Jenny Ha's Changehouse," Alec said. "It's a busy nest of Jacobite activity. They'll not be questioned closely by the City Guards, who avoid confrontation there, though we might be questioned if it were noticed that two Highlanders accompanied us up to my residence."

She nodded, aware of arrangements previously agreed upon.

Jack guided the horses leftward, and they departed the Canongate to climb the mile-long slope of the High Street, the Royal Mile that ran between Holyrood at its lower point and Edinburgh Castle at its peak. Here Kate saw more tradesmen, more caddies and chairmen. Here the grand facades of stately homes and beautiful civic buildings glowed in the rising sun alongside brightly painted shopfronts, taverns, and gloomy tenement buildings that rose so high that, in places, the sunlight was blocked. Even the more exclusive areas of Edinburgh showed the remarkable qualities of tolerance and casual equality that was so common to Scotland and the Scottish character.

Seeing the easy mingling of social levels here, Kate felt keenly and suddenly proud of Scotland and its people, both Highland and Lowland. She felt, too, a renewed sense of purpose and dedication—the Jacobite cause must prevail for the good of the Scots, she thought, and her mission with Alec and the rest, but a small piece of the grander puzzle, must prevail also.

Hearing a series of bells chiming out, she startled. "The bells of the Canongate Kirk, just there. They ring throughout the day," Alec said. "You'll get used to hearing them."

She nodded, having been to the city before. "I'm a bit jumpy. Is that the Tolbooth?" she asked in a hush, as they passed a massive facade that hulked over the cobbled street.

"Aye, the city jail," he murmured. "The Lord Advocate's house is across from it. Hopefield House is a little way ahead, just below Castlehill, on the right. You'll see the Chocolate House, and behind it in the close, Hopefield House."

Kate drew a deep breath. Then she saw the brown fieldstone front of a building with rich brown trim, and a neatly painted sign in gold lettering on black: FRASER'S FANCY CHOCOLATE HOUSE.

A woman was outside sweeping the steps, and as they neared and began to turn, she waved exuberantly. Alec lifted a hand, smiling, and she dropped her broom and ran inside.

"Effie," he explained. "Euphemia Fraser—my uncle's wife."

Kate felt even more anxious as Jack guided the horses into the close, one of the short alleyways common throughout the city. The chaise entered the shadowy chasm between two multistory buildings and followed the sloping pavement downward to a little open court tucked behind the main street.

At the far end of a tree-lined plot, a sandstone mansion of modest proportions and graceful design, with gabled roof and cupolas, rose behind an iron gate.

"That's Hopefield House," Alec said. "The family lives there, and the shop is located in our other building, just on the High Street."

Nodding, Kate drew up the wide hood of her dark brown cloak and smoothed her skirts of forest green wool, which she wore with a close-cut jacket of green-and-blue tartan over a white, ruffled shirt. Sophie had lent her the outfit, encouraging her to wear something more *à la mode* than Kate generally preferred.

Alec exited the chaise and turned to help Kate down, his hand taking hers. Then he kissed her cheek under the shadow of her hood and tugged the rim down.

"Keep it like that if we see soldiers, my love," he said. "There's always the chance that someone could recognize you."

"Her fairy beauty will blind 'em, and she'll charm the breeches off 'em," Jack quipped as he came toward them.

"Let's let them keep their breeches, shall we?" Alec muttered. He turned then, and waved. "Aunt Effie, good to see you! And hello, what's this?"

He smiled and bent down as three little girls in ruffled pink gowns raced toward him from the back door of the building facing the street. Passing the tall red-haired woman in black who stepped outside with them, the children ran across the cobbled yard, the littlest one toddling so fast that Alec stretched out an arm to catch her before she fell forward.

"Miss MacCarran," he said, looking up at Kate. "I'd like you to meet my nieces, and my aunt, Euphemia Fraser."

He stood to embrace his aunt, who was nearly as tall as he was and perhaps close to his weight, and so delighted to see him that she near picked him up off the ground. Explaining quickly that he had injured his arm during a sword practice, but that it was healing nicely, he then turned to Kate.

"Aunt Euphemia, this is Katherine. Kate," he said. "I've brought her to meet you and Uncle Walter."

"Aye? She's special, then?" She smiled, brown eyes dancing under a crown of unruly red hair barely tamed by a cap, her hair either dyed or still possessing a great deal of natural color despite her age.

"Oh aye, she's quite special," Alec answered.

"Welcome, Miss Katherine—?" Effie waited for the rest.

"It's Fraser, Aunt. Or soon will be," Alec said.

Euphemia gaped at him. "I'll hear this now, and so will Wattie! Come inside, we'll no' stand outside with this news!"

They were beautiful, each one, like an assortment of fairies, Kate thought as she was introduced to each child: Rosie, with straight dark hair and serious green eyes; Lily, whose pale blond locks, big blue eyes, and a dazzling dimple gave her an enchanting air; and Daisy, the youngest at two, with bronze curls and eyes as blue as her sister's. Greeting each child, Kate was entranced by their charming personalities as much as their appearance—serious Rosie, ethereal Lily, and bouncy little Daisy.

"Such bonny lasses," she said brightly, looking at Alec.

He smiled, nodded as he looked at them. Rosie stood near him, Kate saw, looking up at him every few moments, and shy Lily tucked her hand in his quietly. Noticing how quickly he took the girl's hand, and noticing how Daisy pulled on the hem of his kilt, watching him with adoring eyes, Kate felt her heart simply melt.

317

"They've missed their uncle Alec," Euphemia Fraser said.

"And I'm sure he's missed them." Kate glanced up to see a flicker of uncertainty, even vulnerability in Alec's eyes. Then he smiled, and it was gone, and he rested a hand on Rosie's dark, shiny locks, so straight they would not stay in the yellow ribbon that held them back.

"She looks more like her mother each time I see her," he said, looking at his aunt.

"You should see her more often," she said with a huff. "Perhaps then 'twouldna be so much of a shock to you each time that you keep away. Come inside, and we'll take some chocolate. It's early yet, and we've just finished breakfast, though you both may want a bite to eat." She gestured for them to follow, and they headed toward the mansion, while Jack, behind them, turned the horses and took the chaise to stable it and the animals down the street.

"What does she mean, come here more often, Alec?" Kate asked as they walked across the yard—cobbled areas and garden plots, lined with fruit trees, compactly arranged—toward the house.

He was silent, letting the children run ahead with their great-aunt, though Daisy fussed and wanted to stay with her uncle. Alec stooped to pick her up, handing her to Kate because his left arm was still in a sling, and the child came readily into her arms to ride there sweetly.

"Their mother was my betrothed. When I returned

from Leiden, I found her married to my brother and already with child."

Kate sighed out. "You mentioned something about it once, but—seeing the girls now, it gives me a stronger sense of what you must have endured."

He shrugged. "Amy and Edward were better suited, perhaps, than Amy and I, for he was a wilder sort and she and I were both a little staid. He needed her calming nature, and she needed . . . well, perhaps some unpredictability. They had these three lovely lassies," he said, glancing at Daisy, who never took her eyes from him as they strolled along. Kate knew, in a way, what the child felt. She, too, had fallen under the spell of Daisy's uncle Alexander, and could not look at him often enough.

"And the more babes they had, the happier they were, and the more I stayed away," Alec went on. "Amy passed away with the birth of that lovely bairnie in your arms."

"Oh, no," Kate murmured. She tucked her head against Daisy's. "I'm so sorry."

"For years, I dreaded coming here, so much so that I avoided it as much as possible. After Edward died early this year, it only grew worse for me. And a few weeks ago, I would have dreaded this visit as much as any other . . . but it feels different now."

Kate glanced at him, and he stopped with her in the yard, just inside the iron gates, while Euphemia let the other two girls into the front door of the mansion, then turned to wait for Kate and Alec. "What has changed this time?"

319

"I am not sure. I do not feel such . . . fear of them, somehow, if you can understand that."

"I do understand. I know you must love them very much."

"I always have, but the hurt was a powerful thing, lasting over years. And now . . . it's as if it has cleared itself away. It has changed . . . I have changed."

Kate gazed at him thoughtfully. "You *have* changed, Alexander. You have let go some of the locks you kept on yourself, I think."

He gave her a little, rueful smile. "I have, my love, and it's thanks to you and your magic."

"Oh, no, not me. It's within you, sir—perhaps it was time to open up your heart again."

He laughed softly and reached out to touch Daisy's reddish curls. "Whatever it was, it's gone now, Miss Daisy Fraser," he said, and the child laughed as if they shared a fine joke. "I've been such a fool."

"Foo," Daisy said, and Kate laughed.

"Love, Captain Fraser," Kate said, "makes its own magic."

"So the MacCarran fairy sort like to say." He put an arm around her. "And it may be true."

"Oh, it is," she murmured, looking up at him.

"But what we do not yet know, Miss MacCarran, is whether your special sort of magic can extricate three men from prison without putting you in their place."

"Let's hope it can," she said, thinking of their plans with keen trepidation. "Or you and I will be back to chains and manacles, sir."

"Let's hope we at least share a cell," he said, in a wry tone as he led her toward the front door.

As she set Daisy down and greeted Euphemia at the door, she lifted a hand to the crystal at her throat. Love had been born in her life and must be given the chance to thrive. Somehow, they must prevail in the dangerous task that faced them. The plans were in place, and she and Alec and the others had only to carry them out— while presenting a pleasant facade for Alec's family.

Chapter 27

"Married!" Euphemia stared at Alec.

"Well," Alec said, sliding a glance at Kate, who turned a bright blushing color. "Kate and I are, ah, married by Highland tradition, and will be formally wed as soon as we can manage."

"I canna believe it," Effie muttered, and looked at her husband, Walter, who sat in a high-backed chair in Hopefield's drawing room, a cozy place with brocade sofas, embroidered draperies, and children's toys scattered in a corner of the room. "What do you mean, married by Hielan' tradition?" Effie had been raised in the Lowlands, and her Scots accent was thick with rolling r's and abbreviated words.

"You dinna want to know," Walter said bluntly,

while Effie gasped and put a hand to the shelf of her bosom. He pushed his brass-rimmed spectacles higher on his nose. "I think 'tis a fine thing, and you'll no' bother them aboot it any longer. Felicitations to you both," he said, nodding.

"Thank you, Uncle," Alec said, and Kate murmured the same.

"It's time you decided to marry," Walter said. "They're happy, Effie, so leave it be. She's a fine lass, and he was lucky to find her, is my thought."

Effie stared at Walter in silence, then sighed and nodded.

"We've only come to stay a day or two, and then we'll be returning to Kate's home for a while. We'll come back here for a longer visit," Alec went on, lifting a hand to his aunt's protest. "I have some important business to take care of in the Highlands," he added in a loud whisper.

"*Och*, something for Mr. Keppick? Good!" Effie used the code name she had created for MacDonald of Keppoch—a lamentably obvious one, Alec thought. Effie looked at Kate. "And you are from the Highlands? Aye? Do you know a place called Jacob's Ladder up north, or Jacob's Stone?" She spoke in a loud whisper.

Kate looked blank. "I suppose they are not near my home—"

"Those are signals from one Jacobite to another," Alec told Kate. "Aunt Effie, it's fine. She shares our sympathies."

"Ah! Verra good. And where did you meet?"

"In London, months ago," Alec said.

"Did you visit White's Chocolate House at the bottom of St. James's while you were there?" Effie asked, folding her hands. "It has a fine reputation."

"Aye, as a gathering place for Jacobites and anyone of a rebellious nature, be it politics or poetry," he said. "Jack and I went there to make a comparison with your establishment here in Edinburgh. We recognized no one else frequenting the place, but I did try a hot chocolate drink in the Spanish style."

"Aye, pepper makes the difference!" Walter looked pleased. "And it's most authentic."

"No one makes it quite like you, Uncle," Alec said tactfully. "I also rather enjoyed the hot chocolate that Kate's friend Mrs. Murray made for me," Alec said. "Hot cocoa made with plenty of thick cream and extra loaf sugar."

"*Och*, that's for bairnies, that," Walter said. "Pepper is the thing!"

Alec smothered a smile as he looked at Kate. She was blinking madly, trying to keep pace with his two eccentric relatives.

"I like it the Roman way, if you take my meaning," Effie hissed loudly to Kate, who leaned back, a little startled.

"Iced with milk, madam?" Walter asked his wife, as if deliberately misunderstanding. "You used to like it hot and spicy—"

"Hush!" Effie waved her hand at him. "I mean, I like James Stuart's *Roman* court," she emphasized. "Do you, Miss Kate?"

"Aye, it's nice. Well, a bit dull, to be honest. I lived

there with my parents for a few years. There was a great deal of praying and reading, and not very much intrigue, which I found so much more interesting." She wrinkled her nose a little, and Walter laughed, low and hearty.

"You were in the court of exiles?" Effie sounded astonished.

"Aye, my father was sent to France, and we went with him. He followed the court to the Muti Palace in Rome, so we lived there, too, as well as in France and Flanders at different times."

"Her father was exiled for crimes of rebellion," Alec said.

Effie clasped her hands together rapturously and leaned over to grab Kate in a hug. Alec's aunt was a tall woman and nearly twice Kate's weight, with a generous bosom and a powerful hug, and she nearly enveloped the girl for a moment. Kate emerged, half-laughing, glancing at Alec as she straightened the little lace cap on her head.

"I like her!" Effie announced as she stood. "You should marry her!" She swept toward the door. "Now, you two will need to rest and refresh, and the maid will have your rooms ready by now. And I'll go fetch the wee lassies. We all need to rest before luncheon, after the events of this morning!" She nodded at all of them, and left the room.

"She's drinkin' too much brown sherry before luncheon, that one," Walter drawled, as the door closed with a theatrical thud. "After you've had your chance to rest and refresh, come downstairs, and I'll show you the chocolate shop," he told Kate.

* * *

Easing open the door that adjoined his room and Kate's, Alec stepped in quietly, expecting to find Kate resting. But she stood at the window and turned, haloed in sunlight softened through curtains, as if she had been waiting.

He knew she had, then, for she wore only a chemise, only that, so that the light behind her gently filtered through the fabric to show her delectable shape. He caught his breath silently, feeling himself surge and harden just at the sight of her. He walked toward her over Oriental carpets that added quiet luxury to the bedchamber.

She moved toward him, the rhythmic sway of her body telling him what she wanted, for it was the same desire he had. She lifted her arms to him as he reached her, and without a word, he took her by the waist, drawing her forward to kiss her. Under his hand, smoothing up and down her back, he felt her warm curves, felt her body press against his own.

Her lips were luscious beneath his, firm and knowing, and she opened for him quickly, the small tip of her tongue sweet and willing. He sucked in a breath and pressed her even closer. Earlier, he had removed jacket, sporran, all but his shirt and plaid, and he could feel her shape meld against his through the layers of fabric, could feel the heat and hardness building in his own body.

She pulled back, then, glancing up at him, glancing at the door. "They're all asleep," Alec told her, "napping in their rooms. They think we are, as well."

"And so we will do," she whispered, "in a little while. But for now," she went on, as her mouth traced over his lips, along his chin, her breath warm and delightful upon his skin, "for now we have a promise to fulfill."

"Aye, what is that?" he murmured, his lips caressing hers.

"First, a promise of marriage," she whispered against his mouth, "and after it, a fixing of the bargain between us."

"Ah," he said, "a bargain we can both agree on."

She laughed softly and took his hand, leading him to the bed. He saw that she had turned down the covers, and as he reached up to draw shut the bed drapes, she sat on the mattress and he sank down beside her, then paused to strip away the cloth sling that encumbered his bandaged left arm. He took her into his arms and reclined in the cool, deep nest of pillows and linens.

As she leaned forward to kiss him, as he returned it and rolled her to her back, where he could most easily sweep his hand up under the long chemise that veiled her body. He felt excitement mounting in him, its beat strong as a drum, but he paused, nuzzling against her ear, licking the delicate lobe.

"I promise to marry you, Katherine MacCarran," he whispered, "as soon as you like. And will you promise the same to me?"

"Oh, aye," she whispered, "I will."

"So that is all we need for the *matrimonio* part of it," he murmured, tracing his lips over the softness of her cheek. "And now for the *consummato*, if you will."

SARAH GABRIEL

"I would dearly love that," she breathed.

He laughed softly and kissed her throat, her upper chest, his next exhalation pooling hot between her breasts. He glided his tongue over one soft mound and found the nipple, and Kate sucked in a breath of pleasure, arching for him. He reached upward with his hand under the chemise to strip away the fabric and draw it over her head. A moment later, she lay nude and exquisitely lovely in his arms, and he let his gaze caress her, creamy skin, golden hair like ripe sunlight, the graceful allure of her body making him pulse and throb for her until he could bear it no longer.

"Now you," she murmured, and with sure, deft hands, she helped him out of the plaid, the shirt, the rest of it, until he stretched beside her, his body pressed beside her own, dark where she was pale, taut where she was soft, hard where she was satiny, and all of it a perfect complement and fit. His fingers traced up and down, circling the smooth hollows and secrets of her body, and she stroked him, kissing and admiring and easing along, while his heart began to thunder within him.

He knew a little more about pleasing her now, knew that she loved to stretch out and arch for him, knew the shape and sweetness of her breasts, so that he kissed and caressed her with a leisurely sureness that he knew would bring him as much pleasure as it would bring to her. Soon he covered her with kisses, then gently eased his fingers inside of her, tenderly coaxing until she began to whimper and rock against him.

When her hand found him, shaping his hard, heated length and teasing even more life into that part of him, he sucked in a breath and rocked toward her, and she moved a little and opened for him, so willing and lovely that his heart leaped just to know it. Lifting, taking her hips into his hands, he eased himself into her, feeling her luscious heat surround him and mold to him, and as he began to thrust, he felt himself shift, pulsing blood and breath, then his very soul rushed through him, and he felt his life open up before him as it never had before.

All of it, suddenly, seemed a miracle to him such as he had never experienced before, and he felt himself surge with the great power of it and felt her move under him like a wave of the sea, sweeping in tandem with him toward a new threshold.

Never before, he thought as he emerged, had he felt so truly joined, so blessed, so deeply in love. He was filled with a renewed, deep certainty that this woman, this union, was what he had been needing, and missing, for so long.

Yet danger still lay ahead for both of them, threatening that union—and he thought she understood that as well as he did.

"We will be meeting our friends at the Chocolate House in a little while," Alec said, when they met Walter in the drawing room an hour or so later. "We'll need a private room to speak with them, if you have that wee room at the back of the shop available."

"Aye," Walter said, as he led them through the corridor to the front door of Hopefield House.

A minute's walk took them across the yard to the tenement building. Walter let them in the back door and through a corridor, past a kitchen, and out into the main area of the shop. "We've been here nearly forty years, when my brother and I started the business of Fraser's Fancies. We started out with coffee and added China tea and chocolate," he told Kate. "We opened this shop originally as a coffeehouse, then added chocolate, and it's since become known as the Chocolate House. It's the brown stone front as much as what we serve here, but we like the name." He smiled and held open another door for Alec and Kate to pass through. Walter Fraser was slightly built, lean and spry and barely as tall as Effie, but his good nature balanced her exuberance.

As they went through, Kate smiled up at Alec. "I like your uncle," she whispered. "Is he one of the staid Frasers?"

He leaned down, knowing Walter was a bit deaf and would not hear their conversation. "He may seem that way, but for his penchant for experimentation, especially with chocolate and cacao, which puts him on the wilder side, I think."

"Hot peppers and such?" she whispered.

"You say you have friends meeting you here today?" Walter asked. "You'll be wanting to take chocolate, then. 'Tis the king o' drinks." He led them into the main room.

Stepping over the threshold, Alec looked around, and his hand clenched on Kate's shoulder.

Three soldiers sat at a table by the front window. Kate caught her breath and nearly stopped, so that he bumped against her. She looked up at him with alarm in her eyes. He recognized two of the soldiers as those who had been at MacLennan's Changehouse.

"Is the private room empty now, Uncle?" Alec asked quietly. Walter nodded and led them to a side door, opening it to show them a small room with four tables, each with a silver chocolate server on it. No one was there, though a fire crackled in the hearth.

"This is the smokin' room," Walter said. "You can use this one for your meeting. Might be others coming in to use it, too, though. We get busy of an afternoon. We see a fair number of clerks and advocates here, and because we're so close to the courts, the justices themselves come here often. The Lord Justice Clerk and the Lord Advocate himself come here for their midday break from proceedings there."

Kate gasped then, and Alec pulled out a chair for her to sit. She shoved back her hood and patted her hair with a shaking hand. "Lord . . . Advocate? Here?"

"Aye, he's Alec's uncle on his mother's side. Lord Hume."

"I thought your mother was a MacDonald," she said.

"She was, but her stepbrothers are Humes. Complicated, but that and other relatives have given me an assortment of uncles. Uncle George comes nearly every day, does he not?" Alec asked.

"Usually. He takes his chocolate here often as he can. Likes Spanish-style with cinnamon and anise, or else chocolate with jasmine, and biscuits. If he has trials and interviews and such, he'll come for the fours and have his cocoa instead o' tea."

"Jasmine?" Kate asked dubiously.

"*Och*, 'tis good, that. Jasmine flowers and vanilla beans with the chocolate. The lassies like it." Walter winked at Kate, and Alec nearly gaped—he had never seen his uncle do that.

But he remembered Kate's peculiar effect on men, and supposed his uncle must have succumbed, in his way. "We've whatever sort you like, lass. With cinnamon, or jasmine, with anise or pepper, or the way the bairns like it, with milk and sugar and vanilla beans. We serve it hot and some days can serve it chilled on ice, when we have the snow brought down from the mountains for the packing. We have medicinal chocolate, with brown sherry frothed with eggs, and we have chocolate soup, as well. What will you try?"

"Chocolate soup?" Alec asked. "We did not have that before."

"Aye, it's but a puddin' over bread, wi' thick chocolate and eggs. Oh, and Effie wants to add a more Continental flavor to our place, so she is offering mocha custards and chocolate liver."

"Liver?" Kate asked, looking at Alec.

"Aye, liver fried up and dipped in a chocolate sauce. And she doesna like my eating chocolates, but she says the liver is fine, see, because 'tis Continental," he added, shaking his head. "What would you like to try?"

"I'd love to try some Spanish-style with the cinnamon, please," Kate said.

"I'd be happy to make it for you myself. We make it in the best chocolatières, large silver pots with *molinillo* sticks to whip up a very thick froth. You'll never have it so good as at Fraser's. Alec?"

"Aye, lass, you'll never have it so good as at Fraser's," Alec drawled. She kicked him beneath the table. "I'd like some coffee, Uncle, if you would be so kind. Strong and bitter, with sugar on the side."

"*Och*, this lad never did like the cacao, though his brother loved it. Edward kept this business thriving, while this lad lets me tend to it and mucks about with espionage," Walter murmured to Kate.

"But Mr. Fraser, Scotland needs men who are willing to muck about with such things, just as we need men who are willing to muck about with chocolate, to create the most wonderful eating chocolate imaginable." She smiled sweetly.

"And you enjoy tending to the business," Alec said. "You manage it much better than I could do."

"When you have time, lad, we'll need to go over the accounting books. Our exports of Fraser's Fancies—cocoa, teas, and coffee—are finally beginning to grow again, though our import costs are climbing quickly, too."

"Flax," Alec said. "I've been thinking. We need to consider investing in another commodity. Flax is a stable industry for Scotland, and can expand very rapidly—if we invest in flax and fabrics, we will better be able to support Fraser's Fancies. And we can contribute to the welfare of Scots who need small industries in their towns."

Walter lifted his brows high, and his glasses slid to the end of his nose. "Of course! *Och*, we'll talk about that. It could be you'll be as brilliant as your brother was in business matters! Now, we'll make these drinks up for you." He smiled and left the room.

Alec reached across the table to touch Kate's hand. "You're anxious, lass. And since I've known you, I've seen a good deal of courage, and temper. What is it?"

She shook her head, smiling a little, then got up to peer through the door that Walter had left open a bit. "The soldiers are still there. But where are Rob and Connor?"

"They will not come inside if they see soldiers here. You may have to go up to the castle as we agreed, to see Ian and the others, and wait for us."

"But our plan depends on all of us staying together. We agreed on it."

"Aye. First Jack and your kinsmen must do their part, and we must wait for them. Is that the one o'clock bell?" Alec rose and went to the door with her to watch for a moment. Soon the door of the shop opened, and several men in black robes and old-fashioned white periwigs came into the Chocolate House. Three or four redcoat soldiers were with them, although Alec could not immediately see them for the crowd of black robes and gesturing hands in the way.

It hardly mattered who they were. Any development involving justice and military could be disastrous if Kate was recognized, or if Rob and Connor were questioned. Walter rushed forward to greet them, and after talking for a few moments, nodded and indicated the private room with an eager smile.

"Aye, he's here," Walter was saying. "And Kate, too.

Oh, aye, you will want to meet her. Come this way, Lord Hume."

"By the devil," Alec muttered under his breath. He looked at Kate. "I hope you have your fairy charm well in hand today, lass. Uncle George is here, and he looks none too pleased. If you've never prayed for a miracle before, this would be the time."

Kate's face went ashen so fast that Alec thought she might faint, but she sat straight, put a hand to her throat where her necklace lay hidden, and smiled. It was like a bit of sunshine emerging.

God bless the lass, he thought in admiration, then he prayed himself—though he had not done anything like it for a very long time—as he stood there looking mild and nonchalant, prayed for a miracle to guide them through this.

For he could not lose her now, not to this fate or any other. He was her fate now, as she was his—and that would be complicated enough where this lass was concerned, he thought, without long-robes passing judgment.

Alec stepped back as Walter and one of the justices approached. And then he saw that the Lord Advocate, one of the most mean-spirited men he had ever known, uncle or not, was walking directly toward the private room.

And behind him was Colonel Francis Grant.

Chapter 28

"**T**his is the man, Lord Hume," Grant said. He had a tight smile on his face as he looked first at Alec, and then at Kate. "Captain Fraser. And this is the girl he stole away from the prison at Inverlochy, ignoring his orders from General Wade."

Kate stared hard at Grant, who gave her a narrow glance, then could not help but sweep his gaze down her body, neatly defined by the snug jacket and flaring skirts. He lifted one brow in a rude acknowledgment of her attractiveness to him.

Beside him, the Lord Advocate had a scowl so deep it carved troughs in his jowly cheeks and in his brow. "Alexander," he said in a gruff voice, "how are you?"

"Fine, sir, thank you, and you?"

Kate looked from one to the other, noting Alec's cool formality as he answered his uncle.

"Alexander?" Colonel Grant repeated.

"Lord Hume is my uncle," Alec told Grant.

"Uncle! Damn you, Fraser—"

"That's no matter to me," Lord Hume snapped. "If he's guilty, he's guilty, nephew or none, and he knows me well enough for that. Where is my chocolate? And who the devil are you?" The Lord Advocate peered at Kate from under shaggy gray eyebrows. His eyes were blue and rheumy and he looked supremely annoyed. She smiled timorously.

"This is Katherine, sir," Alec said.

"Katherine who? I will not play games. Is this the girl who is to be interviewed for treasonous crimes and espionage? The one Wade wrote about in his report to me—and the one this gentleman is whingeing on about?" He peered again at her.

She wanted to take a step backward, but did not, holding her ground and regarding the Lord Advocate calmly and silently.

"This is the one, sir," Alec said. Kate glanced at him, dumbfounded by his open admission, tantamount to a betrayal that left her on her own—but for the fact that he sent her a covert glance that said, inexplicably, all would be well.

"Where's Walter's lass with that blasted cocoa? I do not have all day for this. Well, sit down, all of you, and tell me what this is about. If she is to be interviewed, it may as well be here since I do not even have my chocolate yet and must wait." The Lord Advocate sat down, heavily, for he was apparently a robust man under his voluminous black robes.

Alec pulled out a chair for Kate, and he sat beside her. Grant remained standing.

"Lord Hume, sir, this girl was caught stealing documents from officers' tents," Grant began. "You have seen the reports. She was seen again and again, and she did bodily harm to some of the men, including myself. She is a harlot, to be frank, and though Captain Fraser had her arrested, he has since changed his mind and abetted her escape." He looked so smug that Kate wanted to reach out and slap him.

Lord Hume grunted. He looked from one of them to the other, and at that moment Walter walked into the room carrying a tray with a tall silver pot with a long, narrow spout. He was followed by a servant carrying another tray with a second pot and various cups. "Finally," Lord Hume muttered.

Watching Walter froth the chocolate in the pot by whipping it fervently with the stirring stick, Kate waited, heart pounding hard, dreading the rest of the meeting with the justice.

First Walter poured out Lord Hume's chocolate—steaming and rich, it smelled like heaven—into a small porcelain bowl. Then he set a small bowl before Kate and poured her another serving of the same.

"Spanish-style with cinnamon," Walter said, looking pleased to have such distinguished guests and cherished visitors gathered together. With a flourish, he offered Grant a bowl as well, but the man declined with a curt, dismissing wave of his hand.

The servant girl poured a small china cup full of hot black coffee for Alec, setting it in front of him with a bowl of sugar and a delicate silver spoon. Biscuits on a tray, with marmalade and butter, completed the meal. Bowing, Walter left and ushered the girl out of the room with him.

"Now," Lord Hume said, "go on. I have only a few minutes before I return to the courts." He sipped his hot cocoa, holding the bowl with both hands. "The girl stole documents, et cetera. I know all that. Now I want to hear something I don't know. Katherine who?" He looked at her over the rim of his bowl of cocoa. "What is your name?"

"Uncle George, this is Katherine Fraser," Alec said.

"What! What do you mean? A long-lost relation of yours?" Lord Hume picked up a biscuit and bit into it, crumbs flying.

"If she were Fraser," Grant sneered, "you would have said so earlier."

"Katherine Fraser," Alec repeated. "She is my bride."

Kate sat silent, watching the others warily.

"Bride," Grant growled. "What the devil is this about?"

"You married your prisoner? That was damned foolish." The Lord Advocate sipped loudly. "You could be imprisoned and stripped of your military commission for that, lad."

"Exactly what I think, sir," Grant said. "Treason, lying to the court, stealing the prisoner away without permission. She was arrested in his quarters, and now he's trying to protect her. She does that to gentlemen,

Lord Hume," he said, leaning down. "She's a Jezebel and a strumpet—"

"You're unpleasant to listen to," Lord Hume barked. "So be quiet. I rather like the look of the girl myself. Are you a strumpet?" He peered at Kate.

"I am not, sir, and I've never been," she replied quietly, and thought he began to smile. Lord Hume leaned toward her, but then exhaled loudly and returned his attention to his steaming drink.

Like his nephew, the Lord Advocate seemed immune to her presence and any charm she might have. She watched him, realizing that she was so anxious about her fate, and Alec's as well, that she could not deliberately charm anyone just now. She trembled all over.

"Hmph. Now I want to hear what this is about. Alexander, explain." Lord Hume sipped again, noisily, and munched on another biscuit, then dipped it into his cocoa.

"Sir, when she came into my tent that night . . . I believe she was searching for me," Alec said.

With her own little bowl raised in her hand, Kate stopped, the chocolate scent of the steam surrounding her. She stared at Alec in disbelief.

"I can say for certain that I have been looking for her ever since we met, months ago in London. We pledged our love when we were together there. I gave her my heart, and she gave me hers, if I may be honest with you gentlemen. And then we were separated. Ever since then—"

"We have been searching for each other," Kate said. "It's true. I have looked for him every day since I first saw him . . . I have dreamed about him and feared I might never see him again. Everywhere I went, I felt compelled to look for my Highland officer." She glanced up at Alec. "No matter what I did, I was always looking for him. Only him."

"As I have looked for her," Alec murmured, setting a hand on her shoulder.

"Oh, I can't bear this," Grant said in a snide tone. "And you never looked for military documents?" He snorted.

"Only those with Alec's name on them," Kate said.

Lord Hume, chewing a mouthful of dry biscuit slathered in marmalade and dipped in cocoa, watched them, crumbs spilling from his mouth. "Mm-hmm," he mumbled. "So then you had her arrested?" He sent Alec a sharp glance.

"Lovers' spat," Alec answered.

Kate nodded vigorously. "We had a terrible disagreement."

"That's a hell of a way to punish a lass for disagreeing with you. I should try that with my wife." Lord Hume began to wheeze with laughter.

Grant looked thunderous. "And you never said a word about this?" he fumed.

"I was sure of my heart, but not of hers," Alec replied. "But we were married in a Highland fashion."

"For how long?" Grant snapped.

"It seems as if that happened the moment our eyes met," Kate said. "We committed our hearts to one another."

"Lord Advocate, sir," Alec said formally. "She has

341

never done such crimes as have been attributed to her. She is an impetuous lass and thinks with her heart, not always her head, and so she has done some foolish things—but she's no strumpet, and she's no thief. This girl is loyal, sir, and devoted."

"But she's a spy," Grant said bluntly.

The Lord Advocate slurped up the last of his cocoa and poured another helping from the silver bowl, fragrant mist rising as he poured. He said nothing as he took the last biscuit and dipped it in the hot chocolate.

"Sir, this is utter nonsense," Grant said. He was scowling, his hands knuckled white on the back of the empty chair in front of him.

"So you're vouching for this lass?" Hume looked at Alec, who nodded. Then the old man looked critically at Kate. "And you swear you never took a military document, or any other thing, with criminal or treasonous intent?" His glare was powerful.

"I can say in honesty, sir, that I never entered an officer's tent, or looked at a document, without Captain Fraser on my mind, without him being my sole purpose, my sole reason for . . . doing anything. I can tell you truthfully that he fills my every waking thought, and my dreams. I could not rest, sir, until I found him again." Truthful enough, she thought. Reaching up, she rested her hand on Alec's, which still gripped her shoulder.

"Oh, please, do not expect us to accept this," Grant said.

"It's true," she said. "We have been searching for each other for months."

"Make of that what you will, sir," Alec said quietly. "I only want to clear this matter up and take my wife back to Kilburnie House, where we can begin a peaceful life together."

The Lord Advocate grunted again. He finished the second helping of cocoa, brushed the crumbs off his black robes, and stood. "I am not wasting my time, or the crown's time or money, on a lovers' spat between two besotted fools. This is not worth presenting in court. I am the Lord Advocate of Scotland, not a blasted matchmaker. And if the girl is a spy, she is not a very good one, and again it is not worth presenting this at the Court of Justiciary. We have a burden of cases as it is."

"Sir—" Grant began. "I implore you to pursue this."

"Love and such has no place before my bench. Alexander, good day to you. Katherine, welcome to our family. And Colonel Grant—come with me, sir. You have a report to prepare." Though Grant protested loudly, the old man was intractable. He waved Grant toward the door, then turned.

"Excellent choice in a wife, Alexander—and that was a damn fine story." He smiled then, truly smiled, for an instant.

"Thank you, sir," Alec said, and Kate stepped forward to kiss the Lord Advocate on the cheek. He blustered, said nothing coherent, and left, slamming the door behind him.

Alec looked down at her. "Now that," he said, "was either a miracle or some very fine fairy magic."

She laughed then, with breathy relief and true joy.

She threw her hands around his neck, and he hugged her to him, arm in a sling between them, and she lifted her face for a deep, rich kiss that mingled chocolate and coffee and the sweetest measure of passion and tenderness she had ever known.

Then Alec pulled back and looked down at her. "My love, as much as I would love to continue this, we have another task more pressing to see to."

She nodded. "Alec—if we should be caught removing Ian and the others from the castle dungeon—after the Lord Advocate's leniency here, we would have no more chance for mercy, or miracles. What if it goes poorly?"

He held her then, in silent answer, just held her, and that rock of security and comfort he offered was one of the most wonderful sensations she had ever felt. Then he drew back.

"We'll have to take the risk. We cannot let the lads linger there awaiting their deaths, and Ian will be transferred to the Tower of London very soon, I think. But you do not have to do this if you are anxious over it."

"I'll come with you." She lifted her head.

"Good," he said softly. "We'll need your glamourie up at the castle to shield our way."

He led her out of the little room and through the main room of the Chocolate House. Waving to Walter Fraser as Alec opened the street door for her, Kate did not notice, at first, the group of people standing outside on the pavement, talking to a pair of sedan chair carriers.

344

She looked, and gasped, and looked again. Alec gave a low huff that sounded like a smothered laugh.

Rob, Connor, and Jack turned, all dressed in long, dark, hooded cloaks, similar to the one that Kate had with her. And all of them, beneath the cloaks, were dressed in gowns.

None of them looked particularly pleasant as ladies, Kate thought, trying not to laugh. The situation was desperately serious, she knew. Men could die this day for what they had planned—and she was sure none of them would want to die looking like this.

"Well," Jack said, coming toward them. "We're ready. Let's do what must be done. The chairs are hired, so we can go up to the castle now."

"Jack," Alec said, "you look quite ravishing."

"Go to the devil," Jack growled, and spun to return to the sedan chair awaiting him.

Chapter 29

❧❧❧

The sedan chair rocked, its seat fastened with pinions, so that as the chair carrier went up the hill, Kate stayed level on the leather seat. She gripped the seat edge tightly, and looked behind her. All of her "female" companions rode sedan chairs as well, while Alec would make his way separately.

Ahead, the castle walls loomed dark at the top of the hill, and all four chairmen brought the group easily through the first sentry gate, for Kate explained that she and her friends had come to visit prisoners within, with three of the ladies in danger of becoming widowed. They were waved on to the front gate, where they were passed through again.

As they entered the inner walls and climbed the

slope toward the complex of buildings, Kate glanced toward Rob.

"Up there, straight on," he whispered, keeping his head low. "The dungeons are in that keep."

She nodded and proceeded slowly. Then she heard a voice hailing them from behind, and she turned to see Alec, dressed in red coat and kilt and officer's sash as before—but now there were many like him in this place, soldiers and officers, and he looked anonymous and strikingly handsome. He came toward their group, and her heart flipped to see him.

"Ladies, allow me to escort you. Are you here to see prisoners? Aye, then." He was cool and polite, hardly looking at Kate. Within minutes he had passed them through one sentry post after another and led them down a few worn stone steps to the dungeon area, and finally into a narrow, dark corridor that smelled of oil smoke from lanterns, barely covering far worse odors.

Kate shuddered, remembering her confinement in Inverlochy Castle's dungeons. A sense rose up in her then, all doubt vanishing, that what they were doing here was right—these men could not be left in this place.

"Sergeant, Corporal—these ladies have come to visit the Highland prisoners," Alec said, as two sentries in the corridor stood and saluted. "I suspect they are soon to be widows," he whispered loudly. "We may want to allow them some privacy."

"There's four ladies," the sergeant observed, "and three Highland Donalds in there, so how many wives do these fellows have? Three can go in," he said. "Not four."

"One of them is sister to a prisoner."

"Then she can go in separate-like," the sergeant replied. "We cannot let them all in there at once, Captain." He stood.

"Unless they are prepared to convince us otherwise," the corporal said, holding out a gloved hand. "You know, sir, these Donalds are kept in these lower cells because they've no money to pay for better quarters. They could have fine rooms above, good food, beds with linens, even a servant and postal privileges and books and such, if they had coin to pay. But Highlanders are notorious poor. We had to put all three of those rascals together, and we have to sit down here watchin' 'em." He wiggled his fingers, and after a moment, cleared his throat and stepped back.

"I understand," Alec said, and turned. "Ladies?"

Rob, dressed in a long green cloak and hood, and showing a ruffled blue hem under the cloak, came forward. He held a kerchief to his face and sniffled. He was followed by Connor, then Jack, all in swishing skirts and cloaks, two with handkerchiefs to their noses, Jack with a pretty fan. He sobbed as he went past, fluttering the painted silken fan, and Alec patted him on the shoulder.

"There, madam. Go in, please. The sergeant will unlock the door for you." As the "ladies" left with the sergeant, Alec turned to Kate. "Miss . . . Cameron, you're sister to one of those lads, are you not? Would you mind staying out here and keeping these gentlemen company until the other ladies have finished their

348

visit? Then you can have a few moments alone with your brother."

"Thank you," she murmured. She pushed back her cloak, so that the lanternlight caught the ruddy golden glow of her hair, which she had loosened and taken down during the ride in the sedan chair. The corporal seemed startled, then stared.

"Greetings, Miss Cameron," he said, stammering.

She inclined her head regally.

"I'll take my leave now," Alec said, bowing. "So very nice to make your acquaintance, Miss." He turned and walked away, his footsteps echoing.

Kate smiled at the corporal, who was still staring, his skin beginning to blush. She knew her role—to distract the guards as much as she could while the Highlanders went back and forth in various stages. Jack, Rob, and Connor all wore extra cloaks and skirts under their outer cloaks that they planned to share with Ian, Andrew, and Donald.

The sergeant came back, and she turned to glance at him. He blinked at her, and smiled, and offered her a chair in cordial silence. She declined, and asked after their health, asked after their families, asked about themselves.

They were both eager to talk, young men who were lonely and bored on sentry watch in the dungeons. She showed rapt interest in everything they said, laughing prettily at their jokes.

All the while, they stared, and the corporal's jaw kept slacking open. She knew both men were surrendering to the allure of her fairy gift, with every word, each glance she gave them.

"Miss," the corporal said, "you have a sort of glow all about you like candlelight, did you know it? A very pretty glow." His companion readily agreed, nodding.

"Like a new lantern. We needed such," he said.

She caught her breath at that, and thanked them. Fingering the crystal at her throat, she felt its power in a new way—a confidence she had never had before and a detachment as well.

Suddenly she felt as if she could control this ability as never before. A smile, a word, a touch of the crystal seemed not nearly as powerful, now, as something that came from within. It was different than will, or any sort of awareness. It had more to do, she realized then, with her own conviction that she was loved, her own sense of holding love within her like a vessel holds water, or a lantern holds light.

This had not happened before in her experience with the fairy charm, and she knew now, indeed, that the fairy-blessed among the MacCarrans were those who could carry this love within themselves and give it to others. The thought took her breath away, and she set a hand to her chest, feeling the beautiful power of it. The Fairy Gift was meant to be shared, she knew then, shared in the kindest and most beneficial ways.

Her breath quickened, and her smile deepened, and the men with her seemed completely entranced.

And behind her, first one and then another lady came out of the cell and went back inside. One and then another walked past her weeping, or sobbing; two ran past and down the corridor beset by grief, and one came back sniffling, apparently intent on one last embrace, one last kiss. Back and forth they went, while Kate smiled at the guards, and they smiled at her, and no one counted the cloaked ladies shuffling and sniffling between the cell and the corridor.

"Oh," Kate said, turning at one point. "They seem to have all gone. Beset by grief," she whispered, "my poor friends. I'll go say my farewell, if I may. Oh, no, do stay here," she urged, when the corporal moved ahead. "It is something I must do myself, but I thank you for your courtesy."

She walked down the short length of the passage to the cell, with its planked wooden door and inset, barred window. Stepping into the cell, she stood for a few moments, turning around to enjoy its emptiness.

They were all gone—and all she need do now was linger long enough to give them time to get out of the castle, six ladies, when four had gone inside. With Alec's help, they would be escorted out of the castle compound and be away down Castlehill in sedan chairs before any of the guards realized what had happened.

When she thought enough time had passed, she left the cell, closing the door behind her. Then she walked past the guards, sniffling, giving them a tremulous smile.

She paused, and reached into the small purse she had tucked in a deep pocket. Extracting two gold Spanish doubloons, as arranged with her kinsmen earlier, she handed one each to the sentries.

"Oh, no, we could not accept—" the corporal began.

"Please," she said. "You've been so kind. This is for your trouble. They're quite valuable, I'm told."

"I'd say," the sergeant remarked. "But they don't shine nearly as brightly as you, Miss. It's like a magic about you." He grinned, looking boyishly eager to please.

She smiled, and pressed each man's hand in farewell. "I'm in love. That's all the magic you see." Smiling again, she turned. "You need not accompany me, gentlemen. My friends are waiting outside." Then she glided away.

And around the corner, picked up her skirts and ran.

Outside, as Alec ushered each "lady" into a hired chair, the grateful as well as the grumbling ones, he kept glancing back to watch for Kate. While Jack MacDonald, and Kate's kinsmen were done with ladies' gear and did not want to keep it longer than necessary, Ian, Andrew, and Donald were more than willing to leave the esplanade in any disguise. Finally, seeing them all safe away, Alec turned and headed back to the castle entrance.

Where the devil was Kate? She should have been outside already, he thought, frowning. As he walked forward, he looked up to see her coming out of the arched tunnel entrance and across the lowered drawbridge. She picked up her skirts and ran toward him, her cloak hood falling back to show her hair, shining Celtic gold in the afternoon sun.

He hastened toward her, and she smiled up at him, but he kept back. "No embraces, love, as beautiful as

352

you are to me," he said, "more lovely than even the queen of the fairies. But unless you can vanish into the mist, or fly, we'd best find you a sedan chair and get you gone from here."

Kate nodded, for he knew she well understood the need for caution. He turned with her and walked sedately to escort her to the outer gate. When he glanced down at her, she suddenly gasped and set a hand upon his arm to stop him.

Looking in the direction of the gate, he saw Francis Grant coming toward him from Castlehill like a thundercloud, his brow lowered and dark, fists clenched.

"Fraser!" he yelled, his hand on the sword at his side. "Damn you to hell, Fraser, and the lady with you! What have you been up to in this place?"

"Nothing much, a little sport," Alec murmured.

"Aye, I'd wager one or more Highlanders are gone. You and this one have been about some sort of work, I'm sure of it. And I'll give you sport, sir, if that is what you want," Grant snapped, and whipped his sword from its sheath.

Alec pushed Kate back and drew his own sword, advancing on Grant with such ease and sureness that the colonel stumbled back immediately at first. Then Grant recovered, and threw away his cocked hat and took his stance, a hanging guard.

Countering quickly, knocking back the blade as it came down, Alec began a fast series of lunges and parries. Grant proved to be a skilled opponent, and Alec had to watch every step, every move. He could not spare a glance for the guards who gathered around, hands on swords, two with their fingers set on pistols.

Nor could he watch the lady who stood with them, beautiful and luminous in the midst of the soldiers. Most especially, he could not look her way.

Dance back, quarter guard, parry, and thrust—Alec spun out his moves, scarcely thinking about them. He circled, his balance affected slightly by his injured arm in its sling, so he tore away the confining cloth in one motion, pulling it over his head and flinging it away. Then he extended his left arm for necessary balance, and though pain protested all along his forearm, he hardly noticed it somehow.

Rounding so that his back was to the setting sun over the castle walls, he saw Grant blink furiously. Keeping the man facing in that direction required that Alec step forward and backward, rather than side to side, and he did his best to maintain that position.

Blocking blows, he retreated, lunging, he thrust forward, keeping his back to the brilliance of the lowering sun. Grant tried again and again to shift away, the sun slanting strong gold over his face now, illuminating his eyes, so that Alec saw the deep fire in them and knew he would be killed for certain if the man got so much as an opening.

Hang guard, step forward, thrust—and this time Alec found flesh and whipped open a wound in Grant's cheek. Slapping a hand to his face, Grant shifted, and Alec shifted back again, so that the setting sun was ever there behind him, like a luminous ally at his back.

Grant stepped backward, and Alec followed with a

volley of strikes. The other man stumbled suddenly and turned, whirling so fast that Alec had no choice but to dance to the side—and the movement brought both of them perilously close to the outer wall that flanked the esplanade, with the castle looming to one side and the city sloping away to the other, and not an arm's reach away, a straight drop down a sheer cliff to sloping ground hundreds of feet below.

Beyond Grant's shoulder, Alec saw Kate move with the soldiers who watched them, all of them helpless to stop the lethal sword fight in progress. He shifted and sidestepped, his shoe heels scraping the base of the wall, the wind brisking fresh and cold over the side, whipping his hair across his eyes as it sifted loose of the ribbon that held it back. The wall's sloping base threw him off balance and off guard, and in its curving course along the top of the hill, it was scarcely waist high in this area. As he tried to put a little distance between him and the stone wall and the expanse of air and distance beyond it, Grant advanced again.

This time the tip of his blade caught Alec's injured arm, ripping through bandages, slicing along the wound. Agony seared through him, and for a moment Alec saw the world go gray, but he kept to his feet, ignored the drip of blood along his sleeve, and whirled.

And she was there, like a sunbeam beside him, her back to the wall, her back to the setting sun. When she had stepped forward into the path of danger, Alec had no idea, but he could not look her way—could not, though he felt the lure of it.

"Step back," he hissed over his shoulder. "Get away!"

But she did not. Nor did she need to—for Grant suddenly slowed, and gaped at her, and a look came over his face of such wonderment, such bewilderment, that he faltered for a moment.

In that instant, Alec thrust again. Grant recovered, but now it was Grant who watched Kate with a distracted fascination—Grant who kept glancing her way, who could no longer maintain his focus. Alec advanced again, and turned, and Kate turned with them, circling outside them, several feet away and out of harm's way. But she was incandescent in the setting sun, her hair like a halo about her, and Alec saw it then—the glamourie over her like a glow about her.

But he did not falter this time, was not distracted. In some way, he felt strengthened suddenly, the pain in his arm dissolving, his strength reviving. She was there like a comrade at his back, in her way, her magical way, and he felt strangely as if he, too, were somehow part of that magic, as if he, too, had a touch of the glamourie.

For Grant now stared at both of them, from one to the other, as if stunned. Then a wild and stormy look passed over his face, and he lunged at Alec, sword flashing in the setting sun.

And Alec leaned back as the blade went past his chest and struck out into sunlight. Grant stumbled forward with his own momentum, and tipped over the waist-high wall.

Alec lashed out his left arm to catch the man, grabbing the tail of his coat, leaning forward himself with the effort. His sword clattered to the cobblestones and he snatched with his right hand as well, pulling back with all his strength, knees pressed against the stone wall, his shoulders tipping over the edge with the man who dangled, shrieking now, over the side.

Alec felt Kate's arms close about him, felt her pull back. And he soon felt the strength of two soldiers who came forward with her to grab his arm, grab his coat and waist, pulling backward with him. But the weight of the man dangling from his hands was too great—far too great, and the tail of woolen cloth in his fingers slipped, rasping over his skin as it tore, and the man fell all too silently.

Pounding a fist on stone in desperate frustration, in a genuine torrent of regret, Alec pushed away from the wall and spun, sinking down, his back to stone, his limbs shaking.

Kate dropped beside him in a pool of skirts, looping her arms around him, sobbing out, her breath as ragged as his own.

"Oh, God, Alec," she whispered in a torn voice. "Oh, God, I thought you were gone—I thought you were gone—and you're safe." She gasped and buried her head against him.

He drew her into the circle of his right arm, his left dripping blood from the opened wound, and he pressed his face to hers, his breath heaving for a moment, aware that more and more soldiers were gathering around them and unable to do anything about that now.

They would be caught now, he realized—there would be no getting away, for surely the guards knew

357

by now that three Highlanders were gone from their cell, and the two who had been at the center of the escape sat here, breathless, trapped.

"Go," he urged her in a whisper, pushing her away. "Get out of here—go!" But she clung to him, shaking her head. "Kate, I love you—dear God, I love you," he murmured into her hair. "Get up and run out of here, and lose yourself in the closes and side streets. Make your way to my uncle's shop."

She shook her head. "I cannot leave you—"

"Sir," a man's voice said, and Alec looked up, his arm around Kate. "Captain, sir, some prisoners have escaped. Would you know anything about that?"

"Prisoners?" Alec saw the sentry staring down at him. They all gazed down at him, their expressions accusing.

"They had nothing to do with this, Lieutenant," a man said, stepping forward. Startled, Alec recognized the corporal and the sergeant from the dungeon. "These two had nothing to do with it."

"But you said—"

"Aye, there was a man dressed in military gear, and a lady with him—so beautiful, that lady. But not this lady," the corporal murmured. "Not this one."

He stepped forward and offered his gloved hand. Kate took it and rose to her feet, staring up at the young man.

The sergeant helped Alec to his feet, and both soldiers looked at Kate.

"No, not this one," the sergeant said quietly. "The other was not nearly so beautiful as this lady." He smiled a little, almost sadly.

Kate reached out and touched his arm in silence, then did the same to the corporal. They nodded to her discreetly.

"They got away, whoever they were," the corporal said to the lieutenant, and the rest of them gathered there. "These two were merely caught in the middle of whatever happened here. Poor soul," he added, glancing over the wall.

"Captain, I apologize," the lieutenant said. "We'll need to call a physician for you."

"I'm fine," he said. "I'm fine."

Kate took his arm. "I'll just take my husband home now, sirs. I thank you." She smiled at all of them, looking round her in a circle. And every man there, Alec saw, smiled back at her, knowing and affectionate and flattered, as if she had smiled at him, and him alone.

"Come ahead," Alec murmured, taking her arm to hasten with her toward the gate. "I'd better get you out of here before you have every soldier in Edinburgh at your feet."

She slipped her arm around his waist as they went. "There is only one soldier in Edinburgh I want," she said. "Only one."

He said nothing, though he felt the heat and glow of that within, until they were through the castle gates and outside in the cool blue shadows of the buildings at the top of the hill.

Drawing her into the shadows, he put an arm around her and kissed her, held her hard against him and felt her arms in an endless circle round his neck, felt himself whirl into the magic of that kiss, and into the miracle that had come to him—a string of miracles like a silver chain, and she was the crystal at the heart of it all.

"I love you, Katie-Katherine," he whispered, kissing her mouth again, tracing his lips along her cheek. "You've thrown your glamourie about me, and I never want to come out of it."

"Oh, but you've thrown the magic around me," she said. "And I think you did not even know you could."

"We'll have to stay in it forever, then, admiring one another's gifts," he murmured, and she laughed and pressed herslf deep into his arms.

"You will have to come out of it now and then," she whispered.

"Why? There's no reason that I can think of." He had her laughing now, a silvery chiming laugh that he loved, a healing sound for him.

"You'll have to come out of it and order me a sedan chair," she said. "I rather liked it."

"Aha," he said. "I always thought you were a bit spoiled, my darling." He set an arm about her shoulders and looked along the street. "Here comes one now."

"We'll need two—you're injured." She stepped forward with him and put up her arm, and another sedan chair appeared around a corner, as if by magic.

He laughed. He could not help it. "I truly love you," he whispered, and she made a little sound, her face pressed to his, like a sigh of joy. "And the sooner we are alone, my darling Kate," he murmured, kissing her cheek, "the sooner I can show you just how much."

She laughed sweetly, and when she drew away to smile up at him, Alec saw a soft glow all around her like

a lanternlight, and knew it was the glamourie, the
Fairy's Gift within her.

And he knew that he would see that luminosity
around her every day for the rest of his life—not always
with his eyes, perhaps, but forever with his heart.

Epilogue

~~~~~~∞~~~~~~

February 1729

As he entered Hopefield House from the courtyard, Alec heard a series of crashes and muffled
shrieks so frantic that his heart slammed. Breaking into
a run, he made his way along the corridor in the direction of the screams, shoving his way through the door
that led through a pantry, where cupboard doors stood
open, stacks of china and glasses evident as he went
past—someone's work interrupted, he saw, for dishes
were being sorted in preparation for the wedding
scheduled for that evening.

Where were the kitchen servants—and who the devil
was screaming? He pounded onward, shoving through

another door. Lily, he thought—surely that was Lily. And Daisy was crying—

In his haste, he knocked over a stack of porcelain, hearing it shatter on the floor behind him. The shrieks continued—that next came from Rosie, he realized. He pushed through the half-open kitchen door and pounded into the kitchen, kilt flying, heart slamming.

And he stopped short, glancing about, as loud shrieks echoed off the arched stone ceiling of the old kitchen, and the sweet, rich scent filled his nostrils—

Chocolate was everywhere: puddling on the stone floor, splattered on the scrubbed oak table, soaking into the bricks of the hearth; it had bubbled and dripped over the sides of two black kettles placed on the table. The smell was divine, and he saw no immediate harm to anyone.

Turning, he saw them: three chocolate-smeared little females peeking out from behind the largest of the stout oak tables in the kitchen. His nieces were shrieking, most definitely, but with laughter.

They were nearly coated in chocolate, their little hands and faces smeared, their ruffled gowns of creamy pastels smudged, their hair tousled and sticky with the stuff. Seeing him, Rosie and Lily lifted up their hands, waved, wiggled, jumped up and down. Daisy was too intent on crawling away from Kate even to look toward her adored uncle.

Crouched in their midst, Kate glanced at Alec over her shoulder, a cloth wadded in her hand. She turned her attention to her task: holding Daisy's skirts with one hand, she wiped at the dark mess on Lily's face with the other. The youngest, on hands and knees, challenged Kate's effort to hold on, for Daisy was intent on stretching out her arm to dip her fingers into a sticky puddle of chocolate on the floor, squealing in frustration.

"*Ach*, my wee cabbage, you will not be doing that," Kate said, dragging the child toward her by the tail of her dress. "Alec—help me," she implored over her shoulder.

"Uncle Alec, look!" Rosie, the quiet, serious, dark-haired image of Amy, was grinning from ear to ear.

Alec stopped, arms folded, and watched them, taking it all in. They were safe, they were unharmed, they were lovely, despite being dunked in chocolate, and all of them were so very dear to his heart that he felt the wonderful ache of it bloom in his chest. He laughed.

"You're by far the sweetest sight I've ever seen, all of you," he said.

"Now that is helpful," Kate said, laughing.

"Look, Uncle Alec!" Rosie was jumping up and down now and pointing to the oaken table, where Alec noticed countless blobs, drips, and a lacy web of chocolate adhering to the surface and dripping over the edge.

"Alec, take her!" Kate said as she pulled on Daisy's dress while kneeling in chocolate herself, so that it stained the front of her gown of pale blue satin. She had sticky fingerprints on her sleeves, her fingers were smeared, and she had traces of kisses on her cheeks. "*Tcha*," she went on to Rosie, who was still giggling, "however did you three do this?"

"We made the eating chocolate for your wedding,"

Lily said, between swipes of the cloth, as Kate scrubbed her face.

"Eating chocolate?" Alec said, coming forward to scoop Daisy up under one arm. She giggled and squirmed, wrapped her legs over his hip, and left delicious-smelling smears on his snowy linen sleeve. She lifted her face and pursed her lips.

"Kiss," she said.

He kissed her cheek obediently and felt her sticky mouth on his chin. "Sweet wee Daisy," he said, laughing.

"She's not sweet, she's wicked naughty," Rosie said.

"Rosie," Kate admonished. "Daisy could not have done all this by herself."

"She spilled the pot," Lily pointed out logically. "We were trying to do our work, but wee Daisy spilled it all over the table and on the floor."

"So then you decided to paint yourselves in it?" Alec knelt, Daisy still clutching him, and offered the sleeve of his free arm—the fine lawn was ruined already—to Rosie, so that she could wipe her hands clean.

"We were making wedding chocolates, but Daisy ruined that, too," Rosie said.

"Wedding chocolates?" Kate looked at Alec. "Uncle Walter had been in here earlier making up a batch of something special for the wedding supper."

"Aye, he mentioned that when I just saw him in the shop," Alec said, "but where is Aunt Effie? And where is Cook? And who the devil was watching the bairns?"

"I was watching the bairns," Rosie said. "Aunt Effie said she must nap with the headache, and told us to go to Kate, but Katie was trying on her gown with Lady

Kinnoull—I mean Aunt Sophie because she says we are to call her that—but she was holding wee Duncan, who was crying again," she went on breathlessly, "and I said I could watch the bairns myself."

"I doubt you were supposed to watch your sisters in the kitchen," Alec drawled. "Or watch them muck about in chocolate."

"We wanted to surprise you," Lily said plaintively.

"Aye well, this is a surprise," Alec admitted.

"I came downstairs when I saw that Effie was resting alone and the lasses were nowhere to be seen," Kate explained, letting Lily go and turning to wipe Rosie's face with the damp cloth. "But where is Cook and the kitchen girl?" she asked Rosie.

"They went to the greengrocer's in the Grassmarket," Rosie said, her words muffled by the scrubbing cloth. "They couldna find a caddie out on the street to fetch something for them at the market, and the stable groom went wi' Uncle Jack to fetch our guests from the inns." He knew she referred to Kate's kinfolk and friends, who had come to Edinburgh for their wedding in this new year, staying discreetly at inns in the city that catered to Jacobites. Kinnoull had brought Sophie earlier in the day and gone with Jack to ferry Duncrieff, the other MacCarrans, the Murrays, and MacPhersons to Hopefield House for the wedding itself, and a night of celebration.

"And Cook said there werena enough turnips for the 'neeps for the wedding supper, and they wanted more currants for another pudding, and they would be back at half past the hour. Is it that time yet?" Lily peered at Alec.

"Not quite," he said. "You mean you managed all this in about fifteen minutes?"

"Or less." Kate stood, leaning toward Alec and Daisy to use a fresh corner of her cloth to clean Daisy's round cheeks and tiny fingers.

"Kiss," Daisy said, pursing her lips again. Kate kissed her, then resumed wiping smudges off the child's forehead.

Seeing chocolate smeared on Kate's chin, Alec reached out and wiped his thumb in sensual, gentle circles over her creamy, translucent skin. She glanced up at him, her gaze smoky and deep.

"Kiss," he murmured, leaning down.

She tilted her face, and he cupped her head in his hand, fingers sliding into the silky golden thickness of her hair. Touching his lips to hers, he kissed her, drank in the transcendent sweetness of it, moving his mouth over hers and feeling her lips caress his. He closed his eyes, renewed it, and she made a little mewling sound under his mouth that made his heart and body leap, unbidden and eager.

"Later," he whispered.

"Uncle!" Lily tugged on his kilt, and he looked down, his hand still cupping the back of Kate's head. "Come see what we made for you," she said, dragging on his kilt to bring him with her. Alec followed her to the central table in the big kitchen.

Half the table was littered with bowls of chopped

fruits, smooth brown hen's eggs, cold porridge, currants, and spices, and pitchers of milk and cream to be used for pudding desserts to be prepared that afternoon. There were bowls, too, of creams and puddings. He recognized a lemon pudding by its scent and appearance, though it was slopped over the bowl, a spoon halfway sunk in its depths.

He was vastly relieved to see that the knives were tucked neatly away in a box, with nothing left out that would be dangerous for little girls. In the deep oven, roasted mutton and birds were tucked to keep warm, and a steaming kettle of soup was ratcheted too high for little hands to reach.

But his heart quailed at the thought of what could have happened. "They cannot be left alone," he told Kate.

"I know that," she said snappishly. "I thought Effie was watching them, while Sophie and I were fixing my gown. Her wee son was fussy, being but three weeks old, so we were distracted."

"I know you would have gone to look for the lasses if you even thought they were on their own," he said. "Perhaps they should not be left with Effie all the time. She may be getting a little old to watch them every day."

Kate tipped her head. "We could take them into our home," she murmured. "You are their guardian, after all. We are going to Kilburnie House after the wedding, and we'll see your other kin there. And after that, if winter weather allows, we'll be going to Duncrieff for our wedding there. I want to be married in the tiny chapel in the hills there, according to ancient MacCarran tradition."